IN RUINS

In Ruins

DANIELLE PEARL

FOREVER
New York Boston

Copyright © 2016 by Danielle Pearl
Excerpt from *In Pieces* copyright © 2016 by Danielle Pearl
Cover design by Elizabeth Turner. Cover photography by Shutterstock. Cover copyright © 2016 by Hachette Book Group, Inc.

Forever
Hachette Book Group
1290 Avenue of the Americas, New York, NY 10104
forever-romance.com
twitter.com/foreverromance

First Edition: October 2016

Forever is an imprint of Grand Central Publishing. The Forever name and logo are trademarks of Hachette Book Group, Inc.

The publisher is not responsible for websites (or their content) that are not owned by the publisher.

The Hachette Speakers Bureau provides a wide range of authors for speaking events. To find out more, go to www.hachettespeakersbureau.com or call (866) 376-6591.

Library of Congress Control Number: 2016946398

ISBNs: 978-1-4555-6833-8 (paperback) 978-1-4555-6834-5 (ebook)

Printed in the United States of America

LSC-C

1   3   5   7   9   10   8   6   4   2

For Roman, always.

In Ruins

Prologue

Carleigh

Five Years Old

"Princess," Daddy loud-whispers to draw my attention from the rainbow I'm coloring on the brick driveway with chalk. I don't have all the colors, so I used purple three times. I think I like it better than a regular rainbow.

"Coming, Daddy!" I top off the rainbow with a fluffy white cloud and run to the front of the garage. My face spreads into a super big smile when I see the shiny car with the big red bow.

"What do you think, Princess? Will Mommy like it?" Daddy asks.

The car is big and small at the same time. Sneaky looking. Like it can go really fast without even making a sound. The color is special, too. It's shiny and white, but not just white. Like one of the pretty pearls Mommy sometimes wears around her neck. Like white glitter.

"She's gonna love it, Daddy!" I squeal with giggles as he grabs me and plops me up onto his shoulders.

"Too bad I don't have anything for you," he says in a way that makes me think he's up to something.

"That's okay. It's not my aversity, silly," I remind him.

"Ann-i-ver-sary," he says for the ten hundredth time today, and I say the word the way he said it, even though it still comes out different.

Daddy walks us into the garage going slower than a turtle, and then I see it.

"Yay!" I start clapping and wiggling so much I almost fall, but Daddy catches me—he always does.

"Whoa, calm down there, Carleigh! You don't want to break your neck before you ever get to drive it." He laughs with his big mountain voice, and it booms like a happy drum through the whole garage.

I rush over to what I know is my present, even though it isn't my a-ver-sity. It's exactly the same as Mommy's new car. Only smaller. And it has no top. A *converble*. It even has a big bow like Mommy's car, except this one is my favorite color—purple.

"What do you think, Princess?" Daddy asks. "I had it made custom for you to match Mommy's. They don't sell it in stores, you know."

I hug his leg as tight as I can—it's as high as I can reach unless he picks me up or leans all the way down.

"It's the bestest car ever," I tell him. "I love it so so so much. Can I drive it now?"

Daddy bends down and picks me back up. "In a few minutes. It's all charged up for you, but let's give Mommy her present first, okay?"

"Will!" Mommy calls Daddy from inside the house.

"Come out here, Nik!" he calls back.

A minute later Mommy appears with my baby brother, Billy, in her arms. He is cute and tiny and I just met him a couple months ago when Mommy and Daddy brought him home from the hospital, and I already love him even more than my favorite doll. If I'm super careful Mommy lets me hold him sometimes, but only if I'm sitting down and either she or Nanny Marina is right next to me.

"God, what is it, Will?" She seems tired. Billy doesn't really sleep so good, but Nanny Marina takes care of him at night and Mommy and Daddy's room is so far away they can't even hear him. Sometimes I hear him cry and I wake up, but I don't mind. He likes it when I sing him songs from my favorite princess movies like *Beauty and the Beast* and *The Little Mermaid.*

"Just wanted to show you something real quick," Daddy says, and he smiles back at me in that sneaky way.

"Honestly, Will, I was going over instructions with Marina, and I still have to finish packing." Mommy sounds like me when Daddy tells me I'm whining.

"Well, we could stay home. Celebrate our anniversary with the kids," Daddy says, and he gives Billy a baby kiss. "We've been to the south of France plenty of times. We can take a trip when this little man gets a bit bigger."

"Ugh, stop it. Last summer I just found out I was pregnant and couldn't even enjoy a glass of rosé! It's my turn for some fun," Mommy says, and I wonder why she can't have fun with me and Billy.

Daddy doesn't say anything else; he just tucks Billy into his elbow and holds my hand with his other hand.

And then we can see Mommy's present. Daddy turns around with a giant smile and I yell "Ta-da!"

Finally Mommy also smiles, and not the one that only shows in her mouth. Her eyes are smiling, too.

"Oh, Will!" She runs over to her new car and touches it from the top down to the front like she can't believe it's real. "You got me my Aston Martin!"

"Happy anniversary, Nicole," Daddy says, and Mommy gives him a big hug and an even bigger kiss. "I promised you, didn't I?"

Mommy claps like a little kid and gets inside, and starts pressing buttons and looking around.

"Told ya she'd like it," I tell Daddy, and he pats me on my head like the puppy Mommy won't let him get me.

"Right as always, Princess."

Chapter One

Carleigh

I wait, until my mother blows her air kisses and the door to my dorm room closes behind her, to let the fake smile fall from my face. I don't know which of us is more relieved for her to go, but once she does, I allow the finality of her departure to finally sink in.

Freedom.

I turn to face my roommate and a genuine grin pulls at my lips.

Devin mirrors it. "She's something, huh?" she says of my mother.

I raise my eyebrows in mock exasperation. Nicole Stanger is certainly *something*. I plop myself down onto my narrow twin bed—the smallest one I've had since I was in a crib—and sigh. "Well, she's gone now," I assure myself more than her.

Devin smiles at me in sympathy. We were fourteen when we met on a cross-country teen tour my summer camp was sponsoring, and we connected instantly, staying in sporadic touch despite rarely ever seeing each other. So when we learned we'd be heading to the same college, we put in our roommate requests immediately.

She has never met my mother before, and I'm sure she wasn't quite what Devin expected. We're nothing alike—never have been. I was a

Daddy's girl, though the idea that I might take after him isn't something I especially want to entertain.

"Carleigh, darling, be sure to put your best foot forward for rush week." I repeat my mother's words in a perfect mocking impression, and Devin laughs. I roll my eyes. I may have simply smiled at my mother in response—arguing with her gets you nowhere—but I have no intention of joining a freaking sorority, that's for sure. I'll just tell her none of them wanted me.

"Do you want to go down to the dining hall for dinner?" Devin asks.

"Nah, I want to get to these." I gesture to the excessive number of moving boxes considering the shoebox of a dorm room we now share.

"Okay," she replies. "Just remember we need time to get ready for tonight."

My pulse speeds uncomfortably and my stomach rolls. "I don't know…" I say for the hundredth time. And I hate myself for it. I should be excited to go out tonight. My first night of college, and it's a notoriously huge party night. But Devin isn't the only person from my past here at school with me, and I hate myself even more for being *that girl*. The one naïve enough to make college plans with her high school boyfriend, only to have the relationship implode before summer was out.

But it's so much worse than that. Because ours wasn't your standard high school romance. Sure, it was tumultuous for a time, until we admitted our feelings for each other, but then…then I thought it would be *forever*.

And ours wasn't your standard breakup, either. It was a disaster.

It was *Chernobyl*.

Devin sits down beside me on my bed. She doesn't know that Tucker is here at school with us. All she knows is that I had a tough breakup over the summer, and she has made it her personal mission to get me out of my funk. It's something I would do if the roles were reversed, but hers is a role I could handle. It's this one that has me utterly lost.

Because I'm the strong girl. The one who doesn't need a boyfriend. Who could hook up and walk away. Or so I used to tell myself.

Now I feel like every step I take on this campus is on eggshells, because Tucker knows my secret. He hates me for it, and he should. And I honestly can't fathom why he hasn't outed me as the fraud that I am. Why he hasn't told all of our friends. But he hasn't.

But that doesn't mean he won't.

"Come on, Carl. It will be fun. You'll get your mind off of your ex, and maybe meet someone new," Devin coaxes.

I slip on my fake smile. She doesn't notice. I've been pasting it on for so long, lying for so long, I'm not sure *I* can even tell when I'm faking it anymore.

*   *   *

There are three main parties tonight, and I've managed to convince Devin to go to the one at The Library bar, even though it's the least popular of the three. It's famously lax on ID's, so I told her my fake isn't convincing enough for the others, even though my ID happens to be spectacular. But Morgan's is the bar everyone wants to be at, so that's where I expect Tucker to go. Because that's who he is. He is popularity, and likeability, and utter male perfection, and he will put absolutely no effort into it whatsoever, but by the end of the week, every freshman here at Hofstra University will know his name, and every girl—and some guys—will be fantasizing about warming his bed.

I squeeze my eyes shut to chase off the image of his army green eyes, the way his dirty blond hair falls into them. I try to forget that boyish grin and those dimples that melt my heart. But they only appear when he smiles, so they are decidedly absent in my memory of the last time we saw each other. No, that one features his rare scowl, directed at me with such resentment and contempt that it shocked the air from my lungs. Even recalling it now has my eyes welling with moisture, and I have to blink to fight it away.

I suck in a deep breath and dab under my eyes with a tissue, then fix my eyeliner and concealer. I'm skilled with makeup, and I'll admit I put extra effort into my look tonight. I needed to account for the shadow of heartache staining my features, and I have.

I brush my stick-straight, light golden-blond hair. It's grown quite a bit since I cut it to my shoulders last winter, and it now hits just above my cleavage. I wonder if I should cut it again. Perhaps something drastic. Something to make me feel like someone else. Someone new. Anyone but the girl Tucker Green hates.

"You ready?" Devin asks as she spritzes on a final spray of Hanae Mori perfume. She smells like cotton candy, and she looks beautiful, too. Her chocolate bob is sleek and straight and parted down the side. I did her makeup using a new technique I learned from a YouTube video, and while she looks equally gorgeous without any at all, I'm deeply pleased with the result. Her eyes are almost the same chocolate shade as her hair, and the coral and earthy shadows make them look impossibly large under her long, black mascaraed lashes.

"You look hot," I tell her, and she smirks at me.

"Not so bad yourself, Stanger. Come on, let's go make all the other bitches jealous."

We walk outside, following the throngs of students all headed to the same strip of bars. The girls are dressed to impress in their favorite outfits—short dresses, tight miniskirts, tighter tops. Tonight we will all make our first impressions here, and the air is thick with possibility.

Three more blocks and I can see our destination up ahead—a vintage-y white and green sign that reads "The Library." It may be lackluster in appearance, but it's brilliant with significance. The bar is one of the staples of our new school—a bona fide landmark—and its dull sign glows under the streetlamps; and under that, a crowd of students smokes and chats. A couple of guys pass us and shamelessly rake us both with their gazes. One smirks. I think I hear another murmur something about *fresh meat*.

I try to force myself not to wonder what Tucker is thinking right now. What *fresh meat* he's checking out. Who he might go home with tonight. The truth is it wouldn't be any less painful if he were across the country at some other school. As long as I don't run into him, anyway. But no matter where he is, he'll be doing the same thing. Meeting new people, checking out the girls, and inexorably attracting their attention.

My phone buzzes with a text from my friend Rory, who's in New York City at freshman orientation for NYU.

How are you doing? 10:15 pm

She doesn't know the details of why Tucker and I broke up, but she knows my devastation. She's one of the few people who can actually understand it, as she experienced her own last year when she and Cap couldn't get their shit together. They're practically married now, but then, she hadn't been harboring some monumental secret that would inevitably destroy them.

I text her back.

I'm okay. About to head into some bar. How are you? Cap? 10:15 pm

We're good. Heading to his place now. Miss you though. Call me if you want to talk. 10:16 pm

I text her back a smiley face that in no way reflects my actual mood. I'll call her tomorrow. At least one of us is happy. And Rory and Cap deserve it, especially after all they've been through. I don't know what I deserve, but I fear happiness isn't it.

* * *

The night passes slowly. It's a strange juxtaposition. Because while the dull ache in my chest is always there, surprisingly, I am kind of having fun. I've met a few girls I'll be in classes with, including one in my creative digital marketing class, the one I'm most excited for. Which is ironic since I ended up in the class by default when it was the only one available to replace the class Tucker and I had planned to take together prior to our breakup.

My new friend Julia, on the other hand, has been looking forward to digital marketing ever since she visited campus last year and happened to audit the class, though her enthusiasm is less about the coursework than about Professor Stevens himself, who apparently has a reputation as the hottest professor on campus.

Personally I'm hoping to gain a lot more than eye candy from that class—namely credits toward my major. I love makeup, but I don't just want to own a salon one day—I want to own a chain of them, and a line of cosmetics, too. And for that I need a business degree.

I swallow the last sip of my beer and debate ordering another. As Devin predicted, we have gotten our share of attention from the opposite sex, and I should feel flattered, but honestly, I just feel inescapably lonely.

The place is packed, and the guys are all on the prowl. Most of the girls, too. The guy with the shaved head I've been trying to blow off all night suddenly sidles up to me *again*, and I sigh in exasperation. "You sure I can't buy you a drink?" he slurs.

"I already have one," I say for literally the fifth time.

He shakes his head and taps the glass of my empty beer to make his point. "Not anymore."

Well, nothing gets by you. "I can get my own drink, thanks." I turn away from him.

"Fucking bitch is too good to let a guy buy her a drink," he murmurs drunkenly to his friend, who isn't even listening to him.

I should let it go, I know, but I just don't have it in me. I swing around to face him. "Actually this *fucking bitch* is just too good to let *you* buy her a drink. Who do you think you are, anyway?" I hiss.

Devin turns from the guy she's flirting with, her eyes wide and alarmed, as do quite a few of the people surrounding us. I hear my mother's voice in my head warning me not to make a scene, but I just don't care. I'm not going to take that shit from this douchebag.

Douchebag chortles loudly, spitting beer out of his rancid mouth, and I recoil from his rank breath. "Who am *I*? I'm Ricky fucking Vance, *bitch*!" he says proudly, and I vaguely recognize the name, but can't place it.

I glare at him, unimpressed.

"I'm the fucking number one lacrosse goalie in the goddamn state!" A few cheers erupt around him. "And you're just some fucking slut who should've taken the drink I so generously offered. I—"

"Ricky, shut the fuck up," a deep male voice commands from behind me.

Douchebag—or Ricky, whatever—refocuses his very dazed, inebriated gaze behind me. "Fuck this uptight bitch. She was disrespectful." But the fight is draining out of him, replaced by uncertainty.

I turn to see who seems to have called off the douchebag, and I'm a little taken aback. He's stunning. At least six foot two with dark brown hair and hazel eyes. I noticed him in the bar earlier—a gaggle of girls gathered around him, desperate for his attention, and finally I recognize who he is. Ben Aronin, the captain of our very popular lacrosse team, and a nationally ranked attacker. And he's offering me a conciliatory smile.

"I'm sorry for my friend. As you can see, he's had a little too much to drink."

"The fuck, man?" Douchebag sounds betrayed.

"*The fuck* is right. A girl doesn't want a drink from you so you start cursing her out? You make us all look bad when you act like that. Go back to the house and sleep it the fuck off," Ben orders, his eyes narrowed in censure.

Douchebag starts to say something else, but suddenly there are two guys beside him guiding him toward the door, and I just stare after him, a little dumbfounded.

"Sorry about that," Ben says again. He nods to the bartender and holds up two fingers.

"I was handling it," I murmur. I am not the girl who needs saving. I can handle a drunk douchebag. And at least the douchebag *asked* to buy me a drink. Ben just hands me a beer, and I don't know why I take it.

He's handsome, sure, but all I can see when I look at him is how much more vibrant Tucker's eyes are, how much more thrilling his smile.

"I don't doubt that. But I'm not about to stand by and let my teammate behave like that. Sorry," he says matter-of-factly, as if he wasn't doing it for me at all—like it was simply his responsibility—and strangely, that makes me feel a little better about it.

"Thanks for the beer." I hold it up and turn to go find Devin, but he stops me with a hand on my shoulder.

"Hey, you don't have to run off. Not all of us are assholes," he says sheepishly.

But I already know not all lacrosse players are assholes. I know one in particular who is absolutely wonderful. But he hates me. And he lives in the same house as Ben and the rest of the lacrosse team, and the last thing I need is to get to know anyone who has anything to do with Tucker.

"Hi," Devin says, suddenly beside me as she flashes her winning smile.

Ben grins and tips his beer. "Ben," he introduces himself.

Devin's smile widens even more and she bats her eyelashes flirtatiously. "I'm Devin. This is my roommate, Carl."

Ben signals for the bartender to get him another beer, which Devin accepts graciously. I wonder if he's running a tab, since he doesn't seem to be paying for any of these drinks.

Devin asks Ben about his major—finance—and talks excitedly about classes I happen to know she's not actually excited about. The girl has flirting down to a science.

But Ben hasn't taken any of Devin's classes. "What about you?" he asks me. "Taking anything good?"

I shrug. "Just freshman requirements, and creative digital marketing with Professor Stevens."

Ben's subsequent stare is unsettling, but then he breaks out into unrestrained laughter.

"What?" I ask, but he just continues to laugh so hard he's practically choking. I glare at him, and Devin just blinks at him, puzzled. Irritation crawls up my skin—how did I suddenly become the butt of some secret joke?

"I'm sorry," Ben cries, wiping his eyes as he tries to get ahold of himself.

"Funny how you apologized for *your teammate's* rudeness…" I remark.

He sucks in a deep breath, and, with one last shake of his shoulders, his apparent hilarity finally subsides. "I'm sorry," he repeats. "I just didn't take you for the type." His shoulders twitch with a residual chuckle.

"The *type*?" I raise my eyebrows, still annoyed.

Ben frowns, like he expects me to know what the hell he's talking about. "Oh," he says.

Oh?

"My bad. I just thought…well, Zayne Stevens, you know? It's been the same every semester since he started teaching my sophomore year. Girls signing up for an easy elective so they can stare at his ass. Only to find out it's one of the hardest business classes at the school."

"Well, that's not why I took the class. I didn't even know he was supposedly good-looking until some girl told me tonight." Inwardly I think Julia is probably one of the girls Ben just described, and she might be in for a rude awakening. "I'm here to learn. I'm not afraid of a difficult class."

"*Psh*," Devin scoffs, "Carl will ace that shit."

Ben eyes me thoughtfully, nodding slowly. "Yeah. I'm getting that," he says. "I'm sorry."

"You said that already," I remind him.

He flashes his too-perfect grin. "But this time I mean it."

I offer a flicker of a smile despite myself. At least he's honest.

"Well, good luck, anyway. I took that class last semester. I mean, you learn a lot, but it can wreak havoc on your GPA if you're not careful."

I shrug. "I'll be okay."

Ben smirks. "I don't doubt it."

Devin taps my shoulder. "Uh, Carl, don't freak out, but there's a seriously hot guy over there who's been staring at you all night like he either wants to eat you or kill you," she says, pointing to the back of the bar, and Ben turns to follow her gaze.

I suck in air and swallow down my anxiety. Because I know exactly who the hot guy who wants to kill me is, and I don't know if I can handle seeing him.

But I can't help but look, and I will away the tears that threaten as dark green contemptuous eyes greet mine.

"Hey, that's our new defender, Tucker Green," Ben says, surprised.

Tucker is surrounded by people, particularly girls, who are obviously vying for his attention. But he's distracted by my presence, and he just stands there, glaring at me.

Ben laughs. "You know, Carl, I think it's you he wants to eat, and me he wants to kill right now."

Ben waves to Tucker, who nods once and sips his beer, eyes barely straying from mine long enough to acknowledge him.

"So do you know him, or is he just that competitive over beautiful girls?" Ben asks lightly.

"We went to high school together," I murmur, and I think he expects me to blush or something, or thank him for his compliment, but the only person I care about thinking me beautiful is looking at me like he wishes I would disappear. So I do him the favor.

"Thanks for the beer, but I—uh, need to go. Dev, you stay. I'm just gonna walk back to the dorm," I mutter quickly, and then I turn and rush out of the door before she has a chance to ask questions.

I speed-walk the first half block until I can round a corner, and once the bar is out of sight, I stop and catch my breath. I haven't been running like usual lately. I haven't been exercising at all, in fact. The pitiful truth is, I've barely been able to pry myself out of bed since our breakup.

My throat feels too tight and my chest aches. I hate how he affects me. I hate that I know he will always affect me.

And then a hand is grabbing my arm and I almost scream, suddenly remembering how stupid it is to be out alone at night, until I turn and realize that I am physically safe, though my heart is in mortal danger.

"What the fuck is wrong with you?" Tucker growls.

I shake my head. *I'm sorry*, but I can't articulate it. I shouldn't have to be sorry for being out at a bar at my own college, but I am. I'm so fucking *sorry*.

Tucker slams his palm into the brick wall behind me in frustration, right beside my cheek, the sound making me jump. "Goddamn it,

Carl! You don't leave a bar alone at night, *ever*. You hear me?" He is furious.

I blink at him in surprise. Not at his wrath, but at what's caused it. He's right of course, but he hates me, so why does he even care?

But deep down I know why. What happened to Rory that night last spring traumatized us all, and I should know better.

"I'm sorry." I finally whisper the words.

"You're sorry a lot lately, aren't you?" Tucker sneers, and I wince.

But he's right, and I don't have a comeback. I study my sandals instead. I don't even recognize myself anymore.

"Why were you talking to Ben?"

I shake my head. "I wasn't. He just…his friend was being a jerk and I guess he felt responsible." I shrug.

Tucker inhales, slow and purposeful, as if he needs to calm himself, and if I didn't know without a doubt that he would never lay his hands on a girl, I might be afraid of him. He smells of beer and his sharply familiar aftershave, and the scent ignites a wave of heartache and a twinge of desire in equal measure.

"You can handle a drunk Ricky Vance," Tuck murmurs, and I realize he must have been watching me longer than I thought. "It's Ben you need to stay away from," he adds, and I meet his gaze, confused.

"Seriously?" I ask him. I know our breakup was my fault, but *he's* the one who broke up with *me*. He doesn't get to tell me to stay away from guys, even if I have no intention of hooking up with anyone—even if I still only have eyes for him.

"Seriously." His tone is vaguely threatening, and I try not to—I really do—but my reaction is preconditioned. I only respond to threats one way—I rise to the challenge.

"I'm pretty sure I'm single, Tucker. I don't need to stay away from anyone."

Tucker sucks in air through gritted teeth, and I wait for him to blow up. To yell at me and tell me I'm impossible. To get frustrated past his limits until he can't stop himself from kissing me.

But we're not *us* anymore. He doesn't want me anymore. He doesn't even *like* me anymore. And before I'm even conscious of the fact that I was trying to suck him into our old routine, Tucker takes a step back.

He shakes his head, glaring at me with utter disgust, and I think he'll turn and go back to the bar, but instead he just walks to the street and hails a taxi.

"Get in," he demands, opening the door.

I stare at him in desperation, and I want so much to take it back. To tell him I have no interest in Ben. That I only want him. That I have only ever wanted him.

But even if I could form those words, they would do no good. What's done is done.

"In!" Tucker growls, and I obey.

It's so unlike me, but I owe him at least that. And so I help him make me disappear, so he can get back to his night.

I check my phone and find Devin's worried texts, and when I read that she's out looking for me, I text her that I drank too much but I'm fine, and for her to go back to the bar or to take a cab home—not to walk home alone. God, I'd never forgive myself if something happened to her because of me.

She gets home only about ten minutes after I do, and I pretend to be asleep, my face hidden under my blanket so she can't hear my pathetic weeping.

Chapter Two

Carleigh

Eleventh Grade

The bell rings, shrill and promising, indicating the beginning of summer break and the end of my junior year of high school. Twelve years down, one to go, and then college. *Freedom.*

It's going to be a long year.

I make my way to the student lot, stopping to chat about tonight with Lily and Sarah. I wait for Tina on the concrete steps, where wannabe rebellious seniors celebrate by lighting cigarettes on school property now that expulsion is off the table for them.

I glance at the time on my phone, wondering what's taking Tina so long. But of course, I know exactly what's holding her up, and when she appears around the bend with Andy's fingers playfully stroking the new blue streaks in her hair, I smile wryly. *Casual hookup,* my ass.

"Hi there, Carl."

I turn to find Brian Falco swinging the keys to his Benz in a way he probably thinks comes off as absentminded. It doesn't. "Congrats on your last day," I murmur. *God* it must feel good to be a senior today. I turn away so he doesn't have the chance to hit on me, which he's done quite a few times in the short weeks he's been single.

I continue watching Tina and Andy approach, in no apparent rush, and Cap and Tucker appear behind them, chatting animatedly about something—probably tonight's party to celebrate the end of the school year.

"Thanks," Brian says through a self-satisfied smile. "You coming to Coop's party tonight?" he asks, forcing me to turn back to him. He actually isn't such a bad guy—and damn good-looking too—but he dumped Cap's little sister not too long ago, and Cap's hostility is no secret, and my loyalty lies with my friends. Not to mention that even if he was my type—which he most decidedly is not—I'm completely turned off by how callous he's been about the end of his relationship, when it obviously devastated Beth Caplan. She's only a freshman—or she was until today—and Brian should have been more careful with her heart...and the other parts of her I suspect he took advantage of.

"Yeah, I'll come with Tina. Hopefully the weather holds out." I eye the charcoal clouds warily.

"Falco." Tucker's derisive voice rumbles from behind me. He drops a familiar hand on my shoulder, reminding Brian who my friends are and what they think of him.

Part of me wants to pick a fight over Tucker's staking a claim over me when technically, as my friend, he doesn't actually have one. But I love the weight of his hand on me. I love how his fingers stretch all the way from the nape of my neck, over my shoulder and collarbone. I love the tingles that spread from where his skin touches mine.

"Green," Brian replies, and then turns and walks right out the door.

I suppress a laugh. I wait for Tucker to remove his hand, but he doesn't. Instead, he slips it around to my other shoulder and pulls me to face him. "He bothering you?" he asks.

I shrug. "Kinda, but I can handle myself, Tuck," I remind him, and his full lips twist up into a smirk, his dimples peeking out.

"I know you can, Princess. But you've gotten way too hot for your own good, and all these asshats don't seem to realize that you're mine," he teases, and I roll my eyes.

This is his new M.O. Pretending he wants me. And I both love and hate it.

When we were kids he used to pull my braids. When we were in middle school he upped the ante, teasing me any way he could—putting glitter on my chair, telling everyone I pooped sparkles. He even started a rumor that my mother was Swedish royalty, and started calling me *Princess*. And now he seems to think it's hilarious to pretend he wants me.

And it's annoying. Because deep down—or not so deep down, if I'm honest—I wish it were true.

But if Tucker really wanted me, he wouldn't make it a joke. He would just make a move.

And he wouldn't be hooking up with Sarah Lickman.

We walk out of the building, his arm still draped around my shoulders, trailing behind Tina and Andrew, whose hands are all over each other, and Cap, who's been joined by their other best friend, Dave.

"*God* I can't wait to see you in a bikini tonight," Tucker jokes. "Will you wear a special one for me, Princess? So I have something to imagine when I go home and think about you."

"*Please*, Tucker. We both know you won't be thinking about me when you go home with Sarah tonight." As always, I call him on his bullshit.

Tucker gasps dramatically, pressing his hand to his chest as if I've wounded him. "It's you or my hand tonight, baby, I promise."

I shrug out of his arm. "Enjoy your hand, then." Since we both know he's full of shit.

*   *   *

The weather is still holding out when we arrive at the party later that night, and everyone is in an exceptionally celebratory mood, drinking and laughing. Girls whine about not wanting to get their hair wet while guys throw them in the pool anyway.

I sit in the hot tub, hair sopping wet, waterproof makeup holding strong, while I pretend I didn't wear my sexiest one-piece for the dual purpose of defying Tucker's demand that I wear a bikini, and still wearing something hot enough to get his attention.

Sarah and another girl join Tina and me, but they're only half invested in our conversation. Their eyes betray their true interests by practically stalking Tucker and Cap, who are engaged with Andy and Dave in an overly competitive game of beer pong. I try to ignore the familiar rush of jealousy that swarms my chest.

I grant myself a moment to check him out. It isn't fair really. He's gorgeous; he can have any girl he wants, and the worst part is, he knows it. His skin is still damp from his recent swim, and his muscles glisten in the dim lamp light. He's always played football and lacrosse, but when he made the varsity teams freshman year, he started lifting weights to keep up with the older kids, and boy has it paid off. He doesn't look like a normal seventeen-year-old. He looks like a man.

The water has darkened his blond hair, and he tosses his head to fling it out of his eyes. His biceps flex as he bends his arm to throw the Ping-Pong ball, and then all of his muscles ripple temptingly as he jumps in victory when his shot wins the game. I swallow thickly and chug the remainder of my sugary punch.

"Careful with those," Tina says. "Andy warned me the punch is much stronger than it tastes, and that's, like, your fourth one."

I shrug. She's right, but I don't care. Tonight is a celebration, and I'm celebrating. I try to convince myself of this—that I'm simply toasting the end of yet another school year. That I'm definitely not trying to get drunk enough to numb the emptiness inside me.

Sarah steps out of the hot tub, her friend following right behind as she seductively makes her way over to Tucker, and I have to look away. Andy takes their place, and Tina climbs onto his lap.

"I lost." Andy pouts.

Tina presses a kiss to his dramatically protruding bottom lip. "That's okay," she flirts. "The more you lose, the more you have to drink, and the more you have to drink, the easier it'll be for me to take advantage of you."

Andy's pout rearranges into a delighted smirk. "I'll have to lose more often then."

I laugh at them. Tina has had a crush on Andy for a while, and I love seeing her happy like this.

The water surges suddenly as a big, warm, hard body slides in right behind me, but before I can jump away, his voice echoes gruffly in my ear. "You can never just do as you're told, can you, Princess?"

He's positioned between me and the wall of the hot tub, and I relax against the only boy I'm glad to have touching me, enjoying the buzz from both the alcohol and the sensation of his skin against mine. "Not my style," I remind him, turning just enough to see his gorgeous face and his playful smirk.

"Well, joke's on you. This thing is even sexier than a bikini." His fingers trace the cut-outs of my swimsuit, his palms sliding up and down my bare sides.

I turn away and smile to myself. *Mission accomplished*.

Tina and Andy get out a minute later, leaving Tuck and me alone as they head inside the house for some privacy.

It should be awkward for me to be sitting with Tucker like this, his body stretched behind mine, his fingers teasing the exposed skin of my waist beneath the water. But it isn't.

Tucker leans into my ear, his breath caressing my neck, and I stifle a gasp. "You drive me crazy, do you know that?" His voice is barely a whisper.

I shake my head vaguely, but lean a little closer to his lips, wanting so desperately to feel them on the sensitive skin of my throat. But that would cross a line. That would take us from friends who flirt to something else entirely. That would mean his teasing isn't just teasing, that he really does want me, and even in my inebriated state, I know better than to let myself fall for his game, to get my hopes up.

"You're the one always teasing *me*," I remind him.

His chuckle vibrates through my entire body. "Maybe that's to get you back for how much you tease me without even realizing it."

I turn a little more, and find myself half sitting on his lap. "How do I do that?"

Tucker's smirk, both familiar and newly intent, makes my heart race and my belly flutter. "With this perfect body," he says, deep and husky, his fingers ghosting up my arm and shoulder, and under my jaw. "With this gorgeous face." He runs the pad of his thumb over my bottom lip. "With this smartass mouth. You distract the hell out of me, Princess."

He leans in a little more and I choke in a shallow breath. He used to call me *Princess* to make fun of me, but lately it's been almost…affectionate. And you'd think it would be weird, considering it's the same thing my dad used to call me. But it just reminds me of the last time anyone showed me real affection, and all I feel is grateful to have it again.

But Tucker *is* only my friend, so why is he teasing me like this? "Surely you have Sarah to keep you *distracted*," I counter.

Tucker turns me suddenly until I'm straddling his lap, his features screwed into an exasperated scowl. "What the fuck, Carl? I hooked up with Sarah once, over a month ago. Why do you keep bringing her up?"

I frown, surprised by his frustration, and even more so by his revelation. "She said…" I try to remember what exactly she said, but I'm too drunk, and I think she more *implied* than *said* anyway. I guess my jealous mind fell right for it.

Tucker's brow furrows, luminous green eyes earnest for once, and they completely disarm me. "You really don't know how much I want you?"

I'm too tipsy to come up with some witty response, or some sexy invitation, and my lips part, but all I do is shake my head.

"How can I prove it to you?" he asks hastily.

"Take me home with you." The words are out of my mouth before I have the chance to talk myself out of it. But I don't regret them. This is what I want.

"Fuck, yes," Tucker exhales, and his mouth is so close I think he'll kiss me, but he doesn't. His eyes search around, and then he's pulling me out of the hot tub and wrapping me in a towel.

He leads me around the side of the house until we're alone, and then finally and suddenly, Tucker's mouth crashes down on mine.

I'm held prisoner in my towel as his lips capture mine, and for once I don't fight back. I surrender.

I feel a desire I've never known before, and I know without question that I was right to wait. I didn't hold on to my virginity out of principle, I just never felt like I wanted to have sex. But right now I'm desperate to know what it's like to feel this fire everywhere.

Tucker pulls away, his chest heaving with exertion, and touches his forehead to mine. "I've wanted to do that for *years*," he admits.

My pulse races in excitement and my heart beats wildly, but my buzz is no longer from the alcohol. I am high on Tucker Green. "What stopped you?" I whisper.

"You think I don't know you're too good for me, Princess?" He shakes his head. "But God help me, right now, I can't seem to give a fuck." His gaze drops back down to my lips, and like he can't even help himself, he's kissing me again as if I'm the oxygen he needs to breathe. I shrug off my towel, my fingers aching to touch him, and I rush to trace the lines of his obscenely defined abs.

He sucks in a sharp breath. "Fuck this, let's get out of here."

I nod my eager agreement.

"Stay here."

I hate being ordered around, normally. But right now, I obey him without question, and I don't dwell on what the reason for that might be.

Tucker heads back to the yard and returns a minute later with my cover-up and bag, his shorts pulled over his still-damp swimsuit. I slip my cover-up over my head and Tucker is pulling me around to the front drive before I can even fish out my phone to text Tina that I'm leaving.

We climb into Tucker's car, and he starts texting someone, and my heart plummets at the thought that it might be Sarah.

"I'm designated driver and Cap's supposed to stay at my place tonight," he explains. "Just telling him to Uber it home instead."

"You're just going to leave him?" I ask.

"He'll understand, trust me," Tuck says cryptically.

I don't question him further; I don't want him to change his mind.

We ride in silence. I practically tremble with nerves, but they are the nerves of certainty. The nerves of knowing I won't turn back—the surrealness of being here, with *him*, about to do what I've fantasized about for longer than I'd care to admit.

He pulls into his drive, murmuring something about his mom being away—visiting her sister or something. When we get to the front door, Tucker pauses. A brief, strange look masks his features before he inhales long and harsh, as if he's trying to slow things down. For a moment I worry he's having second thoughts about crossing this line.

But then he kisses me. Not hot and hard like at the party, but slow and deep.

He pulls away and smiles a new smile. Not his knowing, cocky Tucker-smirk, or his carefree, playful Tucker-grin, but something almost shy, almost vulnerable.

A flash of a memory reminds me of the first time I ever saw Tucker look vulnerable. The Father's Day after his dad died when we were in the seventh grade. I lost my father in an entirely different way a few years earlier, and we were the only ones in our art class with no one to make a card for. We bonded that day. It was the day we went from classmates who teased each other to friends. Real friends.

I reach out to trace the curve of his mouth, and instantly he's back. Tucker smirks with lustful intent, and then he's unlocking his door and pulling me up the stairs.

"I've pictured you on my bed a million times, Princess."

I laugh. "I've been on your bed before," I remind him. Never alone. In fact I've never been alone with him in his bedroom at all. But in a group of friends, hanging out, watching a movie, I've been here, and the room is familiar and comforting. His scent fills the air, relaxing me despite the anxiety inherent in what I'm about to do. What *we're* about to do.

Tucker's smirk stretches wider. "Not the way I'm talking about." He tugs me to him, resuming his kiss.

I reach for his T-shirt and pull it over his head, and he maneuvers to help me. His fingertips brush the tops of my thighs as they grasp the hem of my cover-up, then it's gone and I'm standing in my damp swimsuit, which is really just a few scraps of material that happen to be connected by a thin mesh cloth, making it a one-piece instead of a bikini. Tucker's eyes rove over me from head to toe and back again, lingering on a few choice parts, and I watch, riveted, as his eyes darken and his smirk vanishes.

I step closer and let my fingers explore his intricately sculpted body, starting at his chest before tracing the grid of his stomach. He sucks in a sharp breath as my gaze wanders south to where he strains against his board shorts, and I hope he doesn't notice my thick swallow.

He won't know how new this all is to me. I know he'd never suspect that I'm a virgin, and even less so that the extent of my sexual experience was giving my first boyfriend a hand job when I was fourteen. I've kissed plenty of guys, and most of our friends have done far more than that, so people just assume that I have, too. I don't have a reputation for being a slut or anything, but no one would guess that kissing is pretty much *all* I've done.

So Tucker doesn't know how bold it is for me to slowly let my hand continue down past his waistline, and palm him over his bathing suit.

My desire for him is so heady it makes the room spin, and I stumble before regaining my footing. I blink up at Tucker, my vision blurred by lust and alcohol, and it takes me a moment to realize he's looking at me funny. Almost suspiciously.

"How much have you had to drink?" he asks out of nowhere.

I shake my head. Because the answer is *too much*, and Tucker is too good of a guy. If he realizes how drunk I am, I have no doubt he will stop this.

He takes a step back, pinning my jaw between his fingers and bringing his eyes down to my level. I try to appear focused and in control, but his expression confirms that I'm failing.

The room tilts suddenly and I grab on to his shoulders to anchor me. But it doesn't stop me from taking another staggering step, and he catches me around my waist as I fall into him.

"Fuck," he mutters to himself. "I knew this was too damn good to be true…Serves me fucking right."

"Tuck—"

"It's okay, Princess. I'm sorry. I should have realized." He ignores my shaking head. "Come on, let's get you some water." He starts to lead me out of the room, but I dig my bare heels into his plush rug.

"I don't want to go." But my voice comes out strange—a mix of a slur and a breathy plea.

I start to feel dizzy, and I don't want to stand anymore. I walk backward and Tucker accommodates me, guiding me toward his queen-sized bed, its size not distracting from the reality that it is, in fact, still a bunk bed. The thought makes me giggle.

Tucker smiles. "Something funny?"

"When I said to take me home with you, I wasn't picturing the kind of sleepover that involves bunk beds." I laugh louder, and Tucker joins me.

"Me neither, Princess." He sighs, and I can't help but feel like I've let him down. Like I've let us both down. His next words confirm it. "But we're not going to have any kind of sleepover. Not if you're drunk."

I shake my head. "I'm fine," I insist, but we both know it's a lie.

Tuck doesn't bother arguing the point, he just smiles. "I'll bring you some water." And he's gone.

I lie back on his bed, watching as his ceiling spins like a fan set on low. I never would have drank this much if I knew it would ruin our night. And yet, I wonder if I'd even be here if it didn't also give me the courage to tell him I wanted to go home with him. Still, I can't help but feel a little wild thrill that I am here, in Tucker's bed, even if he won't do anything about it now. I replay our kisses in my mind, and I flush with renewed desire and a bit of giddiness. Because it's more than just attraction. I *like* him. I've *always* liked him.

"Sit up," he instructs, his strong arm sliding under my back to help me into a sitting position, and he hands me a bottle of water. "Drink."

Again, strangely, I obey him without hesitation.

"That's my girl," he praises, and I smile. "Do you want me to give you some dry clothes? I'll drive you home."

No. My stomach falls in disappointment and mild panic. I don't want to leave. I don't want to go back to that huge house, far too vast for three people, whose halls echo with the ghosts of a once happy family. "I don't want to leave."

Tucker sighs. He runs his fingers through my hair and it's affectionate and sweet, and when he cups my jaw, I lean into his touch. I wait for his kiss, but it doesn't come. "Do you think I want you to go?" he asks with open frustration. "I've waited years to get you here, Carl. But I'm not going to take advantage of you while you're fucked up."

He shifts uncomfortably on the bed. "As much as my dick might disagree with me."

I gasp a surprised laugh and he smiles at my amusement.

"If you want me, Princess, you're gonna have to admit it when you're good and sober." It's a challenge, and I wonder if it's one I'll have the nerve to accept.

But it's clear tonight's cause is a lost one. I'm drunk, and Tucker is my friend, and a good one, too. It seems my virginity is safe for at least one more night, and I pout my disappointment.

Tucker brushes a soft kiss to my forehead, and it does something to my heart. These tender touches are new for us, and I'm afraid they're turning my crush into something more. Something decidedly dangerous.

"I don't want to go home," I say meaningfully, and he knows me well enough to understand. He knows my house is almost always empty, especially on the weekends, when my mom likes to stay in Manhattan and my kid brother, at his best friend's.

"You can stay here, okay? But we can't do anything."

It means the world to me that he'll let me stay over now that he isn't getting anything in return. Idly I wonder why it would even surprise me, but then I suppose that's just what I've come to expect from guys.

Thank you, Daddy, for the low expectations and abandonment issues.

But, of course, Tucker isn't just some guy who was hoping to get lucky tonight either. He's one of my oldest friends, and my closest guy friend, and I feel a little guilty for momentarily forgetting that just because we almost hooked up.

I avert my gaze in remorse, nodding my agreement to his terms. *The kind of sleepover that does involve bunk beds after all.*

Tucker gets up and retrieves a Port Woodmere Varsity Lacrosse T-shirt and a pair of boxers from his dresser and tosses them to me. "Get changed, okay? I'm gonna grab a quick shower. I'll be right back."

But his shower isn't all that quick, and I suspect I may be the only one going to sleep frustrated.

I'm already in his T-shirt and underwear, curled under his duvet, when he emerges from his en suite bathroom, shirtless and in a pair of flannel pajama pants. He pauses at the foot of the bed and looks between me and the top bunk.

Friends can cuddle, right?

I flip open the duvet in invitation. Tucker only hesitates a fraction of a second before climbing in behind me, and I snuggle back against him. I sigh with contentment as his arms fold around me, feeling unfathomably comforted and protected as I let my eyes fall closed.

"'Night, Princess," he murmurs hoarsely, pressing a chaste kiss to my hair. But I'm already half in another world, the alcohol and my exhaustion, and Tucker's intoxicating proximity, guiding me into the most peaceful sleep I can remember.

Chapter Three

Carleigh

Eleventh Grade

I wake with a start, my erotic dream so real that for a second I still think I'm in Tucker's bedroom. And then my eyes focus, and I realize that I *am* in Tucker's bedroom, and I'm not alone. I blink into bright green eyes, already awake and watching me shamelessly. We're facing each other on our sides, and belatedly I register how close we are, the hard planes of his body pressed right up against my soft curves, my leg curled around his thigh. The hunger I felt in my dream rematerializes with a vengeance, all too real.

"Hi," I breathe, and Tucker smiles. It isn't his smirk, but that new, sweet smile I had barely a glimpse of last night.

Last night.

The memory comes rushing back and my breath hitches.

I almost slept with Tucker Green!

And then I chew on my lip, realizing that, more than anything, I'm disappointed that we *didn't*.

I feel the evidence of his arousal between us, and I wonder if it's for me, or if he always wakes up this way. I wonder vaguely if I should untangle myself from him, but the simple fact of it is—I don't want to.

"I keep trying to think of something smart to say," Tucker murmurs. "Some joke or something. But all I can think is how beautiful you look right now."

And just like that, warmth floods my chest, recalling the comfort I felt in his arms, how well I slept in them.

"We almost—"

"We didn't." He cuts me off, reassuring me, as if he thinks I might be worried that in my drunkenness I made some horrible mistake.

I blink at him.

"You were drunk," he reminds me.

"I'm not drunk now." I gaze up at him meaningfully, flushing with a combination of embarrassment, nerves, and deep desire.

Tucker stares at me for a moment like he's not sure if he's hearing me right. I don't give him a chance to misunderstand. I slide my leg forward over his thigh, one inch, and then another, until my leg is effectively wrapped around him. I brush my fingers over his bare chest, so warm from sleep, and trace the tapestry of muscle and sinew, the soft spattering of light hair.

When I look up at him it's from under my lashes, and I find his eyes hooded and heated. I love that I can feel his need growing between us.

Tucker sucks in a deep breath, and then, he kisses me.

God, does he kiss me.

It is in no way tentative or unsure—no, it is purposeful and inexorably deep. But it isn't hasty or fast. It's like he's taking his time, maybe to give me a chance to change my mind, or to let me know he's in no rush.

But I *am*. I want to do this. With him. Right now. More than I've ever wanted anything.

My palm slides down, down, following the very masculine lines of his body, the trail of hair, until I'm grasping his telltale erection through thin flannel.

The air hisses through his teeth with his sharp inhale. "Fuuuuck," he groans, and then something in him breaks. I'm rolled onto my back and suddenly I am being utterly *consumed*. His lips lead the assault, laying claim to the skin of my jaw, my throat. He licks and sucks his way across my collarbone and my exposed shoulder. I'm lost in the sensations, my stomach trembling as his impatient fingers begin an exploration of their own under my shirt—*his shirt*—and then my knees raise of their own accord, my thighs cradling his hips, and I give in to my instinct to lock my legs around him.

Tucker groans again, and then makes quick work of my shirt, tugging it over my head. My breasts are free and he's kissing me and kissing me, and I feel my bare chest pressed against a man's for the very first time. Tucker's chest is a masterpiece, firm where I am soft, curved but not round, and our hands explore each other as he tongues the shell of my ear.

"You're so fucking beautiful, Princess. Tell me you want me," he rasps. His hand slips between our bodies, tentatively lifting my breasts, feeling their weight. He brushes his thumbs over the sensitive peaks, and pleasure shoots between my legs and I gasp.

"Tell me, Carl," he demands.

"I want you." It's a confession. One that's rung through my head a thousand times, but that I've always hidden behind playful quips and combative challenges.

Tucker's eyes fall closed, like he's savoring my words, and I press light, tentative kisses to his jaw, reveling in the rough sensation of his stubble against my swollen lips.

My hips rock upward all on their own, and Tucker answers the motion with his own. He pulls back to meet my gaze, and then his fingers slip under my shorts—*his boxers*—and he slowly peels them down my legs, never breaking our eye contact as I swallow down my nerves.

His gaze reveals so very much. He's reading me, making sure I'm still with him, and *God* am I with him. But his eyes also blaze with a passionate need, a fire I'm starting to believe has burned a long time, maybe even as long as my crush. And I could be fooling myself, but they may even hold emotion beyond his friendly affection. Or perhaps it's simply the reflection of my own.

No, heart, this isn't about you.

I need to keep my feelings in check. This is about sex. Nothing else. And there's nothing I could do right now worse than fooling myself into hoping for more.

Tucker's gaze finally leaves mine to rake my naked body for the first time. No guy has ever seen me naked before, ever. I'm not an insecure girl, but there's something inherently nerve-racking in this, and I am, after all, human. Tucker must have seen plenty of girls naked before, and for the first time I find myself wondering if my breasts are too small, if my hips are too wide, and I hate myself for it.

He doesn't say anything for a few moments, and his silence doesn't help my anxiety any. But then I notice the change in his breathing as it quickens and deepens.

His eyes fall closed. "Why do you have to be even hotter than I've imagined?"

I flush all over. I have no other response.

Tucker's hand slips slowly down, down, across my hip bone and between my thighs and we both gasp. No one's ever touched me there—except, well, *me*—and I'm so turned on right now, and the feel of his big, rough hand against my sensitive skin is just unreal.

His gaze shoots to mine. "Princess...you're so wet for me," he marvels, and my cheeks flush with heat.

My instinct is to challenge him back. "Take off your pants," I demand. I want to see him, too.

Tucker smirks, but he doesn't hesitate. This is one challenge he's eager to accept.

Then he's naked, but the shadow from the blanket hides him from me, so I kick it off of us. Tucker chuckles as my eyes find their target. I would never admit to him that I'm seeing my first naked guy at seventeen, and I hope my rapt fascination doesn't give me away.

He's long, thick, hard, and darker than I've imagined, and I try not to feel intimidated.

And then his lips are back on my neck, his fingers between my legs, and my attention is refocused. His hand designs a rhythm like a conductor leading an orchestra, and my hips mindlessly play for him like a virtuoso until I think I'm going to explode in a crescendo of harmonious bliss. But he slows his ministrations and the music is hushed but not silenced.

"I want you to come around my dick, not my hand," he whispers gruffly into my ear.

Yes. "Yes."

He grabs a condom from his bedside table and tears it open with his teeth. I watch intently as he rolls it on and positions himself between my legs.

His eyes meet mine and I stare, hypnotized, into my new favorite color—a beautiful deep green that reminds me of spring.

Are you sure? they ask me.

Hell yes, mine reply.

And then he's pushing forward. At first he doesn't get very far, and I widen my hips.

"Fuck, Princess, you're so tight."

I chew my bottom lip, trying not to panic. The last thing I want is for him to suspect I'm a virgin. He won't want that responsibility. He will stop this. I tighten my legs around him and push his ass with my heels, urging him forward, and he pushes harder.

And then he's partly inside me and there's a sharp, almost blinding pain.

"Yes," I gasp to hide it.

Thankfully he stops for a moment, and I take the time to get used to him. Somehow he knows to go slow, and he rears carefully back, and pushes slowly back in, gaining more ground this time as he groans a sexy, guttural sound that reverberates right in the part of me that seems to both resist and welcome his invasion at once.

"Why do you have to *feel* even better than I've imagined?"

Why do his words turn me on as much as his touch?

"Tucker," I breathe his name, relishing the way he responds to hearing it.

His pace picks up, his strokes deepen, and I lose myself. I lose myself in Tucker Green.

I find myself moaning, almost whimpering, and it's utterly shameless. I'm glad he doesn't know it's my first time, that he's not treating me like glass.

The harder and deeper he moves, the more I want to match him.

And then his hand is between us, stroking me where we fit so perfectly together, and I burst.

I pulse around him, moaning his name, holding him to me, holding him *in* me.

He sucks in a shaky gasp, burying his face in my neck as he thrusts himself deep inside me and pants, "Fuck, Princess, *fuck*," and then he stills.

He collapses on top of me, gasping for breath, our chests heaving together with blissful exertion. I'm in no rush to get him off of me. I love the feel of his weight, even if it is a bit crushing, but he rolls to my side, and presses a hard kiss to my lips.

"*God*, Carl," is all he says, looking at me like he doesn't quite know what to make of me now. Like I am some unfamiliar creature he's only just discovered, and he would like very much to study me further.

"Yeah," I breathe, but I can't help wondering if it's always that good for him—if every girl he's been with has experienced the same thing.

He slings an arm around my waist and we just lie there as I cuddle into him, in no hurry to leave his bed. Considering my lack of experience, my comfort level right now is pretty astonishing. I could spend a lazy morning with him, just like this—no clothing necessary.

I just wish I knew what he was thinking right now—if he would even want me to stick around. Because I have nowhere to be. I doubt my mother has noticed I didn't come home last night, and my kid brother Billy is camping with his friend Kyle and his family. Tina is the only one who might worry, so I reach over the side of the bed where my purse has been unceremoniously dumped, and grab my phone to text her that I'm fine. Tucker takes the opportunity to check his own phone, and when I'm done, he's still busy, eyes fixated on his screen.

So I wait. And wait. I try not to watch him, to give him his privacy, but when several minutes pass and he's still texting God only knows who, I'm flooded with self-doubt.

Does he want me to leave now?

And he texts and texts, and doesn't so much as glance my way, and I have no choice but to take the hint. Tucker sits up at the same time I do, but he's out of the bed before I can even get my legs over the side.

It startles me. It's been barely ten minutes and three words since he was inside of me.

He tugs on a pair of jeans, and for a moment I just watch him, a little stunned. And still, his thumbs race over the touchscreen as he fucking texts and texts.

And in this moment I absolutely hate myself. Not for giving my virginity to someone who only wanted me for sex, and not for shame-lessly taking what I wanted from him in return. But for wanting *more*. For being this girl right now.

And to make matters worse, I am at a severe disadvantage. I have no clothing except for a bathing suit and a cover-up, and I am without my car. *Wonderful.*

"Can I—uh, borrow these?" I hold up the boxers and T-shirt Tucker let me sleep in last night, and finally he looks up from his phone.

His expression surprises me. I expect dismissive, even callous, but he looks ambivalent. Worried and remorseful. His eyes have darkened to their usual army green, as if they're waging some kind of internal war as he glances between me and his phone. I am competing with a piece of technology.

Or whoever's on the other end of it.

I am fucking pathetic.

"God, I'm so sorry, Carl, but I really have to go."

I blink at him. Is this some kind of act he puts on for all of his casual fucks? A genius way of getting rid of us while making *us* feel bad for *him*?

Wow, he's even better at this game than I realized.

I hold up the clothes again and raise my eyebrows, all the while trying to be as nonchalant about this as he is, telling myself I don't care. *I don't care, I don't care, I don't care.*

Tucker sighs and pushes his hand through his hair, looking exhausted all of a sudden. "Yeah, Princess, of course," he says of the clothes.

"Thanks."

He drives me home in silence, and I continue to tell myself I don't care—that this is what I signed up for. *Lies.*

I don't look at him when he parks in my driveway, but he grabs my elbow before I can jump out of the car.

"Carl—"

"Thanks for letting me crash," I say brightly, plastering on my masterful smile.

Tucker's brow furrows. "Yeah. Of course."

And then I flee from his car and into my house before the player can spit any more of his game. And I can fall for it.

Chapter Four

Tucker

Present Day

I spend an extra hour in the weight room after the rest of the guys leave. We work out as a team most mornings, but my focus was off today, too busy trying not to glare at Ben. I know he doesn't know about my history with Carl, but I don't trust the guy.

I finish my last rep and head to the showers.

I'm angry. I've been angry for months, and it's a new look for me. My jokes don't come as easily and my patience for bullshit has vanished.

I'm angry that she's here. I'm angry that she's not who I thought she was. I'm angry that she's beautiful, and that my teammates have already noticed her. I'm angry she ran out of that bar alone last night when she should fucking know better. I'm angry that she still affects me—that my dick doesn't seem to care whether or not she's a conniving little liar.

I'm angry that we all go out to the same bars, the same damn parties, and that I will probably see her way more often than I realized. But most of all, I'm angry that a part of me actually wants to.

* * *

The second day of classes begins much like the first. I get in my workout with the rest of the team, shower at the gym, then hurry off to my first Tuesday morning class. But unlike yesterday, this one is in the Communications building, which is on East Campus, the farthest possible location from both the lacrosse house—which is just off campus—and the athletics facilities.

It's an effort and a half not to be late, even with cutting through the student union, and I barely make it through the door before the professor closes it behind me.

I'm expecting another vast lecture hall, and I'm surprised by the small classroom, the desks arranged in a circle like we're here for some kind of support group. The professor himself doesn't look much older than me, and I guess that he's probably a grad student. I also note that he looks less than pleased with my abrupt entrance.

"Nice of you to join us, Mr....?"

"Green," I murmur, already deciding I'm not a fan of the guy. It's the first fucking class, and I wasn't even actually *late*.

Asshole.

A small gasp from across the room grabs my attention and pulls my gaze like a damn magnet, and even before it reaches its target, I know. It wasn't even her voice. It was a gasp—a fucking *breath*—but I know her gasps as well as my own name, used to pride myself on eliciting them, and my chest explodes with violent agony the moment my eyes meet shocked emerald green.

Carl forces her mouth shut, quickly averting her gaze as if something on her tablet suddenly fascinates her. But I don't need to see her eyes to feel her anxiety, and I curse myself for still being so fucking attuned to her every goddamn emotion.

Worse than my awareness of her is the impulse to reassure her, to tell her everything will be okay. Because it won't fucking be okay.

I chalk the instinct up to all those years of caring about her feelings above even my own—which worked out fucking *great* for me.

But instincts can be suppressed, and I defer to logic instead, reminding myself that Carl Stanger is nothing to me anymore. That the Carl Stanger I loved was never real at all. The girl I'm painstakingly not looking at is just another stranger.

I don't let my attention linger, not wanting her to think my interest is anything other than fleeting surprise. Before I even got to campus, I promised myself I would leave that shit in the past. I would leave *Carl* in the past. The constant awareness, the jealous outbursts, the uncontrollable desire—all of it. And I was more than ready to move on. I *am* more than ready to move on. I even convinced the guys to go to the slightly less popular bar last night because I assumed Carl would be at the more popular one.

I saw her exchange with Vance, and watched her talk with Ben for way longer than her bullshit explanation would account for. But she's a skilled liar, so bullshit is pretty much where she shines. I remind myself that I only ever *thought* I knew Carl. That nothing she does should surprise me. Because I used to think I saw through her in a way no one else did, but it turned out that, too, was just more bullshit.

I saunter through the circle of students in a skilled impersonation of the carefree Tucker Green I've always shown the world. Even if the one person I'm acting for most of all is the one most experienced at seeing right the fuck through me.

A glance in my peripheral vision confirms Carl is still intently focused elsewhere, which is a relief. But my practiced nonchalance isn't just for her. I don't want to call attention to myself at all—which I admit is new for me. But I don't want anyone to pick up on my animosity, or to realize there's anything between Carl and me at all. I don't want people to make a connection between us. There is none.

It's the same reason I insisted on avoiding the bar I thought she'd be at, but I guess she did the same, because that backfired royally. As I take a seat at one of the two empty desks—which mercifully isn't too close to Carl's—I realize that's probably how we ended up in this fucking class together, too.

When we were still together, we'd planned to take an Intro to Business class together. But in the wake of the disaster of our breakup, it slipped my mind, and it wasn't until I got my schedule that I even remembered. By then this digital marketing class was the only one available in the same slot. But clearly switching a class to escape an ex was also on Carl's agenda, because here we fucking are.

I take out my iPad and open my notebook app, silently snickering at the irony. Ever since the bar, I'd been worried I'd run into her socially, but I never even considered the prospect of us sharing a class. Of having to see her twice a week, every week, for the entire fucking semester.

Fucking great.

The frat-guy-grad-student professor introduces himself, insisting we call him Zayne. The girl sitting next to me stares so hard I think her eyes may pop right out of her skull, and I glance around the circle, realizing she's not the only one. I take another look at the guy, and realize he's not bad looking—if you're into that sort of preppy, wannabe rich-guy look.

He starts discussing the syllabus, and I try not to look over to see if Carl is as fascinated as the rest of the girls, but I can't help myself. I also can't help my satisfaction when she continues to take notes without even looking up.

"So, as interested as you all are in the subject matter, I'm sure you'd like to hear about my grading process?" Zayne says almost teasingly.

There's a resounding murmur of affirmative responses.

He chuckles, though I don't know what's funny. Why *wouldn't* we want to know how to earn a good grade? Some of us are here on athletic scholarships that have minimum GPA requirements. *Arrogant prick.*

"Okay. It's really very simple. If you do a good job, participate, and actually learn something, you have nothing to worry about."

Real fucking specific, asshole.

It's wide eyes all around, and Zayne waits another couple of beats before he lets out another chuckle. "Okay, okay," he concedes, "I guess I can give you a few more details."

The rest of the class—especially the girls—laugh right along with him. Except for one.

Carl's eyes remain fixed on her tablet, her dark blond brows pulled into a barely perceptible frown, her fingers at the ready to type down notes as she impatiently waits on useful information. It hits me belatedly that I even snuck a glance in her direction, as does my satisfaction that she doesn't seem to be under the spell of our douchebag professor, and I inwardly wince. I shouldn't fucking care either way. I *don't* care either way.

Fuck.

Zayne finally gets to the point. "I'm sure you've all heard the popular misconception that attendance doesn't matter in college. I'm sorry to be the one to tell you that it is, in fact, a myth."

A few girls giggle. I roll my eyes.

"Now, every professor is different, but almost all of us at least take attendance. Some will dock grades for unexcused absences, and while I don't necessarily subscribe to that policy, I do grade on class participation, and it's difficult to excel if you're not actually here to participate."

More giggles.

This is going to be a long fucking semester.

"There will be a few unannounced quizzes to confirm you're all keeping up with the assigned reading, and of course a mid-term. Those quizzes, mid-term, and your aforementioned participation will make up half of your grade."

Carl's long, delicate fingers flit over her screen, and I wonder what the hell she needs to write down. This isn't exactly rocket science, right? Participation, quizzes, and a test. Pretty standard stuff, and no different than high school really.

"In lieu of a final exam, you will all be presenting a project, which I will discuss in more detail in the coming weeks. That project will determine the other half of your grade."

My gaze, along with those of the rest of the class, shoots to Zayne, who smiles wryly. Clearly he was expecting a reaction. Half our fucking grade decided on one single project?

"Now don't panic. You'll have almost the entire semester to work on it, but you're right to take it seriously."

Yeah, no kidding, dick.

He continues on about his goals for the class, but I'm too busy trying to follow his advice and not panic. I'm a fairly good student, but the stakes are high and the pressure is on. Being a college athlete may attract the hottest girls, or get you into the best parties, but there are limits to the special treatment, at least at this school.

We're all required to maintain a 2.8 minimum GPA to keep our place on the team, and if we fail to do that for even one semester, we're automatically benched. Two semesters and we're off the team. But even getting benched would make me ineligible for my scholarship, and there's no way my mom could afford the sixty-thousand-dollar private university price tag.

I feel foolish that it's only really hitting me now. It's not that I didn't know the stakes before, but I guess I never really considered they could be an issue for me. A 2.8 isn't exactly reaching for the stars, and I just assumed that as long as I didn't fuck up in some significant way, I wouldn't have trouble landing the grades I needed.

Even now there's no real reason to think otherwise. I just need to nail this stupid project, and I'll be fine. Which is all the more reason not to let myself get distracted by old ghosts that don't have the decency to just fucking disappear.

*   *   *

I tell the guys I'll see them later and leave the gym ten minutes early so I can get to the Communications building on time. I admit that walking into my first Tuesday morning class to find my lying ex staring back at me really put me off my game. But two days later, the surprises are off the table, and I've got my calm and confidence back.

I'm not looking forward to starting off yet another day with this shit, but it is what it is, and I've had no choice but to accept that for the next three months, Tuesday and Thursday mornings are going to blow.

I glance at my watch and see that I've made good time, so I slow my walk through the quad. Obviously I don't want to be late, but I have no intention of arriving even a single minute early, either. My purpose is to show up, learn some shit, and rush out to my next class. Not make small talk with the other students, or even so much as fucking eye contact with one in particular. Because Carl is the type to make friends with everyone, and the last thing I want is to add yet more mutual friends to the already practically incestuous group we have back home.

I linger in front of the building, not heading inside until there are just under two minutes left before class, and everyone is already seated when I saunter in like I don't have a care in the world.

"Mr. Green, take a seat. We're just about to begin," Zayne says, and I do. I don't even glance Carl's way.

Zayne begins his lecture and I mostly manage to keep my focus, taking notes when necessary.

He talks about *old-school marketing*—he actually uses this term in a blatant attempt to resonate with us undergrads—versus newer campaigns.

He lectures on and on, and I continue to take notes, even trying to participate once or twice. I'm sorely aware that at least part of my grade depends on it, and as arrogant and pretentious as I still find the guy, I know I need to do better than my one-word answers if I want credit for participation.

I do notice the dark-haired girl next to Carl staring at me, and it's a little off-putting. The lacrosse team is practically worshipped at this school, and I expected to get a certain amount of attention as a starter, but I didn't think it would happen so soon. Our regular season doesn't start until mid-winter, and while it's true we're also supposedly famous for our parties at the house, the first one isn't even until this weekend.

I catch the brunette staring again, and she blushes and returns her attention to Zayne, who's still talking. But he only seems to make her blush deepen. I want to roll my eyes. Instead I fix them on my iPad, and try to keep my interest in the lecture. I can participate next week.

"…and the question a lot of these companies grapple with is the farthest reach versus the fastest reach."

"What's the difference?" some guy asks.

"Indeed," Zayne says. "What is the difference? Does it pay to reach a greater audience more slowly, or a smaller, perhaps more targeted audience, more quickly?"

And then I hear her soft, familiar voice. "More targeted," Carl murmurs, and all eyes turn to her.

"Elaborate…" Zayne encourages her, and she shrugs.

"Well, mediums like television and billboards are expensive and broad, right? You're spending a ton of money, much of which is reaching people who will never buy your product. But things like social media campaigns can be really cheap. And you can reach people just based on friends liking or sharing, or whatever. I'm more likely to buy something my friend bought than someone random, right?"

"Well said, Carleigh," Zayne praises, and smiles, and it makes my stomach roll. *I'm Mr. Green, but she's Carleigh*.

He continues on about viral campaigns and how they don't even need to feature an actual product to be effective, but I can't stop thinking about the way he smiled at Carl. Suddenly I stop thinking of him as a professor trying to relate to his students, and I see him as something else. As a twenty-three-year-old good-looking guy whose eyes stray way too often to a hot-as-fuck eighteen-year-old girl. And the fact that she's smart—that she continues to participate and make what he describes as *keen observations*—surely isn't making her any less appealing to him.

This time I don't rush out when Zayne dismisses us. Instead, I stay seated, watching intently as he looks at Carl just a second too long as she heads out the door.

*   *   *

Tonight we're throwing the first party of the year at the lacrosse house, and I'm supposed to help set up, but I'm distracted as fuck. I keep picturing the way Zayne watched Carl's ass as she left class yesterday; and whether it's jealousy or protectiveness that keeps me from letting it go, the fact remains that I have no business with either.

I force the thought from my mind and go make sure the kegs are tapped and the punch is mixed, ignoring a bad joke by one of the second stringers about mixing in something extra to "make the girls better company." *Fucking asshat.* I kick him off of punch duty and decide to keep an eye on him.

A few hours later the house is alive with bodies and music, slurring words and staggering steps.

I can't help but wonder if Carl will have the nerve to show up at a party at the house I live in, knowing she wouldn't hesitate if it were anywhere else.

"Hi, Tucker." Some girl bats her eyelashes at me and smiles suggestively.

"I know you?" I ask, the slight gruffness in my drawl hinting that I'm drunker than I realized.

Her smile grows. "Ben told me you're the new starting defender."

I find Ben across the room, and he holds up his beer in a gesture of cheers—like he's giving me a gift. Like I need his fucking help to pick up a girl.

I'm probably the only guy in the house who hasn't bagged anyone since school started just over a week ago, but that isn't because I haven't had the opportunity. And *for fuck's sake,* it's only been a goddamn week.

I make myself check out the girl in front of me, but she does nothing for me. She's cute, sure, but I just can't get myself interested.

And then I zero in on Carl. She's across the room with that same girl she was at the bar with, and I guess that the two are roommates. I can't believe she had the gall to show up here. She at least has the decency to look nervous, and her eyes dart around anxiously as she clings to her beer.

"Hello?"

I realize that this girl has been talking to me for the last minute and I haven't registered a word. "Huh?"

"You know her?"

Shit. She's followed my line of sight, and I pry my gaze away. "Who?" I play dumb.

The girl—a very unnatural redhead wearing way too much makeup—rolls her eyes. She shakes her cup. "Want to get me another beer?"

Not really. My gaze meanders back to Carl, and this time she's spotted me. She stares at me first with fear, and then with something that looks suspiciously like jealousy when she takes in Red. *Interesting*. "Sure," I lie, and then follow Red back to the kitchen.

First Carl has the balls to show up at my house, and then she thinks she has a right to be jealous that I'm talking to a girl? Especially when she so clearly reminded me she's single the last time we spoke. Sure, I'm the one that ended us, but she's the one who lied from our first fucking kiss. From even before then. Carl's been lying since we were fucking kids.

*   *   *

Everyone in my seventh-grade art class is hard at work on their Father's Day cards, and though Mrs. Finch suggested I make a card for my mother instead, I don't see the point. I gave her one on Mother's Day.

I don't know why this week has sucked even more than usual. My father is no more or less dead just because Sunday is some arbitrary holiday invented by big corporations to drive consumerism. Or at least that's what my father used to say. Though he still happily participated, acting thrilled by the ridiculous macaroni picture frames and other hideous art projects I made him when I was little. When he was still himself.

I try to remember what I got him last year, and it makes me incredibly sad that I can't. Things were already bad by then. He was already sick, and he didn't want to barbecue or see family or go to the beach. We just stayed home, and I know I got him something, I just can't remember what.

The funny thing is I can remember the things I didn't get him. The things I considered before deciding against them. I remember thinking there was no point in getting him a tie, since he was in no condition to work, or the Omaha steaks we got him a year or two before, because he was in no mood to grill. But no matter how hard I try, I can't remember what the hell I got him for his last Father's Day on this earth.

It's then that I notice Carleigh isn't making a card either.

She's doodling her name over and over, but she isn't making anything. Her long yellow hair is pulled back in a braid, and her eyelashes make shadows on her cheeks, fluttering every now and then like butterfly wings. She looks sad, and I go over to sit next to her without even thinking about it.

She looks up and smiles at me. I like her smile. I like that it shows in her eyes as well as on her mouth. It's real. Like her. She always says what she's thinking and does what she wants, and I like that, too. No matter how much I tease her, she always just takes it like a champ and dishes it right back. She never gets mad or cries—not even when we were little. I don't think I'd do it if she did. I don't want to see her cry.

"You're not making a card?" I ask her.

Carleigh shrugs. "No point. My dad's not going to be here for Father's Day anyway." Her dad works a lot, and he's never really around. I honestly don't even remember what the guy looks like, if I've ever actually met him.

Everyone goes over to the glitter station to decorate the front of their cards, but Carleigh stays back with me.

"I'm sorry, you know. About your dad," she says.

"Thanks," I say automatically.

"I thought he was getting better," she murmurs. "You know, that he came home from the hospital and all…"

"Yeah. We hoped. But then…" I don't finish my sentence. She already knows how it ends.

"That really sucks," Carleigh says.

I blink at her for a second, a little surprised. Everyone always says things like "at least he's in a better place," and "he's with God now," and all that. But Carleigh's not one to bullshit. And she's right. It really does suck.

"I'm sorry your dad's never around," I tell her. "I'm sure he would be if he could."

She smiles sadly. "No. He wouldn't." But she's not looking for me to reassure her. She's just stating a fact.

And what do I know? If Carleigh was my family I'd want to be around her all the time.

"Hey, do you want to hang out Sunday?" she asks suddenly. "We could go see a movie or something?"

A movie.

And then I remember what I got my father for his last Father's Day. A DVD boxed set of all the Rocky movies—his all-time favorites. I want to thank Carleigh for helping me remember, because right now, it feels like the most important thing in the world that I did, but all I tell her is that, yes, I want to go to the movies with her, and suddenly this week doesn't feel quite as shitty.

Chapter Five

Carleigh

Last Year

The summer weeks drift by, long and lazy. Tucker has been in East Hampton for the past couple of weeks with Cap's and Dave's families. He's sent me a few texts but I've successfully ignored or blown him off. So successfully that he's stopped texting. Tina is deep into her fledgling relationship with Andy, and though I don't begrudge her her happiness, it does leave me a little lonely.

My mother is away on her usual August tour of the Côte d'Azur, currently holed up in a villa in the south of France, and frankly, it's a relief to not have her commenting on everything I do, everything I wear. I've spent a lot of time with Billy, which makes me happy, but more and more he wants to be with his friends. Typical twelve-year-old. And I'm the makeshift mother at seventeen, watching my favorite little boy need me less and less.

I've been reading a lot, lazing by the pool, and I've gone out a few times with some of the other girls. They flirt, and hook up, and I feign interest, all the while telling myself the reason I can't get Tucker out of my head is because of the sex.

And maybe it is. I've heard enough stories to know mine was not a typical first time. Tina lost it to a senior our sophomore year, a guy she'd been dating about six months, and she says it took her another six months before she ever had an orgasm from him.

Maybe I just need to do it again. To find out if I'm playing it up in my head, or if Tucker really is that good. If he's not, maybe I can let go of this borderline obsession, and if he is, then at least I'll know for sure that it's sex-induced. Purely biological, and maybe excusable?

I ran into Cap at Bagel Boys this morning, so I know they're back, and that they'll most definitely be at Andy's tonight.

I text Billy to check in, and he tells me he's going to stay over at Kyle's, so I text Kyle's mom to make sure it's okay. Really I just want to make sure that those are actually his plans. I know the tricks, I'm only seventeen after all, and, sadly, it doesn't take all that much effort to be a better parent to Billy than my mother ever was to me. Kyle's mom texts me back that she's happy to have him, and I lie back on my poolside chaise and relax.

* * *

Andy's party is packed. Besides partying and hooking up, it looks like Tucker spent his weeks in the Hamptons getting a deep brown tan. It makes his blond hair look blonder and his green eyes shimmer like sea glass in the evening light. And it makes me wonder what those T-shirt-covered muscles my fingers recall with aching detail look like in their darker tone.

It isn't long before Tucker obliges me, when he, Cap, and Andy, strip down to their underwear and jump into the lake. I sit back against the enormous weeping willow and watch their drunken escapades, trying to be nothing other than amused as Tucker tries to convince girl after girl to go skinny-dipping. Maybe it's his ridiculous Tucker tone, but I find myself laughing at him. That is, until he notices, and makes his way over to me.

"Something funny, Princess?" He arches a playful brow.

"Just the lengths you'll go to get any random girl naked," I tease.

Tucker smirks. "Not *any* girl, Princess. Not you. Not here. You're for my eyes only."

I swallow thickly. "Is that so?" I challenge.

Tucker nods, staring intently down at me, as if waiting for what I'll say next. But he should know by now there's only one way I respond to a dare—even a vaguely implied one. *His eyes only? Please.*

I stand up. "So I shouldn't go for a swim, then?"

Tucker shakes his head. "Fuck no. Not here."

"Hmm…but the water does look so inviting…" It doesn't. I have no desire whatsoever to go swimming right now.

"Carl." His tone is suddenly censuring, and I'm surprised by the way his features drain of mirth. But his reaction only eggs me on.

"Teen!" I shout, getting her attention from where she sits on the dock, feet in the water, being splashed by Andy. "Why should these guys have all the fun?"

I grab the hem of my tank top and peel it up over my head. Tina is immediately on board. She hops to her feet and starts stripping. We won't skinny-dip, of course, but our bras and underwear cover as much if not more than a bikini, and *God* do I love the shock on Tucker's face right now.

I shimmy out of my shorts and slip my fingers around to the hook of my bra, just to mess with him.

His face darkens in anger. "*Carl.*" He reaches for me as if he's actually going to forcibly stop me from getting naked, and I snake around him and race toward the dock. Moments later, Tina and I jump into the lake, shrieking with laughter.

We start some kind of equal opportunity stripping and swimming feminist movement, and by the time I turn around to face the shore, half of the girls have joined us.

Thirty minutes later, almost the entire party has moved into the cool, refreshing lake, which does feel pretty damn great after all. A chicken fight breaks out and people watch and cheer.

Eventually I feel him behind me. He doesn't touch me, but I know he's there. I turn my face to him, smirking, and he takes another step so I can feel his chest against my back. He isn't mad anymore, just amused, his eyes alight with challenge.

"I'm gonna get you back for that, you know," he murmurs into my ear.

I shrug. Any time he wants to strip down for me is just fine.

But then I feel his fingertips ghosting along my sides, and I suck in a sharp breath. We are deep enough that the water comes up to my chest, and it's dark enough that it hides everything below it. I can't help it, his touch makes me lean back into him until I am flush against him.

"You see what you've done?" he asks, hands banding around my waist as he presses the conspicuous evidence of his desire against my ass.

I nod, pushing my thighs together as I arch into him just a little bit more.

He walks us slowly and casually back away from the crowd until he is leaning against the now empty dock, his fingers caressing all the while. I just let him. I have no witty words or snarky quips to shoot his way, not when he's touching me like this.

"You tease me, now I'm going to tease you." His voice grows deeper with each word.

I trace my nails gently over the back of his hands, and he takes it as encouragement. He slips a finger into the waistband of my boy-cut underwear, and just slides it tauntingly back and forth, back and forth.

I gasp in a breath, waiting to see how far he will go. His other hand explores, roaming around my hip and then to my ass, his fingers digging softly into my flesh. My head lolls against his shoulder and I feel his chest rise with his sharp inhale.

"You like that, Princess?"

I don't want to admit that I do, because I don't want to be the one to lose this challenge. But more than that—more than *anything*—I don't want him to stop. So I nod.

Tucker lets out a soft growl from the back of his throat, and then his fingers dip slowly into my underwear.

"Tuck," I sigh.

His head drops over my shoulder and he kisses my throat. "I said I was going to tease you, not make you feel good," he whispers. "But fuck, Princess, when you say my name like that…" He trails off, but his fingers start stroking me, and I whimper.

He takes me higher and higher, my hips moving with his hand, my ass grinding into his steel erection, and his breathing races mine. He pushes his hand farther down until he thrusts one, then two fingers inside me, the heel of his hand rubbing purposefully, his rhythm making me gasp for air.

Tucker whispers dirty little things about my body and what it inspires in him, how jealous his dick is of his fingers right now, how he wishes he could do the same thing with his tongue.

And then he takes me over the edge, right there in the lake, our friends no more than fifty yards away. I bite my lip so hard I almost draw blood to keep from crying out, my nails digging into his flexing forearms.

It takes several moments for me to return to earth as Tucker's hand slows and eventually withdraws. He traces his fingers over my belly and around my navel as I try to catch my breath.

"Now I'm never going to be able to leave this lake," he says with a laugh.

"Hmm…?"

Tucker answers by grinding his raging arousal against my ass again.

"I came back into the lake to wait for it to go down, and to get you back for getting me riled up in the first place." He laughs. "And now I'm going to have to spend the night in this fucking lake."

Or…I could return the favor, I think to myself.

I suck in a deep, courage-mustering breath.

I reach behind me and let the tips of my still-tingling fingers graze over his thigh, dipping under the hem of his boxer briefs. Tucker stops breathing behind me. I turn my head, and my lips reach up to the base of his throat, just softly brushing his skin. His Adam's apple rolls under my lips with his thick swallow and his hands grip my sides.

I don't dare turn to face him. If anyone looks over and actually manages to make us out through the blackness, it will look like he is just holding me as we watch our friends party. If I turned, it would look too intimate. We would at the very least look like we were making out, and that would destroy the clandestine ambiance—as if our intimacy is a secret that belongs only to us.

I slide my palm up over his underwear until I find the massive shape of him under the thin, wet cotton. My other hand assaults from above, slipping beneath his waistband and immediately finding its target.

"Princess…*Fuuuck*." Tucker groans into my hair, emboldening me, and I grasp him firmly and start to stroke.

I've only done this once before, when I was probably too young to be doing it at all, and certainly didn't know how to make it especially good. And granted, my knowledge now only comes from the couple of porn videos Tina and I have watched online, but Tucker's rapid breathing, the way his fingers burrow into my waist, the trembling of his taut belly behind me, tells me he likes what I'm doing.

I silently marvel at his size, how he possibly managed to fit *that* inside my body. I move faster, a little stronger, stroking and twisting, wanting so much to make him feel as incredible as he made me feel. He hides his face in my hair, his chest rising and falling fast and hard behind me.

"Fuck, Princess. I'm going to come in your hand." He says it like a warning, but it feels more like a promise.

And then he stops breathing entirely, his fingers root themselves almost painfully into my skin, and he does exactly as he said. I strain my neck to watch him, his face turned upward to the night sky, eyes shut tight, teeth clenched as he fights to keep quiet just as he forced me to do minutes ago.

In those short moments he is perfectly mine, and I revel in it.

He takes a moment to calm his breathing, and then spins me to face him, green eyes shimmering with awe in the moonlight. "You never do what I expect," he murmurs.

I bite my lip to keep my smile from growing into an epically embarrassing grin.

It feels like a victory. But certainly not a defeat for him. And I wonder if Tucker and I have found a new way to challenge each other, one where we can both triumph, and I try to ignore the warmth in my chest as my heart swells with pride and something else—something that threatens to thoroughly unravel this new delicate truce of friendship and wonderful, world-spinning benefits.

Chapter Six

Carleigh

Present Day

As the October air grows cooler and the trees change to vibrant coppers and fiery reds, I fall into a routine. Classes and studying, and a reasonable amount of socializing. Devin and I have befriended a few girls from our dorm and we've formed a kind of group. Of course, they all want to go to the hottest parties, the most popular bars, and that means running into Tucker more than my heart appreciates. Or maybe my heart appreciates it more than I care to admit.

We seemed to have developed a nonverbal truce, where the only indication that there's any history between us is his practiced obliviousness to my presence, only rarely interrupted by his contemptuous stare.

Seeing him twice a week in creative digital marketing doesn't help either. I try to focus in class, participating twice as much as I normally would just to distract myself from his presence, but Tucker takes up the entire room. Our past is a living, breathing entity, a constant reminder of what I've lost, and his hostility is tangible.

The sad part is the class should have been my favorite. Even though I landed there by default, and despite the harsh grading system, I actually find the subject matter interesting—useful for the future. And the professor is pretty cool, too. It's nice to have a professor that re-members what it's like to be a student, and I honestly don't mind that he expects a lot from us. I like being challenged. But Tucker doesn't seem to agree. I hate that I'm so acutely aware of him, but I can't help but notice that he seems to dislike our professor nearly as much as he does me.

Mondays aren't especially known for partying or going out, but some people are just incapable of enjoying a relaxing night in, and I'm starting to discover that Devin is one of those people. She suffers from an obvious case of FOMO—fear of missing out—and seems irritated with me when I tell her I'm just going to study and go to bed early. I win her back over when I offer to do her makeup, and she and Julia head out to the bars looking like they'd fit in better at a Hollywood club.

* * *

The following morning begins like any other Tuesday, with equal parts anticipation and dread, and neither is particularly helpful. It's hard enough to get over the love of your life when you're not sen-tenced to spend an hour sitting across the room from him twice a week.

Class starts out normally enough. I get there about five minutes early and take my usual seat. Julia sits beside me and complains about her hangover, though it doesn't stop her from talking my ear off. Not a minute before class is scheduled to begin, Tucker strolls right past me without even a hint of a glance my way. It still stings, but it also gives me the opportunity to watch him, and I note that I'm not the only one. Most of the girls in the class sneak a peek at Tuck, and I can't really blame them. But I suspect I *am* the only one to notice the subtle clench of his jaw, the tension in his shoulders, and I can't help but wonder at it.

Zayne asks the two students nearest his desk to pass out some memos to the class, and draws a blush from both of them. I have to suppress an eye roll. He's good-looking, but he's our freaking *professor*.

Before I can even glance at the sheets of paper that have just been handed to me, Zayne starts speaking. "For your final project this semester, you will be creating a social marketing campaign for one of the organizations on the list I have provided." Zayne holds up one of the sheets of paper.

"Every semester I choose a different theme, and yours will be nonprofits. The campaign will not focus on selling anything or raising money, but rather on the organization's core values."

Zayne goes on to reference points from his last lecture as well as our textbook, and I'm glad I've kept up. Basically he wants us to create a viral video that will positively and effectively represent the nonprofit's values or messages.

I swallow anxiously. *Well, I wanted to be challenged.*

"For your final, you will create a presentation to showcase your campaign to the class," Zayne continues. "You will be graded on the following: concept, writing, design, execution, editing, presentation, and last but not least, professionalism."

Some guy whose name I don't remember raises his hand and Zayne gestures to him. "Uh, what do you mean by professionalism? Like, how professional it, like, *is*?"

A few people snicker, but I hold mine in. It's not a stupid question, even if it was phrased less than articulately.

Zayne just looks at the guy for a moment. "How professional, like, *what* is?"

The poor kid turns redder than the blushing girls before him. "Like…the project?" His inflection is so unsure it comes out like a question; even more people laugh, and I can't help cracking a smile.

Fortunately Zayne takes pity on him. "Professionalism refers to the way you conduct yourselves during all of the stages of your project.

After all, college is supposed to help prepare you for the workforce—for life—so you will be judged and graded very much the way an employee is reviewed in a professional setting."

I glance around the room, trying to figure out if I'm the only one who doesn't know how one reviews your *professionalism* on a project that won't be presented until the end of the semester.

"The second sheet you've been handed is the list of your groups."
Groups?

"I've divided you into six groups of four. You will be responsible for meeting on your own time, assigning roles, delegating work, etcetera. You'll work together through the semester, and in the final weeks, you will all submit anonymous reviews of your group members."

Oh.

"Now, I'm always happy to act as a sounding board or provide feedback for anyone who wants to take advantage of my office hours, but the onus will be on you. I won't be checking in, or micromanaging any of you. It's all up to you. You're adults. It's your project, and your grade on the line.

"And speaking of grades, I should also mention that this project is a competition."

There's a chorus of surprise and anxiety, and I silently echo it. I'm as competitive as the next girl, but aren't we all here to *learn*?

Zayne goes on to explain that our projects will be graded on a curve. We'll start with a specific grade based on our team's place in the competition, which, of course, he will judge. The winning team starts with A's, the losing team with D's, and the four middle teams will start anywhere from a B+ to a D+ depending on Zayne's assessment of the campaigns and presentations. Everyone in a group will earn the same starting grade, but not necessarily the same final grade. Apparently that's where our "professionalism" comes in. Once Zayne evaluates our peer reviews, they, and his own "observations," will either raise or lower our individual grades, "some considerably," and that will determine the grade for our final project. He reminds us it will account for half our grade for the class itself. *No pressure.*

"I expect you all to work together *professionally*; however, you'd be surprised at some of the behavior that has led to a failing grade in previous semesters."

Silence.

But Zayne isn't finished. "There's more on the line than your grades, as well. After all, what's a competition without a prize?"

And here I thought the A's were the prize.

"The winning team will be presenting their campaign to the executives at Steepman and Boyle, my former employer and one of the largest advertising firms in the country."

I'll say. Even I've heard of S&B. They've been famously behind some of the most creative ad campaigns and successful social media promotions in the past decade.

"All of the organizations on the list I've provided are their clients, and if they're impressed, they could potentially use your video in one of their campaigns, and each of the winning team members would be credited. And paid."

This announcement has the intended effect, and cheers erupt around the room along with excited chatter, before Zayne quiets us again.

"There's more." He smiles at our collective eager anticipation. "From the winning team, the student or students who earn the highest grade on the project will interview with my former bosses, and one will be awarded a paid summer internship in the department of his or her choice."

Wow.

"Now, this is a big deal," Zayne states the obvious. "Thousands of students apply for even the unpaid internships at S&B every year, and whoever is selected will be getting a valuable foot in the door—one that, if you play your cards right, could lead to a job offer and a successful career."

I sit up straighter in my chair. An internship at S&B is beyond anything I ever pictured for myself, at least in the foreseeable future, but I'm sure as hell picturing it now. I imagine what I could learn there—how much it could help me when it's time to get my own businesses off the ground. Suddenly my distant dreams feel tangible, within my grasp, and my competitive spirit awakens and flexes its muscles.

A survey of the room indicates that I'm not the only one suddenly motivated, but I rally to find the confidence that once came so naturally to me, and tell myself I've got this.

I'm smiling to myself when I finally take a look at the group list in my hand, and my smile vanishes instantly.

I stop breathing entirely, the black photocopy ink blurring as I stare right through the paper, but Julia taps my shoulder excitedly, and I try to suck in air and focus as she gushes over our being in the same group.

And then she's whispering in my ear, "And that super hot lacrosse player is with us, too! The one always staring at you—Tucker Green."

My eyes shoot to his icy green gaze to find it locked on mine, completely inscrutable. He works to unclench his jaw, his mouth a thin line of displeasure.

Zayne claps once to get our attention. "Okay. So like I said, you can make your own schedules to work on your campaigns, and in the next couple of weeks I'd like you all to have an idea of what organization your group will choose."

He dismisses us. As always, everyone rushes out the door to get to their next class, except Tucker, who always sits there waiting for me to be long gone before he heads out. But I make my way up to Zayne's desk, all too aware of hostile green eyes on me, and vaguely I wonder why he doesn't take the opportunity to get out of here.

"Hey, Carleigh." Zayne's boyish smile makes him seem younger, more like one of us. I would find it disarming if Tucker's presence didn't make me feel like I need a full military detail.

"Do you have a minute?" I ask him tentatively. I need him to change my group. There's no way Tucker and I can work together—there's too much riding on this project—and he shouldn't have to be the one to switch. But as I stand here chewing on my bottom lip, I still don't know what excuse I'm going to give Zayne for wanting a new group.

His smile falters and his brow furrows. "Is everything okay with you?" Something about the way he asks seems like it's coming more from a friend than my professor, and when he places his hand on my arm in concern, I wonder how obvious my distress actually is. I'm usually so much better at hiding my emotions.

Suddenly Tucker's chair scrapes noisily against the floor as he stands up. But I refuse to turn, trying desperately not to show how acutely aware I am of him.

"Yeah," I assure Zayne. "I'm okay. I just need to talk to you about something. About the campaign," I clarify.

Zayne nods, but he doesn't remove his hand from my arm. "I have office hours in a few minutes, but I do have a couple of students coming. Why don't you drop by my office between four and five this afternoon? That way I can give you my focus."

I nod and thank him, relieved that I'll have time to think of some reason for wanting a new group, and that he seems so reasonable and understanding.

"No problem, Carleigh. I'm always here if you need to talk. About class, or whatever else, okay?" His eyes shine with empathy, and idly I wonder if he really identifies that well with his students, or if I'm actually just that desperate to feel understood by a guy.

I turn to find Tucker glaring at us—or at me, anyway. I swallow thickly and hurry out of the room.

A massive hand closes around my elbow and I'm so startled I almost scream before Tucker spins me to face him. "What was that about?" he demands gruffly. He holds me so firmly it almost hurts, and if it were anyone else, I'd wrench from their grip. But as much as his touch burns me, I crave it. Like a stupid mosquito flying into one of those electric bug zappers, attracted to the very thing that means to destroy me. "*Carl*." His impatient growl reminds me that I'm just standing here gaping at him.

"I—I'm going to change groups," I tell him.

He releases me from his grip, and I expect his relief, but it doesn't come. He continues to glare down at me, and I wish fervently that I could read his thoughts. "Don't do that," he says, his voice deceptively soft and low.

I blink up at him, confused.

"Don't go to his office." He exhales harshly. "Okay?" he adds, amending his order to a request, and it obviously grates on him to do it.

"What? Why?" I ask, bewildered.

"Just don't."

I bite my lip so hard it stings, and I soothe the indented flesh with my tongue. Tucker looks away, and I look down at my sandals, studying my chipped pedicure. "You don't have to work with me, Tuck," I whisper.

Tucker shrugs. "It's not a big deal."

I look up at him.

"I'm working with a group of strangers, what's one more?"

Huh?

He shakes his head. "You're not the girl I thought I knew, *Carleigh*. That girl—she never existed. You and me? We have no history. We're nothing. We never were. The girl I thought I loved…she's not real. She was *never* real. You're just another stranger and I can work on the damn project with you and whoever the fuck else." He takes a step back.

I'm not breathing. I'm not blinking. I don't even think my heart is beating right now. How could it be when he's just so viciously flayed me open and torn it from my chest?

But I hold in my tears. Because if there's one thing my mother taught me, it's how to bury emotions until no one is around to witness them. How to work the façade.

"E-mail me whatever company the rest of you choose. I don't care what we do," he continues, as if he didn't just say the worst thing he could possibly ever say to me. As if he didn't just hit the delete button on our entire history. "But do not go to his office later," he repeats.

He needs to go. I need to go. I'm strong, but I'm not invincible, and the tears, they're about to overtake the levy, and I can't let him witness the flood.

"Okay?" he asks, exasperated, and I realize he's waiting for me to agree.

What am I even agreeing to? That we're nothing? That we never were? That the Carl of *Carl and Tuck* never existed and he never really knew me at all? How can I agree to any of that?

Tucker rolls his eyes in frustration with my silence. "Look, you're not switching groups, so you don't need to go to his office. And I don't understand why the fuck he'd need private office hours to discuss a damn project anyway. So cancel, Carl, okay?"

Something about hearing him call me *Carl* again instead of the scornful way he'd said *Carleigh* unlocks the invisible chokehold around my throat. I nod. Because not going to meet Zayne to switch groups is the one thing he's said that I *can* agree to.

Tucker nods his approval and then turns on his heel, leaving me reeling in the now empty hall. I suck in a deep breath and race to the nearest bathroom to let the dam break, and I cry harder than I have since he ended us. Because I didn't know then that he could do something worse than end us. That he could erase us.

Chapter Seven

Tucker

Last Year

Dave honks his horn obnoxiously and I slow my gait to punish him for his impatience. "Take your motherfucking time," he grumbles sarcastically as I climb into his passenger seat.

"You got it, brother," I retort, and we drive to pick up Cap so we can head over to Andy's for the party.

Cap texted that he just finished his run and needs a few minutes, so Dave and I walk right through his front door without knocking. We both practically grew up here and Cap's house is as much our home as our own.

"Hello!" I call out.

"Back here," Cap's kid sister, Bits—Beth—calls out from the kitchen, and we head straight back to where she and her mom, Elaine, are eating dessert.

"Score!" I grab a chunk of cookie pie off of Bits's plate and shove it unceremoniously into my mouth as she slaps my arm. Dave pats her head as a greeting like she's some kind of cat, and she smiles the weird, shy smile he always seems to bring out of her.

"Sammy's in the shower," she tells us as I hop up onto the kitchen counter and make myself comfortable.

Elaine hands Dave and me our own pieces of pie, and we thank her, but I grab another chunk off Bits's plate just to fuck with her. She pokes her fork into my thigh hard enough to make me yelp in a very unmanly way.

"Will you behave?" Elaine scolds me halfheartedly, and I smirk at her.

"Never."

She smiles. She loves me. And I love her right back, in a second mom sort of way. But I have to admit, if she didn't practically raise me, I would be looking a little lower than her beautiful smile right now. Cap's mom is hot—the reason for the creation of the term *MILF*. And Bits is looking more and more like her every day.

Thing is—when I look at her I still see the little brat with pigtails, whining and nagging until we all agree to munch plastic cookies and sip air-tea out of her little pink tea set.

That's why it was so rough on Cap, and on me, too, when she started high school with us last year. We were juniors and she was a freshman, and it was a hell of a shock to see guys notice her. Not just guys her age, but our friends, too, and one senior in particular.

Brian Falco pursued her from even before the first day of class, and though Cap, Dave, and I gave him a hard time at first, he seemed so sincere. He acted all respectful, and just wanted to take her out, to get to know her, and the idiots we were—we fell for it. Or maybe he really meant it at the time. Or maybe we just had no choice other than to relent. Bits liked Falco—a lot—and she wanted to date him. And damn her, once that stubborn girl decides she wants something, there's no stopping her. She's a lot like Carl in that way.

But in the end, we were right to have tried to protect Bits. She wasn't ready for someone like Falco. She wasn't ready for that kind of serious relationship at all. Who is at fifteen? Because despite his eventual professions of love, which I can only assume led to a physical relationship I'd rather not think about, eventually that "love" died out. Maybe he realized it didn't suit his needs to go off to Dartmouth in the fall with a high school sophomore girlfriend holding him back. Maybe he was just playing her all along. We were all relieved when we heard he was going to the Hamptons for the summer. We thought Bits would finally have the time and the freedom from his perpetual presence to get over him. That's the thing about high school. There's no escaping people you don't want to see. Or in her case, the person she still wanted to see, but who no longer cared to see her. *Fucking idiot.*

But I guess we all underestimated her heartbreak. We knew she was sad—it was impossible to miss—but girls got dumped all the time, and I thought they just ate ice cream, cried, and bashed the guy to their friends until they got over it. Never in a million years did I consider that someone like strong, stubborn Bits could do something like *that*. Neither did Cap, and he's been beating himself up over it ever since. And compensating for it by being obsessively overprotective of her, and God knows I can't blame him for it.

I'll never forget his face that day, or the grief in his voice. How in a single split second, that morning went from the best of my life to one of the absolute worst.

I had Carl—the girl I'd been lusting over since she'd first sprouted tits—in my bed for the first time ever. I'd woken up with her in my arms, her sweet thigh hooked around my hip, her stomach pressed up against my exceptionally vengeful morning wood. I lay in bed that morning just watching her sleep, enjoying having her so close, because I knew the moment she woke up she would be gone. I was positive that even if she did remember the night before, she would regret what we almost did. I didn't consider for a moment that Carleigh Stanger, the girl I've crushed on for as long as I could remember, whose beauty literally takes my breath away, might actually want me when she was in her right sober mind.

And then she opened her eyes. Stunning bright jade glittered sleepily from under those long, thick lashes, and they did not hold regret. They held *desire*. So when she slid her thigh around me and pushed her hips against mine, I thought I might still be dreaming.

But I wasn't. Because not a single one of my many, many dreams and fantasies had ever lived up to what happened next. My limited imagination, it turned out, was unable to conjure up the sheer perfection of her naked body. The magnum opus that was the sound of my name on her sweet, swollen lips, in that breathy, sultry version of her voice. Nothing could have prepared me for the sensation of being inside her, or the vision of watching this girl who only knows how to challenge and spar, give in to me in the most decadent way.

And for the first time in my life, after I was done, I wasn't *done*. Physically sated, the usual urge to move on and out was conspicuously absent. Carl was in my bed. With me. Naked. A multitude of thoughts swirled through my head, all with the same goal in mind—figuring out how to keep her there. But I guess she wasn't on the same page, because her next thought was to check her phone. So I did the same.

And then suddenly the girl in my bed wasn't the one who had my attention.

Over twenty texts from Cap alerted me immediately that something was very wrong. He's never been a guy to chase you down. So as much as I wanted to ignore him and focus on Carl, I opened his messages. And thank God I did.

It was strange—even as I read the words, they didn't register in my mind as quickly as they did in my body. I could feel the exponential acceleration of my pulse and the anxiety explode in my gut, but still my brain refused to make sense of the words the screen revealed. But then my brain did catch up, and I started to panic. Because I needed to *go*, but what the fuck was I going to say to Carl? I couldn't tell her the real reason I had to leave just minutes after sleeping with her, not when Cap's texts explicitly told me not to speak to anyone about it. No one is more private than he is, and no matter could be more private than that one.

But I couldn't even think up an excuse. My mind was bombarded with fear for another girl—one I've known most of my life, and love like my own sister. I was in such a rush to get to the hospital, in fact, that it didn't even occur to me until the following day to be offended by Carl's non-reaction to my abandoning her right after sex.

Nothing could have prepared me for seeing Bits like that. For the pallor of her usually bright pink cheeks and the deep gray shadows under her eyes. The tubes protruding from her nose and the skin of her arm. It wasn't until that moment—seeing her lying unconscious and unstirring in the hospital bed that seemed too vast for her small, delicate body—that my brain finally processed the reality of it.

Bits had tried to kill herself. She almost succeeded. And even though we already knew by then that she would pull through, what gutted me was more than the fact that we'd almost lost her—that she'd almost left us. It was that *she'd wanted to*. And for me, it hit far too close to home.

In fact, if it weren't for Carl coming home with me that night, Cap would have spent the night at my place as planned, and he wouldn't have found his sister in time to make her throw up the pills, or for the ambulance to get her to the hospital so they could pump the rest from her stomach.

That night changed Cap. It was there in his eyes when I finally got to the hospital that next morning, drawn in lines of worry and guilt in the skin around them, and it's been there ever since. Bits rolls her eyes in exasperation when she notices me giving her a once-over. Any other girl would assume I was checking her out, but Bits knows we still worry about her, and it bugs the crap out of her.

I raise my eyebrows, daring her to give me shit for it when she knows full well she's earned my concern. She looks away, glancing at Dave, who's watching her with similar concern and what, if I didn't know better, I might think is attraction. But Dave's been around as long as I have, and Bits is as much a sister to him as she is to me.

"What's up, assholes?" Cap greets us as he emerges from the stairs.

"*Sammy*," Elaine chastens, but he just kisses her on the cheek, which Dave and I mimic before following him out the door.

"Later, brat," I tell Bits, and she gives me the finger.

I grin. But she's not paying me any more attention as she slips on her shy Dave-only smile, and I freeze when I think I see his eyes slide down her body. But a second later Dave is following behind me, and I assume I must have seen wrong. Because Dave wouldn't look at Bits like that.

Right?

* * *

"Never have I ever gotten—or given—road head!" Dave bellows.

I laugh and shake my head at the one friend I can always count on to make me look less ridiculous by comparison. I take a sip of my beer and look around Andy's living room. The point of the game is to force people to admit to things they have or haven't done, but it's all bullshit. Most of the guys will drink even if they've never gotten a blowjob while driving a car. Half the girls who drink do it because they think it will make them more appealing to the guys, and half the girls who don't, don't for the same reason. I know for a fact, for example, that Molly has done it, since I was there and all, but she simply blushes and stares down at her beer. Cap never plays—he's too private—but I also know for a fact it's something he's experienced, and not just once either.

But there's only one person I'm really looking at. Carl doesn't take a sip, she just looks around the room with interest, no blush, eyes completely guileless, and I believe her. In fact, lately I've been wondering if she's even less experienced than I realized. The thought excites me, and it's a strange reaction for me. Normally the more experience a girl has, the better. It means they're more likely to be game for some fun, and that I won't have to show them what to do.

But any time I think of Carl doing any of the things I've done with her—or the things I fantasize about doing with her—with someone else, it makes me a little crazy. Not just jealous. I've been jealous over her for years. But lately it makes me basically lose my mind. And it's frustrating, because as much as I enjoy her friendship, and the new benefits we've started to indulge in, she's made it clear she's not interested in taking it beyond a casual hookup. Because she's *Carl*.

She's not like any other girl in existence, and she never acts the way I expect. Everything I've learned about girls' emotions is utterly useless when it comes to her, and I wonder if in our little scenario…if *I'm* the girl. Not something I particularly want to think about. But she just doesn't seem to want the same things I've been dodging from other girls since hitting puberty. And yet for me, if I let myself go there, with her…I think I would be up for more.

Or maybe Carl does want those things, too. Maybe she just doesn't want them *with me*. Not that I can blame her. What would I know about *more*? Trying out an actual relationship? I'd fuck it up, for sure, and then we wouldn't even be friends.

But casual means I have no real claim on her, and she's free to do whatever she wants, with whoever she wants. And fuck, to think of another guy putting his hands on her, kissing her pretty pink mouth—it makes me want to hit something. When I think about another guy actually fucking her, being inside her, watching her come for him, I turn into The Incredible fucking Hulk…on the inside, anyway.

I swallow the thought back down before it completely destroys my mood. I consider getting up and going to another room so I can stop picturing Carl in every *Never Have I Ever* scenario. The party is slammed, and though there are only about twenty or so of our friends in this room, there must be close to a hundred people around the house and in the back. But I can't bring myself to do it. The curious masochist in me wants to see what Carl drinks to.

"Never have I ever had anal sex," Sarah says with a giggle.

I glance at her, because I've heard that isn't exactly true, but I wouldn't know for sure. Not that I care either way. I look at Carl, who once again doesn't sip, and I have no doubt she's never done that. Only three people sip, and I suspect only one of them has actually done it.

Carl is watching me, though she's trying to hide her interest, and I realize she wants to see if I take a drink. It pleases me deeply, and I smile wryly at her. She scowls at being caught giving a shit, and my smile stretches wider.

"Oh *please*, Dave! Who have you ass-fucked?" Chelsea accuses. She doesn't believe him, but he's probably the only one who drank that has actually done it.

Dave just smirks. "Wouldn't you like to know? Or are you jealous, Chel? Should I take you upstairs and show you how much fun it can be?"

A cacophony of hysterical laughter erupts, and Chelsea tosses some beer at him. She sneers some mumbled words and crosses her arms over her chest.

"Never have I ever had a threesome!" Lily shouts.

Some people drink, some don't. I should take a sip, but instead I just look at Carl. And then my heart stops beating as she slowly raises her bottle upwards.

I feel it. The Hulk. He's bursting within me, shredding his clothing and growling with rage. Suddenly I'm breathing so hard my chest is heaving. My nostrils flare and I don't blink as the small glass rim touches her bottom lip. And then before she tips her bottle to drink, she brings it right back down to her lap and her sweet, pink, devious little mouth curls into a smirk, emerald eyes alight with mischief.

I am practically shaking with relief and residual anger as I narrow my eyes at her. *Well-played, Princess.* But no matter how many times my head tells my body she was just fucking with me, I am still completely on edge. Fortunately people are still distracted by Dave and Chelsea's continued arguing.

But whoever's turn it is—I'm no longer paying attention—ignores them and continues the game. "Never have I ever fucked anyone at this party."

Almost everyone drinks, and I try to stop myself, but my gaze automatically slides over to Carl, who's fucking with me again, lifting the bottle to her lips. But this time, when it reaches its destination, she tips it up and takes a drink.

Motherfucker.

I watch in rapt horror as her delicate neck moves with her swallow. *She took a drink.*

She's not just fucking with me this time. The green monster is back, and he is fucking livid. *Who? Who the fuck has Carl fucked?*

A small commotion unfolds in my peripheral as Chelsea storms off and Lily and Sarah jump up to go after her, Cap halfheartedly censuring Dave for whatever it is he must have said.

I'm standing before I even realize it, and I stalk over to Carl's spot on the couch. She stands to face me, a little nervous and a little confused. Vaguely I'm aware that I have no right to my reaction—that she's not mine and she can fuck who she likes. Not to mention she very well may have fucked this person before we ever even did anything. But I can't help the way I feel. It's visceral. It's crawling through my veins, tensing my muscles and boiling my blood.

I don't even think—I grab hold of Carl's elbow and march her out of the room.

"Tucker?" she asks, but she doesn't try to get away from me. "Tucker, what the hell do you think you're doing?" she hisses.

I pull her past the empty kitchen and into the laundry room. I slam the door shut behind us and she yanks her arm from my grip. I close my eyes and silently count to ten, trying to take deep breaths.

"How dare you drag me in here like a goddamn Neanderthal!" she chides.

She's right. I am a Neanderthal right now. But I can't fucking help it.

"Who?" I demand.

She blinks her pretty jade eyes at me, thin brows furrowed like she really has no idea what I'm asking her.

"You think you're real cute, don't you? Fucking with my head like that..."

"Tucker—"

"Such a little smartass." But that's also what I find irresistible. That she challenges me. Teases me the way I've always teased her. She knew that'd get me riled up.

"Who at this party have you fucked?" I practically snarl.

More confusion. "Seriously?"

Do I seem like I'm fucking kidding?

And then her confusion falls away, her features rearranging into their trademark defiance. She puffs out her chest in challenge, but it only draws my attention to her perfect, perky tits in that tight, low-cut tank top of hers. "You think that's your business, Tucker?" she asks, goading me.

And goad me it does. I take another deep breath. I have no right to be so angry at the fact that she's fucked someone I know, but I am. But there's nothing I can do about that now. I can't change the past, but I can make damn sure she doesn't want to fuck anyone else again. And I've never felt more determined to achieve anything in my life. The raging tension shifts lower in my body, my heated blood traveling south until my dick is harder than it's ever been, desperate to reclaim her.

I stalk toward her and she answers with a slow retreat until I have her backed against the door. I run my fingers down her soft, delicate throat, and let them trail lower over her tempting cleavage.

"You let him touch you, Princess?" My voice is low and hoarse.

Her tongue darts out to wet her lips, and she nods.

I don't let her admission anger me more. Instead, I let it fuel me.

I take another step until my body holds hers flush against the door, until I can feel her soft tits against my chest. She gasps, and I know she can feel how hard I am for her, how much she makes me ache. Slowly I lean down and hold my face barely an inch from hers until she can only breathe my exhales, until her scent is the only air I know.

Her breathing deepens and her eyes cloud with want, molten green that I fight not to lose myself in. *God*, she's just too beautiful. I mean to tease her longer, but I can't stop myself, I slam my mouth against hers—I don't even go slow. But it doesn't matter, she matches my desperation as I nibble and suck on her plump lips. Her arms fly around my neck and she burrows her fingers into my hair and tugs. *Fuck* it feels good. My hands close around her small waist, so tiny I can almost touch both thumbs and middle fingers.

I pull back from my kiss, but leave my mouth hovering over hers, my hands exploring. "Tell me, did you let him kiss you like that?" I ask her.

"Yes," she says, and then pulls my head back to hers, pushing her tongue into my mouth.

I groan, and let myself go. I fucking consume her, drunk on the sweet taste of her, until I can't wait another second. I need to be inside her. I grab her ass and squeeze and she grinds her hips against me. *Fuck, yes.*

I slide my hands down to the backs of her thighs and lift, guiding her legs around me, and she locks her ankles at the small of my back. I set her down on the washing machine, wasting no time before I'm peeling off her tank top. She's equally impatient with my shirt. Her skirt rides up, and suddenly my jeans are our worst enemy. *Fuck you, jeans.*

We both attack them together, her tearing at my belt and me at my fly until my raging erection is held captive by only my boxer briefs. I force myself to calm down to make sure she's ready for me. I remember how tight she is from our first time, and the last thing I want is to hurt her. I stroke the small triangle of thin lace between her thighs, high on male pride to discover they're soaked. *God I want to taste that.*

But I can't wait for that right now. I slip my fingers beneath the fabric and trace them down her center until I push one, then two easily inside her. Carl gasps as I stretch her, her eyes glazed with lust. *Yes.* She's beyond ready. I band an arm around her hips and haul her to the edge of the machine before shoving my underwear down. My dick bursts free, reaching for her, pointing to exactly what it wants like the goddamn needle on a compass.

I take her mouth again, showing her how much I want her, how crazy she makes me. "Did he make you this wet, Princess?" I growl.

"Yes," she moans, driving me even madder.

"I'm going to make you come so hard you forget his fucking name," I promise her. "I'm going to make you forget *your* name," and then I pull her panties aside and line myself up, ready to make good.

"Tucker," she pants. "Condom."

I freeze. *Fuck.*

I almost just took her bare. *What the fuck is wrong with me?* I have never forgotten a condom in my life.

"You make me crazy," I tell her, and I grab my wallet from the back pocket of my jeans, still riding low on my thighs, and I retrieve a condom.

I have it on a second later, and a second after that, I'm inside her.

I groan, long and strangled, but it doesn't drown out her responding moan—a brilliant symphony of answering pleasure. *Why is she so fucking tight? Why does she feel better than anything I've ever known?*

God, I want to *live* in here.

I kiss her, hard and deep, and I take her body with all the determination of a man desperate to be the only one she ever wants touching her like this again. Her legs tighten around me like a vise, like she wants to keep me inside of her, as if there's anywhere else I would ever want to be.

"Oh, God, Tuck," she whimpers, throwing her head back, soft blond hair flying everywhere.

That's fucking right. "Again, Princess. Say my name again," I demand.

"*Tu-ck.*" This time it's a broken gasp, and I can feel her body tightening around me as her hips meet mine, thrust for thrust. She's close, and I feel like a goddamn king.

"Yes, baby, it's fucking *me* inside you. *Me* making you moan. *My* dick about to make you fucking explode," I growl.

I suck on the skin of her throat, and she whimpers again. My girl likes my dirty words. But I like the way her body grips mine in response even more, and I won't be able to hold myself back much longer.

"Give it to me, Princess," I order her. "Let me fucking *feel* you."

I reach my hand between us to where I'm ramming myself inside her, and I stroke her with my thumb.

Carl sighs a choked-out version of my name, and I kiss her, swallowing her moans so no one will hear her as she obeys my command. She spasms around me and it's all I can take. I come like a goddamn freight train, buried as deep as she can take me, gagging myself against her throat.

Our heavy breaths fill the room as we both gasp for air. I stay there, holding her to me, holding myself inside her, and I brush soft, lazy kisses under her jaw and along the column of her neck. I feel her pulse race against my lips, and I wait for it to calm before I disentangle myself from her.

Carl sighs a sound of pure satisfaction and I want to beat my chest like the Neanderthal she accused me of being. She is my perfect fantasy, reclined on the washing machine with her skirt hiked up and panties displaced, tits still heaving as she catches her breath, golden hair loose and disheveled. I avert my gaze before I need to take her all over again.

"Tell me, Princess, anyone ever make you come like that but me?" I ask huskily.

Carl's swollen lips twist up into a small, knowing smile, her eyes a little bemused, like I'm missing something. "No, Tucker," she breathes.

Fuck. Yes.

I lean down to kiss her again.

We both startle when we hear Cap calling for me, probably from somewhere in the kitchen. I glance at my watch and realize he probably wants to leave and he's my ride. Shit.

"It's okay," Carl murmurs. "Go."

But I don't want to go. Especially after I had to run out of bed the last time in a move that's haunted me for months. And I don't want to leave the place where she admitted I'm the only one who's ever made her feel that good.

Cap calls again and I tense.

Carl runs her fingertips along my jaw, lightly scratching my stubble, and it feels so damn good. "It's okay. Go. I need to go, too."

I let out a long-winded sigh and help her down from the washer, and we both find our shirts and fix ourselves.

"Tuck!" Cap calls again, closer this time. I grit my teeth, silently pledging to get him back for this one day.

"You go first, I'll wait a few minutes," Carl suggests.

I ignore the dull sting at the fact that she doesn't want anyone to know she was with me. Because I want to scream it from the goddamn rooftops. But I can't. So I place one more kiss on her forehead and turn to leave.

"Tucker—" Carl stops me and I turn back. Her mouth curves into a mischievous smile and her eyes shine with mirth, twinkling in the dim moonlight streaming in from the room's only window.

Beautiful.

"There's only one guy at this party I've ever slept with," she murmurs in a soft confession.

I furrow my brow, confused, but Carl's eyes are laughing at me. And then my brain—the one that apparently shut down when she played me into thinking she'd had a threesome—starts functioning again.

She meant me.

When she drank to admit she'd fucked someone at this party. She. Meant. Me.

The guy she let touch her.

Kiss her.

Who made her wet.

All me.

My chest swells and I'm on her again, kissing her, and she's kissing me back, laughing her sweet, triumphant laugh. I pull away and shake my head. I don't say anything, but my look promises payback.

The door swings open and the light flashes on, blinding me with its sudden glare. I turn, shielding Carl, before I remember we're already decent.

Cap raises his eyebrows and Carl gives me a little push to encourage me to go, and I feel a strange longing as I leave that laundry room. I fucking love that laundry room.

Chapter Eight

Carleigh

Present Day

I had the dream again last night. I haven't had it in a long time, and today I feel lethargic and unsettled. Because it isn't a dream at all. You get to wake up from dreams. This is a memory.

I'm eight years old, asleep in my old canopy bed with the pink silk bedding. It's late and I'm warm and cozy, tucked into bed, in my favorite nightgown that makes me feel like the princess my father insists I am.

Suddenly there is a cacophony of strange sounds. Tires screech outside my window, doors slam, and men's voices carry in the night. I blink my eyes open in fear, only to find that it isn't night at all.

Morning light filters through my ivory curtains, and I think it must be very, very early.

Bang, bang, bang!

The front door of our house is nowhere near my bedroom, and yet the angry knocking reaches me with ominous urgency.

Daddy!

I call for my father, but he doesn't come. I think about hiding under the bed, but I need to find Billy, and I need my daddy. I jump out of bed and cautiously inch my door open.

Men's voices. This time they're inside the house, their orders echoing through our foyer. I creep down the hall, but Billy's already out there, looking for me, tears streaming down his pink, cherubic cheeks. He's only three, and he is terrified.

I take his hand and whisper not to worry. That everything is fine. Daddy will take care of us.

We creep around the corner to the second-floor landing where we can see through the railing.

Men. Men in black uniforms, with vests and flashlights, and in the holsters around their waists, guns.

Whimpering cries. My mother. She is in her beautiful silk nightgown and matching robe, makeup free in front of strangers for the first time I've ever seen. But she doesn't say anything.

And then there's my father, fully dressed in his suit, hands being locked behind his back in glinting silver handcuffs, while one of the only two men in business suits recites his rights as if it's some kind of poem. Even at eight years old, I recognize the foreboding words from TV—right to remain silent...held against you in a court of law...if you can't afford an attorney...

Charged with fraud—a bunch of different kinds. Securities fraud, mail fraud, investment advisor fraud. I don't understand any of the words at the time. It's all gibberish. All I understand is that my daddy is being taken away in handcuffs, and that he's innocent. He has to be.

I tell Billy to stay on the landing and I rush down the stairs.

"Daddy!" I shriek, and grab hold of his leg. I can't let them take him!

But he can't touch me, can't comfort me with his arms restrained. "Shh, it's okay, Princess. Go with Mommy, okay? Everything is going to be okay."

All I hear is okay, okay, okay. But how is any of this okay?

"Nicole," my daddy says gently.

Mommy is standing in the corner crying like a zombie.

"Damn it, Nicole!" he growls suddenly. "Take care of your daughter!"

She seems to snap out of it, and halfheartedly touches my shoulders, trying to pry me from my daddy.

"It's okay, baby. Go with Mommy. It's okay," he soothes.

But then the men start leading him out the door.

No! Where are you taking him?

My tears soak his wool pants, but I don't let go.

"Ma'am, please get hold of your child," one of the men in suits says, and then my mommy is grabbing me and pulling my waist, and I lock my hands around my daddy's leg, screaming for him until my fingers fail me. My heart shatters into tiny pieces that try desperately to follow my father out our front door, because despite my bewildered defeat, one thing I do know is that my life will never be the same.

* * *

Back in my dorm, I make my way to the bathroom and splash some cool water on my face. I hate that dream. That memory. It always stays with me for days. Days where I am eight years old again, helpless, lost in the destructive riptide of my parents' selfish choices. Selfish choices that, I would learn a few years later, didn't even end that fateful morning.

Some things did end that morning, though; namely my childhood as I'd known it for all of its eight happy years.

The thing about kids is they tend to view their parents as superhuman. Infallible. Even though their naïve little minds can often pick up on evidence to the contrary, it rarely changes their overall perception. It takes something earth-shattering to do that. Of course, that's exactly what I got.

Strangely enough, for me, it wasn't even my father's arrest. It was after. It was begging my mom to drive us to the police station, to go get him, only to be told she knows what she's doing, to trust her, and that *everything will be okay*. It was being told we couldn't go pick him up after he posted bail because no one could see us with him there. He didn't even come home. He had to go to the apartment he used to keep near his office in Manhattan for two days before he could ditch the news cameras and come home. And still, my mother promised she knew what was best. Even when they would lock themselves in their master bedroom suite for days at a time, talking in hushed voices, heatedly arguing, my mother's sobs echoing through the walls, I continued to believe her. And why wouldn't I? They're my parents; why wouldn't they have known what was best?

But without a trial it was less than a year before my father was reporting for his voluntary surrender, and even at nine years old I knew that spending the next fifteen years without him wasn't what was *best*. Certainly it wasn't what was best for *me*.

That was about when I stopped believing that other people—even my parents—could possibly know what's best for me better than I do. When I realized the danger in letting others call the shots.

The memories weigh me down with resentment, and I curse that damn dream once again.

After a long day of classes I just want to fall down onto my bed and take a nap. I want this feeling to go away. But I can't, because tonight we have our first group meeting about the campaign project for Zayne's class, and for the second time today, I will have to see Tucker.

His presence makes the aftereffects of my dream sharpen and

linger, makes the shame and guilt wear me down even more. I almost consider e-mailing them all to tell them I'm not feeling well, but I don't, because I may be a lot of things, but I'm not a coward.

And besides, there's too much riding on this project, and I'm determined to win the competition so I can land that internship. Ever since Zayne's announcement, I've grown more and more convinced that it's my opportunity to show the world—and myself—that I can achieve whatever dream I choose, by virtue of nothing more than some talent and good old work ethic. That I possess both, and I can employ them to forge the future I want for myself—one worlds away from the one my father chose.

The sky has spent the entire day overcast in charcoals and slates in a fitting reflection of my mood, but it only begins to weep a light drizzle after I leave my dorm building to go meet the group. The rain waits to grow heavier until I've gone too far to go back for an umbrella, so I push my hood over my hair and rush through the throngs of students also hurrying to their destinations.

Tucker is the last to show up at the student center, and we're all already sitting around the table, tablets out, when he saunters in, brushing the water from his hair with his fingers. He avoids eye contact as he takes the seat opposite me.

"Hi, Tucker." Julia smiles, tucking her hair—also damp—behind her ear.

Yeah, he has that effect.

I stare at the blank note page on my tablet as Tucker murmurs a general hello. Julia tries to engage him in small talk but he seems in no mood for it and changes the subject back to the project. Our fourth group member, Manny, leads the discussion while Julia makes suggestions. Tucker seems as distracted as I am, both of us contributing minimally and blindly agreeing to almost everything. I catch him watching me with vague disquiet, and I wonder if he can read my distress, my exhaustion.

I excuse myself to go to the bathroom and add some concealer to the circles under my eyes. I don't have blush on me, so I pinch my cheeks a little to bring some color to the surface. I avoid Tucker's gaze when I return, something I've become rather skilled at.

"So Tuck did some research on a few of the organizations on the list. He made some notes on their recent outreach campaigns and messages and stuff," Julia fills me in.

Tuck. My eyes skate his way before I can stop myself, but he's staring at his phone. I guess he participates just fine when I'm not around, and I wonder again why he stopped me from switching groups. His words from last week ricochet in my head, wounding as ever, tearing through my chest like shrapnel. *We're nothing. We never were.*

"That's good," I murmur without looking up, my voice soft and unfamiliar.

"I'll e-mail it out," Tuck mutters to no one in particular.

"Okay, cool," Manny says. "You do that, and I'll look some things up, and we can brainstorm more next time."

We all pack up our things, except Tucker, who only has his phone out.

"So, Tuck, I hear there's another party at the lax house tomorrow night…" Julia tosses her hair behind her shoulder.

Tucker looks up briefly from his phone and raises his eyebrows. "That's what they tell me."

He always used to be such a flirt, even when he didn't mean anything by it. It was just his way of being friendly to girls, which is why I didn't take him seriously back when he first started hitting on me. But he's different now. It's like my lies have changed him in some palpable way, and he's erected a wall around a fundamental part of his nature, effectively caging in his playful spirit. It's as if he's lost a piece of himself—or I've robbed him of it—and it makes me impossibly sadder. God knows I don't want him flirting with Julia, or any girl really, but I never wanted him to be anything other than the

Tucker Green I've adored since childhood. That was the guy I fell for, after all.

"You gonna be there?" Julia asks.

"I do live there," Tucker says with a vague hint of sarcasm, but he tries on a conciliatory smile to soften it up. And it works; Julia blushes the color of a freaking tomato.

I mutter something about needing to study for statistics and head out of the student center.

"Carl."

I freeze in place, not daring to turn, not sure if the low rumble of my name in his voice was even real, or if I imagined it. I close my eyes instead, trying to steady my racing heart. Tucker's huge hand comes down onto my shoulder for no more than a microsecond before he thinks better of blessing me with his touch, retracting it like I'm contaminated or something.

Toxic.

I still don't turn, but I peek back over my shoulder. Tucker comes around to face me, glaring with army green eyes I could once read so well. "What the fuck is wrong with you?" Strangely his question is harsher than his tone, which is flat and low, and as inscrutable as his glare.

Still, his words make me flinch like he's slapped me. But mostly I'm puzzled, because he knows full well what's wrong with me, but I don't know why he suddenly wants to discuss it here. "What do you m-mean?" I stammer the last word. Freaking *stammer*. I've never stammered in my life.

"Do you not give a fuck about our grade?" A slight hint of frustration sneaks into his voice.

"What?" I breathe. "Of course I do."

I don't miss the clench of his jaw. "You think you might want to contribute something next time?" he spits.

My back straightens. If there's any way to get me on the offense, it's to make me feel attacked. "You're telling me to *contribute*? Because you performed a few Google searches? So, what? Now you're in charge of the team?"

Tucker's eyes narrow and he grits his teeth, biting back whatever scathing retort is on his tongue. "No, Carleigh," he says carefully, like I'm obtuse. *Carleigh.* "But no one is counting on *me* or my *keen obser-vations* to pull this project off. In case you forgot, all of our grades are on the line here."

Keen observations. He's making fun of Zayne's praise from one of our first classes. But I don't even blame him. I just got done psych-ing myself up to win that internship, and so far I'm not even pulling my weight to get a passing grade. So much for *professionalism.* But locked in a battle with Tucker, no matter how petty, it simply isn't in my nature to surrender. At the same time I'm just too exhausted to argue.

"Are you sick?" he asks suddenly, his brow furrowing in a parody of concern.

I blink at him. "What?"

"You're all out of it. You were out of it in class this morning, too."

And what can I say? That I haven't slept? That I dreamed about my dad and now I feel like complete shit? That's the last thing I would ever bring up to him.

"Maybe I'm *out of it* because I was just out all night partying." My shrug is so strained that instead of the indifference I was going for, I'm sure it has a decidedly different effect. But still I don't back down. "And don't worry about me *contributing* to the project. If you really doubt I'm going to win that competition and land that intern-ship, then you were right after all. You *don't* know me. And you know what? What if I *am* sick? Why should you care either way? I'm just a *stranger*, remember?" The hurt his words have caused me drip from my tone in obvious bitterness.

Tucker glares at me, muscles tensed. I wait for him to strike back with some cutting words, but instead all I get is a slow nod. "You're right," he says simply, and then he turns and walks away without a single glance back.

* * *

Devin drags me to the party the next night. I don't put up much of an argument. It's not worth it. I've already tried explaining that there's someone at the lacrosse house I don't want to see, but it went right over her head. And I suppose I can't blame her for wanting to go to the hottest parties. This is the only college experience we're going to get, after all.

I'm still feeling out of it, as Tucker described it, and I need a distraction anyway. I've realized recently that Tucker's physical presence is irrelevant. He's here with me regardless, whether he's in the room or not.

Fortunately the party is crowded and it's easy to lose myself in the masses. I bury my troubles deep below the surface, and chat with the girls about nothing important. I'm careful not to drink too much, but I do have a nice buzz going, and I have to admit it helps.

"Hey, Carleigh." Ben Aronin slips from his ever-present crowd of eager girls to say hello.

"Hi."

"Having a good time?" he asks, the dutiful host.

I smile—it comes easily as I look up at his handsome features, trying hard not to compare them to Tucker's. "Beer and music, what's not to like?" I shrug.

Ben's mouth lifts into a grin of white, perfectly straight teeth. It's the kind of grin that obviously gets girls exactly where he wants them, but I can't help but think it's missing something, and I try to convince myself it's not the roguish slant of Tucker's, or that one slightly crooked incisor it reveals. I need to shake myself out of this funk.

To stop wallowing in the reminders of the two men I've loved in my life—the one who hurt me and the one I hurt as a result.

So I focus on talking to the nice, handsome, innocuous guy in front of me.

He asks me how I'm liking school and tells me about fall training. Lacrosse season doesn't start until mid-winter, but that doesn't mean the team isn't already hard at work, in the weight room almost every morning, on the field practicing drills most afternoons, and scrimmaging on weekends.

"But I try to enjoy the freedom now before our schedule gets rough," he tells me.

"I can tell." I gesture to the party.

Ben smiles. "Well, these don't stop during the season. In fact, they only get bigger." He sighs, as if the team having these parties is more of an obligation than something he particularly enjoys, and that surprises me. He seems so in his element.

"You don't like big parties?" I ask.

He shrugs. "They're fine. They were exciting when I was a freshman. But, you know, it's hard to get to know people when it's so crowded, and when you feel responsible for making sure people are having a good time."

I smile wryly. "Seems like you already know everyone," I point out. I nod over his shoulder to the girls who surrounded him a just minutes ago, several of whom are shooting glares my way. "In fact, I think your harem over there is already missing your attention."

Ben follows my gaze and runs his hand through his hair. "They don't know me," he says softly. Again, he surprises me with his sincerity.

"Anyway, how are your classes?" he asks, changing the subject. "Regret taking Zayne's yet?" His smirk is teasing, but his eyes shine with playfulness.

I give him a light punch on his arm, silently noting the firmness of his biceps. Ben is definitely well-built. "You could have warned me about that final project!" I scold, my smile betraying my humor.

Ben throws his palms up in surrender. "Hey, I thought you weren't afraid of a difficult class?"

His amusement is contagious and I can't help but laugh. "I'm not. But it would have been nice to have a heads-up."

"Okay, okay," he concedes. "My bad. Anyway, I'm sure you'll do great."

I sure hope so. "Yeah, well. It would be nice to win and start with that A. The range for the rest of the teams is crazy. Anywhere from a B plus to a D plus? Talk about subjective."

Ben nods. "No kidding. My team came in second last semester, and Zayne thought our video was funny, so he started us with B's. But then he heard about some stupid argument we'd gotten into in, like, the second week, and docked three of us a full grade for not being *professional* enough. I aced all of the quizzes and participated as much as anyone else, and I ended up with a B- in the class because of that damn project," he grumbles.

"But I shouldn't even complain. One of our defenders was on the second-place team and he got a bad peer review from a girl on his team he was stupid enough to blow off after sleeping with at a party, and he ended up with a D on the project. He got a D+ in the class, which dragged down his entire GPA, and he ended up benched the entire season."

"Benched?" What does one have to do with the other?

Ben nods. "Yup. All NCAA athletes have to keep a 2.8 minimum GPA. He's just lucky he wasn't here on an athletic scholarship, because that would have been gone as soon as he got benched."

Ben takes a sip of his beer, oblivious to my stunned expression. Because *Tucker's* here on an athletic scholarship. Which means he's got a hell of a lot more riding on this project than I realized—far more than I do. Sure, I want that internship, but Tucker's entire college education could depend on it. And he wouldn't even be stuck in Zayne's class if it wasn't for me. If he hadn't been trying to escape the one we'd planned to take together.

Familiar guilt threatens to crush me, but I force it away.

"Have you been to Bottega?" Ben asks out of nowhere.

I blink at him.

"It's a great little Italian place. It'd be nice to get off campus. Let me take you." His confidence is back in full force, and I'm a little taken aback that he's asking me out.

"I just got out of a pretty serious relationship," I murmur, and I peek over his shoulder to the crowd in the next room. Like I summoned him, Tucker stands in the corner, flirting with that same redhead from a few weeks ago.

"All the more reason to get out and have a good time," Ben offers.

My gaze strays back to Tucker, redhead's pink manicured claws on his arm, and I wish I could say it's not what makes my decision, but that would be a lie. "Okay," I tell him. "Sounds like fun." It doesn't really, but that's my problem. Because it should, *shouldn't it?*

My eyes find Tucker again, and this time, he finds me in return. I expect his disinterest or his usual disdain, but what I don't see coming is his anger. His eyes widen and he glares—not just at me, but at Ben, who doesn't even notice I'm not paying him attention anymore. When Tucker starts marching through the faceless bodies in our direction, I tell Ben I need to use the restroom and get the hell out of there.

I do go to the bathroom. I fix my makeup and reapply my lip gloss, if only to take the time to let Tucker get over whatever suddenly pissed him off, which was most likely simply my presence.

It's getting late, and I wonder if I should just leave. I head down a hall toward the backyard, which is far less crowded now that the air is getting colder. On the way, I walk right into a stocky, solid body. Ricky Vance, the drunk douchebag who basically cursed me out for not letting him buy me a drink that first night out, turns to see the klutz who bumped him and I wince. I don't want another scene; I just want to leave.

"Hi—uh, Carleigh, right?"

Fortunately he doesn't seem to be drunk tonight. "Uh, yeah," I murmur.

He looks sheepish, and I think he might be about to apologize, but then his gaze veers over my shoulder and his brows slip into an anxious frown. "What's up, Green?" He directs his words behind me, and I tense.

I turn to face Tucker, but he's staring at Ricky. "Those chicks from SDT were looking for you," Tucker murmurs, but it feels like he's saying something else.

"Gotcha," Ricky replies, and just like that, I'm alone with Tucker.

"Didn't he call you a bitch or something a few weeks ago? Now you're flirting with him?" he sneers.

"I wasn't flirting with him," I say defensively. And I really, really wasn't. But it isn't Tucker's damn business either way.

"And what about Ben? You weren't flirting with him either, huh?" Tucker's tone is hateful and accusatory and my hands clench into fists. I wasn't flirting with Ben—not really. But I did agree to let him take me out.

"What do you care what this *stranger* does?" I hiss.

Tucker's nostrils flare and I watch frustration color his face red. Suddenly he grabs my elbow and leads me farther down the empty hall and around the bend to a row of closed doors. "And Ben's not a stranger? You don't know him!" Tucker growls.

"This is my school, too!" I snap. "I'm allowed to have the same college experiences as everyone else!"

Not the right thing to say. Tucker's eyes widen and he grits his teeth, and then he drags me roughly through one of the doors and slams it shut behind him. He sucks in a deep breath to calm himself, and then he's stalking toward me until I'm backed up against the wall. "College experiences, huh? Like hooking up with a stranger?" His voice is low and vaguely threatening, and for the first time, I'm frightened. I know he'd never physically hurt me, but the predatory glint in his eye makes me think there's something to fear other than violence.

"That wasn't—" My voice is too soft, too shaky, but my words are cut off by his touch as he trails his fingers down my throat, over my racing pulse.

"You think he can touch you like I can?" Tucker asks hoarsely.

No. No one can touch me like he can; I know that. I shake my head.

Tucker runs the pad of his thumb roughly over my bottom lip, watching its progress with a hunger I've missed desperately. Instantly my body responds, and I sag back against the wall in surrender. But his eyes are filled with more than desire. The anger, the contempt—they're still there, perhaps stronger than ever.

He holds my jaw in place and leans down slowly, completely out of synch with the fervor in his gaze, and softly brushes his lips over mine. "You want to be kissed by a stranger?" he breathes into my mouth.

I don't know if he means Ben or himself, so I say nothing.

His free hand skates down my side, lingering on the side of my breast before continuing to my hip. "I can kiss strangers, too," he growls, and then his mouth slams savagely over mine. He kisses me with all of his frustration and rage, taking no prisoners as his tongue plunders my mouth.

I kiss him back just as fiercely. My heart might ache with his abuse, but my body—it is completely his, and it responds the only way it knows how—it attacks right back. We're all hungry hands and pressing hips, and then suddenly Tucker wrenches his mouth from mine and spins me to face the wall. I gasp as he pushes his hips into my ass, and I feel the vigor of his arousal, and it's a heady feeling after all this time. I hate that I take pride in it, but I do. I love that no matter how he despises me, he can't stop himself from wanting me any more than I can him.

His lips slide harshly up my throat. "You wanna get fucked by a stranger?" he rasps into my ear. He glides his teeth over my earlobe, and God help me, I *do* want him. Even like this.

But I won't admit he's a stranger. He will *never* be a stranger. "Just you," I breathe.

I feel his sharp intake of breath, and something in him breaks. His hands explore and claim, slipping under my skirt and over my ass until they're teasing the front waistband of my panties.

"This means nothing," Tucker growls. And maybe it doesn't. But right now the pain in my chest is overshadowed by the need between my thighs.

I can't agree with him, but I know better than to argue. Instead, I grind my ass back against him, and he groans my favorite sound.

His arm shoots up and he fists my hair in warning. "You are not in control here. This is my house, my bedroom, and this is just a hookup between strangers. Understand?"

His free hand slips inside my panties and starts stroking me the way he knows drives me crazy. He knows my body like a connoisseur, and he works me expertly. *Stranger, my ass.*

"Do. You. Understand?" he repeats, and he gives my hair a soft tug. It doesn't hurt, but it makes his point. I hear a rustle behind me and I know he's putting on a condom. This is really happening.

"Yes."

He takes my thong from behind, pulling the front taut against me and the middle out of his way, and then his fingers are inside, testing me before his erection replaces them, positioned to take me. I try reaching back to touch him, but I get another tug on my hair, and I let out a short, startled yelp.

"Hands on the wall," he orders gruffly.

I obey without hesitation, as he knew I would. When Tucker makes love to me, it's the only time he can count on me not fighting him.

But this isn't making love, I remind myself. He's about to hate-fuck me, and it both disheartens and excites me in the strangest way. He grabs my hips and yanks me backward two steps, and I keep my hands pressed painstakingly against the wall. Only now can I feel that he's removed his shirt and shoved away everything else that separated us.

He strains between my thighs and rubs himself back and forth against me, taunting, promising.

I whimper a desperate plea.

Thankfully, he heeds it, thrusting himself deep inside me. He chokes off his amorous groan, but I sigh with both need and relief. He's the only man I've ever wanted, the only one I can fathom ever wanting, and I know this is only a fleeting moment, but at least physically, for now, I have him, and I try not to think beyond the merciful present.

Tucker moves with raw perfection, his arms curling around me, his hands taking full advantage, touching and molding. He withholds the dirty whispers I've come to expect from him, replacing them with soft growls and grunts into my hair and throat.

His hips are rough and his rhythm is almost punishing, but this is one punishment I revel in. And then his fingers find the place he knows will seal my fate, and I explode around him, shamelessly moaning his name.

He freezes at the sound, as if it vexes him to hear it, but I'm only half aware, my ears rushing with the sound of my blood pumping and my vision blurred by stars. His arms band around my waist and my feet leave the floor, and then I'm facedown on the bed and Tucker is behind me, slamming back inside.

His arm slides under my belly, lifting my hips slightly from the bed, and he takes full advantage of the angle, pounding me into the mattress. His hand slips down, down, and I suck in a gasp. And then I'm coming again, so hard my eyes water and I muffle my cries in the comforter beneath me.

"Fuck, fuck, *fuck*!" Tucker chants until he thunders his release, burying his face in my hair.

He collapses on top of me, but only for a moment before he hastily rolls onto his back as if he can't get away from me fast enough—as if I am some kind of trap he refuses to fall victim to.

We both gasp for breath, and I keep my face turned into the mattress. I don't want to look at him—to see his look of regret, or contempt, or anything else I know he still feels for me despite what we just did. My heart couldn't bear it right now. I may be strong, but even I have my limits.

So instead, I fix my underwear and pull my clothing back in place, take a moment to finger-comb my hair, and swipe under my eyes and around my lips with the pad of my thumb to sort out any smeared makeup. And, without so much as a glance back, I climb off his bed, and walk out the door.

Chapter Nine

Carleigh

Last Year

"I don't know, Teen. I'm not really feeling well," I murmur. I don't have to fake the exhaustion in my voice, only in reality it's more emotional than physical. We just got back from visiting my father, and I'm really not up to anything at all.

"Carl, you never get sick. What's wrong?" Tina's concern crushes me with guilt, but there's no way I'm up for Andrew's tonight.

"I feel like I'm coming down with something," I lie. "I'm just gonna stay in and go to bed." *Not a lie.*

"You sure you don't want me to come over? Are you alone?"

Yes, and *yes*.

"I'm sure. Have fun tonight," I murmur, and hang up.

Billy's staying over at a friend's house. He seemed fine when we got home. He was so young when my father voluntarily surrendered for his sentence that I'm not sure he remembers a life before this one. A time when we were a normal family. When our relationship with our father consisted of more than a weekly phone call and a visit every few months at most.

The visits have grown less frequent the more my mother travels, since we can't go without her, and the truth is, ever since I found out what he did to our family, I've avoided the phone calls as much as possible, too.

I used to think my mother callous, that choosing vacations and "girls' trips" with her friends over visiting her husband more often, especially on an actual holiday, was purely selfish. But for the past few years, I've wondered if it's actually completely justified. After all, my father made his choice.

I feel withered and worn, like my faded, chipped nail polish. So I sit on the floor of my bedroom and paint my nails a midnight blue that reflects my mood—one of several mindless tasks I always turn to on days like this.

It had always been difficult visiting my father—worse even than living without him. But almost exactly five years ago I learned the details of his plea agreement and visits became almost unbearable. That year, our holiday visit came in mid-January—also due to one of my mother's trips. Before then, even though I understood he was guilty of defrauding his clients, I was able to separate the man from the crime—to forgive him. I knew what he did was wrong, but it didn't feel personal—like he did it to *me*, even if in committing the crime he ended up condemning me to life without a father. But I knew he regretted it—that if he could go back and make better choices, he would. That he would do anything in his power to be with us again, to be my daddy again.

Sometimes they let us visit outside, but that day was cold, and we sat across a table in a crowded visiting room, my mother prattling on about needing more access to finances and accounts—a common complaint from her—while Billy and I tried not to look as bored as we felt. Eventually my mother got whatever information she needed, and I got to spend a couple of hours telling my dad about school, about Billy's basketball season, and whatever other mundane things were going on in my twelve-year-old little life, and my father had the grace to act deeply interested. Or perhaps he really was interested. After all, it couldn't have been more boring than his current life.

It was when the correctional officer told him his time was up that I got the idea. "Stanley," the guard called, "work duty in fifteen."

I always knew that my father had gone by Will Stanley instead of Will Stanger. He thought it sounded better, and eventually he changed it legally "for business reasons" I can make guesses about now. He still went by Stanger in his personal life—on school lists and things like that. It's how we avoided attention when he was arrested. Will Stanley was indicted, the news reported, and no mention was ever made of his family. I knew this already of course, but for some reason, that day, hearing the guard call him *Stanley* gave me the novel idea to Google him.

So after a long, exhausting day, I sat down at my laptop and typed "William Stanley" into the search box.

It was a mistake.

I never expected to actually learn anything new. I thought I already knew everything worth knowing. I suppose I was just curious about what the media had said about him, and mostly, it was what I'd expected.

Wall Street Exec William Stanley Accused of Defrauding Clients out of Millions

No Trial for Disgraced Wall Street Whiz: William Stanley Accepts Plea Deal

Shocking Plea Deal: Stanley Refuses to Give Up Stolen Funds, Chooses More Time

The last one made no sense, so I immediately clicked the link.

At first I didn't believe what it said. So I typed "William Stanley Plea Deal" into the browser, and up popped more articles. And they all said the same thing.

Apparently the FBI was only ever able to recover some of the stolen money, and the federal prosecutor wanted my father to tell them where the rest was. Some of the assets, like our house and certain bank accounts, were in my mother's name, and they couldn't tie them to my father's dealings, so they couldn't seize them. But that wasn't enough to account for the missing funds.

It was leverage. And they expected my father to use it.

The offer was for six years if he gave back the money.

Six years.

Six. Fucking. Years.

He could have gotten out when I was fifteen. He would have already been home for three years. I would have had a father.

But he didn't take that deal.

He kept the money. Where—I have no idea. They never located it. No one but my father knows where it is. Not even his old business partner, Art, who he started Stanley Stevens Investments with when they were still in college.

God knows my mother doesn't know, or I wouldn't have to listen to her complain about it at every freaking visit. But I've overheard enough to know it's in a trust, somewhere overseas, and that there's some foreign lawyer who makes transfers to another offshore account in my mother's name "as needed." Or as my father deems is needed. Because it's more than obvious my mom wants more control, and as the years push on, I suspect she's starting to wear him down.

But the fact remains: My father refused to return that money in exchange for less time.

Instead, my father took another deal. A guilty plea to avoid a trial and the potential for twenty plus years, and he was sentenced to fifteen. He could potentially get out after ten, but unless he gives up the missing funds, it isn't likely. It's hard to claim good behavior when you continue to refuse to pay back your victims.

So instead of getting my dad back at fourteen, I will be twenty-four when he gets out. Instead of a teenager just starting high school, I will be a college graduate. Hell, I might finish grad school by the time my father is released. I could be married, though I doubt it. But whatever I do by twenty-four, the reality is, he willingly sacrificed being a part of my childhood…for money.

He isn't the father I knew. It turns out that man never existed at all.

I never confronted him about it, and I suppose he's attributed my standoffishness since then to teenage hormones. But despite putting on a good show, I know he doesn't really care. If he cared, he'd be here.

By the time my nails dry I just want to go to bed, but I know there's no hope for sleep now. I put on pajama shorts and a camisole anyway, and go to the kitchen to make myself some hot cocoa.

I'm so startled by the doorbell that I jump, sloshing some of the chocolatey liquid onto my shirt.

I can only guess it's Tina coming to check on me after all, and I'm fresh faced and practically indecent when I swing open our giant mahogany front door to find Tucker standing on my doorstep. His gaze rakes me from head to toe, a surprised and very appreciative rogue grin stretching from dimple to dimple, and a blush rises to every very exposed surface of my skin. I have to silently remind myself that he's seen me naked, but that memory only makes me flush even more.

"Hi…?" My brows raise to ask what he's doing here.

Tucker holds up a white paper bag. "Soup."

Huh? I blink at him.

"Tina said you were sick."

Oh. "So you showed up here with soup?"

Tucker shrugs sheepishly, and my heart does that melting thing it's been doing for him lately. "That's what friends do, right?" he says uncertainly. "Tina said your parents were both out of town. Thought you could use some company."

I open the door wider and gesture for him to come in, suddenly at a loss for words. I don't like lying about my father, but Tuck still thinks he's just a neglectful workaholic, and I can't bring myself to tell him—or anyone—the truth.

As he steps through the front door, Tucker's gaze never strays from me, either unimpressed by the opulence of my ridiculously sprawling home, or immune to it after all these years.

"I was just having hot chocolate," I tell him. "Want some?"

"Tea would probably be better if you're not feeling well," he murmurs absentmindedly.

"I'm just feeling a little tired, Tuck. I'm not dying of consumption."

Tucker chuckles and I feel my mood lighten marginally. It's instant, and a far more effective cure than any tea. "Sure, I'll have some."

I fill a second mug and hand it to him and we sit on the couch in the adjacent den, where I have the fireplace softly roaring with the click of a remote. He sits next to me, but not too close. I don't know what our boundaries are now. We've hung out plenty in recent weeks, though rarely alone, and on those rare times we were alone, we hooked up. But we haven't had sex since Andrew's laundry room.

Attraction buzzes between us, but it's dulled somewhat by my dejected mood. Tuck watches me as if he's trying to solve some kind of riddle, and I find myself averting my gaze.

"So if you're tired, why aren't you in bed?" he asks.

"Some jackass rang my doorbell with a soup delivery," I remind him with a smirk.

His lips quirk into a smile. "You were making hot chocolate, Princess. Not sleeping."

God, he always has to call me on my bullshit. I shrug. "Couldn't sleep."

Still, he stares at me as if trying to figure me out.

"Why aren't you at Andy's?" I ask.

Tucker shrugs. "Damsel in distress needed a soup delivery."

A laugh bubbles its way out of my mouth and I shake my head.

"There it is," he murmurs, as if my laugh is all he's after tonight, and I find myself both relieved and disappointed.

"Well, thanks, Prince Charming," I tease. "You don't have to stay. Or if you want to we could watch a movie," I offer. I want him to stay. But I don't want him to know how much I want him to stay. That would ruin our game.

Tucker sets his mug on the coffee table and leans back on the couch. "What are we watching?"

I start flipping through channels, enjoying his unusually quiet company. I think he suspects I'm more than just tired, but he doesn't pry. He just sits with me, sipping his cocoa.

I land on FX, which is running a *Sons of Anarchy* marathon. "You good with this?" I ask.

"Hell yes," Tucker replies. His arm stretches along the back of the couch and I find myself curling into him. If we'd never been intimate, it wouldn't mean anything. But I don't know what it is now. I don't know what *we* are now. Friends with benefits, sure, but my heart and my brain don't always see eye to eye when it comes to Tucker.

"You're the one girl I can count on to not turn on some chick flick." He says it with warmth, and I know he means it as a compliment, but all I hear is that I'm one girl of many he's been *Netflix and chilling* with.

I have never been this girl. I have never had a reason to suffer the sharp spikes of jealousy, but here they are all the same. It's unnerving. It makes me feel vulnerable. It's not something I'm used to, and I scoot an inch away from him, needing to get back some of my independence. Because if there's one thing I know about men, it's not to let your heart rely on them. It'll only hurt more when they choose someone else, or something else.

"Your parents coming back for the holidays?" Tucker asks nonchalantly. He's watching the TV, but he looks at me out of the corner of his eye.

Part of me wants to tell him the truth. That my father is a criminal whose greed destroyed lives. That he chose his money over his family—over *me*—and my mother has taken his prison sentence as an excuse to act as if she doesn't have a family at all. That she spends so many nights with her divorced, wino, pill-head girlfriends in Manhattan—the ones who think it's not a drinking problem if it comes in the form of three-hundred-dollar bottles of champagne, and that it's not doing drugs if they were prescribed by a doctor. That those same snobby bitches are the ones she chooses to travel with, never caring that she's missing my volleyball games or Billy's entire childhood, or in this case, the holidays. Not that it stops her from texting critiques about my outfits or hair any time I post a photo on Instagram.

But even if I could get past the humiliation of admitting what my father did and where he is, I wouldn't even know how to begin to tell Tucker I've been lying to him—and everyone else for that matter—for basically our entire lives. Why would he ever trust me again?

And the truth is I'm ashamed. I guess deep down, the fool that I am, I still hold an inkling of hope that Tucker could someday see me as something more than just a fuck-buddy, and I don't want to give him a reason to think I'm not good enough. That I'm not worth it. Because why would Tucker give up his playboy ways for a girl whose own father loves her less than he loves fucking money? Why would *any* guy love that girl, when the man who's supposed to love her the most clearly had no problem giving her up? What does that say about me? But it is Tucker, so while I keep my secrets, I do give him a hint of truth in my bitter tone. "Nope. They like their travel this time of year...*Every* time of year," I add spitefully.

My head spins to Tucker, guilt warming my cheeks. What the hell is wrong with me? I'm so busy feeling sorry for myself that I didn't even think of what he must be feeling. My shame is obvious, and an apology is on the tip of my tongue, but I don't know the right words to say I'm sorry for complaining about my absentee parents when his father is dead. Especially when he died right around Christmas, too.

"Tuck—"

"Don't, Princess," he whispers, his brow furrowed in sympathy. "It sucks not having them around. For whatever reason," he adds.

I chew on my lip, subconsciously recovering the inch I took back just moments ago, and his hand slips tentatively onto my far shoulder and squeezes. It's my undoing. My head drops onto his biceps and I fold my knees in front of me and sit sideways to face him, Jax Teller and SAMCRO forgotten on the TV.

"You must really miss him." My voice comes out an uncharacteristic whisper. Tucker never talks about his father, and I hate that he has to hold it all in.

Pain flashes through army green, and also a smidgen of resentment. I suspect it's for his mother. I know she doesn't handle the holidays all that well, and surely it takes a toll on Tuck. He looks conflicted, and for a moment I don't know if he's going to change the subject back to me. I don't think he knows either, but then he sighs. "Yeah," is all he says, but it's a concession. Something honest, something true, about something I know he never talks about.

My fingers find a loose thread in the hem of his white T-shirt, and I absently twirl it around my knuckle, staring at the stark, light-colored string against the dark blue of my freshly painted fingernail. That's what Tucker is. He is light in darkness. The comic relief, quick to fill the role of the joker, eager to lighten any mood. But I want him to let go of that responsibility. I want him to feel, too. So maybe I can be his light.

"So what will you and Billy do?" Tucker asks. "For Christmas and New Year's and whatever?"

I shrug. "I'll decorate with him. Order a dinner. I try to make it normal, you know. I think he'll probably be with his friends for New

Year's this year, though. He's starting to be too cool for me. What about you and your mom?"

Tucker smiles sadly. "She'll insist on me being home, that we're going to have a family Christmas, just the two of us, and then she won't get out of bed. Or she'll plan for us to go to my aunt's and be with their family, and then cancel at the last minute and claim an illness." His words are riddled with resignation, but there's no scorn, and I realize his resentment from earlier wasn't aimed at his mother after all. He shrugs. "I'll probably end up at Cap's in the end, after she goes to bed."

"That sucks, Tuck." I don't let go of the thread, but I do meet his gaze, looking up at him from under my lashes, my eyes saying more than my words ever could.

"Sure does, Princess," he breathes.

I let his scent of aftershave and the faintest waft of cologne blanket me. It is pure comfort with a whisper of thrill, and I wish I could just melt into it—close my eyes and sleep in his perfect, male scent.

"Your dad on business or vacation?" Tucker asks.

I sigh. "Business." I ignore the spark of guilt at yet another lie. But he *is* away because of how he chose to do business. And his plea deal was very much a business deal. "And before you say he'd be here with me if he could, he wouldn't."

"Carl—"

"No. He wouldn't. He could be here, Tuck. He chose not to." I give him this bit of truth, cursing the moisture pooling in the corners of my eyes. I never cry. What the hell is happening to me?

Tucker's large palm cups my cheek, his thumb brushing under my lower lashes, saving me my dignity before the one rogue tear can escape, and I'm infinitely grateful. "I was going to say that that says something about him. Not you. Okay? Him choosing not to be around."

I stare at my lap and nod vaguely. But it does say something about me. About me, and Billy, and my mother. It says that we weren't enough for him. "At least your dad would be here if he could," I murmur. I find his eyes again. "I'm sorry, Tuck. It's so unfair. My dad could be with me and chooses not to, and your dad…I'm so sorry he got sick." I choke out the words.

Tucker's jaw clenches and he glares at me. Intensely. Unblinkingly.

Shit. Did I overstep? I do that sometimes. I just talk, blurt whatever I'm thinking. I just thought we were connecting and…*shit*. "I'm sorry, I didn't mean—"

"He wouldn't." Tucker's voice is so low and toneless that at first his words don't even register, and I just frown up at him. "He wouldn't," he repeats. "Be here if he could."

Huh? Tucker's father died of cancer when we were in middle school. "What—"

Suddenly Tucker sits up, his back straightening and his energy changing like he's preparing for something. He radiates intensity, and when he leans his face closer to mine I can feel the nervous current buzzing through him in the cells of my own body.

"You remember when my dad was sick?" he asks.

I nod. Of course I do.

"He was in the hospital for a few months," Tucker says, but of course I already knew that.

"For chemo," I offer, but Tucker just exhales harshly.

"We thought he was doing better. The doctors said…" He trails off. "He came home. And then right before Christmas…"

"I know, Tucker," I whisper. I place my hand on his forearm meaning to soothe him, but his fervor is making me anxious, and my hold is almost desperate.

He shakes his head. "He wasn't getting chemo." His stare bores into me, willing me to understand something beyond my grasp.

"Carl, he was sick, but…he didn't have cancer." He watches me carefully. "He was depressed and…he tried to kill himself."

Holy shit.

"He was admitted to an in-patient mental facility. He was in therapy and on anti-anxiety meds and antidepressants, and he came home."

Oh, God.

"And then, a week before Christmas Eve, he took my mom and me to pick out a tree, helped us hang all the decorations, hung up the lights on the outside of the house. We were going to a movie but my dad said he was too tired. The meds had that side effect. So he said good night and then went upstairs, and my mom and I went to some stupid Christmas movie she wanted to see. She didn't want to wake him when we got home so she just got quietly into bed, and when she woke the next morning, he was already cold."

I gape at him, searching desperately for the right words, but I'm not sure they exist.

"He downed both bottles of his meds. While we were at the movies."

It's then that I realize my grip on Tucker's forearm is so tight it's leaving marks on his skin, and I retract my hand immediately.

"God, Tucker," I breathe.

"He was planning it. The whole time we were picking out the tree, decorating—all of it. And we had no idea. But then, looking back...He kept saying things about how it had to be the best tree we've ever had. He insisted on buying my mom a bunch of fancy new ornaments even though we were having money problems. I mean, he hadn't worked in months and he was buying her this ridiculously expensive crystal tree topper we didn't need."

Tucker shakes his head, still incredulous after all these years. "He just sent us off to the movies, knowing it would be the last time we saw him and—" His voice breaks and he slams his mouth shut, swallowing down his grief.

But I don't want him to swallow it down.

After all, I know something about spinning stories and hiding shame. I know the toll it takes. And all this time, Tucker was hiding this. Living with *this*.

I don't think. I just climb into his lap and wrap my arms around his waist, tucking my head under his chin. Because nothing I say will help, but *this*, hopefully this can offer him some consolation.

He doesn't hesitate. He just envelops me in his arms, holding me so tightly it almost cuts off my breath, and buries his face in my hair.

"Princess," he breathes, and I pull back to look at him.

I know the right thing to say is *I'm sorry*, but I've never been good at saying the right thing. "He was sick, Tuck. He—"

"I know, Carl," he says gruffly. "I know he was sick, that he wasn't in his right mind, that he was chemically imbalanced. I know all of it. But whatever the reason, he still chose to do it. He could have stuck it out and fought. But—"

"Tuck—"

"I *know*." And this time his voice is just despondent, like he's given up.

I can't bear it. I press my lips to his, hard. His hands cup my face, his fingers thrust roughly into my hair, and he holds my mouth to his. His lips are firm and desperate, molding mine, stealing my breath, and for once I just let him lead. I let him take from me whatever he needs.

But he doesn't deepen the kiss. We're just lips and breaths, breaths and lips. It's more reverent than passionate, and when he ends it, he holds his forehead to mine until our breathing calms.

Tucker strokes my hair, and subtly I feel the tension in his corded muscles dissipate. I lay my head on his shoulder and his grip around me loosens as he repositions me more comfortably on his lap.

"Thank you for telling me," I whisper into his neck.

"Only Cap knows."

I nod. He doesn't have to say anything else. He doesn't have to ask me not to repeat what he's confided, and I don't have to assure him I never would. It goes without saying. And for the first time I wish I had the courage to confide in him in return. To confide in *anyone*. He said Cap knew about his father. Even Tina doesn't know about mine.

I am a coward.

But then, what my father did is far more shameful. He destroyed families—*lives*. Tuck's dad was ill. Mine was just plain greedy.

Without another word, we go back to watching motorcycles and gunfights, and it isn't long before the rise and fall of Tucker's breathing lulls me to sleep.

The next thing I know, the TV is silent and I'm being carried up the stairs, half conscious. He lays me gently onto my bed and tugs my comforter up to my chin. It's when I hear his descending footsteps that I manage to speak.

"Tuck…"

His footfalls grow heavier as he comes back to the bed. "Yeah, Princess?" he whispers in the dark.

"Stay."

There's a moment of hesitant silence, then a soft sigh and the rustling of clothing, and then Tucker is climbing into bed behind me in only his boxer briefs, and I drift off to sleep in his arms.

I wake the next morning alone, but the way his scent clings to my pillow proves his visit wasn't a dream. I turn my face into it and inhale deeply.

My phone buzzes and I reach for it blindly on my nightstand. The screen announces texts from Tucker, the first of which are from about thirty minutes ago.

Had to go meet Cap for gym. You looked so peaceful I didn't want to wake you. 8:15 am

And also I knew it was the only way I would ever get the last word in ;) 8:17 am

And then, almost ten minutes later:

Tucker: And the last kiss...8:26 am

And then there's a photo. A selfie of just the bottom half of his face pressing a soft kiss to my sleeping forehead.

I melt into a puddle on my bed, a grin stinging my cheeks as I laugh down at my phone. It's funny how context is everything. If it were any other guy, that photo would be the creepiest thing in the world. But because it's him, because it's *us*, it's just completely and utterly perfect.

I twist the phone behind me and snap a photo of my shorts-covered ass.

Kiss this 8:52 am

Twenty minutes later he responds.

I know you're trying to be a smartass, but I'm pretty sure any time you send me a photo of any part of your body, I win. Especially that one. 9:15 am

And for the record, I would happily kiss it. 9:16 am.

Chapter Ten

Tucker

Present Day

Halloween is the one holiday I don't loathe. The one holiday that has nothing to do with family. That is instead about dressing up and getting fucked up and pretending to be someone else for a night. I am definitely down with that.

Of course we're hosting tonight's party. The theme is favorite characters from TV, movies, and books. Pretty broad. And still, the guys just had to choose costumes for us that remind me of Carl. But then, I liked *Sons of Anarchy* before I ever watched it with her, and fuck it, I'm taking it back.

We've all applied our fake tattoos, including the giant one on our backs of a grim reaper holding an M-16 with a scythe blade in one hand and a crystal ball in the other—pointless since we're wearing shirts, but whatever. I pull on jeans and a white T-shirt, then slip on my faux leather cut. They actually look pretty authentic, considering. My dirty blond hair has gotten a little long, and when Ben announced our costume a few weeks ago, I decided I'd put off cutting it.

I go out with a couple of the guys to pick up the kegs and some liquor, and by the time I get back, people are already showing up. An hour later the house is completely packed. I'm already on my fourth beer when Carl walks in with her friend Devin, and my traitorous dick instantly swells in my jeans. My brain tries to remind it that we don't want her anymore. That she's a liar. That she sat back and listened to me confide every last heart-wrenching family secret while hiding her own behind smiles and sex. But my dick doesn't care any more now than it did a few weeks ago, when I apparently lost my damned mind and shamelessly dragged her into my bedroom. That particular memory doesn't help the situation in my jeans. Neither does the fact that she's dressed like a wet fucking dream.

She's dressed like Daenerys Targaryen from *Game of Thrones*— Khaleesi—and from the first season, too, in a badass nomadic getup with her flat midriff peeking out for all to see.

Motherfucker.

Her golden hair is already longer than she used to wear it, and she's added something to it—like extensions or something.

I head back to the keg before she sees me, and refill my cup, deciding that tonight would be a good opportunity to get completely shit-faced.

"Hi, Tuck."

I turn to find Courtney, the redhead Ben tried to hook me up with at our first party, smirking at me.

"Or should I say Jax?"

I offer her a forced laugh, as if I haven't heard that one five times already tonight. She hands me her cup and I fill it for her. She's dressed in tight black leggings and a matching tank top with a Pink Ladies jacket from Grease draped over her shoulders. She matches about five other of her friends I've seen traipsing around the party.

Original.

"You just get here?" I ask her. I notice a couple of the guys checking her out, and I push myself to do the same. She *is* a cute girl. Physically, anyway. Hot in all of the typical ways—small waist, big tits, lean hips. Problem is, I've spent what feels like a lifetime developing a very specific taste for very particular proportions, and it's hard not to think this Courtney chick's tits are just a tad too big for her frame, and that I prefer a slightly plumper ass.

And blond hair and green eyes.

Fuck.

"So tell me, do you have your member tattoo?" she asks, lashes batting like a demented pair of dragonfly wings.

"Sure do," I reply, and she follows me as I start walking through the kitchen.

"Can I see it?"

I laugh. "I'm not taking off my shirt in the middle of a party. Go find Ricky. I'm sure he'd be happy to accommodate you." I've already seen him stripping his cut and shirt off to show three other girls.

Courtney shakes her head. "I want to see *your* tattoo."

I'm not an idiot. I know she's flirting with me. Maybe even offering me something. And I should be into it—I *know* I should—but I'm not. Instead, I keep thinking of Carl in that damn costume. And it's because of that that I give in.

"Follow me." I lead her down the hall and around to my room. I'm not planning to try anything with her. I'm just trying to…I don't know what I'm trying to do. Just not think about Carl.

I slide off my cut, and Courtney is behind me, reaching under my T-shirt before I even flip the light switch on. The lights are so bright they're almost blinding, and as I grip the hem of my shirt to take it off, I change my mind. I'm not a fucking stripper. I let her push the material up instead, and have her look.

Her fingers trace the fake ink. "This is so hot," she murmurs in a way I'm sure she thinks is seductive.

But I just want to shout at her, "It's fucking fake, you idiot." And I know I'm being a jerk, at least internally. She could be a nice girl for all I know. But I never *will* know. Because I don't fucking *care*.

Her nails are too long, and pointed, like those of a witch, and they scratch gratingly along my skin as her fingers continue to trace past where I know the tattoo ends, and along the lines of muscle in my back. There is nothing erotic about it; it's just fucking creepy. I can't take it anymore, and I shrug her off and she lets my shirt fall back into place as I turn around to face her.

"You really do look like him. Jax Teller. Has anyone ever told you that?"

"You know he's not a real person, right? That *Sons of Anarchy* was a TV show?" I'm being an ass, this time out loud, and even though I know she's done nothing wrong, she's irritating me.

But the corners of her mouth curl wryly, like she thinks I'm playing with her. Her fingers find the hem of my shirt again, this time in the front, and they slide along the top of my jeans.

I wait for a reaction from my dick. Anything. Please. Because it would be so much easier if I could just be into this girl. If I could have some fun with her. Take the first step in actually moving on.

"He doesn't have to be real," she coos. "He's a character. A fantasy. And isn't that what Halloween is all about?" Her fingers slip under my shirt again and over the grid of my abs.

I wait. I will my body to give a shit about her touch. And it does—but in the wrong way. Her nails might as well be scraping a blackboard. I give up; I grab her wrists and stop her exploration. "Sorry, Courtney. Not gonna be your fantasy tonight." I try to be nice about it, but I've had enough. I want her the fuck out of my room.

"I don't have to be Courtney, you know. I can be whoever you want me to be."

I frown at her, but she starts lowering herself to her knees.

Well, *shit*.

Her fingers move tentatively to my belt buckle.

Can I do this? I haven't hooked up with anyone but Carl in over a year. Obviously this girl isn't expecting anything other than a good time. Rationally I know the vague sense of guilt rising in my gut over the fact that I had sex with Carl only a couple of weeks ago isn't warranted. She knew it didn't mean we were getting back together. She was just looking for *a normal college experience*—a one-night-fucking-stand—and in a fit of rage and jealousy I convinced myself I could be the guy to give it to her. But I made it damn clear she shouldn't expect anything from me. I've never lied to her. I'm not the liar. And she got the message, and obviously agreed wholeheartedly, since she got up and walked out barely minutes after I finished inside her.

And neither of us has mentioned it since.

But I look down at this cute girl, her fire-red hair falling over her shoulders, brown eyes shining up at me with lustful promise, and her sharp claws clanking against my belt buckle, and I know I can't go through with it. The lights shine too bright in the room, highlighting the glaring differences between this girl and the one I had in here a few weeks ago. The only one I've had in here. And I have to accept that, for whatever reason, I just don't want this girl. I don't want her mouth on me, and I certainly don't want to fuck her. Because she *can't* be whoever I want her to be. She can't be the one girl I do want. The one who never really existed in the first place.

I step back from her and offer a smile of consolation. I shrug. "We should get back to the party," I murmur, and then I turn and walk out, leaving my door wide open, hoping she'll follow, but I don't really care either way at this point, as long as I get the hell away from her.

I grab myself another beer and try not to scan the party for the reason *I'm* unable to have a normal college experience. I spot her friend Devin dressed as The Girl with the Dragon Tattoo, complete with fake piercings. She's chatting up one of our attackers, Max Brighton, and Carl is nowhere to be found. I could just ask her where Carl is, but then she would tell Carl, and Carl would think I give a shit.

I take a lap around the party. The house is big, but it's not that big. There are only so many places someone can be, and an anxious fury starts to build when I realize I'm looking for Ben as much as I am her. If I don't find either of them, I might completely lose it.

I know Ben asked her out. And I know she agreed. It had me seething for days. But then I heard it didn't come to fruition. She kept blowing him off, making and canceling tentative plans, or fabricating excuses. But while that knowledge calmed me somewhat, I think it's only made Ben more interested. He's accustomed to having pussy served to him on a platter, and Carl's elusion is only making hers more desirable. And though rationally I knew being at school with her would be like this—that she'd attract attention, including probably from my own friends—knowing it and living it are two different things.

When I find Ben in the garage getting more vodka from the freezer, my relief is palpable. But it still doesn't explain where Carl has gone off to, and though I have my doubts that she could be hooking up with some random guy, the truth is I don't really know.

I suck in a shallow breath and make my way over to Ben.

"Hey, bro," he murmurs. "Grab this." He hands me an icy supersized bottle of Smirnoff, takes two more out, and then replaces them with new bottles from a crate to chill in the freezer.

I should bullshit with him a little, try not to be so transparent, but I don't have time. "You seen Carl around?" I ask as we make our way back into the party.

He eyes me sideways, and I doubt he's buying my attempt at nonchalance one single bit. "Saw her earlier. That costume, dude. She is fucking something, huh?"

Yeah, she's something—*she's fucking* mine *is what she is.* But I don't say that. I just swallow down my bitter, possessive growl, and try to keep my cool. Because she isn't mine. Not anymore.

"You know where she went?" I ask instead.

Ben stops walking, so I do the same. His brow furrows and I wonder if he's onto me. "You knew her in high school, right?" he asks.

I'm not sure how he knows that, but I guess it isn't really a secret. "Yeah."

"Is there something I should know about, Green? I mean, I haven't hidden the fact that I've been looking to take her out. But if you have a thing for her—"

"No." I cut him off. "No thing. Just some history. But it's over and done with. I had a question about a team project we're working on for a class, and I was wondering where she went off to." *So much for not being a liar.*

Ben nods, placated. I'm not sure he actually believes me, but he doesn't really care. He only offered to back off because he knew I wouldn't take him up on it.

"Well, I don't know where she is," Ben says. "We were talking, and then we saw you walk off with Courtney, and we started taking shots. She got a phone call and went outside to take it, and when she came back she was all upset and looking for her friend—the roommate. Girl shit, I assumed, so I left them to it." Ben's report only sets me more on edge, and I have no fucking choice but to ask Devin what the fuck is going on. Because like I said, I am apparently incapable of just letting her go.

Letting *it* go. I meant *letting it go*.

Devin is still standing in the living room with Max, flirting heavily, and I wonder what the fuck kind of friend she is standing around looking to get laid when her friend is supposedly upset.

"What's up, Brighton," I interrupt them.

Max grins brightly, his eyes heavy with drink and gleaming with lust. I don't really blame him; Devin is an attractive girl.

"Green. Or should I say Teller," he slurs, and I roll my eyes at yet another reference to the *Sons of Anarchy* character I barely even resemble. "You know Devin?"

I try on a smile. "Nice to meet you." Technically I know who she is, but this is the first time I've been introduced to her.

"You too. *Green*, is it?" Her smile is surprisingly almost kittenish, and I guess that she's just one of those girls whose default mode is flirty.

"This is Tucker," Max interjects, slapping my back as his lopsided grin stretches wider. "Team's new badass defender."

I force a laugh. "Thanks, man." Max starts to say something else, but I interrupt him and look to Devin, who's still smiling at me. "Do you, uh—know where Carl is? Ben said she got a call and was upset. He's worried about her." *And the lies just keep on coming.*

Devin's chocolate eyes narrow playfully and her smile turns coy. "*He's* worried, is he?"

I don't have fucking time for this. "Do you know where she is or not?" My tone relays my impatience.

Devin sighs and rolls her eyes. "She had a family emergency. We've all been drinking so I was going to take a cab with her, but there were none available for over an hour with Halloween and everything. Anyway, she got a ride."

"The *fuck* do you mean she got a ride? With who?" I'm the only person on campus Carl didn't just meet for the first time a matter of weeks ago.

"Dude. Take it easy." Max glares at me, but I ignore him.

Devin blinks at me like she doesn't understand why I'm overreacting. "She didn't say," she says a little defensively. "She got a text or an e-mail or something, and said she got a ride, and she got picked up like five minutes later. I offered to go with her but she insisted I stay. She had it under control; she's a big girl."

If Carl was texting or e-mailing with whoever picked her up, then at least it wasn't someone she just met tonight. It should pacify me at least marginally that she didn't just get in a car with a drunken stranger, but I can't escape the feeling that something might be seriously wrong. I can't guess what her *family emergency* could be, but Carl's love and loyalty for her family—even for those who don't deserve it—is relentlessly fierce, and I learned the hard way she sets it above all else. So the idea that she would take a risk with her safety, whether knowingly in her desperation to reach them, or unconsciously—distracted by panic—isn't exactly implausible. And if she's as wasted from those shots with Ben as I suspect…

Fuck.

I need to keep a cool head, because losing my shit won't help either me or Carl. But I can't stop myself from shooting Devin an irritated scowl before I leave them how I found them.

Carl's judgment might have been compromised by her distress—and Ben's goddamn liquor—but what the fuck is Devin's excuse? She should have known better than to just let Carl get in a car with someone without at least letting her roommate know where she's going. Don't girls have systems for this kind of shit? Devin should have gotten a fucking license plate or something, or at the very minimum asked Carl who her goddamn ride was.

I look around the party, and it doesn't take long to realize that everyone I've known Carl to hang out with is here. So who the fuck texted her and picked her up? The campus is only about thirty minutes away from our hometown, but almost all of our friends are away at school, and even if someone happened to have gone home for Halloween—not fucking likely—it would take them longer to get here than five fucking minutes.

I have no choice. I have to do something I've resisted doing since the day she obliterated my heart. I have to fucking call her.

But her phone goes straight to voicemail. It doesn't even ring. Like it isn't even on. My heart pounds like a snare drum. It isn't a bad sign in itself—Carl is constantly forgetting to charge her phone. But coupled with her family emergency and her mysterious ride, it has me on the verge of panic.

I try calling two more times with the same result, and on the fourth attempt, I surrender and leave a voicemail.

"Carl. I... *fuck*. Just—call me. And charge your fucking phone!" I growl into the mic.

I rub my temples, trying to soothe my suddenly raging headache. Then I try calling her again. Same result.

I storm through the living room looking for Leo—a freshman second stringer who doesn't live in the house—to demand a ride. He got stuck being sober driver tonight, and he's supposed to be hanging out on the first floor waiting for people who need a safe ride. But he isn't here.

I shoot him a text and find out he got stuck at some drunk girl's dorm when she started puking after he walked her to her room. He promises to be back within fifteen minutes, but I'm starting to freak out. Anger, anxiety, fear—it's a potent combination and my blood is thick with it, every muscle tense. I head out the front door to the porch, where a few smokers shiver in the autumn chill. I make my way down the walkway to wait on the curb, where four hours later according to my internal clock, but only twelve minutes according to my phone, Leo pulls up and I jump into the passenger seat before he even comes to a full stop.

"Stuyvesant Hall," I order him. I overheard someone mention which dorm Carl lived in a few weeks back. Though I don't know why I'm going there now. It's unlikely she's there if she's dealing with a family emergency. But I don't know what else to do.

Leo doesn't move. "Why you wanna go there? Everyone's out partying and anyone else is only there because they're too drunk to be any fun." He smirks. "Or they're the perfect amount of drunk, depending on—"

"Stuyvesant. Hall," I repeat through a clenched jaw. I'm really not in the mood for his motherfucking date-rape jokes. My tolerance with his bullshit has already been wearing thin, and tonight's the night I just might fucking snap. Then I won't have worry about Zayne's class ruining my GPA and losing me my scholarship, because I'll be expelled for ramming this douchebag's face into the goddamn dash.

Leo finally gets that I'm not in the mood and takes off east toward campus. I don't even bother thanking him as I make my way through the courtyard to the front of the building. Leo was right about one thing—it is dead tonight. It's just after midnight and everyone is out having a good time. And here I am, standing in front of my lying ex-girlfriend's dorm—a lying ex-girlfriend I *can't stand*—with absolutely no idea what to do next.

I check my phone again. Crickets.

I text her to fucking call me back.

Still nothing.

Only residents of the dorm have the key fob to get in, so I search the directory for her room, and buzz the ringer five times before I accept that she's not there. Anyone else I know who could possibly let me in is currently at the party I just left.

With no other options, I settle myself on a bench near the entrance that Carl will have to pass when she gets back, and resign myself to wait.

*   *   *

I must have fallen asleep, because dawn is already breaking when I'm woken up by the idling engine of an obnoxiously loud sports car. The sound jars me awake and I jump into attentiveness. My back is sore as fuck from falling asleep on this stupid wooden bench that I now hate with every cell in my body, and I blink the grogginess from my eyes as they try and locate the source of the noise.

A glance at my watch tells me it's almost seven in the morning, and the small courtyard is already beginning to show signs of life—a student heading out for a jog, another enduring a particularly grueling post-Halloween walk of shame, dressed in the remnants of a very skimpy cat costume.

And then I blink again—this time in disbelief—as Carl emerges from the souped-up Mustang idling at the entrance to the walkway. My gut churns as I take in her weariness. She's changed out of her costume and into sweats, but a man's jacket is draped over her slumped shoulders. I don't recognize the car. I'm about to head over to her when the driver's door opens and out climbs—of all fucking people— our *professor*. Fucking *Zayne*.

What. The. Fuck.

He comes around to her side of the car and I watch them as she smiles sheepishly and he rubs the back of his neck. He murmurs something and she nods. He shrugs, smiling now, and Carl returns it, but hers is forced, and it gets my hackles up.

I start marching toward them but they don't see me, and Zayne squeezes Carl's arm and then just gets right back in his car and drives off. Carl walks with her head down and doesn't see me until the last second.

"Tuck?"

"What the fuck was that?" I growl. I don't mean to come off so accusatory. She looks stressed, and exhausted, and I don't want to make it worse, but I'm fucking tired, too.

Carl responds to my tone the only way she knows how. She straightens her back and narrows her eyes, and I wonder if it's just my tone that's got her on the defense or if it's guilt.

"What the fuck was *what*?" she snaps back.

What the fuck happened with your family, and where have you been, and what's going on? "Did you fuck him?" *And that.*

Carl's eyes widen indignantly. "Did you just ask me if I *fucked* our professor?!"

Well, you did just get out of his fucking premature-midlife-crisis-mobile in different clothes than you were wearing last night. I raise my eyebrows expectantly.

Her mouth gapes open incredulously before her eyes narrow again. "Yes, Tucker. I did. You know, I was at your Halloween party and

while you were busy with that skanky redhead I just thought to myself, *Hey, I've only ever been with one guy in my life, what better idea
than to have a one-night stand with my fucking teacher*. Because I'm just
such a fucking slut. And, you know, he was all for it. Because screwing some random student is totally worth losing your job, and—"

Goddamnit I can't take another fucking sarcastic word out of her
mouth. "Enough!"

"Oh it's *enough*, is it?" she hisses.

Rationally I know it was a ridiculous thing to ask her. She may be
a liar, but she's also a good girl. I know that better than anyone. Because I *know* she's only ever been with one guy. *Me*. Or at least I'd
hoped that was still true. And fuck the damn wave of relief that surges
through me at hearing it confirmed. Because I'm not supposed to care
anymore, goddamnit!

"What happened, Carl? Why did you leave the party?" I try not
to ask the final question, but I can't stop myself. "Why were you with
him?"

Carl sighs and her confidence deflates before my eyes. "Look,
Tuck, I've barely slept. I'm exhausted, and…I just can't do this right
now."

She can't do this right now? I just spent the night on a goddamn
bench outside her dorm imagining God only knows what and she
shows up here first thing in the morning in new clothes with our
young-stud professor, and *she* can't do this right now?

Well, *fuck this*.

"See you in class," I spit, and then I turn to leave.

"Hope you had fun with your skank," she mutters, and it's all I can
take.

"I did have fun with my skank," I lie. "And I will continue to have
fun with whoever the fuck I want. Have fun with our *professor*."

Chapter Eleven

Carleigh

Present Day

I watch Tucker walk away, his hostility radiating off of him in waves. I just don't have the energy for his childish bullshit right now. All I want to do is get into my bed and crash.

I don't understand what the hell he was even doing here. My brain is too tired to do any quality thinking, but if he's outside Stuyvesant Hall this early, chances are he's leaving some girl's dorm—maybe that Red Skank for all I know—and just the thought alone makes my already disheartened mood plummet into downright depressed. It was bad enough watching him flirt and walk off with her earlier, and I don't know why I was surprised. I knew he'd move on. I knew sleeping with me a few weeks ago didn't mean anything to him. But seeing it unfold before my eyes…it was more than I could bear.

And I didn't have *fun* with Zayne, either. I just needed a ride and he did me a favor. But Tucker hates me, and he's obviously moving on with other girls, so why the hell would he care even if I did go and do something crazy like hook up with Zayne?

Like that would ever happen. He's my professor and, as it turns out, a really nice guy on top of it. He didn't have to come to my rescue last night. He didn't have to offer his help. But he did.

My heart practically stopped beating in my chest when my phone buzzed with a call from Billy. I've always told him if he or his friends ever did anything stupid and needed help, that he needed to call me. And to his credit, he did call.

Hearing his slurred voice sent me into panic mode. He's only thirteen. I didn't have my first drink until well into high school, and the guilt of how my being away at school, even if I'm not very far, might be affecting him haunts me even now. Especially now. He has no one. My mother was in the city doing God knows what, and Billy's friends were supposed to be staying at our house. Instead they went to a party, and they got drunk. But they couldn't get back home. There were no cabs available, and their friends are all too young to drive, even if they hadn't been drinking.

But my mother wasn't answering her phone, and the no-cabs problem applied to me, too. And there I was, standing outside the lax party, practically pulling out my hair while I waited for an Uber that said it would be an hour—the shortest quoted wait time.

I figured I'd have to stay at home with Billy and wouldn't make it to my morning classes, so I decided to e-mail the professors of those two classes—Zayne and Professor Farley—to let them know I had a family emergency and wouldn't be in class the next morning. Because contrary to popular belief, attendance *does* count in college. So I e-mailed, and hoped they'd let it slide.

I didn't expect either of them to respond, certainly not that night, but Zayne did. And when his e-mail asked if everything was okay, and I replied that my little brother was in trouble and he had no one else to help him, Zayne asked if I needed anything. I wrote back joking that unless he had some sort of power over the availability of taxis on Halloween, I was on my own. But then he replied that while he had no power in the almighty world of Uber, he did have a car. And how could I turn him down? Billy was so drunk he was barely coherent and I was panicking.

Zayne got me to Billy in less than thirty minutes, and got us to my house just in time before Billy started puking into my mother's hydrangea.

Zayne helped me get Billy and his friends into the house. I thought he would leave then, but instead he helped me get them cleaned up and into bed. It was embarrassing as hell, but I couldn't exactly refuse his help when most of those kids already weighed more than I do.

But having Zayne in my house was surreal. I was struck by how easily I forgot he was my professor, and we fell smoothly into friendly conversation. Of course, once you share the experience of cleaning vomit from a squad of barely conscious thirteen-year-olds, your relationship skips a step or two.

I ended up making him a cup of coffee, and the more we talked, the more I had to remind myself that this man was, in fact, my professor, regardless of how friendly he seemed.

He was finishing his coffee when my mother finally texted me back:

Got your messages. Sorry my phone was off. I'm on my way home now, you can go back to school. 2:03 am

I growled at my phone.

"Everything okay?" Zayne asked, and I buried my frustration for his benefit.

"Just my mother," I murmured. "She's on her way home now."

Zayne frowned. "Well, that's a good thing, isn't it?"

"Yeah. She told me I should go back to school. Like I should just leave Billy and a bunch of drunk thirteen-year-olds alone in the house. She just...aggravates me sometimes." I regretted giving him that insight into my dysfunctional family the moment I said it, but Zayne managed to make even that less awkward. He noted that I seemed like more of a mother to Billy than our actual mother. He's observant, and kind, and it made me confide even more about her.

It turns out Zayne's mother and mine have a lot in common. "Materialism to the extreme," he called it. But when he tentatively asked about my father, I just shook my head and changed the subject back to his family, asking if his parents were still together. A part of me knew it was inappropriate, but still, I felt strangely connected to him in that moment.

Zayne shook his head. "My mother tends to go where the money is," he told me, "And my father was a businessman. Self-made. When he lost his business, he didn't have any family money to fall back on, and he lost my mother as well."

My heart ached for him. At least my mother stuck with her marriage, even if it isn't much of a marriage, what with my father in prison and all. But then again, he didn't lose all the money. I wonder if that's why he put such stock in keeping it—to keep *her*. So much so that he traded nearly a decade of his own freedom. Even now the thought makes me cringe. That isn't love. At least not a love I would ever want for myself. I would have lived with Tucker in a shack if he'd have had me.

Zayne and I talked for a long time, and only when I had to fight to keep my eyes open did he suggest we call it a night. He offered to drive me back to my dorm, but I didn't feel comfortable leaving before my mom got back, and when he offered to pick me up at the crack of dawn just to give me a ride, I couldn't exactly turn him down. After all, my car was back at school, and I didn't want to ask my mother to drive me—I wanted her to stay home and be a goddamn mother to her son.

I must have thanked Zayne a hundred times, but he just blew it off, as if the fact that his student needed help was more than enough reason for him to offer it. Apparently he'd once had a student advisor who regularly went above and beyond for her students, and it's obvious that that's the kind of teacher he wants to be. I'd say he's doing a damn fine job.

I think of the final words of advice he left me with last night: "Everything happens for a reason, Carleigh. It's trite, but it's true. I know it doesn't feel like it on days like these, but hey, if my father hadn't gone through his hardships, I would have inherited a disgustingly handsome trust and would probably be partying on a beach in Ibiza right now. Instead, I found a calling in teaching I never even would have known to look for."

From another man the words would probably have been sardonic, but from Zayne they glowed with earnestness, and I can't help but wonder if they might be true for me as well. If, in the long run, it's possible something good might come of all my regrets.

*   *   *

I enter my dorm room quietly and plug my phone in to charge. I already changed into sweats back at home, so I fall right into bed without waking a comatose Devin, who still appears to be wearing a smudged variation of last night's makeup.

Sleep doesn't come easily, though. Tucker's accusations ring loud in my mind, and the more I think about them, the angrier I get. I'd worried over how much I'd imposed on Zayne, but it never occurred to me that from the outside, him dropping me off early in the morning in front of my dorm might appear scandalous. Because it *wasn't* scandalous. It was all thoroughly innocent, and I can't help but feel outraged for Zayne that Tucker suggested otherwise.

The more I think about it the more disgruntled I get. How *dare* Tucker? While he was screwing around with Red Skank, I was dealing with Billy with no one to help me except one nice guy who really, really didn't have to offer. A really handsome, really sweet, really nice guy. Who I didn't even look at. And the sad thing is—it wasn't because he's my professor. The reason I didn't look twice at Zayne is the same reason I've been blowing off Ben Aronin since he asked me out a few weeks ago. It's because of Tucker, and the realization makes me want to punch a wall.

And suddenly, I'm done. I'm done apologizing and I'm done feeling sorry for myself. I'm done drowning in guilt and I'm definitely done sleeping with him. Especially now that he's been with Red Skank. I'm. Just. Done.

I close my eyes, fueled with a new determination, and I drift off to sleep almost instantly, ready to finally embrace my new single life when I wake. I am finally ready to get over Tucker Green.

* * *

Over the next couple of weeks Tucker and I seem to succeed in what I once thought was the worst possible thing—erasing us. I won't pretend it doesn't still hurt. But if there is anything to be gained in being Nicole Stanger's daughter, it's the ability to bury emotion and feign composure. My new plan of action is a simple one—trite but true—*fake it 'til you make it*.

And so I go through the motions of what I would be doing if I actually felt the emotional stability I'm working so hard to portray.

Tucker seems to have come up with an identical game plan. He flirts with girls and contributes in our group meetings for our creative digital marketing project, though he never addresses me directly, nor I him. And I'm pretty sure he's screwing The Red Skank, whose name I've recently learned is Courtney, and while she may very well be a nice girl, I'm still calling her *The Red Skank*—at least in my head.

I have also learned, however, that she does not in fact live in Stuyvesant Hall, which has led to an ever-growing snowball of internal speculation as to what in the hell Tucker was doing there that morning. At first I suspected he just ended up going home with another girl that night. Going home with some random girl after hooking up with someone else is certainly a slutty thing to do, but not out of the question for a single guy in college. But then I remembered the voicemail. The one he left me that night, demanding I call him back and sounding decidedly frantic. The one I decided to ignore, since I had already decided on my plan of action to move on. But it does make me wonder.

Then I remind myself again of my new mantra, which sounds unsettlingly similar to one I used to invoke after Tucker and I first hooked up.

I don't care.

I don't care, I don't care, I don't care.

Zayne wraps up his lecture and dismisses us. As I pack up my books, he casts me a warm smile, its soft curve of familiarity the only hint of our shared experience. I return his smile, and his familiarity, adding in a personal note of gratitude.

Zayne is a genuinely good guy, a fact I've come to realize more and more. In the weeks since Halloween, as the stress of the night itself—and the following morning—has faded, I've finally had opportunity to process just how much I'd inconvenienced him, and how selflessly he'd acted in turn.

Even Zayne's explanation for his kindness—his outlook on teaching—was exceptionally noble. The man has a gift, and his ability to forge connections with people—with *me*—isn't something to be taken for granted.

But Tucker, it seems, still isn't a fan. He still watches Zayne strangely, but at least he no longer glares at him as if he suspects he's some kind of serial killer. I realize he thinks Zayne is harboring some kind of inappropriate interest in me, but it's like he simply no longer cares. And why would he? I suppose that even if it were true—which God knows it isn't—it wouldn't be Tucker's problem anyway. *I* am no longer Tucker's problem. And I have to get used to that.

So tonight I make my first proactive effort in doing that.

I go through the rest of my classes and then catch up on my reading assignments, and by the time evening rolls around, I'm inevitably nervous, but I'm determined not to cancel.

Ben picks me up at Stuyvesant at precisely eight o'clock. *Punctual*.

After my hundredth excuse why we couldn't go out, Ben finally called me on my bullshit. And what could I say? He was right. So I told him, again, that I'd only just gotten out of a relationship, and I was hesitant to date. So tonight is not a date. We are two friends, going to dinner.

But as we drive off campus in an awkward silence, the air is thick with the discomfort of a first date. Ben tries to make small talk, but I can't seem to come up with more than one-word responses that seem to halt the conversation every time I open my mouth. By the time Ben hands off his car keys to the valet outside Bottega, I'm already regretting agreeing to this at all.

But I don't suppose I can back out now.

Ben's hand closes gently around my wrist, stopping me as I'm walking into the restaurant.

"Carleigh, if you don't want to be here, we can leave," he offers, his handsome face etched with sympathy, and it only exacerbates my guilt.

I look down at my shoes. "It's not that I don't want to be here. It's just…" I trail off. What can I say? It's just…*I wish I were here with someone else*?

Ben gives my wrist a small squeeze. "Hey. Stop over-thinking so much. I'm dying to eat something other than campus food, and I'm happy to do it with a new friend. Okay?"

I appreciate his words, and they do help me relax a little. I give him a half-earnest smile. "Okay," I agree.

* * *

Ben isn't just talk. He's careful not to make me uncomfortable, chatting amicably throughout dinner just like an old friend would. There are no first-date, getting-to-know-you questions or anything like that, and by the time we've finished our appetizers, I've managed to drop my guard and enjoy myself. There's absolutely no attraction or romantic chemistry, but that's fine. I don't have to get over Tucker in one fell swoop. Even just going out and enjoying myself with a new friend is a step forward from drowning in guilt and heartache, and I give myself a figurative pat on the back.

We both agree to skip dessert and I insist on splitting the bill.

"Just to be clear, I'm going along with this because we're not on a date. But if we were, I would not be letting you pay. Just for the record," Ben says through a brilliant, playful smirk.

"Duly noted." I laugh. "I will spread word that you are nothing if not a gentleman."

Ben's smirk widens. "You do that. Be sure to tell all your freshmen girlfriends," he teases.

"You got it, buddy."

"I think this is the beginning of a beautiful friendship."

And who knows? Maybe it is.

We get our coats and Ben hands his ticket to the valet.

My phone buzzes with a message, and I swipe the screen on. But there's no new text, so I check my e-mail app instead, expecting to find one from some online store I shopped on all of once, probably advertising some sale *exclusive* to me and its million other customers. But the sender isn't an anonymous marketing distribution service. It's Zayne.

The subject reads: *Checking in,* and I blink at my inbox, my brows knitted together in thought. It isn't the unexpected e-mail that takes me aback. What surprises me is the barely discernible spark of excitement that flickers in my belly, and I stare down at the screen, wondering where it came from.

A glance to my left confirms that Ben is still busy waiting for the parking attendant to make his change, so I open the e-mail.

Hey Carleigh,

I keep meaning to catch you after class, but one of us always seems to get caught up with something, don't we? Anyway, I don't want to put you on the spot, but I admit I've thought about you a lot in the past couple of weeks, and what you've been dealing with at home. I just wanted to check that you're doing okay. And to let you know that if you ever feel stressed, or need help with anything, you can come to me, okay? Whether it's school related or not. It's clear to me that you're an exceptionally capable woman, but I know how demanding a freshman workload can be, and sometimes our family or personal life can add to its weight. The last thing I want is for you to feel overwhelmed.

I'm here. Even if you just need to talk.

Z

"Ready?" I'm still staring at the words when Ben's voice startles me. I hadn't heard him approach and I jump, hastily shoving my phone out of sight like I was looking at porn or something. And I don't know why; Zayne's e-mail was perfectly innocent.

"Yep," I reply, finding myself. "Let's go."

Ben and I resume our easy company, chatting comfortably as we drive back toward campus.

"Do you want to come chill at the house for a little?" he asks.

This takes me aback. I don't want to be presumptuous or anything, but then, how many reasons are there for a guy to invite you back to his place after dinner?

Ben narrows his eyes playfully. "Get your head outta the gutter, young lady. There are a bunch of people hanging out there tonight and I thought you'd like to come make some more new friends."

My relief must be written all over my face.

He shakes his head. "God, you freshmen and your filthy minds."

I laugh. He's funny. And it's not that late and I would like to socialize a little more tonight. But there's one massive reason why I probably shouldn't do that at the lacrosse house. "I don't know if I should."

Ben frowns. "Why not?"

I shrug, not quite meeting his gaze.

"Let me guess—something to do with Tucker Green?"

My eyes flash to his. How could he know that? Has Tucker said something? "What do you mean?" I ask hesitantly.

"Come *on*. I see how he stares at you. But then, I can't really blame him for that. And you did tell me you went to high school together."

Right. I forgot about that.

"And anyway, he mentioned you two had some history. But he said it's over and done with, and he didn't seem to have an issue with it. You've partied at the house before; what's the big deal?"

Over and done with. I try to numb myself to the sting of his words. Maybe he's not *acting* over us, he really *is* over us. And if he doesn't care, then why should I?

"I guess I could come by for a little bit."

Chapter Twelve

Carleigh

Present Day

Ben and I walk inside the lax house and some eyes turn to us, but mostly people just continue their drinking and socializing.

"Just tell me when you want to go, and I'll drive you home," Ben whispers, and I smile in gratitude.

Two girls I know from my dorm are here, and they immediately call me over to chat. I do end up meeting some new people, and I'm in a good mood until Red Skank walks in and sits down next to one of my new friends, joining our conversation as if she has every right to be a part of it.

The worst part is—she's nice. She's not especially intelligent or witty, but she's not the raving bitch I've concocted in my mind, and I'm ashamed that this disappoints me.

I know Tucker is in the other room playing video games—someone mentioned it earlier and I've heard his loud booming voice sporadically cheer at his apparently victorious digital exploits—and so I haven't dared venture off the living room couch for the two hours I've been here. But now my throat is suddenly desert dry, and I need a bottle of water or something. Or maybe I just need to get away from

Red Skank—whom I now can't even insult in my head without feeling like a pathetic, bitter bitch.

I smile when I hear Ben's voice from outside the kitchen, but stop dead in my tracks when I hear who he's talking to.

"You kick Vance's ass again?" Ben asks breezily.

"Obviously," Tucker says with patented cockiness. If he knows I'm here tonight, he doesn't seem to care one iota.

"Courtney's here," Ben says suggestively.

"I know." Tucker's tone gives nothing away, and I try to ignore the swirl of jealousy stirring in the pit of my stomach. "How was your—uh, dinner?"

"Fine. She's a cool girl. Made it clear she's only looking for friends, though."

I don't know who the long exhale comes from—if it signifies Tucker's relief or Ben's frustration, or nothing at all.

"She's here, too, you know," Ben says cautiously.

There's a pause, then, "Yeah. I know."

"You're not, like, friends or anything?" Ben asks, presumably trying to get to the bottom of the *history* Tucker mentioned.

"I don't know," Tucker replies. "We're not anything really."

It's nothing new, but that doesn't lessen the sting of his words.

"You want to go say hello?" Ben presses.

Another pause, and then, "You know what? Yeah, I think I will go say hello."

Tucker wants to say hello to me? Surprise instantly gives way to excitement, and I scurry off before I can be caught eavesdropping. I rejoin the conversation on the couch, my chest practically bursting with foolish hope, even as somewhere in my mind I vaguely register that Tucker's tone wasn't exactly friendly.

I keep my gaze trained on the girl talking, not hearing a word she says as he approaches. I'm careful not to look like I'm expecting him, and only when someone says "hey" do I even turn in his direction.

"Wanted to say hi," he murmurs with practiced nonchalance, and my mouth battles a small smile as I finally look up.

But Tucker doesn't come over to me at all. Instead, he detours to my left, to Courtney, and wraps her up in a hug. He leans into her ear, and my throat tightens so viciously I can hardly even breathe as his whispers pull a smile from her lips.

"Come play with me," he says, loud enough for me to hear. He holds his palm out to her and she takes it eagerly, greedily, as nausea rises in my stomach, making me want to gag.

Red Skank doesn't hesitate, and I can't even blame her. And that's the worst part. As they leave the living room I find myself wishing I could sincerely hate her—silently call her even worse names and curse her to hell. But I can't even do that. Because she's just as helpless against Tucker's charm and masculine perfection as I've been my entire life. Instead, it's myself I blame. For letting hope drown out reason, and setting myself up for yet another round of heartache.

Tonight was supposed to be about *getting over* Tucker. About *moving on*.

I am so disgusted by my pitiful self that I realize it isn't even Courtney I should be hating or calling names. It's me. And I won't be that girl for another moment. I fucking *refuse*.

I leap to my feet and go look for Ben—the guy who actually *wanted* to spend time with me. I find him still in the kitchen, leaning casually back against the countertop, sipping a beer straight from the bottle as he chats with one of their teammates whose name I've forgotten.

"Hey," he says. "You ready to leave?"

Yes. But I'm on a mission to move on from my old, destructive relationship, and running away isn't the way to do that. So I shake my head instead. I nod at his beer. "Can I have one of those?"

Ben's mouth lifts in a pleased smile, but before he can respond, his friend opens his mouth. "Free alcohol at all times for hot bitches—house rules," he slurs. Apparently that beer is far from his first of the night.

Ben grimaces his disapproval, rolling his eyes in exasperation. "Dude."

The guy raises his eyebrows, utterly clueless.

Ben seems to realize it's a lost cause. "Get lost," he orders, and the fool simply shrugs and walks away.

I watch the entire exchange with quiet interest, until Ben and I are alone in the kitchen, and the moment we lock eyes, we both burst into laughter.

"Sorry…" Ben chokes out through more full-body chuckles, "he's kind of a clown, even sober."

"Clearly." I laugh. "Your friends are pretty misogynistic drunks," I point out.

Ben snorts. "They're misogynists all the time, Carleigh," he admits. "They just forget to hide it when they're drunk." He opens the fridge and grabs me a beer, slamming it against the countertop at the right angle to pop the bottle top like a pro.

Someone calls Ben's name from the hall, and then Ricky walks into the kitchen, pausing when he sees me. "Oh, hi, Carleigh."

"*Ricky fucking Vance*," I greet him with a smirk, reminding him of the crude way he introduced himself that first night in the bar.

Ricky smiles sheepishly, his cheeks heating with obvious shame. "I'm never gonna live that down, am I?"

"Not likely," Ben agrees, and we all share a laugh at Ricky's expense, himself included.

Ricky tells Ben it's his turn to play whatever video game they've all been busy with, and Ben tries to take a pass, but I insist I'm fine and that he should go. I tell myself it isn't because I know Tucker and Courtney are in that room, and if Ben is there, too, then they won't be alone.

God, it's like I can't escape Tucker. Or…

Or I haven't really been trying to.

It strikes me that I've been lying to myself. That I haven't actually been trying to move on from Tucker at all. It's the only explanation. Otherwise I wouldn't have opted to go shopping for new friends on his lacrosse team in the first place. I wouldn't choose to socialize in his own house.

Clarity is sudden and harsh, and the walls of the house start closing in without warning, chasing me into finally finding that escape after all. I hurriedly slip out the front door and onto the porch, before sitting on the top step and sucking in a deep breath. I shouldn't be here. Not if I want to move on with my life.

But the last thing I want to do is walk back into that house of breakup horrors to ask Ben for a ride back to my dorm. I don't really want to see Ben right now at all, in fact. He's as much a connection to Tucker as the house itself. And I know it's unfair to Ben, and I'm not going to drop a friend, newly made or otherwise, because of an ex who no longer even cares enough to hate me. But I just need away from it all right now—everything that currently links me to the boy who is apparently my kryptonite, with the power to render me unrecognizable to the capable woman Zayne spoke of in his e-mail.

Zayne's e-mail.

I slip out my phone and open it, rereading the thoughtful words, and I don't know if it's those words themselves or the thought of their author that reignites that strange spark, but it flickers excitedly in my belly as I try to think of a response. I'm not as eloquent as Zayne, so I simply write the truth.

Hi Zayne,

I'm out at a party, but I just wanted to reply and thank you for your email. It was very thoughtful of you to check in. I'm doing okay, mostly. Billy is doing better, too, I think. Though I haven't had much luck getting him to talk about the drinking, which is an irritating new development in his race to grow up. I guess it's typical

for a teenager, though. But we're hanging in there. Thanks again
for your help on Halloween, and for reaching out. It really means
a lot.

Carleigh

I'm not expecting him to respond, at least not tonight, so I'm surprised when my phone announces a new e-mail, and I don't hesitate to read it.

Carleigh,

You're too young to be stressing about teenagers with attitude.
But I'm glad to hear you're doing well. Enjoy your party. You're
better off than I am right now, but hopefully I'll soon find an excuse to sneak out of the most boring dinner party in the history of
the university's business department. As far as checking in with
you, no thanks needed. I did it because I care. Like I said, I'm
here.

Z

I did it because I care. It makes me smile. But I feel vaguely guilty.
Because Zayne has been nothing but forthcoming and honest, even
confiding about his parents' divorce, and here I am, true to my old
form, pretending everything is just fine when I feel anything but. But
that's the behavior that lost me Tucker. That got me *here*. It's the influence of my mother, and if there's anyone I don't want to emulate,
it's Nicole Stanger.

Zayne,

Full disclosure—The party I'm at is more of a get-together than an
actual party, and I'm not enjoying it so much as hiding on the porch

from my ex, waiting until my ride is ready to leave. So I'm not sure
I'm better off than you after all. But I appreciate the thought :)

Carleigh

Maybe it was too much information, too personal to share with a man
who is, first and foremost, my professor. And I suppose technically I'm
not waiting for Ben to be ready to drive me home so much as I'm giving myself a reprieve before seeing him, and inevitably being reminded
of Tucker, yet again. But my e-mail was honest and real, and I can at least
feel good about that.

This time I'm not surprised to receive a quick reply, but it doesn't
make me smile any less.

Carleigh,

That's no way to enjoy a Thursday night. These years go by fast,
you know, and then you have to get a real job and be a grown-up
like me :(. So enjoy them while you can. I do still need that excuse
to escape, so if you don't want to wait for your ride, feel free to
send me the address and I'm happy to drive you to your dorm. I'll
be passing through campus anyway. Let me know.

Z

Though the speed of the reply didn't surprise me, two things do.
The first is the sad-face emoji, which makes my smile stretch wider.
But what makes that excitable little spark flare in my tummy is his offer to drive me home. It shouldn't, of course. I know it doesn't mean
anything. But a small voice in my head whispers that maybe it's more
than just innate generosity. Maybe he actually wants to spend time
with me. Even for just a five-minute drive. And that thought makes
the spark ignite into a low flame.

It's not romantic, or sexual, or anything inappropriate. It's just the longing to connect with another human being, someone I feel an affinity for, and the vague thrill of thinking he might return it in kind.

Zayne,

You've done enough for me already, don't you think? I really don't want to impose on you any more than I already have. Of course, if you really need that excuse then I suppose I'd be the one doing you the favor, so I'm at 741 Park Street, if you feel like you need to insist.

Carleigh

His response is almost instant.
I'm on my way.
Nothing else.
My heart beats wildly with anxiety and that same spark of thrill. I don't know why I'm nervous. Or excited, for that matter. But I am, and as the image of his clear blue eyes floats through my mind, I can't help but smile.

*   *   *

The roar of Zayne's engine announces his arrival several blocks before he reaches me, and I'm waiting on the curb when he pulls up, not wanting to give Tucker a chance to see me climb into Zayne's car. I'm not doing anything wrong, and neither is Zayne, but whether Tucker still cares or not, I don't want to give him any fuel for his ridiculous suspicions.

Zayne greets me with kind eyes and a knowing smile. "Eager to escape?" he asks when I all but leap into the passenger seat.

I force a laugh. "Something like that," I admit.

Zayne takes off toward campus.

"How was your dinner party?" I ask. "Was it really that bad?"

Zayne shoots me a look that says not to doubt him. "Carleigh, I wish I could say it was the single most boring evening of my existence, but unfortunately almost every party hosted by my department head has been equally dull."

I laugh. "Sorry to hear that."

"Let's be glad boredom isn't fatal." He sighs, shooting me a glance as he turns right onto Washington. "Can I assume your night wasn't the best?"

I chew my bottom lip, considering how much to say. "*The best* is definitely not how I would describe it," I agree.

Zayne nods thoughtfully. "So here's the deal, Carleigh. You have a choice. I can drop you at your dorm right now so you can end your *not the best* night…"

I blink at him.

"Or, if you're not in a rush, we can take a thirty-minute drive, and I can let you in on a little secret of mine, and show you how to make a *not the best* night still end on a sweet note." He stops at a red light and turns to me. "The choice is yours."

"As long as it's legal, I'm in." *And as long as it wouldn't violate any university policies.* I wince inwardly for even thinking it.

"In that case…" Zayne speeds up, purposefully passing the turn onto University Drive and heading toward the highway.

Just like on Halloween, conversation with Zayne is friendly and easy. He asks after Billy again, reassuring me that I'm doing things right with him. But he also seems to think I take too much on my own shoulders, and I don't really know how to respond to that. My brother isn't exactly a burden I can unload. Nor would I ever want to. If I had to make a choice between him and the college experiences Zayne thinks I undervalue, I would move back home in a heartbeat. But I really hope it doesn't come to that.

I'm relieved when the conversation veers back to my classes, and Zayne asks after my workload.

"It's not actually all that bad," I admit. "Or, I have a handle on it, at least. Except for a certain final project I have for this one marketing class. The professor is a real hard-ass," I joke.

Zayne chuckles. He has a nice laugh. A man's laugh—deep and rough. "I'm sure you'll come up with something great," he says. "Don't worry too much; the right idea will come to you—or one of your team members—and you'll make it work."

I sigh. "I hope you're right. Because word on campus is that your grading style is…harsh." I smirk.

Zayne raises his eyebrows. "Word on campus?"

"Mmm-hmm." I nod.

"Whose word?"

"Just a friend of mine who happens to be your former student," I say flippantly.

"Which former student?"

I shake my head. "No way. I'm not ratting."

Zayne smiles. "Fine, fine. At least tell me what they said then."

I guess that's a reasonable request. "He just said that you grade very subjectively."

Zayne nods. "Fair assessment. Life is subjective, Carleigh."

"I know." I think. "But you can see how that kind of uncertainty might make someone nervous when so much rides on our grades. And when you add the internship…" I trail off, because my mind is inevitably back on Tucker, and the possibility of him losing his scholarship.

"Hmm…" Zayne makes a sound of understanding, but that also says, *life is* uncertain, *Carleigh*.

"And it's also the professionalism thing. B— *My friend* told me about his friend who took your class a few semesters ago, and had a girl in his group give him a bad peer review as, like, revenge for…well, sleeping with her and I guess not following up."

Zayne eyes me sideways, the only acknowledgment that I just brought up the subject of sex with my professor, even if not directly. "And…?"

"And his grade suffered."

Zayne pulls off Route 27. "And you don't think that's fair…"

Really? "That some vindictive one-night stand took advantage of your system to ruin someone's GPA?"

Zayne throws me another glance. "I'd argue the system worked as designed."

Huh? "How?"

Zayne shrugs. "My purpose is to help prepare you for the real world, Carleigh. And in the real world, it's not considered professional to screw one's co-workers. Because it can cause drama, and affect one's work. So you can blame this girl because you say she abused the power of her peer review, but I'd say that whoever this guy is, he had the power to keep it in his pants, at least until their project was complete."

I swallow thickly. Because he's right. But also because I'm guilty of the same unprofessional behavior with Tucker. "Yeah, I guess you're right," I force out. "But I still don't think it's right to give someone a platform they can use to ruin someone's grade with a lie."

Zayne watches me thoughtfully. "Duly noted," he says, and then his eyes return wordlessly to the road.

He turns into a parking lot, and I note it's exceptionally full for the middle of the night. He parks in front of a storefront with a chic brushed aluminum sign that says "Sweet Chill Gelato."

"You drove twenty miles to take me to an all-night ice cream shop? In November?" I ask in disbelief.

"Gelato," he corrects me, like it's significant. "Come on."

I follow him out of the car and into Sweet Chill. It isn't completely full, but there's an impressive crowd for past midnight, including a short line at the counter. But Zayne places his hand on my back and guides me around it right to the front.

"Zayne!" the proprietor, who can't be more than a couple of years older than me, calls out in greeting. "Move aside, people, this is the man responsible for me dropping law school to make this bitchin' gelato!"

There's a small chorus of cheers, and I stare at Zayne, who smiles humbly, and shakes the owner's hand over the counter.

He gestures to me and holds up two fingers, and he's handed two bowls full of creamy gelato, and gives one to me. "Give me your phone," he says, and I hand it over, confused. But he pulls up the camera app, tells me to hold up my ice cream, adjusts the cups so they're showing the Sweet Chill logo, and snaps a photo of the two of us.

He hands it back. "It would be great if you could Instagram that," he tells me.

I blink at him. *Is that such a good idea?* It's late, and us being out together…It might not look so good to some people. But Zayne seems unconcerned, so I decide to just go with it, and I open the app and do as he says.

"Hashtag Sweet Chill, hashtag world's best gelato."

I narrow my eyes at him playfully, but follow his instructions. I'm happy to support the store.

The owner smiles and thanks me.

"Digital marketing lesson number one seventy-four—get beautiful girls to Instagram your product." Zayne smiles wryly, and I can't help but return it. And it's back, the spark of thrill.

We take our gelato—which I again call ice cream, and get passionately corrected—to an empty table in the back of the store. As I lick the last of it off of my spoon, I notice Zayne smiling at me indulgently.

"Good?" he asks.

I practically moan. "Mmhmm."

Zayne chuckles. "Did it improve your night?"

I meet his gaze meaningfully, and nod.

He smiles approvingly, but also a little regretfully, and I wonder at that, too.

The drive home is quiet. I'm stuck in my head, with Tucker's ghost, and I want so much to just stop thinking. I want every thought to stop leading back to the same person. I want everything to stop reminding me of him. But I don't know how. And the thought that keeps haunting me is—why isn't *he* feeling like this? How is he moving on so easily? Ever since our breakup I've doubted so many things, but for the first time I wonder if Tucker ever actually loved me as much as I once thought.

"That was the lacrosse house, wasn't it? That I picked you up from?" Zayne asks out of nowhere.

I swallow thickly. "Yeah."

He nods. "The team's rented the same place for years. Since I was an undergrad."

"Hmm." My response is ambiguous and noncommittal.

Zayne eyes me warily from the side, and it has my nerves on high alert. "That ex of yours—the one you were hiding from. He was a guest? Or a resident?"

I slide my teeth over my bottom lip. "Resident."

Zayne hesitates, but it doesn't stop him from asking, "Is he one of my students, by any chance?"

I wait almost a full minute before answering. "Yeah," I say softly.

Zayne nods thoughtfully. "I thought so."

I hug my jacket tighter around me. I don't want to talk about Tucker.

"I do wish I knew that before I assigned your teams for the project," Zayne murmurs. "Though I've noticed it since. But why didn't you ask to switch? I would've understood. I could have put you in a different group."

"He told me not to," I practically whisper, and vaguely I wonder why I'm even telling him this. But I do appreciate that Zayne doesn't pry. He doesn't ask me what happened between us, or who was to blame. He simply sympathizes without saying much at all.

It's several minutes before I think to ask, "You said you've noticed it before? Noticed what?"

Zayne's gaze flicks between mine and the road. "You know, the way he watches you," he says matter-of-factly.

I frown at him.

"Oh, come on, Carleigh. Don't tell me you don't see it? He's always watching you, even when he's not looking at you. He even watches *me* when he thinks *I* might be looking at you." Zayne laughs a little sadly.

And I get it. The whole thing is definitely very sad. My heart hurts so badly I barely even register the flicker in my belly at him saying Tucker thinks Zayne looks at me. And I'm glad when the conversation dies off, and Zayne drives me back to Stuyvesant Hall in relative silence. I thank him for the gelato, and I don't even bother to question the curious way he looks at me as I climb from the car.

* * *

The next day Devin is beyond disappointed by my account of my non-date. She is quite the Ben fan, and an even bigger proponent of the advice that the best way to get over a guy is to get under another one. But that's just not me.

I hadn't planned on mentioning my midnight ice cream excursion, but that Instagram photo sold me out before I ever even got in last night. Devin was waiting up to interrogate me about it, and in my emotional state, I ended up telling her about Tucker. And isn't that just fucking perfect? My boy-crazy roommate wants to know about the famously hot professor who took me on my second non-date of the night, and my response is to recount my sad and sordid history with my ex.

But this morning I'm in better spirits, and after waking to an e-mail from Zayne thanking me for my company last night, I find myself gushing about him to Devin. I tell her about his desire to really help his students, to go above and beyond what's expected of him, about how funny he is, how smart.

"Someone's hot for teacher," Devin teases, and I roll my eyes. "Oh admit it!" she presses. "Someone's got a crush on her sexy, young professor, and I have a thought or two on how you can get an A…" She smirks suggestively.

I toss a pillow at her, but can't help my laugh. "This isn't a romance novel," I chide. "Or a porno."

But I wonder. Not about exchanging sexual favors for a grade, but if I am nursing the beginnings of a crush. Not real feelings or an actual desire for something to happen, but just an innocent schoolgirl-type crush on a man I admire and happen to find attractive. Maybe that's what that spark is about.

Unless…

Unless it's more than that. After all, I am a known champion at denial. And I just don't know the answer. I'm not even sure I'm asking myself the right question. But whether it's just admiration, a crush, or something else, it doesn't change the fact that nothing could come of it.

But there's that tiny glimmer of hope in the corner of my mind. Not for something to happen with Zayne, but for the implications of me possibly wanting something to happen. Because if I've developed even a whisper of feelings for him, then maybe I am on the path toward finally getting over Tucker.

I can't talk about myself or my feelings or non-feelings for another moment, so I change the subject to Devin's favorite subject—*Devin*.

She's been talking nonstop to Max, one of the lacrosse players she met on Halloween, and they finally went out last night to one of the bars. Which is why I was a little surprised to find her home last night. I knew I wouldn't see her at the lacrosse house, because she never leaves a bar before two a.m., but I assumed that when she did leave, she'd be doing it with Max.

I ask her how it went and she gives me a look that tells me it could have been better. She says they got into some kind of argument at the end of the night. It seems Julia and a few of our girlfriends were there along with some of Max's teammates, one of them said something obnoxious, and sides were taken.

"So we're drinking the last drinks of the night, and one of the guys who's been flirting with Julia for, like, an hour, asks her if she's had too much to drink. So I'm thinking he's being responsible, but then he goes 'or should I put a little something extra in there to get you in the right headspace.' And at first I think I didn't hear him right, you know? But then another one of them goes, 'what headspace? You mean unconscious?' And he laughs. And the first guy, who's holding Julia's fucking hand, goes, 'works for me.' Can you believe this shit? And the guys start laughing!"

I gape at her. It's almost unbelievable that they'd joke about drugging a girl's drink directly in front of her. Almost. But then, it's also not that shocking. "Max laughed at that?" I ask her, horrified.

"Well, no. But he didn't say anything to his boy about it, either. He just kind of smiled uncomfortably and pretended he didn't hear. So I asked if he was really going to let the kid talk like that, and he just brushed it off, saying it was just talk, that they would never really do something like that."

"How the fuck would he know?" I ask her. "Why would they even think there's something wrong with it? When everyone seems to think it's either hilarious or harmless to joke about." I try not to seethe, but it's infuriating.

"Yeah, well. That's what I said. And Max just didn't want to start drama, and well, you know me. I started drama."

Normally I'd disapprove of Devin's propensity for causing a scene, but for once I don't think her reaction was for attention. It was certainly more than justified, and if it had been me, I've no doubt I wouldn't have stood for it either.

"And the sad thing is, it isn't even the first time I've heard one of them say that kind of shit. At the parties, you know? And it's like, I'm supposed to willingly take a drink from these asshats? From someone who's friends with them?"

I shake my head. I have no words—she's one hundred percent right. "I just don't get it. How *they* don't get it. These aren't bad guys…mostly. They'd be horrified to hear if their friend raped some-one. But suggest getting her fucked up so her judgment is off, or so she can't fight back? Well, that's just strategy, right?" I grit my teeth in frustration. "It's this ridiculous idea that it's so cool to get laid, that it's also cool to take advantage of a girl to do it, you know? It's like they don't even realize they're glorifying *sexual fucking assault*. Or they don't care." I laugh humorlessly. It's so openly insane that it would al-most be funny if it wasn't so fucking *horrible*.

Because I've heard these comments too, in passing. In *passing*! And when I stop to actually think about the reality of rape being joked about so flippantly, I become genuinely outraged. I think about Ben's friend's comment last night about "free alcohol for hot girls." I can't help but wonder if that "house rule" is about selective hospitality, or something more sinister, and a shiver crawls up my spine at the thought. And yes, Ben had the presence of mind to know it was of-fensive, and to vaguely chasten the kid, but he didn't actually explain what was wrong with what he said, and I wonder if Ben even knows.

"And like, they're grown men," Devin continues. "People don't say this shit in the real world, do they? It has to be a college thing." But she sounds uncertain, and I don't have an answer either.

Devin huffs. "And it's freaking 2016! These guys wouldn't approve if their friend said something racist, or homophobic, but it's fucking *hilarious* to suggest rape as the next evening activity."

I don't think I've ever seen her so up in arms about something so legitimately relevant. As infuriating as the subject is, I'm actually glad to connect to this side of her. I guess it's a universal concern, at least for college-aged women, and how sad is that?

"Why do you think that is?" I ask Devin, who blinks at me. "I mean, why do guys consider it hilarious to joke about? What's *cool* about drugging a girl?" It's beyond my comprehension, and idly I think it's probably a question for a guy.

"You think I understand the idiotic minds of guys?" Devin rolls her eyes. "I *wish*, Carl. Honestly. It makes no sense whatsoever. If I were a dude and I needed to get a girl fucked up to get laid? I'd never admit that. I'd be ashamed as fuck."

"What did you just say?"

But she doesn't even hear me. She continues complaining about Max not thinking he did anything wrong, lets out an exasperated growl, and then without even taking a breath, she hops up from her bed and says she has to get to class. She does a little wiggle like she's shaking off her frustration, blows me a kiss, and heads out the door, just like that.

I don't bat an eyelash at her abruptness; I've grown used to it by now. But she's got me thinking about the last thing she said that wasn't entirely self-centered. That she'd be ashamed to imply she had to resort to drugging someone to get laid. And she hit the nail on the head. That's what doesn't make sense. Guys are all about bragging, and there's nothing impressive about having no choice but to incapacitate someone to sleep with them.

You'd think it would be the opposite. That guys would brag about having a girl want them enough to sleep with them without any mind-altering substances. *That* would make sense to me.

And suddenly, an idea takes shape in my mind. A montage of the awful jokes I've heard, and potential replacements for them. Because if we want guys to change their humor, maybe it wouldn't hurt to provide them with some material.

*   *   *

I'm so proud of my idea that I'm tempted to grab my team members before class rather than wait until tonight's meeting, but I hold back. Not that Tucker arrives with enough time for even a short conversation before class starts anyway.

Zayne announces a revision to his peer review process, and all ears perk up. He says that any student who makes specific accusations of unprofessional behavior beyond the basic questions of the provided form will be required to supply some kind of proof for it to be taken into consideration. He throws me a subtle nod, and I can't help my smile, but Tucker's less than subtle glower wipes it away almost instantly.

But I don't let it get to me. That afternoon, I focus on preparing to present my idea to the group, and by the time I meet them in the student center that evening, I have no trouble ignoring my Tucker-induced nerves.

Julia and Manny arrive before me, and I catch Julia in the midst of a familiar cautionary tale. It's the one about the lacrosse player that got benched after "he drunk-bagged some girl in his group and she gave him a bad peer review," and went on to lose his scholarship.

"Too bad Zayne's rule about having proof wasn't in effect," Manny murmurs.

"I don't think it would have made much of a difference," I tell him.

"What do you mean?" Julia asks, as Manny stares at me, confused.

I shrug. "I asked him about it. That story about the lacrosse player. He said if the guy hadn't been unprofessional and slept with his teammate, then he wouldn't have been in that position, basically."

"You asked him about it…" Manny repeats, his tone mildly incredulous with a hint of accusation.

I frown, puzzled for a splitsecond before Tucker's words rush through my mind—*did you fuck him?* Manny has already made a remark or two painting me as teacher's pet, but never with the shadow of hostility he's casting now.

I bristle defensively, but before I can respond, Tucker walks in. He's the last to arrive as always, and I try not to watch as he saunters toward our usual table looking utterly delectable in dark jeans and a fitted gray T-shirt. His jacket is unzipped and it's too easy to see the way his hard torso is cut with muscle, especially knowing what it feels like beneath my fingers. But before I can get too hot and bothered at the sight of him, I force my mind back onto the project at hand.

We've had several ideas before, but ended up nixing them all for one reason or another, and with only a couple weeks until Thanksgiving break, we are really letting it get down to the wire. After that it will only leave us with a week or so to finalize and execute a concept.

"So what's your idea, Carl?" Manny asks, his tone still vaguely irritated.

I reach into my bag and dig out the materials I had printed. "So on Zayne's list, there's this nonprofit called SAVE. Sexual assault Awareness and Victim Empowerment." Tucker looks at me for the first time at the mention of Zayne's name, and I try not to tense. "It was on the e-mail Tucker sent after our first meeting."

I hand out Tucker's notes.

"So I think it's pretty obvious what they're about, but what's interesting is that their recent focus has been awareness on college campuses."

"So if they're already focused on campuses, how would we do something original?" Manny asks in annoyance. Aside from being the second guy in my group to think there's something up with Zayne and me, he's also still a little bitter we didn't like his last idea, which much like his first three was centered around sports.

"Well, they're focused on teaching about affirmative consent, and how it's more than just 'no means no.' That 'yes means yes,' you know?"

"And?" Manny asks impatiently.

"Let her talk." Tucker's voice is so low it takes me a second to realize he actually spoke, and another to realize it was in my defense. It makes my pulse race and the nerves I thought I had under control flutter wildly in my stomach.

"Right," I murmur, trying to regroup. "Okay, well, I think their message is great and all, but I'm thinking more in terms of campus culture, and how we all relate to one another. It's one thing in a classroom setting to understand what constitutes rape, and how serious it is, but what happens when we're in a less formal setting?"

"I think that ship has sailed, Carl. I mean, we all get it, you know?" Manny drops the attitude marginally, but he's obviously still not into it.

Tucker watches thoughtfully and Julia sits quietly, and I wonder if she's making the connection to the joke made last night at her expense.

"I don't think you do all get it," I say honestly.

"Excuse me?" Manny replies indignantly.

"Not you personally. But guys. Girls, too. I mean, yes, we all know rape is serious, when we're in a serious setting, but when we're at a party, joking around? Sometimes it becomes a joke. And then it's a slippery slope. One guy hears his buddy joke about it, and then thinks his friend thinks it's cool, and so he takes it less seriously himself, and so on."

"I think you're reaching," Manny says dismissively. "People don't joke about rape."

"No?" I ask.

Manny shoots me a skeptical look.

"So you've never heard a friend joke about slipping something into someone's drink? Or getting a girl drunk to make her more compliant? Or suggest giving more alcohol to hot girls so they can get them into bed?"

Manny shifts in his seat, looking decidedly uncomfortable. Finally, he sighs. "Fine, yeah, sure. But a joke's a joke. No one takes that shit seriously."

"You don't think so?" Tucker suddenly interjects, and Manny glares at him. "You don't think hearing someone joke about getting his girl drunk so he can get some makes his boys less likely to be concerned if they happen to spot him carrying her drunk ass up the stairs later?"

"Do you?" Manny counters.

"Yeah. I fucking do."

And then Julia sits forward in her chair, and all eyes turn to her. "Well, whatever effect it has or doesn't have, there's nothing okay about a guy saying he should drug my drink to get me 'in the right headspace,' or the rest of his friends laughing like fucking me while I'm unconscious is just fucking hilarious." She purses her lips shut and her eyes shine with restrained tears, so I take over for her.

"Whether the guy making the joke would actually go through with it or not isn't the point. The point is that we know it happens, right? So someone in that crowd hearing that joke could very well be the guy considering doing something like that, and hearing it talked about like it's no big deal is not going to push him in the right direction."

Manny stares at me, and finally he sighs with reluctant acceptance. "Okay, I hear you. So what'd you have in mind?"

I tell them. I hand out the rest of my printouts of the articles I found from the past decade, of incidents where frats or sports teams got into trouble for rape or joking about rape. I point out that these are only the people who got caught.

I mention some of the jokes I've heard, and we all go around the table, recording some of the better—worse—ones. Then we come up with jokes that send the opposite message. Even Manny contributes, and hours go by as we make more progress in one sitting than we have in all of the previous ones combined.

Tucker makes a joke about the size of his dick—how it's so big girls don't need alcohol to want to sleep with him, but they need it afterward for relief. I burst into laughter, but inwardly I'm blushing, because I remember how sore I was after my first time, and several more vigorous times since.

Although it still hurts to remember, I can at least appreciate that we're sitting around the same table, joking and laughing together. And I think of last night's realization about escaping him. About how I haven't really been trying to escape him. But it's as I watch his head fall back and his mouth drop open, his eyes crinkled with body-wracking laughter at Julia's joke, that I realize I don't want to escape him.

I've never wanted to escape him.

Chapter Thirteen

Tucker

Present Day

I sit down outside Stuyvesant Hall on the bench I hate. Now that we have a concept—and a damn good one at that—we've been spending a lot of time on our creative marketing campaign, and today we're filming in Carl's dorm room. We've been shooting at the lax house, too, since most of the scenes take place at a party, and well, we throw a lot of fucking parties.

I glance at my watch. Carl will be here any minute and I need her to sign me in. It's weird that we've been getting along, but then, we've mostly just been working, and like I told her since the beginning, I can be professional. With her, and the other strangers in our group. Only they're not really strangers anymore, and Carl never was.

And then she's running down the pavement, muttering apologies for making me wait. I get up from the bench. "No worries," I tell her. Because the way she's trying to catch her breath after obviously rushing here, the way her cheeks flush with exertion as her pretty blond ponytail bounces behind her, has me remembering just how well the whole *just friends* thing worked out the first time around.

I follow her to the elevator and up to her room and we wordlessly start setting up for today. I've taken care not to be alone with her like this until now, and as her bed glares at me, taunting me with the knowledge I will never be in it, I remember exactly why this isn't a good idea. Fortunately Julia and Manny show up a few minutes later, and not long after that, we're ready to shoot.

Today it's just me and Manny filming the second version of the scene we did yesterday, where we acted out actual jokes we've heard guys make. I always feel nasty as fuck after playing that role, and I'm glad that today I get to be more like myself.

In the scene we talk about our fictitious girlfriends, competing over whose wants us more.

"My girl wants me so much, I give her nonalcoholic beer and tell her it's regular, just to give her an excuse to be all over me," Manny says with a convincing smirk.

I laugh, and respond with my line. "Whatever, man, *I* can go all night. I can go so long that I convince my girl to be sober driver so she has more energy to keep up with me."

It goes on like that. We do a few takes, and then we wrap for the day.

Manny gets his laptop out of his bag and checks the camera's auto upload of today's footage. He'll work on editing it over the upcoming Thanksgiving break. I've written a general outline for the story we want to tell, and Manny is a whiz with Final Cut Pro, and we will have a couple of days when we get back to campus to shoot more footage if we need to.

I suspect Zayne will give Carl an A regardless of what she turns in. I still can't believe she called him to pick her up from the lax house the night she went out with Ben, but I saw her get in his car with my own two eyes. I don't trust fucking Zayne or his intentions. But I know Carl, and she'd never sleep with her professor. Or at least I convince myself I know at least this about her.

"Are you doing anything for break?" Julia asks Carl, who averts her gaze to straighten up her bed.

"Usual." She shrugs, but I can sense her discomfort. Because I know what *the usual* is for her when it comes to family holidays. The same as it is for me. My mom is incredible, especially considering all she's been through, but holidays get to her, and ever since my father's death we've kind of had an unspoken agreement to all but ignore them. Which is fine with me, frankly, but I don't have a kid brother to put on a show for. "You excited for your trip?" Carl asks Julia, expertly diverting the attention from herself.

Julia has blabbered on for the past month about her upcoming trip to Grand Cayman—a Thanksgiving family tradition, apparently—down to detailing the new bikinis she's purchased for the occasion. Even now her eyes light up at the subject. "Ugh, I can't wait. It's so cold here already!"

Well, yeah. It's November in New York.

"You going to do the whole turkey and football thing?" Julia asks.

Carl's mouth opens either to spit some lie or to uneasily tell the truth, and I save her without even thinking about it. "Such an overrated holiday," I murmur.

Carl turns to me, her eyes equally grateful and surprised.

"What are your plans?" Julia asks me.

I shrug. "Mom's out of town visiting my aunt. I'm going to my friend Cap's house. They do the whole family thing."

In fact, this will be the first time in a long time Cap's whole family will be together for a holiday and he's nervous about it. And on top of that, Rory and her mom are joining them, too.

Carl's gaze darts away and she studies the floor as we pack up our equipment, and the Thanksgiving talk mercifully dies off.

Julia, Manny, and I say good-bye and head to the elevator just as my phone buzzes with a call. *Speak of the devil.*

"What's up?" I ask Cap. It's strange that he's calling. We're in regular contact, but we usually text, and I wonder if something's wrong.

"Hey Tuck. You got a minute?"

A vague seed of dread plants itself in my gut. He sounds serious, and my mind goes straight to Bits. "Everything okay?"

Cap sighs. "Yeah. Fine. Relax."

"So then, I repeat, *what's up?*"

"Thanksgiving."

I exhale my relief. He's so stressed out about that stupid fucking holiday that he's going to give himself a heart attack if he keeps this up. Can't say I really blame him, though. His parents have met Rory's mom before, but this is some serious shit, and for a guy who a year ago was our high school's most infamous bachelor, it's a lot of change for him. "It's going to be fine, man. Your family loves Rory. And her mom loves you. Just don't be an ass and everything will go great, and if it doesn't, then at least I'll be there to watch you crash and burn."

"Shut up, moron," he quips. "I'm not nervous about that. Not really, anyway. It's just…look, don't chew my head off, okay?"

Huh? "What?"

"I know this is a lot to ask of you. But Rory's upset about Carl being all alone for Thanksgiving. Her mom's away, obviously. And it's just her and Billy. And Billy's been having a tough time lately—"

He has? I didn't know that. But then, why would I? I miss that little dude. But I couldn't exactly keep in touch with him after what went down with his sister. Maybe I should reach out to him anyway.

"And she's Rory's best friend. And I get it if it's still too raw, so—"

My exasperated sigh cuts him off. "Dude. Get. To. The. Point." Even though I've already gathered what it is.

"Fine, asshole. Rory wants to invite Carl and Billy for Thanksgiving and, frankly, so do I."

Yeah. That's what I figured.

"But we both understand if you have a problem with it. So just think about it, I guess, and let me know later—"

"It's fine, Cap. You can invite them." The words are out of my mouth before my brain has even formed them. But what am I going to do? Say no? I'm not going to tell Rory she can't spend the holiday with her best friend if that's what she wants, and I'm not going to condemn Billy to another lonely, depressing Thanksgiving with just him and his sister. Even though I know Carl does everything she can to make it special for him, there's only so much pretending you can do in a massive house whose size only shouts of its emptiness.

"You sure?" Cap asks with only thinly veiled skepticism.

"Yeah, man. I mean, I'm not gonna pretend I'm thrilled about it, but it's cool. I've been working with her on this project and we've managed to get along. No reason we can't do that at your house, too."

"Okay…"

"Plus, I'd like to see the kid," I admit. I'd been proudly molding Billy into a bit of a mini-me before my relationship with Carl went to shit. If he's having a hard time, I want to find out why, and see if I can help him out.

"That's good, man. I'll tell Rory. It'll make her happy."

Which obviously makes him happy—I can hear it in his voice. "Don't say I never did anything for you."

Cap snorts. "Yeah, you're a real saint."

Chapter Fourteen

Carleigh

Present Day

I check myself out in the mirror and sigh. I'm casual enough in jeans and an emerald blouse that brings out my eyes, but I went all out on my hair and makeup. I didn't do it for Ben; I did it for myself. We're having dinner tonight with Devin and Max, and as much as I like Ben as a friend, Devin's the reason I agreed to this evening out.

I made her up first, because she's desperate to impress Max tonight, though she could have probably done so in sweats and a fresh face for how into her the guy seems. Ever since their argument he's been playing contrite and attentive, via text anyway. But they haven't gotten together since, and she wants to knock his socks off…or his underwear.

But after finishing Devin's makeup, I decided that I, too, deserve to feel good about myself. I'm not actually wearing that much, but I've used a new technique that plays up my lashes and uses less liner and I'm liking the look. But now I worry Ben will think it's all for him.

Devin slaps my denim-clad ass. "Sexy mama," she teases. She looks in the mirror one last time and runs her fingers through her straight, glossy hair. "You almost look as good as me."

I laugh. "Well, that's the goal, right? We wouldn't want Max to forget where he's supposed to look," I joke.

"Pshh. I'm not worried," she says breezily. And she shouldn't be. She's freaking gorgeous. And she knows it.

Max is driving tonight and his truck is already waiting at the entrance of the courtyard as we leave Stuyvesant. He and Ben lean against the car, chatting. We all exchange kisses on the cheek, and Max holds the passenger door open for Devin.

I climb into the back with Ben and we head to Sweeney's Bar and Grill. Dinner is equally comfortable and not. Ben and I have fallen into an easy friendship, but Devin and Max's flirtations add an extra layer of pressure to the whole situation. I try to ignore it, and Ben seems to be doing the same, but then Max will whisper something to Devin, she'll giggle, and Ben and I will exchange a glance. Mine is only meant to silently comment on our friends' chemistry, but I wonder if there's more behind Ben's. I get the feeling his gaze lingers after I pull mine away.

So I drink.

I'm not driving, and I'm due a fun night out, so there's no reason not to. When Devin orders shots of tequila for us all—excluding Max—I down mine hastily. I take another shortly after, and then switch to beer. It does the trick. Suddenly my veins buzz with the light weight of alcohol, and my own laughter reverberates in my ears, slow and easy. Ben's smile is wide and far too perfect. Symmetrical. Not like Tucker's lopsided, roguish grin.

Don't think about him.

I shake him from my thoughts. Or try to. So when Ben asks me to dance, and I look around to find Max and Devin already going wild on the dance floor, I agree.

The music is loud and fast, and we join our friends and move drunkenly to the eighties music blaring through the bar. There is nothing romantic about it, which makes me even more comfortable—or maybe that's the alcohol.

I'm dehydrated by the time we sit down, and I chug ice water while Ben laughs at me and tells me to slow down.

But my head starts aching. It happens every time I drink hard liquor, though I'd hoped having only two shots would be okay.

I don't say anything, though. Max's arm is wound intently around Devin's shoulders, and he murmurs softly to her—words I can't hear—and I don't want to cut short her night. Her smile is secretive and bright, and I know the evening is progressing just how she planned.

But the pounding in my head grows stronger, and I find myself counting down the minutes until we leave. Ben eyes me curiously, but it isn't until we've paid the bill and are walking back to Max's car that he asks if I'm okay.

"Fine," I lie.

"You guys want to come chill at the house?" Max asks.

"Sure," Devin says.

Ben looks at me.

"Um, actually, my head hurts pretty bad," I admit. "Maybe we should just go back to the dorm."

Devin gives me a *don't do this to me* look, and I feel guilty. She's been looking forward to spending time with Max since their last outing ended in a dramatic failure.

But my temples twinge with pain and I wince.

Ben's arm comes around my waist and I realize I almost stumbled, reminding me that I am also still pretty drunk. "I can give you something for your headache at the house if you want."

I look at Devin's pleading gaze, then back to Ben, who looks sincere and concerned.

"Up to you." He shrugs.

I sigh. "Okay. Just for a little, though." Just long enough for Devin to make out with Max so she can call the evening a win. Hopefully a couple of aspirin will do the trick.

Fifteen minutes later we're walking into the lax house. The living room is empty, many of the guys having gone home for break, and I wonder if Tucker is still here. I don't know if I hope he is or isn't. The more time we spend together working on our group project, the more we seem to get along, but as much as I find myself basking in his company, it doesn't actually ease my heartache. It's jarring to miss someone when he's right beside you, and the thought of us both spending Thanksgiving at the Caplans' makes me consider canceling for the hundredth time since I accepted the invitation. But I don't. Because Billy deserves to experience a traditional family holiday for once, even if it isn't with our actual family.

Devin and I sit and Ben disappears down the hall to his bedroom to get me aspirin. I down them greedily, eager for the pounding waves in my head to dissipate. We sit and talk, joined briefly by Ricky, and it isn't long before my headache begins to clear. I'm still kind of drunk, but my head does feel much better.

Actually all of me feels better. Including my mood.

We're not talking about anything important, but I can't stop chatting. I watch Max make subtle moves on Devin, and the two of them try to pretend like they're not waiting for an excuse to make an exit to his bedroom.

It makes me extremely happy for some reason. Thrilled even. Devin is a cool girl, but the truth is, the more we've gotten to know each other, the more I've realized we're not likely to become especially close. I enjoy her company, but our friendship is the kind that comfortably skims the surface, and I suspect if it ventured too far into the deep, it would probably founder.

"Headache gone?" Ben smirks.

I smile. "Yes. That was some good aspirin you gave me. Thanks!"

Now that I'm feeling better, the warm glow of alcohol runs lazily through me, easing my earlier concerns. Easing all of my concerns, actually.

Ben bristles a little, and I wonder if he's not as relaxed. If perhaps he's still thinking about moving our friendship into something else. Something decidedly physical.

But right now, I don't care. I'm just not interested. I wish I was. I wish I was ready to move on from Tucker with someone new. And Ben is certainly a prime candidate if there ever was one. Gorgeous and sweet, thoughtful, and obviously interested. But he isn't the one thing I want. The one thing I've always wanted.

Tucker.

I feel strange. Fuzzy. My limbs feel heavy—*that'll be the alcohol*—and my euphoric mood is starting to succumb to the weight of reality. I wonder if my buzz is beginning to shift into the hangover phase. Though it's a little soon for that, surely. But I'm definitely feeling a bit woozy. My stomach rolls with nausea, and my head doesn't so much spin as it blinks, moving like a strobe light, skipping about the room.

My eyes land on the cable box by the far wall, and I'm surprised by how much time has passed. It's nearly two in the morning.

I peek over at the loveseat where Max and Devin were earlier, and realize they did, in fact, disappear into his bedroom. But I've no clue how long they've been gone. It could have been hours.

I don't want to interrupt her, but I need to get back to the dorm. It's late, and even though it's now been a couple of hours since my last drink, I'm feeling too out of it in a way that's remarkably unfamiliar. Like a curious combination of physical exhaustion and a wakeful dream.

I lean back on the sofa and let my head fall onto the headrest to try and regain my senses. My eyelids drop heavily, slamming me into blackness, but also not. Thoughts still swirl, but they take me far from where I know I'm meant to be—the lax house, with…Ben?

But I'm not thinking about him anymore. I'm thinking about who I'm always thinking about, whether in the forefront of my mind or buried in the deepest crevices of my soul.

Tucker is talking to me. But I force my eyes open and, of course, he isn't there. It's Ben. Good old Ben. Mouth downturned in a frown of concern, full brow furrowed, eyes still shining with an alcohol-induced haze of his own. But, unlike me, he seems to have retained most of his awareness.

I don't even know when he sat next to me on the couch. Or how the minutes on the cable box have managed to jump a full half hour in the two minutes I had my eyes closed.

He's asking if I'm okay. If I need anything.

I shake my head.

Or I mean to. My neck barely moves. So I do it again with rallied focus and effort, and this time, instead of its intended shake, it kind of rolls side to side. I feel far too warm. Almost feverish. I think I hear the mumble of my own words voicing this, or maybe it's just the echo of my thoughts.

My eyes open again. Ben has magically procured a cold glass of water, and I startle as he holds it to my lips and asks me to drink. *When did he get that?*

My chest rises and falls too slowly, my breaths too shallow to give my lungs any real satisfaction. It's scary. I just want to breathe normally.

"Carl, you need to lie down. You can stay over," Ben says.

Stay over? Where? Where are we? Why am I with Ben again?

He's pulling me up, but my legs feel bizarrely like liquid.

Ow.

"Steady, Carl," Ben says when the wall bumps into my hip. *Stupid wall.*

He leads me past the kitchen and then suddenly we're in the hall that leads to the first-floor bedrooms. I stop walking—*stumbling*.

"You need to sleep, Carl. You'll feel better in a couple hours. I'll drive you back to your dorm in the morning."

I think I shake my head, but I don't know. I'm so damn tired. My eyes won't stay open for more than a few seconds at a time. I must be getting sick. I know I drank a bunch earlier, but this is something else; I must have caught some kind of bug or something.

But even in the haze of drink or illness or both, I know I can't let Ben take me to his bedroom. I think he's a good guy, but I don't know him well enough to actually trust him.

I'm too fucked up right now. I can't make sense of anything, but rising just above the clouds are giant, gleaming red flags.

"No," I mumble. I want to explain myself. To say I want to go home.

Not home. To my dorm.

Or home. I don't know.

I don't know fucking anything right now. I can't think straight, but I can feel.

And I feel fear.

I twist out of his steadying hold and then I'm falling. But his arms catch me and start pulling me again in the direction he wants me. His bedroom.

"*N-no.*"

"It's okay. You just need to lie down. I'll keep an eye on you, you'll be fine."

Yes. *Lie down.* That's what I need.

My feet move, somehow, but then I'm looking down the hall, past what I recognize as the slightly open door to Tucker's room, and toward an unfamiliar bedroom, and I remember—I don't want to go in there.

I pull away and manage several steps back before I trip. I barely catch myself on the wall, and I crush my eyes closed to block out the glaring lights that suddenly burst from overhead. Ben's large hands close firmly around my shoulders, and dread knots in my stomach. Because I need help. Everything is fucked up, and I can't even walk straight. I need him for balance, but at the same time, he is what

I'm afraid of. Him, and this feeling of being out of control of my body.

I am helpless, and it's a new feeling for me, one I loathe with every cell in my compromised body. One that echoes of a time when I was just a little girl, gripping my father's legs as he's stolen from me, just as surely and desperately as I now grip this damned wall, which, for a stationary object, is doing a damn good job of evading my hold. But even through the fog, I have a tiny out-of-body vantage of perspective—as if through a kaleidoscope—observing the cliché of the drunk college freshman, helpless and being led to the bedroom of a boy she does not want to go to bed with.

The lights assault my head even through my shuttered lids, and Ben's incessant murmuring booms in my temples, and then, a lion prowls onto the scene, roaring wildly.

Tucker.

Either I'm imagining him, or he's here, but I don't open my eyes to check. Because if it's only my imagination, then that's where I want to live. Because everything spins and blurs now, and I can do absolutely nothing to help myself other than cling to the corner where the wall of the hallway meets that of the kitchen, my nails digging so fiercely they must chip the paint.

"'The fuck is *this?*" Tucker's volume makes me wince, but the sound of his voice, even in obvious rage, is a quilt of comfort. It is safety and refuge and it helps me suck in deeper breaths.

More murmuring from Ben. I make out words like "fucked up" and "bed."

"You've lost your damn mind if you think you're taking her to your fucking bedroom," Tucker seethes.

The floor tilts beneath my feet as I'm ripped from Ben's grip. My eyes squint open but process very little. All I hear is Tucker's fury at Ben and his whispered words of comfort to me, and I let him tuck me into his strength, and silently beg for his mercy.

Chapter Fifteen

Tucker

Present Day

I can barely see straight through my rage. The only thing keeping my clenched fist from ramming itself into Ben's face is Carl. She needs my hands to keep her fucking upright. I shake my head, my jaw so tight I don't know how I manage to grit out words.

"What did she drink?" I demand.

Ben shakes his head, concern drawn across his face.

"She had some shots of tequila at dinner and a few beers," he murmurs cautiously, thoughtfully.

Fuck. She's shit with hard liquor. I look down at her, her delicate features flushed and skin clammy. Her breathing is too slow, its rhythm off—something doesn't seem right. I know Carl, and she should be dizzy and slurring if she drank too much, or passed out, but not like this. Her eyes—when they actually stay open—are dazed and unfocused.

"Carl." I try to get her attention. "Are you okay? How much did you drink?" I don't fucking trust Ben.

Carl whimpers and blinks, and then her eyes are wet and she looks like she might cry. And Carl never cries. Up until our breakup I had only seen her cry a handful of times, and the sight of her tears sends warning signals rushing through my veins like white water.

My gaze charges back to Ben. "What the fuck is going on, Aronin?" And then a thought shoots through my brain.

I go from angry to enraged, and I hold my breath to keep The Hulk at bay. "Did you fucking *slip her something?*"

Ben's eyes go wide, horrified at my accusation. "Of course not! Fuck you, Green!"

"Fuck *me?*" I nod in the direction he'd been trying to drag her. "Why the fuck would you take her to your room like this? Why is she *like* this?"

Fuck, my heart is racing. I'm *scared*. Carl is more fucked up than I've ever seen her and what if she isn't okay?

My fear compounds my anger and I refocus it back onto Ben, whose eyebrows pinch together in concern as he nervously shifts his feet. I know there's something he's hiding, and I realize he still hasn't answered my question. So I repeat it. "Why. Is. She. Like. This?"

Ben chews his lip. "She had a headache. I told her I'd give her something for it. It knocked it right out, but...I think she took too much."

"Too much *what? Tylenol?*"

Ben shakes his head, his shame apparent in his reluctance to answer. "Percocet."

I lose my shit. "You motherfucker!"

Carl winces at my snarl and I pull her tighter to my chest and whisper an apology before settling my wrathful gaze back on Ben. "You gave her a *narcotic painkiller?* And let her mix it with fucking *alcohol? What the fuck is wrong with you!*"

Ben looks away.

I can't believe this. Fucking *Percocet*. I had them prescribed to me when I sprained my wrist during football season last year. They are fucking *strong*. Not something you take for a goddamn headache. "How much?" I demand.

Ben frowns sheepishly. "Two," he answers. "Ten m-g's. Each."

Shit.

One five-milligram pill is the dose she'd be prescribed if she needed it. Like if she got hurt, or had a root canal or something. But four times that? And Carl is a skinny little thing.

Fucking *shit*.

It's not enough to put her in real danger—like for her to overdose or anything like that. But it's enough to get her seriously high. And with alcohol? Forget it. She's in outer fucking space.

"Was this your plan? Take her out and get her fucked up? Give her pills and then drag her to your room?"

Fuck.

Fuck, fuck, fuck, fuck, fuck!

Ben opens his mouth to defend himself, but I'm not fucking interested. I need to take care of Carl.

"Come on, Princess, let's get you to bed. You're going to be okay," I promise her. I nail Ben with my gaze. "If I didn't have to take care of her right now, you'd be a dead man, Aronin. You know that, right?" As it is I will have to wait to resolve this. But I *will* resolve this.

"It was a mistake, man. She had a headache. I thought it would help. I gave one to Courtney last week when she had a migraine and it totally worked. And she felt better, too." He nods to Carl. "But then she started acting all out of it and I got a little worried. I was just gonna put her to bed and keep an eye on her. That's all."

He seems earnest, but I don't give a shit. He put Carl at risk. And he could just be a good actor. Guys like him usually are. For all I know he had every intention of waiting until she was fully passed out, and then fucking her.

God, just the thought of it makes me *murderous*.

But what the fuck was Carl thinking taking fucking painkillers? And when she'd been drinking? It's so unbelievably out of character for her. I'm so frustrated with her lack of judgment I could kill her myself.

But none of that matters right now. All that matters is making sure Carl is okay, because if she isn't, I never will be again.

Ben takes a step forward, watching Carl with ostensible concern. "And what's it to you, anyway? Carleigh's my friend. I may have fucked up, but I thought she was nothing to you—isn't that what you told me, Green? Why should I trust you with her? A few weeks ago she's nothing and now I'm supposed to let you take her to your bedroom to 'take care of her'?" He shakes his head. "I don't think so."

Has he lost his fucking mind? I'm so stunned by his gall that it takes me a second to even process that he's reaching for Carl's wrist.

"I got her, Tucker."

I yank her behind me. "Like fucking hell you do!" I growl.

Carl starts trembling. "T-tuh," she squeaks. Fuck, she can barely even get my name out.

"Get the fuck out of my way, Aronin," I demand. God, if I thought she could stand without my support I would end this now, with my fucking fist.

Ben stands tall in my path, but if he thinks I'm going to allow him to take Carl to his room like this, he better be prepared to kill me. "Carleigh," he says, his voice slithering with an attempt at comfort. "I shouldn't have given you those pills. I'm sorry. You'll be fine, though, I just want to look after you. Will you come with me?" He offers his open palm, and for a split second I'm terrified she's going to take it. Because who the fuck am I to her anymore, anyway?

But her shaky fingers just grip me more fiercely, and I feel her already compromised breathing skip even more. "T-uck."

I lean down so my eyes are just in front of hers, ready to beg. "Carl—"

"Please. D-don't leave me." Her liquid jade eyes plead as much as her words, and I'm done.

I shove Ben out of our way, my glare speaking volumes.

Carl's legs barely hold her upright, and halfway down the hall I scoop her up to carry her instead. Her arms wind weakly around my neck, and I whisper to her that she's going to be fine, and that she just needs to sleep.

I slip off her shoes and lay her gently on my bed, tugging the comforter out from underneath her.

Jeans on or off?

Shit. I can't just strip my ex-girlfriend.

"Carl, open your eyes," I encourage her.

She moans softly.

"Just for a sec. Please?"

They dazedly flutter open.

"Do you want to sleep in your jeans, or do you want me to take them off?"

Her eyelids drop back down like they're being pulled by weights. "Off," she breathes.

I sigh. I don't know how much of her judgment she currently retains, but she had enough to choose me over Ben—who she barely fucking knows—so I hope she means it.

I undo her fly and pull off her jeans. She makes no move to help me. I don't know if she even could right now.

I hang her jeans over the back of my desk chair and sit beside her on the bed. I pull out my phone and Google the drug to make sure my assumptions about the amount she took were accurate, and breathe a vague sigh of relief to confirm that they were. That she definitely overdid it, but she doesn't need a hospital or anything like that. I just need to keep an eye on her—make sure her breathing doesn't become too depressed.

"T-Tuck." Her eyes stay closed.

I lie on my side to face her. I brush away the hair that fell over her cheek and tuck it carefully behind her ear. "Yeah, Carl?"

"I…I…don't feel good."

I run my hand soothingly through her hair like she's a small child. "I know. But you're gonna be fine. You just need to sleep, and tomorrow you'll feel okay."

Her hand slides slowly and tremulously forward until it makes contact with my T-shirt, and her fingers bunch the material, like she wants to make sure I can't get away, but still, her eyes remain shut.

"Please stay with me," she breathes.

It's like a knife to my chest—her thinking that I would just leave her like this.

"Not going anywhere, Princess."

She takes a deep breath for the first time since I found her with Ben in the damned hallway.

"How do you feel?" I ask her.

Her eyelids press together, her brows pinching in a frown before her eyes flutter open. "Dizzy," she groans. "Nauseous."

"I'm sorry," I whisper.

"And…high," she adds. "D'he do it on purpose?" I wonder if she's asking if Ben got her this fucked up on purpose or something more nefarious. I have my suspicions, but I know it's not something she needs to hear right now.

"Did *you*?" I counter.

"Mmm mmm," she mumbles. "Ass pin."

"What?"

"'S'perin."

"Huh?" *The fuck?*

And then I realize what she's trying to say. "Aspirin?"

Her head falls forward in a weak nod.

So she thought she was taking aspirin. I'm going to fucking murder Ben in his sleep. I glance at the east wall of my bedroom, knowing that only about forty feet in that direction, Ben is probably sleeping soundly, completely unconcerned with the consequences of his actions. I roll my jaw in an attempt to unclench the tension.

I try not to let Carl's fingers on my stomach affect me in the usual way, but it's hopeless. The way her fingers twitch over my abs makes the thin cotton between her skin and mine evaporate, and just being in her proximity has me swollen and aching. In just the T-shirt and boxers I was wearing when I came out to check on her, my arousal is obvious, but she's too out of it to notice.

It's going to be a long night.

I think she may have fallen asleep when she speaks softly.

"Please don't hate me, Tuck. Just for one night." It comes out something between an exhale and a wistful sigh, but it hits me hard.

"I don't hate you, Carl." Fifty/fifty she won't remember this conversation come morning. Still, I'm not sure I should admit how I feel—which is that I have no fucking clue how I feel anymore.

"Sometimes I hate me."

I don't think she means to say it out loud. She may not even realize she's said it at all. But it fucking guts me.

Carl is not that girl. She's never entertained an ounce of insecurity or self-loathing. She's not vain or conceited. Instead, she's always been filled with a healthy sense of confidence and self-respect. It's part of the reason I'd fallen in love with her in the first place.

"No you don't, Carl. Don't say that." I sound equal parts pissed and pleading.

"Mm…" She doesn't agree. She doesn't *say* anything really, it's more her tone that speaks volumes. It's just matter-of-fact. And I realize how much our demise has really changed her at her core. And it twists the knife gutting my insides, ripping me apart turn by turn.

"Carl, you're impossible to hate." I stare at her sweet, heart-shaped face, eyes shuttered, but somehow her expression more open and honest than I've seen since the night she first told me she was in love with me. I stroke her soft cheek with the pad of my thumb. "Trust me, Princess," I breathe. "I really fucking tried."

Chapter Sixteen

Tucker

Last Year

I'm completely overwhelmed. Drowning in an ocean of emotion, wave after wave cresting in surges of pure fucking ecstasy, only to crash in fear.

Carl is mine. I love her, and I have her. She's all I've ever wanted, long before I was even cognizant of the fact, but now that I know I have her love, another inevitable fact comes with it. I have her, and that means I have her to lose.

As I lie here on the soft hotel mattress, wrapped firmly around—as of last night—*my girlfriend*, I still can't bring myself to close my eyes.

This spring break trip to Miami was supposed to be about carefree fun—a bunch of friends blowing off steam before finals. But Carl and I had reached our breaking point, and after almost a year of push and pull, denied emotions and an attraction that's come to border on fucking obsession, something was bound to give. Of course it would take us one of our trademark blowouts followed by an epic wake-up call to get us to confess our feelings, but now that we finally have, I just can't seem to stop staring at her—as if letting her out of my sight might make it less real.

Ungodly early morning light filters through the small crack in the blackout curtains, highlighting the soft glow of her golden hair, and I press my lips to her temple for what must be the hundredth time since we lay down together only a few hours ago.

I've never felt so goddamned vulnerable in my life, and I don't fucking like it.

Loss isn't unfamiliar to me. Its force has been a perpetual presence in my life since I was thirteen years old. So I need no reminder of how exposed I suddenly feel.

When she said the words I never imagined I'd hear from her perfect lips, I couldn't quite believe it. But there it was.

She fucking loves me.

All these years I'd accepted it as a given that I could never deserve her. But Carl obviously doesn't see it that way. She never did. She *loves* me. And for the first time, I let myself imagine a future my subconscious has never before allowed. And it's fucking beautiful.

I stare down at her perfect sleeping form and my chest swells with possession and pride.

I miss her. It's stupid as fuck, but right now, even right next to her, I actually miss her.

I shouldn't wake her up. It's barely dawn. But I miss her, and I just want to talk to her for a few minutes—reaffirm that she's really here, really mine. Then I'll let her go back to sleep.

I sweep my lips along her long, delicate throat, dragging them down to her exposed collarbone. Carl has always been a light sleeper, and she stirs instantly.

Her skin is unfathomably soft against my lips, and I slip my tongue out for a small taste.

"Tuck?" She exhales.

Already I regret waking her. My mouth is busy with the curve of her shoulder. "Go back to sleep, baby," I tell her, kissing my way up her neck and the underside of her chin.

Her breath hitches. "Tuck…" It comes out more like a moan this time, and her breathy tone makes me change my mind again. I want her up after all.

"You taste so good, Princess. I fucking love your skin."

"Mmm…" Carl turns her head to give me better access. "Just my skin?" she teases, her fingertips dancing on the back of my neck.

My heart beats a little faster and my boxer briefs grow even tighter. My girl is up and she wants to play.

"Hmm. Let me think," I taunt right back, my hand finding her lithe thigh and sliding upward. She slips her leg around my hip, welcoming my greedy hand on her tight ass as I climb over her. *God* I love her ass. "This is okay, too," I tell her.

"*Okay?*" She feigns offense. "You don't love it?" She shrugs that perfect shoulder. "Well then, you don't have to—"

But before she can torture me with a mock denial, my fingers dig into the sweet flesh and I attack her mouth with mine. She responds instantly, lips devouring, conquering just as much as they welcome my own. This is my girl. She gives as good as she gets, always, and I fucking love every single bit of her, inside and out.

I pull away, suddenly overwhelmed by emotion. By the weight of my love for Carl, and the thrill of knowing I own hers in return. I stare down at her, wishing I could articulate what I'm feeling. But either the words don't exist or I just lack the enlightenment to express them. "I love you, Princess," I say simply. But she gets each of the million words I'm not saying, because her eyes soften, watering ever so slightly, and I press my lips to each one.

"I love you too, Tuck."

I kiss her forehead, her cheeks, her chin before finding her lips again. I want to kiss her everywhere. I grasp the hem of her tank top and tug it off of her and she lifts her arms to help me. Her bare tits are supple and full beneath me, and the feel of her softness yielding to the firm planes of my chest makes me so hard it's almost painful. I peel her underwear down her legs, barely lifting my weight enough to get them off.

Carl's fingers slip beneath the waistband of my boxer briefs, gripping my ass like she owns it, but she's trapped underneath me, and she can't do much more without my allowing it. She snaps the elastic against my skin, but it only makes me push myself against her, and she moans as my dick presses against her center.

"Tuck…*off*," she demands, tugging harder at my underwear, and I obey.

My erection springs free, swollen steel pointing like a fucking arrow at what it wants. It knows its way home.

Carl's legs wrap around me, silently hurrying me along, but as much as I want inside her, she's going to have to wait. First I want to taste her.

I've only ever gone down on her as foreplay, but right now we're in no rush, and I'm desperate to make her come on my tongue.

I brush my lips over the swell of her cleavage and pay extra attention to her perfect tits before continuing down her flat stomach. I dip my tongue into her navel, soaking up the way her body writhes under my attention. When I reach my destination, Carl holds her breath.

My tongue starts its slow, easy rhythm, and I hear her suck in deep, calming breaths. I smirk against her bare skin, because I'm about to make it impossible to keep calm.

I swirl my tongue around and around, faster and faster, until I suck her into my mouth. She cries out as I push my tongue inside her. My eyes roll into the back of my head at her taste. There's fucking nothing like it.

Her hips start moving with me, and I slide two fingers inside her, working her with my mouth all the while.

"Tu-ck!" She's gasping now, her thighs caging my head between them as her hips move mindlessly, and I know she's close. She says my name again. She's warning me. Because every other time this is when I would move to fuck her. But this time there's no parent who might come home, no friend who might be looking for us, no kid brother to worry about—there's nothing but her, and me, and hours to say with our bodies what I couldn't quite articulate with words.

Her climax is sudden and beautiful. I'm caught in the impossible choice of watching and tasting, and I do my best to do both. And only when she's given me every last drop and I've drained every aftershock from her do I lazily kiss my way back up her body.

I have never been more aroused in my life, and I smile when I realize how often I've had that thought with Carl. It's been nearly a year since we first hooked up, and it's only gotten better. I could happily spend the rest of my life being with her and only her.

But one thought nags at me. I know it doesn't actually matter one way or the other, but I also know I'm going to ask, because apparently I'm some kind of masochist. "Princess…"

She raises her eyebrows, lids still at half-mast—a look that strokes both my ego and my arousal.

"Tell me, baby, was I the first guy to put his mouth on you?" From her stunned and anxious reaction those months ago I'm pretty sure I was, but I want to hear it from her.

Her lips curve into a small smile. "Tucker, you're the only guy ever to do that."

My chest expands with my sharp breath, and I want to beat it like a fucking caveman. That is the best news I've heard in my life.

"And what about this beautiful mouth?" I brush a kiss to her red, swollen lips. "Am I the only man who's been inside here?"

Carl's gaze holds mine with more intensity than I expect, and an uncharacteristic blush steals over her skin, from her cheeks down to her delectable chest. "Tuck," she breathes in a tone that makes my own breath stop. "You're the only man who's ever been in any part of me."

I blink at her. Is this some sort of metaphor? Does she mean inside her heart?

"You're in my heart, too, baby," I say softly, suddenly ready to move on from this topic.

Carl shakes her head. "No, Tuck. I don't just mean figuratively."

The only one to be in any part of her? Literally?

It hits me like a load of bricks. "You haven't slept with anyone else?"

Her head shakes in slow motion. My heart races at warp speed.

"That morning in my room—"

"Was my first time," she confirms.

My. God.

I remember thinking how incredibly tight she was—but then, she's felt just as perfect every time since then, too. I knew she was inexperienced. But *how*? *How* could I have had no idea she was a virgin?

I'm slapped with a spectrum of emotion. Awe. Humility.

But I'm also angry—perhaps irrationally. Perhaps not. How could she have kept that from me? Not just that morning, but all this time?

And then I'm back to pride and possession. Carl is mine. She's *so* fucking mine. And she's *always* been mine.

But still...*why*? "Why?"

Carl's pretty neck moves with her nervous swallow. "Because I wanted to." She shrugs. "You're the only guy I ever really, you know, wanted like that. And you'd been teasing me with your flirting, and I just thought you were messing with me like always. But I wasn't sure. And if you weren't, then...I didn't want to miss out."

She didn't want to miss out. *On me.* What is this alternate universe I'm living in where Carl is in love with me and where *she* didn't want to miss out on fucking *me*?

"You're crazy." I shake my head at her, incredulous. "But why didn't you tell me? I didn't know...I just assumed..." And I feel like an asshole for it now. Why would I just assume she wasn't a virgin?

Another shrug. "Honestly, Tuck, I didn't want to make a big deal out of it. And I thought if you knew, then it would be like, a whole thing, and you would back out."

Back out of fucking her? Does she not know me at all? "God, Carl, you could have told me you were a serial killer plotting to murder me the second I came and it wouldn't have deterred me. But I do wish you'd told me, Princess," I say wistfully.

Her fingers play with the short hair at my nape. "Why? If it wouldn't have made a difference either way?" she asks.

"I didn't say it wouldn't have made a difference, just that it wouldn't have stopped me from being with you, baby."

"What do you mean?"

I brush my lips along her jaw line. "I don't know. I would have tried to make it more…" *More what?* "Special, I guess."

She lets out a teasing laugh. "With *what*? Rose petals? Candles?"

I smirk down at her. "Maybe." She's the only girl alive I would consider doing those kinds of things for.

Her smile fades. "Or maybe you wouldn't have just left right after?" she says quietly, gaze averted in obvious vulnerability.

Well, *shit*. That must have really hurt her. She acted like she didn't care, but Carl is nothing if not skilled at hiding her true emotions.

What would I have done differently had I known? I *couldn't* not leave right after. God knows I wouldn't have if I'd had any other choice anyway. But Bits had almost died and Cap needed me. "I still would have left, Carl."

I'm still lying half on top of her and I feel her deflate beneath me. I need to explain. But how can I? I promised my best friend I'd keep his sister's secret. And up until now, I have. But he's not the only important person in my life. He's not even my only best friend anymore. I'm staring down at the other one—the one I'm fucking in love with—and she's still hurting from something I had to do almost a year ago.

Can I trust her with this?

I gently nudge her chin to meet my gaze. "You deserved better, Princess, but I didn't have a choice."

She frowns in confusion.

"Something happened the night before. I didn't want to leave you,

Carl—I had just slept with my fucking dream girl, I could have died in that bed and done so a happy man."

She tries to hide her small smile, but I don't miss it. "What happened?" she asks.

I sigh. *Here goes.* "When I checked my phone that morning I saw texts from Cap. Like, a lot of texts. Beth…she was in the hospital."

Carl's eyes go wide. "Beth? What happened?"

I swallow anxiously. I know I can trust her. And I know she would never do something to betray that trust. Still, I've kept this to myself so long it's like my mouth is physically opposed to forming the words.

"She tried to kill herself." My voice comes out a whisper, and I'm surprised by the emotion choking them. It still hurts to think of Bits like that.

"God, Tuck," Carl says simply.

She must sense how the memory affects me, because she pulls my head to her shoulder in a fierce hug. "Yeah," I breathe.

Minutes pass like that, and neither of us pulls away. It feels good. Just being this close to her. Like it's where I'm supposed to be. Like it's always been where I was supposed to be. "I wouldn't have left, Carl. But Cap was freaking out, and Bits—"

"Shh," she soothes.

"He asked me not to say anything to anyone. So I couldn't even tell you why I had to—"

"Tuck, it's okay. I get it."

Of course she does. She knows what Cap's family is to me. How much of a sister Bits is to me, blood or not. And she's one of the only people who know about my dad, and how close to home the whole thing would've hit. I lift my head enough to meet her compassionate gaze. "Still, I'm sorry. You know that, right?"

She brushes off my apology—like she deems it unwarranted and so she won't accept it. My lips twist up into a small smile. My stubborn girl.

"Fucking Brian Falco." She spits his name out with sincere distaste.

"Yeah. But, you know, it was deeper than that. He must have triggered her, but…you don't do something like that just over a guy."

Carl doesn't ask me to explain, and I'm grateful. It's Bits's and Cap's business, and their asshole father and family issues have no place here, in this bed, with this beautiful girl. I sweep my lips tenderly from her ear, along her jaw, until they reach hers. We're both still naked and I'm still dying to be inside her.

Her mouth opens for me and our kiss deepens until we're both practically gasping for breath.

Her leg winds around my hip in invitation. I pull back and climb off the bed.

"Tuck…"

"Yeah, Princess?"

"I have something else I need to tell you."

"What, baby?"

"I started the pill a month ago."

I freeze, my eyes widening and my heart racing. She already knows I got tested at my last physical before lacrosse season began. We'd gotten into one of our many pointless arguments when she thought I was flirting with some girl at a party. It ended with her calling me a manwhore—little did she know I hadn't slept with anyone since first sleeping with her—and telling me she wouldn't touch me again until I got tested. I thought she was kidding, but a week later she asked if I had my results yet.

So I got tested. Because when the only girl you want to fuck declares conditions in order for you to do so, you fucking do them. I also knew I had never had sex without a condom, so I was confident I was good.

We've never discussed her going on the pill. So the fact that she did, and that she's telling me about it…

"What are you saying, Princess?" I don't want to presume anything, but my male brain can't help going there, and the thought of being with her completely bare has my dick straining so hard I think it might detach from my body just to jump inside hers. I wouldn't blame it if it did.

"I'm saying you don't need to get a condom."

Fuck. Yes.

But that wasn't the only reason I got up. I smirk down at her. "Noted." I head to the en suite bathroom.

"Where are you going?" she whines.

"Patience, Princess." I grab the two candles the hotel has laid out by the tub, and Carl eyes me suspiciously as I lay them on the night tables by the bed and quickly light them. Then I grab the two violet flowers that came with yesterday's room service tray and yank the petals from the stems. My hands are rough and they come off torn, but the effect will hold, and I scatter them around Carl on the bedspread.

My girl giggles relentlessly. "What are you doing?"

I climb back over her, savoring the sound of her amusement. I want to hear that sound every day for the rest of my life. "Petals and candles for my Princess," I murmur as my mouth meets the column of her throat.

Her giggles instantly morph into moans.

I kiss my way back down her body, silently telling my impatient dick it will have to wait just a little longer, and this time when I go down on her I don't do it to completion. I wait until she's panting and writhing and then I shift back over her and position myself.

She stares up at me, jade eyes practically screaming their love for me, and I soak it up like a starving man. I enter her slowly, as if it's her first time, and our usually passionate, almost combative lovemaking is decidedly slow and sweet. And as much as I love how we usually are together, I realize I love this, too. I love making love to her. Because as I slide in and out of her perfect body, my weight pinning her beneath me, her limbs snaked around me and holding me to her like vises, I can feel everything. Even as my thrusts grow in power and pace, even as her breaths become gasps and her lips moan my name, all I can think is that she is mine, and I am hers, and at only eighteen, I am done. This is what I want, and this is who I want it with, and I will never want anything else. And as she spasms around me, I fill her with myself for the first time, and I can't help but feel as if I'm staking some primal claim.

Mine.

*   *   *

We make love a second time and still make no move to leave the hotel bed. The early hour of my sexy wake-up call is finally starting to take its toll, and after Carl sucks in another adorable yawn—her third in as many minutes—I suggest we try and get some sleep, and pull her back flush against my chest.

But ten minutes later, she's still awake, eyes trained thoughtfully at the small crack in the curtains. "Princess?"

She doesn't move. "Hmm?"

"You thinking about Rory?" I guess. Last night was traumatic as fuck.

Carl's head shakes gently. "Beth, actually," she murmurs.

I shift and turn Carl to face me. Now that I've told her that truth, I feel strangely unburdened, much like I did when I told her about my father's suicide. It's incredibly comforting to have someone you can trust implicitly. Someone you can give your most heart-wrenching secrets to—someone you *want* to confide in, if only for them to know every piece of you. And it's equally gratifying to know not only that she'd never betray my confidence, but that she gives me her deepest, darkest truths in turn. Because I know full well that Carl lets me see parts of herself she keeps hidden from everyone else. I think she always has.

"She's doing much better now," I assure Carl, who nods vaguely.

"I know you said it wasn't really about Brian Falco, but I just can't help thinking if he'd been more careful with her heart...or better yet, if she'd never met him..." She trails off.

"You and me both," I admit. "And, I mean, there's plenty of things to blame on that fucker. But what Beth did that night isn't one of them—not totally, anyway."

"I guess."

"A lot of girls get dumped, Princess. And they don't down a bottle of sleeping pills." The anguish in my voice is obvious, because I can't help but think of my father, who chose a similar way to end his life. But with Carl here, one of the few people I can really talk to, at least I have some consolation. "She was dealing with other issues, for a long time, and when Falco came along, and gave her all that attention, it distracted her, you know? The other issues were still there, but Falco made her happy, and that masked the rest of it." I shrug. "When he took that away, and added to it a broken heart...it was too much."

Carl wears her empathy in the lines of her frown. She cares. Deeply. And I love her even more for it. It makes me want to keep talking, to tell her everything she still doesn't know.

"It's like, with my dad. He always had issues. He would get in these low moods for no reason. But he managed them, you know? He was successful right out of college, and money, it doesn't buy happiness, obviously, but it sure as hell makes shit easier."

Carl drops her gaze, and I think she's ashamed. But I didn't mean to guilt her for being born into a wealthy family.

I nudge her chin. "Hey."

She looks at me.

"You think I don't know you wish your mom cared about more than designer bullshit and fancy trips? That you'd burn that big-ass house you live in down to the fucking ground if it meant you'd have your dad home with you more?"

Carl chews her lip, saying nothing. But I don't need words. She's given me enough already. She's complained to me about her mother's judgmental comments and snide critiques. She's confided in me about her dad—not much, but enough that I know her heart. That she resents his constantly being away on business, and I silently vow never to be that kind of man. That I will always put my family first—put Carl first.

"When my dad's business was doing well, he was able to cover up his problems by spending—you know, buying my mom jewelry, and me ridiculous toys, floor seats for the Knicks—shit like that. I think it made him feel more whole. Like he had an idea of what a provider was, and as long as he filled that role, he could manage his lows." I suck in a deep breath, holding Carl's eyes, making sure she's still with me.

"Then the economy tanked, and just like that it was all over. I mean, he was a business consultant, and half his clients were bankrupt within weeks, so his business went to shit. I was only like eleven, but I remember everything. It was like living in a different house. Suddenly all he could talk about was 'making payroll,' and he was in a constant state of panic, and you could feel it, you know? Like we were all on edge.

"When he finally had to close down, I thought things would calm…" I trail off, remembering the muffled shouts behind my parents' closed bedroom door, my mom's hysterical sobbing. I remember when I finally understood what had happened. My anger. My contempt for someone I didn't even know, but hated with every bone in my eleven-year-old body. I feel a shadow of it now and it tenses my back and clenches my jaw.

Carl's fingers gently brush over my stubble, scratching softly, and my rage eases marginally.

My voice is quieter, strained when I tell her, "I figured he would just start something new. Or maybe get a job. That we would get by on our savings in the meantime, and whatever. I didn't really know any details about our finances, but I knew I had a college fund, and I remember thinking I would tell them to take it. That I would get a sports scholarship for lacrosse or football, that they didn't need to worry."

"Tuck," Carl whispers, and I can feel her hurting for me, and that helps even more.

"But, it turned out, I was wrong. I didn't have a college fund. They didn't have any savings. Not anymore."

Carl's thin brows pinch together, but she stares without blinking.

"My dad had invested it. With some hotshot broker. Supposedly. But when the market got fucked, the guy couldn't pay back the money, and it turned out he'd never invested it at all. Or he invested some of it, but lost it, and then just lied on statements or some shit. I don't know exactly. But he did it to a lot of people."

Carl's eyes shine with tears. She must see where this is going—get that this piece of garbage who stole my family's last dollar was my father's trigger. His Brian Falco. Except no one was there to find him before it was too late. My mother and I couldn't force the pills from his stomach and get him to a hospital in time to save his life. My father is dead. And even though I know that technically justice was served, the bastard was never punished for *that*.

I slide my palm up the side of Carl's neck, trying to return the favor and relieve the strain my story is causing. But she's tense and anxious, and I wonder if I should stop talking.

But I know she's already guessed where this is going, so I might as well just say it. "My father couldn't handle living like that. Begging extended family for money to pay the gas bill every month. Debt collection letters, threats to foreclose on our house. Yeah, he also had issues before, like I said. But the stress of it all…Whatever, if it wasn't for Stanley, my dad would probably be alive. That piece of shit killed him."

I don't hide my hostility. I don't want to hide from Carl anymore, ever. "And you know, he never paid for that. Sure, he's in prison, and they recovered some of the stolen money, but the little we actually got back was barely enough to pay some past due bills, and even that came too late. My dad was already gone," I sneer. "That scumbag deserves far worse than fucking prison. He deserves to suffer like my dad did. His *family* deserves to suffer like we did. Like we *do*."

Carl winces as though my words cut her, and I pause to take a settling breath. It's hard not to get heated when talking about the man who ruined my family. I wonder if he even realizes the fallout he caused—the devastation. My emotions return to that time, watching my mom suffer the loss of her husband, but instead of having time to grieve, she had to worry about mounting bills and funeral expenses.

"And to top it all off, we couldn't even get him a normal fucking headstone because of that bastard," I tell Carl. "But my dad had always loved the water—lakes, ponds, whatever—and Beth Moses Cemetery has this small pond, but the plots near it were way more expensive. It destroyed my mom—having to choose between a nice headstone and the burial plot near the water because we couldn't afford both. My mom agonized over it for days, but…I knew he'd have wanted to be there. Near the water."

"Water is peaceful," Carl says shakily after a beat, swallowing around the emotion lodged in her throat.

"Yeah. Still, I hate the stone we ended up with. The smallest size, the cheapest material. Just a slab of rock, really. I second-guess it every time I go visit his grave. But then I look out at the water…" I trail off.

Talking about my father has made me wonder again about Carl's, and I want to give her the opportunity to return my confidence—to reveal one of those cards she plays so close to her chest. I've begun to suspect there's more going on with her dad than just working constantly, and it's not that I'm nosy——though I do want to know what his fucking deal is—but more than that, I want Carl to feel like she can open up to me. I know she must have some feelings on the subject, but she never entertains anything other than the vaguest sense of resentment.

But as I take in her obvious distress, the way her jade eyes fill with renewed tears as they dart desperately between mine, I realize that now isn't the time. She's too busy processing everything I've just confided, and I press a soft kiss to her temple and decide to change the subject.

"Tuck—" Carl's voice is fragile and hesitant.

But my phone buzzes before she can get out the rest of her words, and I think we both welcome the distraction as I reach over Carl's shoulder to grab it from the nightstand.

I don't want to think about the goddamn past anymore, anyway.

Chapter Seventeen

Tucker

Present Day

The sound of a whimper jolts me awake. I hadn't meant to fall asleep at all, and my gut rolls frantically, though it takes me a moment to recall exactly *why*. Then my heavy arm registers the warm, tight stomach it's resting upon, and my eyes fly open.

Carl squirms, and I push up onto my elbow to face her. Her eyes widen in a regretful startle. Was she trying to make an escape?

"Trying to sneak out?" I accuse. I know I should reel it in, but I'm already pissed. What was she going to do? Just disappear so I could wake up and worry my damn head off?

Carl's mouth opens silently and her cheeks flame in a rare blush.

"What the fuck?"

Her shoulders sag. "I..." She trails off and I raise my eyebrows expectantly. She sighs. "I'm *mortified*, Tucker."

Oh. I blow out a slow exhale, telling myself to relax. "You have nothing to be embarrassed about, Carl," I murmur as I sit up, effectively releasing her.

She rolls her eyes. "Yeah, okay." Her tone drips with bitter sarcasm. "It's not remotely embarrassing to become a pathetic college freshman cliché, and to have to be rescued by my ex who fucking hates me."

I balk at hearing her say I hate her again—absurd, really, since it was me who worked so hard to put the idea in her head. "We went over this last night," I remind her, and I wonder how much she actually remembers. The way she watches me makes me suspect she does remember, only she's not sure if it's an actual memory or not.

When it becomes clear she's not going to ask, I decide to ease her worries. After last night, I just feel like she needs a goddamn break. "I don't hate you, okay?"

"You don't?" she asks softly.

I shake my head. "Look, Carl. I was angry. Still am angry most days, to be honest. But we were friends for a long time before we ever started dating, and I don't know…maybe we can be friends again at some point," I offer.

Dating. It sounds like such a foreign word. Completely inadequate for what we were doing.

For nearly a full minute, Carl doesn't so much as breathe. "How?" she asks.

"I don't know, Carl. Obviously we can't go back to how we were, you know, *before*. I'm not even saying I forgive you. But our best friends are all either best friends or together. And I do obviously still care about you. Beyond that, I honestly don't know. I don't know how I feel. But I do know it isn't hate, okay?"

I hope that's enough. It's all I have to offer.

She nods slowly, and from the look on her face, I'm not sure if I've put her at ease or hurt her even more somehow.

I let another minute pass before I speak again.

"How are you feeling?"

"Hungover," she admits. "But not like a normal hangover. I mean, I'm okay. I just feel kind of, like, slow. And a little lightheaded, actually."

"Yeah, that's pretty normal for what you took. I think you'll feel more like yourself in a few hours."

"Great," she grumbles, eyes trained on the bedspread. "And what did I take, exactly?"

I sigh. "Painkillers. Percocet."

Carl nods slowly, like she should have known.

I realize I'm still in just a T-shirt and my underwear, and I grab her jeans from the chair and toss them to her, and hastily pull on a pair of my own.

I order myself not to watch as she dresses, but mostly I fail. Carl is still wearing her shirt from last night, and as soon as she's got her jeans on, I reclaim my place beside her on the bed.

"I'm really sorry about last night, Tuck. You know that, right? It's so humiliating."

"Why?" I ask her. Ben's the one who should be sorry, and I have every intention of seeing that he is.

Carl blinks at me, as if the answer should be obvious. "Because. I shouldn't have put myself in that position. And you certainly shouldn't have had to come to my rescue, of all people."

Of all people?

"I'm so stupid. Ben got my guard down. *Ugh!* So *stupid!*" She drops her head into her hands and rubs her face in frustration.

But I can't dwell on the *of all people* comment anymore, because my brain is pouncing on the idea that Ben got her guard down.

Because *how?* Did she fucking *like* him? *Does* she fucking like him? And why, if my intentions are to be nothing more than a friend at best, does the thought make my stomach roll with unease?

"How did he get your guard down, exactly?" I try to keep my voice as monotone as possible.

Carl shrugs. "You know, with the whole *friends* thing. I told him I…" She looks me over as if she's only just realized it's me she's talking to, and she's wondering if she should continue.

I raise my eyebrows expectantly.

Carl sighs. "I told him I'd just gotten out of a relationship and I wasn't really ready to date or anything, and he acted like he was totally fine with it. That we could just be friends. And he really did seem cool with it, you know? He joked about me setting him up with my fresh-men girlfriends, and we've hung out several times and he's never tried anything or made me feel even remotely uncomfortable."

I resist rolling my eyes. For all Carl's intelligence and competence, she doesn't get that there just isn't a straight man alive who wouldn't want more than a friendship with her, no matter how *cool with it* he acted.

"So when he handed you those pills…"

"I didn't even think twice about it," she admits. "I thought they were aspirin." She shakes her head in self-reproach. "So stupid," she adds under her breath.

I scoot closer and take her chin between my thumb and forefinger, pointing her gaze to mine. "He told you they were aspirin?" I ask carefully.

Her brows pinch together in thought. "I'm not sure I remember."

"Think, Carl," I order. "This is important." If he actually told her they were aspirin, then there's no question his actions were intentional. In which case golden boy Ben Aronin is going to spend his Thanksgiv-ing holiday in jail, with enough injuries to put him out of commission for the year, let alone the lacrosse season.

"I don't think he did," she murmurs. "I think I just assumed—"

"Maybe it will help if you start from the beginning. He said you had a headache," I prompt.

Carl nods. "We were at dinner, and we were drinking, and danc-ing, and…we did tequila shots." She throws me a tentative glance.

"I thought I was fine, but then my head started hurting. Devin wanted to come back here to be with Max, but I wanted to go to the dorm. Ben said he'd give me an aspirin—"

I nearly jump off the bed, ready to commit murder, but she corrects herself.

"No. Actually, no. He said he'd give me something for my headache," she amends.

I stare at her meaningfully. "Are you sure?"

Her eyes hold complete sincerity. "Yeah." She nods. "I'm pretty sure. I mean, I was drunk, but so was he. We got here and he just got the pills and handed them to me. I don't think he ever said the word *aspirin*."

"Did you ask?"

Carl chews her bottom lip as she slowly shakes her head.

I nod thoughtfully. But I don't know how to figure out whether Ben is simply a fucking thoughtless idiot or something more sinister.

"What else do you remember?" I ask her.

She shakes her head. "Not a whole lot. Honestly? At first I felt really good. Which makes sense, being as I was apparently *high*," she says derisively. "How did you know?"

"Know?"

"That I needed help."

I sigh. "I was just checking who was still here," I lie. "And when I saw how fucked up you were, and realized Ben was trying to get you to his room…" I trail off.

In truth, I ran into Devin and Max on my way to the bathroom some time earlier and knew Max was meant to be Carl's ride home. I went to check on Carl and found her in the living room, talking and smiling with Ben, and spent the next hour or so staring at my ceiling, mercilessly awake. I listened for the sound of a cab outside my window since Ben was in no shape to drive her home, and though I doubted Ben had even a remote shot at getting Carl to his bedroom, I left my door cracked just in case, knowing they'd have to pass it to get there.

At around two in the morning I heard voices outside the kitchen and came out to check on them. I wasn't even suspicious at first. It wasn't like there was screaming or anything particularly alarming.

Just muffled whispers in the dark, and it sounded like they were just trying not to wake anyone. I launched myself out of bed at the thought of them hooking up, and while there wasn't time to form a conscious plan, I suppose I hoped my interruption would be enough to make Carl second-guess going through with whatever she was considering doing with Ben. But I'd flung on the lights and my heart froze at the sight before me.

I avert my gaze. I don't want Carl to see how affected I still am by the memory of her eyes, distant and dazed—when they actually managed to open—and lined in fear. I can't bear to think of her so helpless.

I make my way over to my window and check for Ben's car. His usual parking spot is empty. Smart move on his part.

I stretch my arms over my head and turn back to face her, sighing. "We should get moving," I tell her. Cap's family will be expecting us in a couple hours.

Carl peeks sheepishly up at me from her place on my bed. I try not to think about how it feels to have her there. Not to let myself picture an alternate reality—one that not so long ago I believed would be my future, where she'd wake up in my bed every damned morning.

"Do you think you could give me a ride back to Stuyvesant?" she asks hesitantly.

I glare at her. I thought that was implied.

"I mean, I don't want to impose after—"

"You're not," I cut her off. "I'm just surprised you thought you had to ask," I admit.

That earns me a small smile.

"Let me just grab a shower and throw my things together. You can shower here if you want. I'm pretty sure everyone's gone by now anyway. Or I can wait for you back at your dorm."

Carl blinks at me. "Wait for me?"

"I'm driving you to Cap's," I clarify.

Her mouth gapes slightly before she catches it. "Tuck—"

"Don't start, Carl." I'm really in no mood for one of her arguments.

"But—"

"You already admitted you feel slow and lightheaded. I'm not letting you drive to Port Woodmere. Period." I try to unclench my jaw, but what the fuck? Does she want to get away from me that fucking badly?

"I'm supposed to pick up Billy at a quarter to three."

"Then we'll pick up Billy."

Carl nods tentatively, and I breathe a silent sigh of relief.

*　　*　　*

Two hours later, Carl is fast asleep in the passenger seat as I drive us to her house to pick up Billy, and she doesn't stir as the three of us make our way over to Cap's for Thanksgiving like everything is perfectly normal.

Somehow I get the feeling that today is going to be one of those days where everything changes, and I think to myself that I've had far too many of those in my life.

But after that one day just over five months ago, I guess there isn't much that can shock me anymore.

It was a gray, wet day when my phone rang far too early, Cap sounding all hesitant and somber. I remember thinking something must have happened with Rory, or Bits, and my heart raced in dread as I demanded he tell me what was going on.

"My dad called this morning," he said.

I don't know how, but I knew then it was about Carl's father. I'd recently had the idea to have Cap ask his dad—who is a high-powered attorney—to use his resources to find out what he could about William Stanger. I hated the look that Carl got every time he came up, and when he didn't show up to graduation, I'd begun to suspect something more than work was keeping him away. I'd been looking around for him when it hit me that I wouldn't even recognize him if I did see him. And I've known Carl most of my life. I'd tried to get her to talk about it, but I could tell it hurt her to even mention him, so for some reason it made sense to me to find out on my own. For some reason that didn't seem like sneaking around behind her back…

But the moment I thought I was going to learn what was really up with him, I felt suddenly uneasy. Still, I couldn't imagine what Cap's dad could possibly have learned that would have Cap sounding like someone died.

Now I can't count how many times I've wished I could go back to that moment before that call—before I knew anything at all—ignorance being bliss and all that.

"Tell me," I demanded.

"Let's meet up," Cap countered. His insistence made my stomach drop—not only because he wanted to discuss it in person, but because he didn't seem to want to tell me anything until then.

I lost my cool. "Just fucking tell me, Cap!"

"He's in prison, man."

Still, I didn't know then what it meant. Had no idea what kind of bastard had fathered the girl I loved. No idea what she'd been so careful to lie about from the very beginning.

"Prison?"

"I'm on my way over."

Chapter Eighteen

Carleigh

Present Day

"Shh, kid. Let her sleep. There's some flu going around campus and she hasn't been feeling well." Tucker's voice breaks through my dreamless slumber.

"But we're almost there," Billy whines.

My eyes flutter open to trees and telephone poles flying past the car window my head rests against. I groan.

"Finally!" Billy exclaims.

I lean around back to look at his adorable face—thirteen, yes, but never more than seven or eight in my eyes. "Hiya, Billy boy," I croak. I clear my throat to rid it of the residual sleepiness.

"Carski." He uses his childhood nickname for me. "Are you sick? You kinda look like shit."

"Billy!" Tucker and I chide in unison, but Tuck's lips twist into an amused smirk. "You never say that to a woman," he admonishes.

"She's not a woman, she's my sister," Billy corrects him. "And she does look...*under the weather*."

I flip down the vanity mirror and determine that Billy actually had it right the first time. I look like shit. I grab my overnight bag from under my feet and rifle through it until I find my emergency makeup kit and blend some concealer under my eyes. I brush some bronzer and blush onto my cheeks to counterbalance the lingering pallor. Then I add a light shimmery shadow to my eyelids and smudge a deep brown line above my lashes, finishing off with some mascara.

I turn back to Billy and raise my brows.

"Much better," he approves.

I slip Tucker a tentative glance as I turn forward again, and his smile of appreciation makes my chest swell.

"Beautiful," he mutters.

I turn away so he can't see my smile.

We pull up to Cap's right on time, a beautiful red-brick mansion, impressive in its own right, yet still only about a quarter of the size of my own monstrosity of a home.

Billy heads straight to the guest bathroom off the Caplans' grand foyer, and Tucker and I head around the bend toward the kitchen, where I expect people will be. We both stop in our tracks at overhearing what seems like a mildly heated conversation between our respective best friends, and we exchange an uneasy glance.

"I just don't get why you're being so fucking stubborn!" Cap growls.

"I'm not being stubborn, Sam!" Rory replies, her swirling southern accent sliding off her words as it does when she's worked up over something. She's the only one besides Cap's immediate family who calls him *Sam*, and it comes out more like *Say-um* in this moment. "I'm never around anymore, and it's Thanksgivin', and it just isn't right!"

I feel bad for listening; Rory is such a private person that she can barely kiss Cap in front of someone without blushing bright red. I take a step forward to make ourselves known, but Tuck catches my elbow and shakes his head. "Let them finish."

I acquiesce, but it unsettles me. They're not the kind of couple you'd expect to break up over some petty fight—or at all, for that matter. When two people are so inherently created for each other, you like to believe their love can endure any hardship, great or small. But I know better than most—sometimes it isn't enough.

I'm so put off by the thought of Cap and Rory fighting that I actually start to sweat. Tucker's hand squeezes my shoulder.

"They'll be fine," he assures me, careful to keep the rumble of his voice below a whisper.

My gaze swings to his as I try to regain control of my emotions—something I used to excel at. *What the hell is wrong with me?* "How can you be so sure?"

Tucker scoffs, his mouth slipping into an ironic, crooked smirk, obviously trying to put me at ease. "Because, Carl. Cap loves that girl more than his own life. He isn't letting her go—not for anything," he assures me.

My breath blasts from my lungs in a sudden rush of air. It's like a sucker punch to my stomach. Because he's right. Cap would never leave Rory. I've seen his love for her firsthand. And when you love someone like that, you don't let anything steal that from you. Not a fight, not a lie—even a devastating one. Nothing.

And for the first time, I consider that maybe I'm not entirely to blame for my and Tucker's downfall. Because I know I loved *him* like that. So if we couldn't make it, then it's very possible Tucker never loved me that way in the first place. Not like Cap loves Rory. Not like I loved him.

Love him.

The realization shatters the tattered ruins of my heart all over again, and I know I have to escape before the moisture in my eyes becomes too much to pass off as concern over our friends. But by the way Tuck's eyes widen and his mouth parts, it's apparent he's realized not only what he just said, but its implications. But he can't even bring himself to deny it; he just watches me with a mixture of pity and regret.

Well, now I know.

I murmur something about needing the bathroom and head in the opposite direction, through the den, before I realize I can't go any farther without either running into Cap and Rory or turning back and returning to where Tucker still waits. It's just as well, since my legs need a moment before they can be depended upon anyway.

I mold myself to the wall and suck in deep breaths, telling myself nothing has actually changed. The knowledge that Tucker never quite loved me the way I thought he did should make our breakup easier to stomach, shouldn't it? If anything, it should at least explain why he was so quick to end us. No discussion, no chance to explain—nothing.

God! Why does this hurt so damn much?

Cap and Rory have been arguing this whole time, but Tucker was right; it doesn't sound like anything they won't resolve by the day's end, and after another minute or so, Rory tells Cap she's going to help his mother in the kitchen and for him to "just let it go."

I peek around the corner to see if the coast is clear, but not only is Cap standing there running his hand through his hair in aggravation, not two seconds later, he's joined by Tucker.

Fucking great.

"Trouble in paradise?" Tuck asks.

"Fuck off," Cap snaps back.

"Whoa, man. Chill."

Cap sighs. "Sorry," he mutters under his breath. "She's just being fucking stubborn. She's giving me a hard time about staying here tonight. She wants to go home with her mom after dinner."

"And you're worried about her nightmares?"

Rory suffers from night terrors. Debilitating ones. But she confided to me—and Cap to Tuck—that somehow when she sleeps with Cap, he manages to keep them at bay. Maybe it's knowing he would kill to protect her. Maybe it's simply the comfort of his love for her. I remember what it was like to feel that secure, brief as it may have been.

"She says they've gotten better," Cap replies. "But she hasn't spent a night without me since I moved into the apartment. Since *we* moved in."

"She's still keeping the dorm?"

"I think she'll give it up next semester. The fucked-up part is she's worried about *me*. Like I'm suddenly going to feel pressured and it's going to fuck with us. You know—backfire on our relationship or something."

"And it pisses you off that she still doubts you."

"Yeah," Cap says simply, but the word carries weight. "How's Carl feeling?" he asks.

I startle at the tone Cap uses, and I realize Tucker must have called Cap at some point today and told him what happened last night.

Tucker sighs. "Better now, I think. She slept in the car."

"You figure out what the guy's deal was?"

"No." The single word hums with frustration. "But I motherfuck-ing *will*."

"I still say you report him either way. It's not your job to play detec-tive, man. He put her in danger—he should pay for that whether he intended to or not."

"Yeah, Cap. And he will. But it's his *intentions* that I need to figure out. Because if they were what I suspect, then you know I'm not going to handle it by fucking *reporting him*."

Shit.

"You could lose your scholarship." But Cap's warning is half-hearted. I know it wouldn't stop Cap if he were in Tucker's shoes, but that's different. Cap loves Rory. "You could end up in jail."

And then I hear Billy's voice echo through the foyer, his end of a phone conversation—what must have kept him so long—and judging by the way he lowers the cadence of his voice, I suspect he's talking to a girl, and I almost let loose a giggle, grateful for the comic relief he's unwittingly supplied. *My baby brother*.

He ends his conversation and calls out a greeting to Cap.

"Billy the Kid," Cap replies, and I retreat back into my hiding spot while they exchange playful male teasing and friendly ball-busting comments. Moments later Cap's sister Beth emerges from the kitchen and joins in on the fun.

I need to get myself together.

Billy instantly focuses his attention on Beth, who very much resembles her older brother in her own feminine version of his trademark gorgeousness, only her hair is dirty blond where Cap's is chocolate brown. Billy targets her with a smooth smile, and asks her what she's been up to, telling her how much better school would be if he had her beautiful face to pass in the halls. Beth doesn't take him seriously since he's three years younger, but she's clearly amused by his attention.

Beth says she's going back to the kitchen to help, and my little brother follows after her, murmuring facetious, furtive admonishments about how misogynistic the other guys are to let the women do all the work while they stand around and bullshit.

Tucker places his hand over his heart and smirks. "Damn, he's doing me proud."

"Can he *do you proud* on someone other than my fucking little sister?" Cap grumbles, but his eyes smile with amusement.

I use the distraction to make my way to the guest restroom, where I quickly retouch my makeup, fixing the minor smudge caused by the tears that pooled but never fell. It takes me no more than five or so minutes to pull myself together—at least outwardly—a testament to my talent at concealing my feelings.

Shortly thereafter I join the others, and I'm welcomed warmly by the Caplans and friends. It's weird seeing Mitch—Cap's dad—here. I haven't seen him since Cap's parents divorced back when we were in middle school.

Billy stays within five feet of Beth, attentive and helpful, and while I'm fully aware that he's mostly motivated by Beth's pretty smile and tight sweater, I also know most guys his age would go about flirting in a decidedly different manner, what with chivalry being dead and all.

While the guys park themselves in the den to watch football, Rory and I offer to finish setting the table, and when the last glass is set down, she pulls me aside in the dining room.

"Are you okay?" she asks, careful to keep her voice contained to the otherwise empty room, and I swallow anxiously, wondering if Cap told her what happened last night, and what the hell would possess him to do such a thing when she still has her own demons to deal with.

"I know it must be weird to be here with Tuck, but Sam said you guys were trying to be friends, right?"

I breathe a subtle sigh of relief. "Yeah," I agree. "Friends."

Rory smiles in sympathy. "It seems to be going okay so far, right? I mean, you drove over together…?"

"So far so good," I reply noncommittally.

"I'm glad you're here," she murmurs.

"Me too."

We spend the next thirty minutes catching up, and when we notice that the boys have been enjoying bottle after bottle of beer, I ask Elaine how she feels about us having a glass of wine. She starts laughing, embarrassed that she hadn't thought to offer. We're only eighteen, but she's fully aware that a little drinking is par for the course for college students. Or more than a little drinking, depending on the person and situation. Frankly, between last night and spending a family holiday with my ex today, I could use a glass or two.

Or four.

The end of the third quarter sends Tucker into the kitchen to retrieve more beer and snacks. He reaches for the artfully arranged platter of Elaine's famous butternut squash mini quiches, and starts stacking them three deep on an appetizer plate before her spatula meets the back of his hand with a resounding *thwack*.

"Ouch!" he whines through his chuckle. He manages to snatch two more before she lands another smack, and he grins smugly as he side-steps her to escape mostly unscathed back toward the living room.

His gaze meets mine as he flees with his haul, and my eyes return his bright smile, even if my lips can't quite manage it. I can't banish the memory of hearing him so sure that Cap wouldn't let his girl go for anything, knowing that Tucker *did*.

But his eyes drop to the maroon liquid in my glass, and they go instantly stern, delivering some silent message I don't receive. Rory hands me some cloth napkins to take to the dining room, and when I turn back to where Tucker stood, he's gone.

By glass number two, thankfully I'm starting to relax. But it doesn't last long. Tucker corners me on my way from the bathroom and tugs me into the empty study.

"What's wrong?" I gasp, startled.

He shakes his head, expression impassive. "You need to stop drinking."

I narrow my eyes, programmed to react to his bossiness only one way. "I don't need to do anything, Tucker. What is your problem? How many beers have *you* had today?" Apparently he's decided to go all hypocrite on me, and I'm just not up for it right now. I turn on my heel and walk out the door, but he catches me in the empty hallway no more than three steps later.

Tucker sighs, raking his hand exasperatedly through his soft, dark blond locks, and my own fingers itch with the memory of how his hair feels against my skin. The feel of it locked in my grip, against the sensitive skin of my inner thighs...

I blink the memories away, shocking myself with my own wayward thoughts. What has gotten into me? Maybe I should cool it with the wine after all.

"Look, I'm not trying to be a dick," he says, suddenly sincere. "Just, after last night, maybe you should take it easy, you know? Those pills could still be in your system," he warns.

I shake my head. "They were gone after a few hours. I Googled it."

His look of disappointment makes me suspect he already knew that. He was just hoping I didn't. But why the hell does it matter to him if I drink?

"Still, Carl—"

"Look, Tuck, last night is the whole point. Or part of it. I'm stressed the fuck out, and right now I want to forget it ever happened." I sigh. "And being here with you…I almost turned Cap down when he invited me for today. Even when he said you were cool with it. But I couldn't exactly turn down the chance to give Billy a real Thanksgiving. I doubt he can even remember ever having one before, since he was only a toddler when my dad, you know, went away. But with us…" I gesture between the two of us. "I'm still figuring out just how to be around you now, you know? And it means so much to me that you'd consider us maybe being friends again at some point, and I don't want to fuck that up, and even that is stressing me out. And look, I just want to have a good time, in a safe place, with people I know I can trust, okay?" And apparently I've been reduced to a rambling idiot.

Tucker reluctantly considers me, fighting the urge to dig in his heels. But I suspect it's my earnestness that gets him. "Yeah, okay," he agrees halfheartedly.

"And not that I've been stalking you or anything, but you've had more than your standard couple of 'good time' beers," I point out, belatedly realizing that I probably shouldn't have admitted I've been paying him enough attention to notice.

He runs his lip between his teeth, considering. "I guess I'm kinda stressed, too." He lets out a short, ironic laugh. "You know what? I think last night traumatized me more than it did you."

I frown, remembering his implied threats to Ben. "I'm fine," I remind him.

"Thank God for that," he murmurs. Then, that quickly, he shakes his head as if to rid it of his grim thoughts, and locates a half-smile. "All right, Carl. My bad. Do what you want. Just be careful, okay, friend?"

I find a small, bittersweet smile of my own. "You got it, buddy," I whisper.

Chapter Nineteen

Carleigh

Present Day

An hour later, we all sit around the beautifully set dining table. There's no preamble to dinner, just everyone digging enthusiastically into the impressive meal, talking with full mouths, laughter echoing off of the damask-papered walls.

The ringing of silverware against glass resonates across the room, and we all turn to where Mitch Caplan stands at the head of the table, holding up his glass of sparkling mineral water with a contented, sober smile. I noticed that he's the only one in this house—besides Beth and Billy of course—who hasn't had any alcohol today. The rest of us are all brightly buzzed, and we hold up our glasses in turn when Mitch makes his toast.

He thanks his "beautiful wife"—strange, since last I checked they were long since divorced—and "her mini-me, Bitsy" for the beautiful setup and incredible meal. Beth beams up at him from her adjacent seat, obviously thrilled by the compliment. Observing her makes me feel wistful, because while I'm happy for Beth, I can't help but think of a time when I used to look at my own father like that.

We all raise our glasses and exchange clinks and cheers, and then

Elaine offers her own toast to her family and friends, thanking her guests for coming.

"Ooh, let's go around the table and say what we're thankful for!" Beth exclaims, suddenly seeming much younger than her near-seventeen years.

Cap rolls his eyes and there's a collective groan.

"Oh come on, it's a good idea." Billy, who sits to Beth's right, smiles indulgently. "Nothing wrong with being a little cheesy on Thanksgiving," he offers, and I can't help my burst of laughter. If I'd been the one to suggest it he'd be groaning along with the worst of us.

Beth pushes her lips into an exaggerated pout, and at that, Cap is the first to surrender.

"Okay, brat, put the lip away," he teases, and she grins triumphantly. "I'm thankful this year for…being wrong, I guess. I had some preconceived notions about…some things. And it's humbling when people come into your life—some new"—he looks adoringly down at Rory—"some not so new"—he meets his father's gaze across the table—"and completely redraw the picture you had of your life in the course of just a few months."

He doesn't elaborate, but the people he's speaking to obviously receive the message, and Rory blushes scarlet as he wraps an arm around her and presses a chaste kiss to her forehead.

Tuck thumps his fist to his chest and slips on a mask of mock sentimentality. "That's deep, bro," he teases, wiping an invisible tear from his cheek. "I love you too, man."

A chorus of laughter erupts, and Cap tosses a pumpernickel roll down the length of the table in a perfect arc, hitting the target of Tucker's face in true quarterback form.

"Okay, Rory's turn," Beth interrupts.

Rory's not a fan of being the center of attention, and her voice is low and tentative. "I'm thankful for new beginnings, new friends—"

"And sexy-ass boyfriends!" I add for her, reviving the laughter around the table.

Rory blushes but smiles widely, peeking sideways at Cap. "Yeah, those too," she agrees, burrowing into his side.

"Okay, me now," Bits announces. "I'm thankful for having the whole family together. Including those who aren't technically related. I'm thankful my manwhore of a brother finally got put in his place by a girl, and—"

"Okay, *next*." Cap cuts her off and she sticks her tongue out at him.

We all look to Billy, who blinks back at us. "Oh, me?"

"Not so into the idea now, are you, Billy boy?" I tease.

"Yeah, kid. Let's hear it. It's cool to be cheesy on Thanksgiving, right?" Tuck goads.

Billy shrugs, all cool and smug, obviously for Beth's benefit, and I suspect that if he were older, she'd be eating it right up. But it's me he directs his smile to. "I'm thankful for my smartass big sister." He turns to Beth on his left. "And for the seating arrangements," he smirks.

This time Cap's roll hits Billy square in the jaw.

Rory's mom and Elaine go next, followed by Mitch, who is thankful for "second chances." *Yeah, we don't all get those, Mitch.*

Then it's Tucker's turn, and I'm careful not to make eye contact. After listening to Cap and Rory essentially thank the universe for each other, I don't really feel like watching Tucker *not* do the same of me.

"I'm thankful for all of you losers. It's good to have you all as friends." He subtly emphasizes the word *all*, and when I peek up, he's looking at me.

And then it's my turn, and somehow I've managed to be caught off guard. This whole time, I forgot to think of something to say. "I'm thankful for my friends, and for my annoying kid brother, who keeps forgetting he's still a *kid*. And for you guys inviting us today. We really appreciate it," I murmur, and I glance at Tucker, because even though I'm here at the hospitality of the Caplans, it was Tucker who could've revoked my welcome—who had fair reason to—and who blessed it instead.

His warm smile makes my heart flutter, like it has for as long as I can remember, and I look away, reminding myself that it's no longer an appropriate response.

Dinner continues like that, with jokes and laughter, and increasing inebriation. I have more than a few glasses of wine, and I feel the stress of the past day float into oblivion, where I'd very much like it to stay.

We all help clear the table and set out dessert, and by eight o'clock the parents have left us to our own devices in the den, where Cap, Rory, Tucker, and I continue drinking—Tucker and me most of all.

Rory and Cap's earlier argument resolved itself when her mom got up after dessert, and started saying her good-byes.

Rory stood, startled when her mother said good-bye to her as well. "Uh, I thought I'd come with you, Mom. Stay the night at home," she murmured.

Her mother was obviously surprised. "Oh…uh…really? I thought you'd stay here with Sam," she stammered.

Cap stood behind Rory, where she couldn't see him nod his encouragement.

"Oh. I mean, I could. I just thought—"

"Actually, Rory, honey…I wasn't planning on going home just yet."

Rory's puzzled look was priceless.

"Well, you see, Mark's just finished dinner with his kids, and we thought we'd get together."

Rory's jaw fell slowly before she caught it. Mark is the man Amy's been seeing. He's divorced and, according to Rory, remarkably handsome.

"Oh, okay. That's cool, I guess. You're sure you don't mind me staying here?"

"Why would I mind? You stay with Sam every other night. And anyway, you're all coming over for brunch tomorrow, right?"

"Of course," Rory replied, turning around just in time to catch the tail end of Sam's self-satisfied smirk, and jabbing his side with her elbow.

"Carl, if you and Billy aren't busy, we'd love you to join us. Just a small, casual brunch. Noon."

I accepted, because why not? Lord knows I sure don't have any parents looking to spend time with me this weekend.

Now we sit around doing much of nothing. Billy and Tucker battle it out on the Xbox, while Beth shows me pictures on her phone from a post-season Mets game Mitch took her to last month where she got to meet David Wright, her favorite player, who also happens to be her father's client. Cap reaps the spoils of his win, even if Amy handed it to him, his arm possessively glued around Rory's waist, which she doesn't seem to mind in the least.

"Oh yeah!" Billy hoots suddenly, in time with Tucker's "God-damnit!"

"Take that, Mother-Tucker!" He jumps onto the couch like Tom Cruise professing his love for Katie Holmes to Oprah, and punches both fists into the air in celebration of his digital victory.

"*Billy*," I halfheartedly chasten.

He ignores me. "Totally just kicked your ass," he boasts.

Tucker does some maneuver—I can't tell from my vantage behind the back of the couch—that has Billy falling out of nowhere and landing sideways onto the cushions. "Want to see if you can kick my ass in real life?" he smirks, knowing that Billy isn't stupid enough to even pretend to consider that challenge. Billy may have grown a lot in the past year, but Tucker is still six foot two and one hundred and ninety pounds of pure lean muscle. I shake my head, trying to rid it of the image of the way those muscles flex with certain physical exertions. God, why do I keep going there?

"Billy, it's cool if you want to bring a friend to brunch tomorrow," Rory says. It's nice of her. We'll all have each other, so it would be nice for Billy to have a friend of his own there as well.

"That's a good idea," I tell him. "Why don't you invite Kyle?"

Billy rolls his eyes. "Fuck Kyle," he murmurs.

I gape at him. Billy and Kyle have been inseparable since kindergarten. "What do you mean, 'fuck Kyle'?" I ask.

He shrugs. "We're not really talking right now."

What?

My glare demands an explanation, and I'm surprised when he seems hesitant to give me one. He's always confided in me about everything.

Finally he sighs. "We got into a fight after he said something that pissed me off."

"Elaborate," Tucker interjects.

Another sigh, this one of reluctant resignation. "He was sleeping over a few weeks ago, and he was in the bathroom—showering, I thought. I left my phone charger in there so I go in to get it and he's holding a TV guide with a picture of Daenerys from *Game of Thrones*—"

"Who?" Rory asks.

"Khaleesi," I explain. "The one with the dragons."

"Yeah," Billy continues. "Anyway, he was totally jerking off to her."

"Jesus, Billy," I practically squeal. This is not where I saw this story going. Somehow I still see Billy as my sweet little boy in his Batman costume begging me to play with his action figures.

"You wanted to know!" he whines.

I gesture for him to continue, though suddenly I'm not sure I actually want to hear the rest of this story.

"So obviously I left, and then later when he came downstairs, I started making fun of him."

"Naturally," Tucker agrees.

"I joked that he was pathetic because he had to jerk it to a fictional character because he couldn't get a real girl. He said the girl he was thinking about was very real, and some other things…"

"I don't get why that would get you into a fight. You guys bust each other's balls all the time," I admit.

"You remember he was there on Halloween," Billy murmurs, his cheeks flushing.

"Yeah…"

"Oh, that motherfucker!" Tuck growls before falling into a bout of hysterical laughter.

"What?" Rory asks.

"Yeah, what?" I echo.

Tucker looks at me, eyes dancing with mirth, smirking wryly. "Your costume."

Oh…

Oh.

Oh! Ew!

"Gross!" I shudder at the thought of the kid I've watched grow up since he was five think about me that way.

Tucker chuckles wildly while Billy glares at him, unamused.

"I don't know whether to kick his ass or give him a high five." Tucker laughs some more.

"Tuck!" I chasten.

"Well, I went with hitting him," Billy admits.

"Billy, *no*." My voice drops in disappointment. How could he punch his best friend over something so stupid? What has gotten into him?

"Relax, Carl. Cap and I have gotten into it plenty. They'll get over it eventually," Tucker assures me.

I chew on the inside of my cheek, not knowing what else to say.

"On that note," Cap murmurs as he pulls Rory up from their seat and starts leading her toward the foyer. "We're going to go see if my mom needs help cleaning up."

Yeah, I bet that's where they're going.

"I should go see if they *actually* need help," Beth says, and excuses herself after them, and then I'm alone with Billy and Tucker.

"What happened on Halloween?" Tuck asks suddenly.

"Huh?"

"On Halloween," he says more slowly. "You were at our party, and then obviously you were with Billy…" He stares at me, his eyes saying more—reminding me of the following morning, when I ran into him outside my dorm building, when he accused me of fucking our professor. They don't accuse now. Now they seem almost regretful. Which makes sense, I suppose. Now that he knows I was with Billy, he must finally realize I wasn't doing something scandalous with Zayne.

But I can't help but still feel resentful that he ever thought I was. So I don't answer right away. But it doesn't matter; Billy does it for me.

"Nothing happened."

"Nothing?" Tuck asks skeptically.

"Me and some of my friends just got too drunk. There were no cabs 'cause of Halloween, so we kinda got stranded. Had to call Carleigh for help. You couldn't get any either, right Carski?" He turns back to Tucker. "She had to get a ride from some guy from school."

Tucker's gaze lingers on mine for an extra moment, and I know it's as much of an apology as I'm going to get.

"So not really *nothing* then," he says to Billy.

Billy rolls his eyes. "Whatever, man. You know how it is."

"How is it?" Tucker counters.

Billy eyes him with vague irritation, and it surprises me. He's always looked up to Tucker as if he were some kind of superhero, and while he briefly wanted to kick his ass for breaking up with me, I made it clear to him I was the one to blame. "Like you weren't doing the same thing when you were my age. Bullshit."

"Billy!" I chide, but I'm willfully ignored.

"I was," Tucker admits. "But only because I was having a hard time. I was hurting, and angry, because my father had just died and I didn't know how to handle that."

My jaw drops. I can't believe he would confide something like that in Billy. Even if he hasn't given any details. But even just discussing his father, and how his death affected him—it's not something Tucker would ever take lightly, and he's doing it because he's worried about Billy—because he cares—and it means the world to me. I pray that it helps get Billy to talk about whatever's been bothering him, that Tucker can reach him where I seem to have failed. I've tried to get him to talk since Halloween, but he always blows it off—pretending all is well and making me seem like I'm overreacting.

But Billy doesn't open up. "That's *your* life, Tucker. Not mine. Sorry and whatever, but don't put your issues on me. I'm just having a good time."

Sorry and whatever? Who *is* this person?

I'm so stunned by Billy's callousness that it takes me a second to form words. "Billy, how could you act like this? Tucker's just trying to talk to you. To figure out what's up with you, because he cares."

And then Billy gets visibly pissed off, and it throws me even more off guard. "Yeah, he cares so much that he just dumped your ass and then fucking disappeared," he spits.

I gape at him. It hits me hard—realizing that I've been so caught up in my own loss that I somehow didn't realize that when we broke up, Billy lost Tucker, too. He's always been around as a close friend, but when we started hooking up last year, he became kind of a fixture in our lives, and even more so when we made it official.

"Whatever," Billy says bitterly. "I don't need this shit."

"Billy!" But this scolding apparently holds no more weight than the others.

Tucker doesn't look angry, just concerned; and I feel guilty that he tried to help only to get burned.

Billy stands up, and I think he's going to leave the room, but then he turns back. "Can you take me to visit on Sunday?" he asks.

My nerves come alive in my veins. I can't remember ever feeling this angry with Billy before, but even more than that, I'm hurt. And now he's asking me to take him to visit a man I can't stand to be in the same room as? In front of someone who really doesn't need to be reminded of his existence. Even if Billy couldn't possibly know that Tucker probably has a pretty good idea who we're talking about, we're usually so careful about talking about our father that I don't understand why he's now gone from callous to utterly thoughtless.

"No," I say simply. I glare at Billy, admonishing him for so much, and for the first time in his almost fourteen years, he doesn't seem to care how I feel one way or another. Out of the corner of my eye I notice Tucker silently excuse himself, but he doesn't go far. Instead, he stands in the doorway like a sentinel, offering us a false sense of privacy while still standing guard, as if he actually believes Billy might go too far and hurt me. Not physically, I'm sure, but Billy's been known to lash out with cutting words when he's upset—something he's learned from our mother.

I'm grateful Tuck cares enough to stay, but it does mean he can hear us, and I'd rather he not overhear this particular subject. I'd rather he forget it even exists.

"It's been months. It's a holiday weekend and I want to go," Billy argues. He knows this is a big ask. I haven't gone to visit my father more than a couple times a year since I learned the real reason he's still there, and I'm not due to go again until Christmas week.

"Mom will take you when she gets back." Part of me just wants to tell him he's being an asshole and to cut it the hell out, but the other part can't stop searching for the little boy who's always been so exceptionally thoughtful and sweet.

"Just fucking take me!" he shouts.

"I'm not fucking taking you to see Dad!" I lose it. I've never cursed at him before. Ever.

Billy lifts his chin to Tucker, who's standing calm and observant in the background, and has yet to so much as flinch. "So he does know," Billy accuses. "I have to keep it secret from everyone I know—from my best fucking friends—but you told your boyfriend?" He turns to Tucker with a sneer. "That's why you left her, huh? You liked dating the rich little princess, but once you found out where her dad really was you booked it real fast, didn't you, *Mother-Tucker*?"

"Don't talk to him like that!" I hiss.

"You're *defending* him?" Billy erupts in disbelief. "He broke your fucking heart! *Now* you suddenly care so much, Tucker? Where were you when my sister was crying herself to sleep every night? When she couldn't even get out of bed?"

"Damn it, Billy, what happened between Tucker and me is none of your business!" I snap. I'm idly aware of Tucker's gaze boring into me from my peripheral vision, but Billy and I are in a stalemate, and it's an unfamiliar position for us. "I'm sorry you got hurt in all this. And it's my fault. I should have been stronger for you. But you can't take it out on Tuck, Billy, okay? Him and me—we were a mistake from the beginning. We're friends. We always should have just stayed friends. He cares about you, and I love you, and you've got to stop acting out. Please," I plead with him.

Billy visibly deflates, and I feel a flare of hope. "Just take me Sunday, okay? It's a holiday weekend and he just wants us for a couple hours. He said you haven't even taken his calls since you left for school."

My mouth gapes open. I thought he'd just been asking me for a ride, but this is more than that. My father is manipulating Billy into trying to facilitate a visit, and the thought that he would do that—

play on Billy's sympathy when he's obviously already dealing with so much—it infuriates me.

"I spoke to him after graduation," I defend, even though rationally I know it's beside the point. But at the end of the day, I just don't want to see him. I can't help it. I don't hate him, but it hurts to be around him. I resent him for his choices. For choosing his money over us, and for the choices he made in the first place that a decade later would cause me to lose the love of my life.

"That was five months ago!" Billy shouts, and I'm just done.

"Why do you even want to see Dad?" I cry. "He doesn't give a fuck about us! He doesn't care who he hurts or what the fallout might be! We're better off without him and you know it, and acting like an asshole isn't going to change that!"

Billy's eyes widen in shock. I've always bitten my tongue when it comes to my father, and I can't bear to watch my brother's face crumple in denial. I turn on my heel and rush away. I need to calm the hell down. Before I say something I can't take back.

Something else.

Chapter Twenty

Carleigh

Present Day

I find myself alone in the Caplans' laundry room, forcing deep breaths down my throat. I don't even bother turning on the light. I can't remember the last time I lost my cool like that with Billy. Already I'm flooded with shame. Even if every word I said about our father was true, that doesn't mean Billy needed to hear them. Especially when he's obviously already dealing with so much.

God, I can be such a jerk sometimes.

It's another minute before I even realize I'm crying, and probably ten more before I manage to get control of it. I don't actually know how much time has passed. I don't wear a watch and I left my phone in the den. I need to grab it and order a cab to get us home.

A knock sounds on the door and already I know it's Tucker. He doesn't wait for me to invite him in, just tentatively opens the door.

He's backlit by the soft glow from the hall and he looks impossibly tall and looming. The planes of his face are shadowed and hard, and utterly unfathomable. My stomach twists. The last thing I would ever intentionally do is remind him of my father, and Billy and I have just thrown the man smack into his handsome face. I'm surprised he even came looking for me. Unless he's here to revoke his offer of friendship, after all.

"You okay?" he asks gently.

I shrug. "I don't know what to say, Tucker," I murmur. "I don't know what has gotten into him." God, all the things Billy said to him. It's humiliating. Especially the picture he painted of my state after our breakup, which incidentally was pretty accurate.

Tucker looks around, his lips quirking in vague amusement. "What is it with us and laundry rooms?"

I let out a short laugh. "I don't know."

He takes a few steps closer, into the darkness I've been hiding in. I wish he wasn't so damn good-looking. His jaw and cheekbones are angled with perfect roughness, the deep green of his eyes almost celestial in the dim room. Men who look like him aren't like this. They're not kind and caring. They're cocky and frivolous. And he's those things, too. I suppose we're all all things. But Tucker is an impossibly perfect combination of those things. Perfect to me, anyway.

"Is he okay?" I ask him, only now realizing how selfish it was of me to leave Tucker with Billy after the way he treated him.

"He's texting on his phone and grimacing like a surly teenager." Tucker smiles vaguely.

I run my fingers through my hair, digging them into my scalp. "Thanks for trying," I murmur. "And I'm sorry he was such a…"

"Dick?" Tucker offers.

I sigh. "He's had his moments, I'll admit, but he's never been so intentionally hurtful before, you know? And I'm sorry he brought up, you know, our dad. And—"

Tucker's abrupt step forward cuts off my rambling. "Don't worry about me," he says softly, his brow furrowing deeply. "I didn't realize you weren't speaking to your father."

My stomach rolls at hearing him mention the man. I don't want him reminded of what I come from. "I'm not *not speaking* to him. I just haven't spoken to him in…a while." *Since we broke up.*

His jaw clenches as he considers me, and then he blows out a long breath. "Look, I know this is weird coming from me of all people, and the irony isn't lost on me, I assure you, but maybe you should take Billy for that visit, you know?"

I stare at him. That is probably the last thing I ever expected him to say.

I clear my suddenly dry throat. "I don't want to see him, Tuck. I don't even get why he would want to see me." I hate how shaky my voice comes out.

"Come on, Carl." I hate Tuck's pity even more. "For all his bravado, Billy is still just a kid. He needs his father, in whatever capacity he can get him. And your dad…whatever the fucked-up choices he made…It doesn't mean he doesn't love you guys."

"Doesn't it, though?"

"Carl." My name comes out like an admonishment.

"I lost everything because of that man."

"Did you?"

I blink at him. Why the hell is Tucker defending my father?

"You have friends who care about you, a kid brother who adores you—despite his current attitude. So your parents suck. They've always sucked. And you've always been okay. You'll always be okay. You'll get through it, whatever it is. You and Billy will work it out."

I stare at him. He's right. My father is to blame for a hell of a lot, but the more time passes, the more I realize he's not responsible for my losing Tuck. That was all me. For all those weeks he spent supposedly hating me, it was my refusal to tell him the truth he couldn't forgive, my choice to look him in the eye, even after he unknowingly revealed the significance of that truth, and continue to lie instead.

But it wasn't until I knew he returned my feelings that I felt secure enough to consider confiding in him, and I'd only just begun to work up the nerve to do just that when Tucker dropped the bombshell. And his hostility, the contempt he harbored, not only for the man he didn't know then was my father, but for his family—*me*—choked back my words every time I came close to forcing them out.

So I can resent my father all I want, but when it comes to my breakup with Tucker, the reality is, the blame is all mine.

And now I've let my resentment affect my little brother. I can't believe I said those things to him. Tucker is right. He needs our dad. And I told him the man doesn't care about him.

I flush with remorse. All Billy wanted was to see his father, and I selfishly denied him. Out of what? Spite?

"I need to talk to Billy," I murmur.

Tuck nods and steps out of my way. Vaguely I'm aware of him following me out of the laundry room and back toward the den. But all I find is Bits picking up our wineglasses.

"Have you seen Billy?" I ask her.

"He just headed to the front. Said his ride was here."

His ride?

I hear the front door slam shut and I rush around to the foyer after him. I fight with the lock on the door and Tucker has to step in to disengage it for me, and then I'm outside watching Billy climb into an unfamiliar car.

"Billy!" I call after him.

He turns back to me briefly. "I'm going to stay at Sadie's," he says in a defiant tone that sounds familiarly like my own. Sadie is Billy's other "best friend," aside from Kyle, though I've long suspected she means even more to him than that. I recognize her older brother, a high school senior, in the driver's seat, and as I take the steps to the car, Billy shuts the passenger door behind him. I see him mouth "let's go," and they drive off without a backward glance.

My feet crunch onto the gravel driveway as I realize three things. One—that I'm not wearing any shoes. Two—I don't have my car here. And three—that even if I did, I'm still way, way too drunk to drive.

I feel powerless, like I'm trying to swim with my arms and legs bound and weighted, and instead of resolving this thing with Billy and me, I'm just sinking further and further into the muck. I run back into the house, Tucker quietly following as I make my way back into the den to search frantically for my phone. I need to call Billy and order him back here immediately.

Where the hell is my phone?

It's not on the sofa where I left it, so I start tossing around throw pillows that Bits must have just straightened up, then start digging around in the couch cushions.

But I turn up empty.

"Damn it!" I slam my palm into the armrest.

Big hands grip my shoulders, halting the trembling I hadn't even registered. Tucker's deep, familiar voice urges me to calm down.

"I need to call Billy," I explain. "I can't find my damn phone."

Tuck turns me around, fingers rubbing my muscles until I submit, releasing the tension.

"He went to Sadie's," Tucker says.

I nod. "I know."

"Let him cool off."

I blink at him. "But—"

"You're just going to call and start shouting and demanding he come back here, and he's just going to refuse. You're just going to fight more tonight. And that's if he even answers." Tucker tells me what I already know, and unfortunately that makes it no less frustrating.

I sigh. "Yeah," I admit.

"Why don't you stay here tonight, and tomorrow I'll drive you over to Sadie's to talk to Billy."

"I should go home," I murmur.

"No. Beth already asked me if I was cool with you and Billy staying over, seeing as we're all too drunk to drive you home." He smiles wryly.

"I was going to order an Uber."

Beth walks in at that moment, obviously having overheard. "I already made up the second guest room for you, so enough of that. Let's open more wine. My parents finally went to sleep and now I can have some."

"Can you?" Tucker challenges, all overprotective big brother.

Beth pouts. "Oh, come on, Tuck. Just a little. Carl obviously needs someone to drink with." She winks at me and I offer her a smile.

"She can drink with me," Tucker counters.

"Oh, give it a rest, Tuck. She's almost seventeen. Remember what we were doing two years ago?" I remind him.

Tucker just sort of grunts, but Beth takes it as his approval, and she retrieves a bottle of Chianti from behind the bar.

"Here," Tucker mutters as he slips my cell phone from his pocket and hands it to me.

I gape at him, before adjusting to an indignant stare. "You let me ransack the place when you had it the whole time?"

Tucker shrugs shamelessly. "Didn't want you to flip out on Billy and make things worse."

I huff and walk over to Beth, turning my back on him, though rationally I know he probably did me a favor.

But with the next glass of wine, and the next after that, the evening rolls into night, and we slip into a comfortable tipsiness, talking and laughing about everything except our actual problems, and I'm grateful for it.

* * *

After we've all said good night, I lie awake in bed, staring at the ceiling, watching it lazily spin. I am most decidedly drunk. And I don't regret it for a second.

I feel so grateful to Tucker. For rescuing me last night, for his attempt to get through to Billy, and for his friendship. I want to thank him again, and I regret that we've already said our good nights and gone to bed. I can't stop thinking about his lopsided, intoxicated grin, his charming dimples, or his bellowing laugh. But I also think of the way his arms flexed under the sleeves of his T-shirt as he turned the corkscrew in the wine bottle. The way his breath whispered off my skin when he stood closer than necessary in the laundry room.

I think of the way he took me in his bedroom at the lacrosse house. Back when we were both still convinced he hated me. It was brutal, and punishing, but it was also unbelievably hot. That heat unfurls within me now, craving the only man who has ever been able to light its flame.

I find myself climbing out of bed in only my nightie before I even process what I'm doing. It's almost two in the morning, and as I creep out into the dark hall, I tell myself I just want to see if he's still awake. To thank him again. Though that doesn't explain why I don't bother to wrap a robe around myself.

Chapter Twenty-one

Carleigh

Present Day

It's only when I reach the door to his guest room that I admit to myself what I'm really here for. I'm not thinking with my heart. I've packed it securely away, along with my brain, which shut down and went dormant a good hour or so ago. My decisions are being made by a part of me that has been woefully neglected since the night I submitted to a heated and heartbreaking round of hate sex—well, hate from his end, anyway—all those weeks ago.

But his hate has fizzled, and now, he claims, we might be friends. It certainly felt like it tonight. And friends can hook up, can't they? We certainly did, when we were meant to be just that.

It's been so long since I've been touched, and only ever by him, and with this new version of friendship still so undefined, I wonder if we could possibly have the casual physical relationship we failed so epically at before. If only just this once. I cling to my hope that his desire for me didn't die with his love. That he can see past the resentment I know must still consume him, just enough to succumb to the attraction that has simmered between us since we were old enough to recognize it.

So what if he never really loved me? At least not in the way I'd understood. This—*this* is undeniable.

I curl my fingers into a fist, shaking with drink and nerves. And desire. But I think twice before knocking and drop my hand. Instead, I push the door open and creep into his room. I close it hastily behind me, forgetting to be quiet, and the soft bang sounds utterly explosive in the silence of the slumbering house.

But Tucker isn't asleep. The screen of his phone casts a spotlight on his face, his brow furrowed and his jaw clenched in a familiar look of fury, before it's eclipsed by his shock at my sudden interruption.

And then my gaze follows a little lower to where his hand emerges from beneath the bedspread, and I realize why his expression felt so familiar. Not fury after all, but raging lust.

It echoes between my legs and I rub my thighs together unconsciously. I bite my lip as he silences his phone, cutting off the moans of whoever he was watching so intently.

"Carl?" Tuck's husky voice resonates through my veins, scorching my blood.

"Hi." *God,* I seem to have completely forgotten how to be sexy.

Tucker scoots back and props himself up against the headboard. My gaze is transfixed onto his hand—the one that was just on the part of him I can't seem to stop thinking about—as it rakes his bed-mussed hair.

"What I said," he starts, "about Cap and Rory—"

"No, Tuck. I don't want to talk about that." Why would he bring that up *now*?

"But—"

"It doesn't matter. I get it, okay? I should have always gotten it."

"Carl—"

"*No.* Don't, Tuck. Please," I plead with him. "It doesn't matter now. Nothing does. Not the past. Only now, today. If we can be friends, then let's do that. Otherwise—"

"I do want that, Carl."

I stare at him and swallow anxiously, ignoring the sting of the wound he just so carelessly reopened. It's one thing to lose the thing you cherished above all else, but to discover you never had it at all? That it never even *existed*? That's a profoundly different burden to bear.

But I force those thoughts away. They serve no purpose, certainly not now, when all I want is to seduce him. But I'm realizing belatedly that in this new, unfamiliar dynamic of ours, I have no idea how to go about doing that.

I shift my weight between my bare feet, nervously running my teeth over my bottom lip as I wonder how to let him know what I'm really here for. But I can't help fearing his rejection, and I'm not sure I can bring myself to risk the humiliation it would bring.

Or maybe it's more than that. Maybe I don't want to risk finding out I was wrong—that his attraction to me expired along with our relationship after all.

He glances down at where he impressively tents the sheets. Of course, I know very well the extent of that impressiveness. But Tucker doesn't embarrass easily, if ever, and he smirks.

"Sorry about that, *friend*. I wasn't expecting company."

"Don't stop on my account." I mean to sound suggestive, but instead I come across as shy, almost submissive.

Tuck's nostrils flare, and I wonder if I'm actually turning him on. More.

I take two tentative steps toward the bed. My steps are slow and tremulous, but not out of reluctance or uncertainty.

"Don't tempt me, Carl," he warns. "I've been suffering this thing since you took your sweater off before dinner." He gestures to his arousal as his voice drops to a gravelly timbre that vibrates up my legs and settles in my lower belly.

I continue forward. "Maybe I want to tempt you."

One more step and I'll reach the foot of the bed. Tucker crawls toward me, his huge body needing no more than one movement to meet me.

"I can't be held accountable for my choices right now, Princess. You know I've been drinking all night. My judgment is a little slanted."

"So are your words." I giggle. "You're slurring a little," I slur at him. *A fine pair we make.*

"How drunk are you?" he asks cautiously.

"No more than you," I counter.

He eyes me warily, fists clenching the bedding on either side as if to keep them from grabbing for me.

This is on me now. And I know what I want. "I'm so lonely, Tuck. I know it doesn't mean anything. That we're just friends. But I'm sick of my vibrator and I don't want to go out and have some one-night stand with a stranger that will probably leave me disappointed and worse off than before. I—"

He jumps me. I'm hauled onto the bed and in one quick maneuver I'm pinned beneath him on the mattress, my arms held above my head, clasped at the wrists by one of his strong hands. My legs open of their own accord and his hips settle between them, my nightie riding up to my trembling belly.

"No. Fucking. Strangers," he growls, and then his mouth is ravaging my own, lips sliding and sucking, his tongue claiming and making its point with an angry possession.

Oh, God, yes.

"No motherfucking one-night stands." His mouth continues its assault along my jaw and down my throat, and then back up until he bites on my earlobe, more aggressive than he's ever been before—even the last time—but I revel in it. I need it. Because I was right. Love or not, this is real. This always was.

"Okay," I moan as his boxer-covered erection rubs along the center of me like throbbing steel, the flimsy lace of my underwear doing nothing to mitigate the heat between us, both figurative and literal.

"Fuck, you drive me crazy, Carl. I'm not sure if this is Thanksgiving or fucking Christmas. One minute I'm watching porn, imagining you tied to my headboard, and the next thing I know, you appear in this fucking thing that makes my dick nearly explode on the spot." He takes the satin of my nightie in his grip. "And I just want to rip it right open like a goddamn present."

I love the way he talks in bed. "So do it," I tell him.

He pulls back, eyes seeking confirmation. I nod and he tears the satin down the middle with one long, slow, panty-melting rip.

He slides the two straps down my shoulders and I expect him to dive into my breasts, but he doesn't. Instead he lets his eyes do the caressing, taking in my body like a long-lost love. It's almost romantic and I have to forcibly extinguish the false hope I know better than to believe in.

This is about sex, I remind myself. *Only sex*. But the message rings loud and clear when, the hunger in Tucker's gaze—no, *starvation*—is punctuated by his low growl of appreciation as my panties go the way of my nightie, discarded onto the bedside in tatters.

"You have no idea how much porn I've been watching lately."

I expect to see a smirk, but he's completely deadpan.

"And every time, Carl—every *motherfucking* time—no matter how much I tell myself to stop, I find myself closing my eyes and picturing *this*." His fingers trace lightly from my collarbone down between my breasts, circle around my navel, and then slowly trail lower and lower until they linger between my thighs. "And then only when I give in to thinking about you do I come like a goddamn freight train."

Tucker kisses me again, but it is decidedly slower, if not softer. He pulls back, his gaze blazing with promise as I await his lead. I'm so turned on I couldn't hide it if I wanted to. The evidence lingers on his fingers as he uses them to tease me.

"On your hands and knees," he orders. "I'm going to fuck you so hard you won't be able to take a deep breath tomorrow without feeling me."

No threat of romance there. Well, good. This is how this needs to go. The last time we hooked up, hate sex made sense for us at the time, and this needs to as well. None of that slow and passionate lovemaking. That's not us anymore. I'm no longer sure it ever really *was* us.

I comply with his demand immediately, wild for the pleasure I know he's good for, and he inhales a sharp breath of satisfaction. He loves me like this. Eager and obedient. He loves it because it's so at odds with who I am outside the bedroom, and he knows it's because of how much I want him, how good he makes me feel.

He folds his body over me, skin scorching skin, his hand fisting my hair and pulling my head back so his lips can worship my throat. I close my eyes to the sensation of his hot, wet mouth. He is a master with it. His hands wrap around to reclaim what's always been his, and a soft moan falls from my lips.

His hand slams over my mouth and I gasp, and then his voice is right in my ear, warning me to keep quiet, reminding me where we are. But I'm not in a guest bedroom in the Caplans' house. I'm in an alternate universe, removed from place and time, nowhere and everywhere, with someone I have no right to be with, the only man it feels right to be with.

Tucker tugs on my hair. "Can you keep quiet for me, baby?" He uses his fingers to make his request nearly impossible, and my voice hums against his hand, still covering my mouth.

"*Tsk, tsk, tsk*, Carl." He pulls his fingers away as punishment and I groan my grievance.

He chuckles softly before tentatively renewing his ministrations. I bite down on my bottom lip to keep my pleasure on mute.

Again he brings me close to the edge, and just as I'm about to tumble over, he slows right back down, and I let out a small growl, but Tucker doesn't seem to care. He's too busy enjoying his little game.

Another terse whimper as I close in on blissful oblivion and another cruel denial.

"Damn it, Tucker!" But it comes out a muffled mumble under

his massive palm and I nip at it to accentuate my frustration, and he laughs again, but removes his hand.

"Don't move," he orders, and starts kissing his way down my spine, tracing each vertebrae with his tongue. He palms both ass cheeks, administering a gentle slap to one and I flinch. It earns me another slap.

"I said *don't move*," he says, openly amused, as he squeezes and kneads. "*God* I love your ass. It is singularly the greatest ass in the history of asses."

I giggle, and he leans down to gently bite the ass he claims to love so much. But the sting vanishes as he redirects his attentions lower, and suddenly his mouth is between my thighs. He doesn't start out slow either, he just goes for it, licking and sucking, taking no prisoners, and it's barely a minute later that I grit my teeth so hard I feel it in my cheeks so my climax doesn't wake the entire household.

My limbs liquefy and I'm still half in outer space when he leans over me to whisper in my ear, "I'm going to fuck you now, Princess."

A soft whimper of agreement is all I can manage.

Tucker holds my hips in place as he slowly enters me. I hold my breath until he's fully seated inside me, listening to his long, strangled groan of relief.

"*How*, Carl? Huh? How do you feel even better than I fucking remember?" he growls.

I could ask him the same question, if I could form words.

Tucker moves in and out of me in long strokes, making sure I feel him in every way possible. He cages me with his vast body, owning and possessing me on the outside as he does within.

"Oh, *God*, Tuck," I croon.

"Yes, baby, that's right. *Me*. Not some stranger. Not some fucking one-night stand." He punctuates his words with powerful thrusts that grow in speed and force until he is utterly ravaging me. "No one could make you feel like this but me. You know that, right?"

I answer with a moan, and his strokes become punishing, utterly untamed.

"Answer me!" he commands.

"Yes. God, yes, Tuck. I know," I choke out. Of course I know. That is why I'm here, after all.

Tuck groans his satisfaction, and then suddenly he pulls himself from me, and I'm being thrown onto my back. But there isn't a moment to register his movement as he shoves inside, and my legs instinctively wrap around his waist.

And then I'm soaring over the edge, bursting in a rainbow of color and light, only mildly aware of taking him with me as he swallows the sounds of my release with his kiss.

Tucker collapses on top of me, making no move to relieve me of his weight. My arms and legs remain painstakingly wound around him, holding him to me, not yet ready to let him go.

I'll never be ready.

I banish the thought. It's a frightening truth that promises a lifetime of misery, and accepting it has implications I'd rather deny.

Eventually he does roll off of me, and I wait for his direction. If he wants me to leave now, I will. I offered him a casual hookup, and I can't begrudge him for holding me to that.

But he pulls me to him instead, tucking me neatly against his feverish body, and I sag into his embrace.

But most of me knows I really shouldn't. That we shouldn't be doing this at all. Friends don't cuddle—at least not after a mind-blowing round of passionate sex. Still, the rational part of me hasn't regained its control, and I snuggle into him, afraid to say a word, not wanting to break this spell.

He doesn't say anything for a long while either, and I wonder what he's thinking—if he's thinking at all.

Finally I risk turning my face up just enough to see his beautiful, pensive face watching me.

"Princess?"

"You probably shouldn't be calling me that," I reluctantly remind him.

"I know," he sighs. "But I called you that long before we were ever something more than friends, right? When we were just kids. It's like muscle memory, you know? There's just something that feels so wrong about not calling you that."

My eyes sting and my chest grows heavy with a sense of hopelessness at what we've become. "So much feels so wrong, Tuck." I hate the wistfulness in my voice. I hate that it sounds like I might cry. But most of all, I hate that I actually might.

"Carl—"

"I know. I'm sorry. I should go." I try to sit, but his arms tighten around me in protest.

"Stay," he says simply.

"Tuck…" I should argue, but there isn't a cell in my body that wants to.

"Just tonight." His voice is vaguely pleading, and I inwardly laugh at the irony. "This once. We'll chalk it up to being drunk."

"I don't think I'm drunk anymore."

"I don't think I was ever all that drunk, Princess."

And with that, he pulls me to his chest and I surrender to the bittersweet torture of it all.

I close my eyes, but I don't fall asleep. I don't really try to. Okay fine, I fight desperately to stay awake. To savor every moment of being back in his arms, achingly aware that it may very well be the last time.

If you told me a year ago that I would become this pathetic creature, starved and desperate for the slightest ounce of affection he might grant me, I'd have cackled like the overconfident, independent feminist I fancied myself. And maybe I'm still that, in most aspects of my life. But not now. Not here.

I try not to gasp as Tucker's arms tighten around me, revealing the fact that he's still very much awake. As does the reawakening of his body against mine.

I lift my chin to look at him, too stubborn to pull away from his chest to make proper eye contact. He's staring down at me, eyelids lowered, his expression uncharacteristically unscrupulous, serious, and I can't get a read on it.

His hand starts moving, his fingers ghosting along my cheekbone, tracing the lines of my jaw and throat. "You really are the most beautiful woman in existence," he murmurs.

My instinct is to scoff at that, but for some reason, it doesn't feel right. "Do you really believe that?" My voice is too small to be my own. It belongs to this new heartbroken, pathetic, desperate version of me I barely even know.

Tucker smirks ironically. "Well, it's not a line to get you into bed," he points out.

Touché.

His face softens. "Come on, Princess, why would I tell you anything other than the truth?"

I flinch. "Right. Lying is my job."

"I didn't mean it like that."

But it doesn't make it any less true.

Tucker sighs. "Let's not go there tonight."

I nod meekly. Because it's very much in my own interest not to go there tonight.

"So beautiful," he breathes. "Even the innocent parts. Especially them."

"Innocent parts?"

A smile. "Yeah." His finger sweeps down the line of my nose, doing a small jump off the end. "Like this little nose. Almost too small for your face, but not. Like a tiny ski slope," he murmurs. He continues downward, his finger dancing along my upper lip. "And this perfectly shaped bow."

He clasps my chin between his thumb and forefinger, lifting my gaze to his. "And your eyes. Flawless gemstones. Sometimes more emerald, sometimes jade. But always fucking captivating."

I can't help my blunt giggle. "When did you become so poetic?"

He smiles sheepishly. "Maybe I am drunk after all."

I return his smile.

"Or maybe I'm just a glutton for punishment," he murmurs, almost to himself.

But his words echo in my chest. "Is that what I am? A punishment?" I ask tentatively, trying to hide the sting of his words.

"Sometimes it feels that way," he admits.

I nod vaguely, frowning.

Tucker's fingertips absently continue their path downward, feathering along the column of my throat and along the swell of my breasts.

His lips quirk sideways into a lopsided smirk. "And then there are the parts that make me make bad decisions."

I know he's trying to lighten the mood, but all I register is another barb. "So now I'm a bad decision," I grumble.

He doesn't answer. We both know that's exactly what I am—what tonight is. Because nothing has changed. I am still the daughter of the man responsible for his father's death—the reason we could never have any real kind of future. And I'm still the girl who swore her love, only to lie to him for months even after I knew how profoundly the truth would affect him.

I wait for him to make his next move—to move his hand lower or roll me onto my back—but he doesn't. His hand instead finds the back of my head and he tucks my face into his neck, securing it with his chin, his fingers digging into my scalp like he'd do anything to keep me here. His other arm slings around my waist, and I both love and hate the fervor with which he holds me. It says so much and so little at the same time. Because I know it can't mean what it feels like it does.

Chapter Twenty-two

Carleigh

Present Day

Despite my attempts to evade sleep, the firm, warm pillow of Tucker's chest rises and falls with his slowing breaths, soothing me into unconsciousness. But it's when I drink that my dreams are most vivid, and tonight is no different. Unfortunately my subconscious chooses to bring me back to one of the worst mornings of my life.

I jog back toward our colossus of a home, in through the open, cast aluminum gates that are designed to pass for antique wrought iron. They are much like the rest of the house, and everything—and nearly everyone—in it. A veneer meant to portray wealth and success. Good fortune to be coveted. In reality, of course, they are fabricated from cheap material. Not salvaged from a French chateau, but manufactured in eastern Asia, likely by child laborers.

I set my foot on the front step and bend into a lunging stretch. I pushed myself more than usual on this run, and my hamstrings burn a little. Usually when I exert myself like this, it's motivated by frustration or distress. But not today.

This morning, when I woke up and pulled on my leggings

and sports bra, I did so wearing the perpetual grin that's barely left my face in weeks. The one that's left my cheeks as sore as certain other parts of me—all welcome side effects of Tucker Green.

I didn't know I could be this happy. It sounds trite, but it's completely true. Me, Carl Stanger, abandonment issues and all, is in love, content, and excited for the future.

Well, the near future, anyway.

Because just under the surface, the malignant truth of who my father is, and his connection to Tuck's family, ticks away like a time bomb, a constant threat of devastating ruin.

I've tried to tell him so many times. At one point I even convinced myself he could somehow get past it. But every time I opened my mouth, my mind would conjure the memory of his derisive scowl, his scornful words wishing my father a punishment far worse than prison, and equal suffering on his family—me. And every day I let pass, I just became more and more of a liar, hammering yet another nail into the coffin that will one day be the end of us.

But presented with the choice of losing him now or later, when my father is released and the truth inevitably comes out, I've made the selfish decision to keep him as long as possible. To embrace what we have while we have it, living in the moment, because living in constant fear of being found out would destroy the time we do have.

I stretch my arm over the front of my chest, and I'm startled by the roar of an engine, tires squealing too quickly to be safe for a driveway, and I spin to see who's so impatient.

Tucker's truck comes into view, and my heart, which has only just begun to calm from my run, jolts into warp speed as he steps out of his vehicle. My gaze trails up his denim-clad thighs, past narrow hips, and takes in the way the cotton of his T-shirt clings to his broad chest and shoulders. He was always gorgeous as a boy, but watching him grow into this—the epitome of masculine beauty and strength—has been nothing short of a privilege. And he's all mine.

I freeze when I finally pry my eyes from his body to catch his expression. It's remarkably unfamiliar and it takes me aback. It's utterly inscrutable, serious and solemn, and it is completely alien to me. Tucker has always worn what he's feeling freely on his face. Joy, anger, amusement, frustration, desire…But right now his face appears carved from stone—hard and unreadable—and fear coils deep in my gut.

Tucker takes in the house behind me, one he's seen a hundred times, but this time his lip curls with disdain.

It strikes me like a bolt of lightning, obliterating my fragile denial. He knows.

I've lied to Tucker for years, even when I knew just how monumentally my secrets would affect him, and any hope I might have that he could forgive me for it is snuffed out by the look on his face.

When he finally speaks, his voice is low and calm. "Tell me, Carl, where is your father?"

It takes three attempts at opening my mouth before words finally scrape their way out. "You know where he is."

Tucker nods.

"How did you find out?" I ask tremulously, though I'm not sure that it even matters now.

Tucker breathes out an ironic laugh. "I was worried about you." He shakes his head in self-reproach. "Had Cap's dad look into your dad…So you know where he is, I assume you know why he's there, then?"

I stare at him, waiting to wake up from this nightmare, but I know there's no escape. That I don't get him back at the end of this conversation.

Tucker takes my silence as the affirmative answer it is. "So every time you said your dad was away on business, or traveling, you just lied right to my face?"

I have no defense. I just stand here, blaringly silent.

"Every time I confided in you about my life, about my own dad, you just looked me in the eye, and lied, again and again?"

I say nothing.

"You knew exactly who your father was, but you just continued to lie, even in Miami, when..." He shoves his hand through his hair, shaking his head in condemnation, both for himself and for me. He huffs out another sardonic laugh. "When I thought I was confiding my darkest secrets to the girl I thought I fucking loved." He chokes on a sharp exhale.

The words echo cruelly in my mind—the girl I thought I loved...

"And you never said a goddamn word. Every time you told me you loved me—"

"I do love you, Tuck!" I cry. I may be as guilty as he says, but I never lied about that. Tucker has had my heart since we were kids. He will always have it, even if he doesn't want it anymore.

"You were the only person I talked to about him!" he snaps. *Were.*

"I know," I breathe.

"And you never thought you should speak the fuck up?" he snarls, but behind his fury lies a glimpse of betrayal, of the hurt I've caused him, that I can never take back.

"You would have hated me." *We were doomed no matter*

what I did, and I suspect that deep down, Tucker knows that, too.

"As opposed to now?" he sneers.

I flinch. "I didn't know what to do," I say pleadingly. "Tuck, I love you—"

"Did you know, or didn't you." It's a question, but not. Because he already knows the answer.

And I know without a doubt that it doesn't matter what I say. No excuse or explanation could ever suffice. For Tucker it is as simple as that one question, and the only answer I have is the one that will solidify our end.

There's an eternal pause while I try to go back in time and change the facts—rewrite our past to save our future. But that's not reality.

"I knew."

Tucker's jaw ticks and he swallows down his rage, his Adam's apple rolling between the tensed cords in his neck. "We're done," he says simply.

My throat dries up and my lungs seize. I can't speak. There'd be nothing to say even if I could. How can I argue? He deserves better and I deserve...this.

Devastation.

Tucker turns on his heel, heading toward his truck, and my tears well so thickly that my vision is blurred when he turns back, though unfortunately not enough to hide his ire, his blatant disgust. But it's more than that. More than just hatred. Tucker is looking at me like he doesn't even know me. Like I am unrecognizable—a stranger. It pierces through my chest, and his next words only slice deeper, gutting me until there is nothing left of what makes me me—until I am a stranger even to myself.

"Your father is evil," he spits. "He knew exactly what he was doing. He knew, and he took my dad on as a client any-

way. Knowing it would eventually ruin him. And it did. And my dad is dead because of it."

My heart stops beating; my stomach is weighted with lead. It's no worse than what he said in Miami, but hearing him repeat it, attribute it to my father…it guts me.

"That's who your family is. Who you are. Stangers—Stanleys, whatever your fucking names are," he spits. "Just put on a convincing smile and hide your betrayals behind it, right? And you're the worst of them, Carleigh, because you claimed to fucking love me." He chokes on the word, the only sign of vulnerability in his armor of derision. "And all along, you looked me in the eye, knowing what he did, distracting me by spreading your fucking legs. Never mind that my father was dead because of yours."

Every word cuts me deep, carving away another piece of me. The man I love has essentially just called me a traitor and a whore. But it's his calling me Carleigh that stings most of all—as he knew it would.

Yet I deserve every word.

"Liars, all of you," he mumbles before walking back to his truck. He stops at the driver's door. "I never want to see you again, Carleigh Stanger. Do you understand me? I fucking hate you. Fuck, I don't even fucking know you!"

He opens the door, and finally my feet manage to free themselves and I take an automatic step in his direction. And then another. I don't have a defense, but my body is physically incapable of just letting him walk away from me without trying to do something—anything.

But his palm slams against the roof of his truck and his warning thunders through the entire three-acre property. It shocks my bones, paralyzing me except for an insuppressible trembling.

"Stay the hell away from me," he orders. "I mean it." And then he climbs into his truck and peels out of my driveway.

*   *   *

I linger half in a dream, wondering why I feel as if I'm waking up inside my past. My fingers automatically reach to the base of my throat for the white gold crown charm Tucker gave me before graduation last year, a reminder that I would always be his *princess*. But *always* didn't last, and my fingers come up empty as I recall tearing off the necklace and stuffing it unceremoniously into my bathroom drawer minutes after he broke my heart.

The subtle scent of fresh spring soap, aftershave, and the faint musk of last night's sweat ambush my senses. My eyes flutter open to find dawn breaking in through the window shades. It's still early enough that I doubt anyone else will be awake for a while, but I know that whether it's minutes or an hour, once Tucker's eyes open, it won't be long before I'm asked to leave.

It takes no more than another second or two to register the pattern of his breathing, too lively to indicate sleep, and I stiffen above him. I swallow anxiously and reluctantly look up.

He's watching me, gaze impassive, but his arms don't move. His fingertips dance, feather-light along the small of my back, and I wonder if that's what woke me. I clear my throat, though I have no idea what to say in this moment. But Tucker speaks first.

"This can't happen again. You know that, right?"

I nod. Because I do know. We'll never be friends if we blur the lines with this. Not just the sex. Not even mostly the sex. But *this*. This intimacy. This is what could break us. Break me.

In an instant, the haze of last night's lust begins to lift, and anxiety settles in its place. Because I doubt I could survive his breaking my heart a second time, and that's precisely what I'm setting myself up for. I've laid my own trap, and I need to free myself before it's too late.

"We shouldn't be lying in bed like this," I tell him.

His smile is wistful. "I know."

But he makes no move to disentangle himself from me. Instead, he does the opposite, his hand leisurely roving up the avenue of my spine, as if it's going for a Sunday drive.

I shrug it from my body and sit up, startling him. "Stop doing that," I snap.

"Touching you?" His brow furrows.

"No! *Yes*. Touching me, and agreeing with me but continuing this…this *affection* anyway."

"Sorry," he murmurs halfheartedly.

"No you're not."

He frowns as I yank the sheet out from under the bedspread and drape it around myself.

"Maybe it was wrong of me," I admit. "Coming here last night. Maybe I was stupid to believe we could just hook up and walk away. Or that I could. But Tucker, if you wanted to fuck me, then why couldn't you just fuck me?" My words drown in regret. "You can't say these things—about my eyes, how you think about me…You can't stare at me the way you do, or call me *Princess*. It isn't fair."

"Carl—"

"*No*, Tuck. You know how I feel about you. And you said it your-self. When you love someone more than your own life, you don't let them go for anything." I stare at him meaningfully. "*Anything*."

Tucker shakes his head, eyes lined with exasperation. "Carl, I tried to talk to you about that last night—"

"No, Tuck. I get it now," I assure him. "And maybe I always should have known. But *you* must have, right? Or at least you do now."

"Know what?" His brow furrows deeply, vaguely bewildered.

I glare at him, trying to determine if he's undermining my intelligence or if I'm somehow not making sense. But I know him better than that, and as easy as it would be to vilify him right now, I can't lie to myself. "Maybe you really did believe it at the time," I admit. "That you loved me back."

"Carl—"

"Or maybe you really did love me. Just not enough, you know?" I don't bother fighting the tears. He's seen them plenty of times now anyway, and if there's ever been a time to let them flow, it's now.

And Tuck stops his attempts to explain. He blinks at me, stunned silent, and I suspect he's finally grasping the weight of his own words. And I realize that even though he's the one who said them, it's only now that he's really understanding their implications. The truth is obvious and cruel, and with it I can stop wondering. I can stop analyzing his words and guessing at their meaning. Because now I know.

Eventually Tucker sighs, raking his fingers through his hair as he searches for words to placate me. But I don't want his guilt, and I definitely don't want his pity.

I avert my gaze and it lands on his overnight bag, three feet to my right. I force in a deep breath and shove my hand inside it, pulling out the first piece of clothing I can grab, grateful to discover it's a T-shirt—fitted for him, but oversized for me. I hastily slip it on.

I look back at him, feeling utterly defeated. "You let me go."

We both know now what that says about his love, but this isn't about blame—this is about acceptance. It's about moving forward. "So *let me go*," I beg him, and then hurry out the door.

Chapter Twenty-three

Carleigh

Present Day

Mercifully I make it to my room without incident. I walk numbly to the en suite bathroom and brush my teeth. I wash my face and for once don't bother with even the most basic makeup. I just don't care. I hastily yank Tucker's T-shirt over my head, desperate to rid my body of his scent, but it clings to my skin, and I wonder if I will ever truly be able to wash it away. I eye the shower, but decide I'd rather do that at home; I need to get out of here as fast as possible.

I put on clean underwear and a bra, and pull a pair of jeans from my overnight bag, absently checking my phone, which I'd left charging overnight.

I freeze. *What the hell?*

I have more than twenty missed calls from both a local number I don't recognize and my mother, as well as several texts.

Call me.

Call me Carleigh.

Where are you

Call me now.

And more of the same, all starting around three in the morning.

I'm vaguely aware of light knocking on my door, but I can't

respond. Instead I tap my phone to listen to one of the several voice-mails.

The anxiety ripping through me makes it difficult to process the messages, but I make out key words.

North Shore LIJ Hospital.

William Stanger, Junior.

Critical condition.

My throat dries and my lungs seize and I suck in gasping breaths.

"Carl?" I think I hear Tucker's voice, but I'm frantically trying to dial my mother. *"You have reached Nicole Stanger…"*

I hang up and tap her contact again, and again it goes straight to fucking voicemail!

Her son is in the goddamn hospital and she can't be bothered to answer her goddamn phone?

"Carl?" Tucker's inquisitive voice is right behind me, but I don't turn. I can't deal with him right now. I need to focus. I can't panic. I need to get to Billy.

I try to force in a deep breath and open the contact for a cab company I have in my phone.

"Carl!" Tucker growls, and he grabs me and spins me to face him.

I watch his expression morph from frustration to concern.

"What is it?" he demands.

"Long Island Taxi," the man on the other end of the line answers.

I stare at Tucker as I speak into the phone. "I need a cab from— Shit. What's the address here? 14 Briarcliff? Or 16?" I ask Tucker.

But instead of answering me, the asshole grabs my phone and hangs up!

"What the fuck are you doing?" I shriek. I try to grab for my phone, but he dodges me.

"Carl!" he snaps, holding my phone behind his back with one hand, the other gripping my shoulder and giving it a firm shake. "Tell. Me. What. Happened," he says carefully.

"I don't know!" I wail frantically. "Billy's in the hospital, and I need to get there. *Now*."

Tucker's eyes widen in shock for a split second before he grabs my jeans from the bed and tosses them at me. "Get dressed," he orders.

"I need my phone to call a cab," I plead with him.

"Clothes, Carl. Now. I'm driving you." His tone brooks no argument, and I'm in no position to turn down a ride.

The moment I fasten my jeans, he's already pulling a shirt over my head, holding it while I shove my arms through the sleeves. I don't take the time to even look at what he selected, but the scent tells me it's the T-shirt I just removed—the one that reeks of my past.

He hands me my phone. "Meet me downstairs." And then he rushes off, presumably to dress himself.

Five minutes later I'm frantically pacing the Caplans' foyer when Tucker races down the stairs.

He doesn't stop his momentum, just wraps his hand around my forearm and keeps moving. "Let's go," he murmurs, dragging me along, and I have to jog to keep up with his purposeful stride.

"North Shore?" he asks, and I nod as he pulls out of the Caplans' circular drive, the tires kicking up gravel as they spin into speed.

My knee bounces with nerves and I try dialing my mother twice more before I accept that her phone is obviously turned off. I rake my fingers through my long, unkempt hair, over and over as I try to steady my racing pulse.

Billy has to be okay. There is simply no other option.

I listen to voicemail after voicemail, each as vague as the last. All I am able to deduce is that Billy was in a car accident with one other minor, that there was alcohol involved, and that he is in critical condition. Finally I get to the last message from my mother telling me that she was getting on a plane home, which explains her phone being off. I hadn't even considered that she would fly home, and how sad is that?

Tucker pulls off the exit to the hospital, but at least on the highway we were in constant motion. Now, on the local streets, every red light makes me want to pull my hair out. Tucker squeezes my thigh to get my attention.

"Hey. We're almost there. Try to stay calm, okay?"

"You stay calm, Tucker!" I hiss.

"Carl—"

"No! You know what? This is your fault!" I accuse. "He was drinking again! This is all your influence! He fucking idolizes you, and your bullshit party-boy attitude!"

Tucker just keeps driving, and his non-response agitates me even more.

"I knew I shouldn't have just let him go last night," I growl. "I can't believe I listened to you! You have no idea what it's like to have responsibility! You just do whatever the fuck you want without any thought of the consequences." I lay into him, consumed by guilt that I let Billy go last night, to risk his life in his adolescent stupidity while I was busy screwing my ex.

"Carl." Tucker doesn't say anything more, and my frustration compounds.

But instead of scolding him more, I abruptly break out into desperate sobs, and I hide my face in my hands, hating that he's seeing me in such a vulnerable state. Despite the fact that I just essentially attacked him, blamed him for a fucking car accident like a raving bitch, Tucker still offers me comfort. He wraps his hand around the nape of my neck, his thumb soothing back and forth over my skin, his grip rubbing muscles tensed in dread.

I keep my face shielded by my hands, suffocating in self-loathing, drowning in fear and shame. Because I know—knew even as I said those horrible things to him—that this isn't Tuck's fault. It's mine.

But I don't have the courage to take it back. I can't do anything except surrender to the sensation of Tucker's hand, which I'm quite certain is the only thing holding me together.

Tucker pulls up in front of the emergency entrance to the hospital five minutes later, and I'm out of the car before he even comes to a complete stop, leaving him to go find parking.

My head is spinning, but my feet carry me forward to the reception desk, where a nurse is typing something into her computer. My disembodied voice tells her Billy's name, and answers her obligatory questions.

Who am I? *His sister.*

Am I a minor? *No.*

Where is his legal guardian? *Our mother's out of the country.*

And your father?

My patience expires suddenly and explosively, and then I'm screaming at her, demanding to see my baby brother, barely registering that the alien hysterical wailing is actually coming from me.

I'm grabbed from behind and I twist violently, trying to wrench myself from his grip.

It's his scent that gives him away.

"Carl. Stop." Tucker's voice issues the sharp command.

I stop squirming and he turns me to face him, bringing his face down to my eye level and blocking out the chaos of the room.

"I need to see him!" I plead.

He nods, unwavering army green steadying me. "Take a deep breath for me, okay?"

I do. I force my lungs full of air, and when I release the breath, my pulse seems to settle just the slightest bit.

Tucker nods his approval. He grabs my hand and leans over the desk. "Billy Stanger. William. We need to see him."

"And you are?"

"Tucker Green."

"Are you family?"

"Uh—"

"Yes. He's family," I interject.

The nurse sighs. "If you could both have a seat in the waiting room, I'll let the doctors know you've arrived, and someone will be out to speak with you—"

"Why can't we just see him?!" I snap, and Tucker squeezes my hand—in support or in warning, I have no idea.

"William Stanger's family?" a Middle Eastern woman in blue medical scrubs calls from the double doors, and I rush over to her, hauling Tucker after me.

"I'm Dr. Solamed. I'm the trauma surgeon assigned to William's case."

"Billy," I automatically correct, for no relevant reason I can discern.

"Billy," the doctor agrees. "You're his sister, I presume?"

"Yes." My voice is a shaky whisper, betraying how ill-equipped I am to handle the stress of the situation. Tucker takes it as his cue, squeezing my hand once more before taking over.

"Carleigh is Billy's sister. I'm Tucker Green, her fiancé. Can we see Billy now?"

"Billy is currently in surgery…"

She keeps talking, but her words whirl together in an undertow of senselessness, only the most terrifying crashing into my consciousness—*blunt trauma, internal bleeding, blood loss, surgery*—but they swim around in no particular order, and I can't decipher any sense. I'm vaguely aware of Tucker asking questions, but all I deduce is that Billy lost a lot of blood, and that they're in surgery trying to find and repair the source of the internal bleeding.

Before I can even focus enough to speak, let alone verbalize any of the infinite questions rolling around in my head, Dr. Solamed is excusing herself, and I'm staring at the new face of a nurse, who tells us to follow her. It takes me another second to understand, and I hold on to Tuck as we dutifully follow her down the bright, fluorescent hall.

The nurse gestures ahead to a small family waiting room more private than the main one of the ER, and tells us to have a seat—that we'll be updated when there's news. Tucker thanks her. I say nothing. When she's a distance away, he squeezes my hand to get my attention, and I look up at him, terrified he's going to leave me now. That he's going to drop me off in that room to await news of Billy's fate without him.

"Please don't go." My voice quakes in distress, and Tucker's brow furrows, deep and daunted.

"Go where, Carl?"

I bite my bottom lip to stop its pitiful quivering. *Anywhere but here.*

He shakes his head, eyes wide with incredulity. "I don't know whether to be offended that you think so little of me, or feel guilty that I've caused you to."

I open my mouth to tell him I think no such thing, but he holds up his hand to stop me.

"Hey, it's fine, okay? Now's not the time anyway. But to be clear, I don't go anywhere until you want me gone, got it?"

Today, I silently correct him. He won't go anywhere *today*. Because my brother is fighting for his life and Tucker is loyal and supportive in ways he's only ever found me lacking. But still, the concrete dread weighing me into the ground eases marginally with his promise.

"What I was going to say, is that I didn't want you to be freaked out about the fiancé thing. I just had to say it, so they would talk to me, you know? If they know I'm not family they might make me wait out there." He gestures in the direction we came from. "It was just the best way I could think of to be able to help you. If you want me to, you know, talk to a doctor, or whatever you need."

I nod dimly.

"I mean it, Carl. Anything you need from me, you tell me."

Another nod. Tucker's unease is palpable. And I get it. Me frozen in fear, unable to form coherent sentences—he doesn't know this me. *I* don't know this me.

My vision blurs with tears, blinding me with fear and guilt. "I'm sorry I said those things in the car," I tell him. "I didn't mean them."

Tucker smiles sadly. "I know, Princess."

"I'm so sorry," I sob, apologizing for so much more than he knows.

He draws me into his arms in a way I don't deserve, consoling and protecting. But he can't protect me from the stifling regret squeezing my lungs, suffocating me. I can't force my legs to work—to walk into this new room where I'm meant to await news that could change everything, forever. Where they'll eventually either tell me that Billy will be okay, or…I can't even finish the thought.

Billy has his entire life ahead of him. And it's my fault he's here right now, fighting for it. How can I ever forgive myself for our argument? For driving him away and out into the night, upset and reckless. And I just let him go, got drunk like the pitiful excuse for a role model I apparently am, and distracted myself with sex.

I choke on another sob and Tucker's arms band tighter around me.

"He's a tough kid, Carl. A fighter. Like his big sister. If anyone can pull through this, it's Billy," Tucker promises. But right now I don't feel like the strong girl he makes me out to be. I feel like I'm crumbling.

"I called him an *asshole*, Tuck." I cry feebly into his T-shirt. "It's the last thing I said to him."

I look up at Tucker to find his gaze flowing with deep, army green sympathy.

"What if it's the last thing I ever say to him?" My voice shatters and I bury my face in his chest as I choke on more sobs, my body racking with them.

"Billy knows how much you love him, Carl. One fight can't overshadow the lifetime of love you've shown that kid. Anyone who knows you guys can see how much he adores you, and how lucky he is to have you. He's in that operating room fighting his ass off because you showed him how."

I try to let Tuck's word comfort me, but I'm just so fucking scared. Billy's just a kid.

Tuck runs his hand up and down my back, soothing me, before he takes my hand and leads me into the fated waiting room. In it, huddled together, are Chris and Gina Lahey, Kyle's parents. I blink at them in confusion. Did the hospital call them when they couldn't reach me? Or was Kyle the other minor in the car? All the doctor was able to tell me is that another minor was driving and was also injured.

Gina slowly stands and pulls me into a hug. Her movements are delayed, her eyes a little dazed, and it seems like more than just fear for her son. Like she's been sedated.

"I'm so sorry, Carleigh. So sorry," she apologizes over and over, tears washing more mascara down the charcoal trails on her cheeks.

"They wouldn't give us any updates on Billy," Chris—who is either calmer or just in better control of his emotions—explains.

"He's in surgery." My voice sounds like it's coming from someone else, the words still so foreign that it's easier to deny they belong to me at all.

"Is he going to be okay?" Gina asks.

My lip trembles as I open my mouth to speak, but a sharp exhale replaces my voice, which I seem to have lost in my tightening throat.

"He lost a lot of blood," Tucker answers for me. "They're doing a laparotomy to deduce the extent of the internal injuries, and, you know, close them up."

My gaze swings to his. He obviously caught more details than I was able to, and I'm eternally grateful for it.

"Kyle?" The one word is all I can manage.

Gina's eyes rush with more tears, and even Chris's voice is choked by fear. "He tore his spleen in the accident. They're probably going to have to take it out."

"Oh God," I gasp.

"He can live without his spleen," Tucker assures me.

I nod at him. Yes, we watched that episode of *Grey's Anatomy* together.

"Why don't you sit down, sweetie," Gina offers, but I shake my head. I need to stay on my feet.

"What happened?" I ask them. Because I don't understand. Billy was supposed to be staying at Sadie's. I saw him get in the car with her brother myself. So why was he out, in the middle of the night, drunk, with a thirteen-year-old behind the wheel—and one he told me just hours earlier he wasn't even currently speaking to?

"Billy got into a fight with Sadie. He texted Kyle and asked him to come get him. Told him to bring a forty-ounce. It sounded like they've done this before, Carleigh. Stolen my car and driven around at night. Drinking at Memorial Park. I had no idea. I swear I had no idea!" Gina dissolves into sobs.

My heart races in shock and shame. How could I not know my brother was acting out so badly? I knew he was having a hard time. But *this*?

"What do you mean it sounded like they've done this before?" Tucker demands.

Chris digs into the pocket of his slacks and pulls out what must be Kyle's cell phone.

I shake my head. "They didn't give me Billy's phone." They didn't give me anything of Billy's. My pulse skips erratically in panic and my chest constricts painfully as my brain refuses to conclude what it might mean that Kyle's phone survived the accident and Billy's may not have.

But Gina is shaking her head. "He left it at home."

I suck in a gulp of air as the relief settles over me—a temporary reprieve. "Why would he do that?"

"He knows we have an app that tracks it. We've caught him sneaking out before. He must have left it in his room so if we checked, it would show he was there," Chris explains.

"Billy texted him just after one in the morning saying he got into a big fight with Sadie. He said he left her house and was walking north on Lincoln, and for Kyle to pick him up. According to the chat it was the first text he's sent him in weeks. Unless Kyle's been deleting them."

"No. They got into a stupid fight. They weren't talking," I tell them.

Gina rakes her artfully manicured fingers through her disheveled chestnut hair. "I didn't know that. How didn't I know my own son wasn't speaking to his best friend? What kind of mother am I?" Her voice grows progressively more hysterical with each word, and Chris pulls her into his chest and murmurs soft reassurances.

I have to look away. Because I am equally at fault. *What kind of a sister am I?* Tucker wraps his hand around the nape of my neck, resuming his soothing ministrations of earlier before tugging me into his side.

"I swear to God, as soon as he's all healed up, I'm going to kick his ass," Tucker promises.

Yeah. Me too.

A doctor I don't recognize enters the room. "Mr. and Mrs. Lahey," he says.

I hold my breath.

"Kyle is out of surgery. We were able to do a subtotal splenectomy. Meaning we removed only part of his spleen."

"He's going to be okay?" Gina asks, her voice pleading.

"Barring any complications, yes."

There is a collective exhale of relief.

"Can we see him?"

The doctor calls a nurse over and directs her where to take the Laheys. Gina turns back at the last second to ask me to keep them updated on Billy. I nod numbly.

I'm relieved Kyle is okay. Truly I am. But I'm also envious. I hate that I am still in limbo. I just want the doctor to come back and tell me that Billy is going to be fine. To have a nurse take me to go see him. So I can hug him and scold him and apologize to him. Is that so much to ask?

Tucker pulls me to a chair and urges me to sit with him. We don't speak. We just sit, his arm curled around my shoulders, keeping me in one piece.

An hour passes. Then another. No one updates us. Tucker offers to get me coffee, but I refuse to release his hand. Eventually I get a text from my mother telling me she's landed and is on her way to the hospital. She asks about Billy, and I text her back what I know.

It's the moment I stop staring at the door that Dr. Solamed suddenly appears. I jump up so fast I nearly topple over, and Tucker's strong hands dart out to brace me. But even he can't steady my racing pulse as I realize I can't get a read on the doctor's expression, and I hold my breath as my stomach rolls with dread.

Chapter Twenty-four

Carleigh

Present Day

I open my mouth to ask how Billy is, but Dr. Solamed is already talking.

"He's out of surgery. The blunt trauma from the accident caused two bleeding sites, which we were able to locate and repair. We also gave him a blood transfusion."

My mouth gapes open. "So…he's…"

"He's okay then, right?" Tucker translates for me.

She nods. "He's being transferred to a private recovery room. He'll be out for a while still, and then he'll need to stay here for at least a few more days for observation, but barring any complications, William is going to be fine."

It's a physical unburdening. I can feel the weight of my terror lift from my shoulders, feel it ease from my joints and muscles.

Billy's okay.

I fling myself at Tucker and he catches me in a bear hug and presses his lips to my forehead.

"I told you, Princess," he whispers. "A fighter. Just like his sister."

"Can we see him?" I ask the doctor.

"As soon as he's done being transferred I'll have someone show you to his room."

"Thank you. Thank you so much," I tell her.

She smiles warmly. "Carleigh, do you by any chance know your blood type? Billy's already had a transfusion, but it would be great to get some more, just in case."

"Um, AB positive," I tell her.

"Oh, okay. William is AB negative," she says. "What about your fiancé?"

My fiancé.

"O negative," Tucker says.

Dr. Solamed grins widely. "Ah, a universal donor. Please consider donating; we could always use more O neg."

Tucker nods. "Whatever I can do to help."

"Fantastic. A nurse will be by in a minute to take you, if that's all right?"

Tucker nods and the doctor leaves.

"Sorry," he murmurs. "I know it's weird. The fiancé thing. But it was the only way—"

"I know," I interrupt him. "You said that already. I get it. It doesn't bother me, Tuck." Not that he called himself my fiancé, anyway. What bothers me is knowing that whisper of happiness I get from hearing it will never be real.

"It does bother you, Carl," he challenges.

I frown at him.

"Maybe not that specifically, but you made your thoughts pretty clear at Cap's earlier. And we need to discuss it."

Huh? "Tuck—"

"Not now. I know not now. You need to focus on Billy. But we need to talk, Princess. Don't think you get to say that shit to me and walk away. I get a chance to respond. Just, *fuck*, not right now." He runs his hand through his hair in frustration.

But I don't get why. Why do we need to discuss this more? And why won't he stop fucking calling me *Princess*?

A nurse knocks softly on the doorjamb and asks if now is a good time to take "the universal donor" to give blood.

"Is that all I am to you people? A bag of blood?" Tucker teases, and the twenty-something nurse smiles and bats her eyelashes. I don't miss her blush, either.

I roll my eyes. *A bag of blood, and a piece of meat, apparently.*

"You good if I go do this now, Carl?" he asks.

I nod. "Yeah. My mother will be here any minute," I assure him.

He squeezes my shoulder, and then leaves with the blushy nurse.

Then I'm alone, pacing back and forth, waiting for someone to come tell me I can see my brother.

"Carleigh!" my mother cries, and I turn and run to her. She wraps me in a hug and I'm surprised to find her face red and tear-streaked. "Have you heard anything?"

"He's okay!" And then I'm crying, too, and we hold each other in comfort and narrowly avoided tragedy, and vaguely I think that I can't remember the last time my mother sincerely embraced me, or offered me any kind of affection outside of her trademark air kisses. But her emotion right now is genuine, and I glimpse a piece of Nicole Stanger I never knew existed.

*   *   *

My mom and I make small talk to ease the tension as we're led to Billy's hospital room. She talks about her awful flight, and even though she focuses on the "unbearable" experience of flying coach, the strain in her eyes tells me her fear for her son was the real reason for her discomfort. She apologizes for me having to wait out the news alone, and I tell her that I wasn't alone. That Tucker is here. Her only response is a vague sound of fleeting interest and a passing mention that she wasn't aware Tucker and I were even speaking.

The nurse outside Billy's hospital room warns us that he isn't expected to wake for a couple of hours still, and gestures for us to go on in.

I startle when I see him. He looks so pale, so young. A youthful face attached to a body that's too big for a child, too small for a man.

My mother settles in a chair at his bedside, but I find myself unable to sit. I stare at her as she holds his hand, and tells his unconscious form that he's going to be okay. It just feels so inauthentic. Even if her emotions seem real now, I can't help but resent her arbitrary parenting. As if she can pick and choose when to actually be a mother. Sure, she flew home as soon as she learned he'd been hurt, but the fact that I was surprised when she did—that speaks volumes. And the reality is, if she wasn't so goddamn absent most of the time, Billy wouldn't be acting out like this in the first place.

We could have lost him.

I could have lost him.

I swipe angrily at the tears that well in my eyes, banishing them in frustration.

"Kyle's okay, too, though they took out half his spleen," I murmur, and my mother looks over at me. "He was driving the car. They were both drinking."

Her eyebrows pinch together as best they can through the Botox freezing her facial muscles. "Why would the Laheys let him drive? He doesn't have his license."

I gape at her. *Is she serious?* "Of course he doesn't have his license! He's fucking thirteen!"

"Carleigh—" she admonishes my expletive, but I ignore her.

"And what do you mean *let him drive?* The same way *you* 'let' Billy drink. They didn't *know*! He snuck out of the house and stole the damn car!"

My mother swallows anxiously. "Boys acting out," she says uncertainly.

I shake my head. "This is more than that and you know it. Billy needs to talk to someone. He needs a *parent*."

My mother sighs. "I know you're upset about Billy, but that doesn't give you the right to say hurtful things."

Oh, that's rich coming from her. "Right. I forgot you're the only one allowed to criticize. But at least your opinions are about things that *matter*. I mean, who cares how your lifestyle is affecting your kids, as long as I wear the right clothes, right, Mom?" My sarcasm is harsh, but I'm sick of biting my tongue. I can't be Billy's mother, especially now that I'm not even living at home.

My mother rolls her eyes, as if I'm just some hormonal teenager acting out. "*Now* Billy was drinking because of my *lifestyle*?" she says dismissively. "Is he the first teen to ever try alcohol?"

"Are you for real?" I snap. "Billy didn't just *try* alcohol. He's *been* drinking! Remember Halloween?" My God, if denial were an Olympic sport, this woman would hold every world record.

She sighs. "Okay, Carleigh. I hear you. He's obviously going through a phase. I'll talk to him about his behavior."

I glare at her. "What about your behavior?"

She frowns—or she would if she could move her forehead—but instead of the righteous indignation I expect, she seems anxious. But she hides it quickly and expertly. "And what behavior would that be, exactly?"

I rub my palm down my face. "How about spending more time abroad than at home? Billy needs a mother."

My mother glares at me. "There's nothing wrong with raising independent children. My parents traveled all the time, and I turned out just fine."

Debatable. "I think the operative word, Mom, is *raising*."

Her eyes narrow. "You know what, Carleigh? You may be an

adult, but you're only eighteen. Despite what you seem to think, you don't know everything. My life hasn't exactly been all cupcakes and caviar, you know. For all intents and purposes, I am a single mother, and in spite of your attitude, I'd say you turned out pretty damn well."

No thanks to you. But it's the first compliment she's paid me in recent memory that wasn't entirely backhanded, and as I take in her pursed lips and squared shoulders, I realize I'm not being fair. For all of Nicole Stanger's faults, she did teach me pride and resilience, and if I'm going to blame her for her shortcomings, then surely I can acknowledge her strengths. But she doesn't give me the chance.

"You know, I love your father, but it isn't exactly the life I always dreamed of—being on constant guard to keep up appearances, to protect our family's reputation. Do you think I enjoy being separated from my husband? Barely seeing him every couple of months? It's hardly ideal."

I stare at her, incredulous. "*You're* the one who's so obsessed with *reputation*! Maybe if we just told people the truth, we wouldn't have to be on constant guard! Maybe if Billy didn't have to lie to even his best friends, he wouldn't be under so much goddamned stress!"

"For such a know-it-all you really are delusional, Carleigh. What do you think your childhood would have been like if all of your friends knew where your father was? Do you think they would have been compassionate and understanding?"

"Maybe." But it's only part true. Because my closest friends wouldn't judge me for my father's choices, but not all "friends" in high school necessarily do the word justice.

My mom scoffs. "They would have judged us all for it, not just your dad. They would have read the articles, and believed all of the terrible things they said, even the exaggerations, and they'd have reserved their sympathy for the people who lost their investments, Carleigh. Not us, I assure you."

I swallow past the lump in my throat. Because I know that in many ways she's right.

But she can't resist taking things a step too far. "Look what happened with Tucker. And *he* was supposed to love you."

Chapter Twenty-five

Tucker

Present Day

I pause outside the room the nurse told me Billy was moved to, still munching on the sugar cookie they gave me after I donated what looked like a hell of a lot more blood than I'd been expecting. A little sugar in exchange for the flow of life—*seems like a fair trade.*

It's Nicole Stanger's haughty voice that's stopped me outside the door. It echoed down the hall as I approached and it almost made me turn back in the other direction.

"Whatever, Mom. I don't want to talk about Tucker." I flinch at the sound of my name. I should probably just go. Carl doesn't need me anymore now that she has her mom, but I don't want to abandon her on the off chance she might need me again.

Nicole sighs, long-winded and dramatic. "Still blaming yourself for the entire breakup, then?"

"Just leave it alone, Mom." Carl already sounds exasperated. It's probably because they're talking about me, and it stings that I'm a sore subject for her.

Another sigh from Nicole. "You know, I'm not heartless. I know it's hard to get over your first boyfriend. But *that's* what he is, Carleigh. Your *first* boyfriend, probably of many. I know when you're a teenager you feel everything times a hundred, but all this *love* and *soul mate* business…it's not real. If it was, he'd still be here."

I am still here! I want to shout.

"Figuratively, I mean," she amends. But she's still not right, and I grit my teeth, restraining myself from barging in there and correcting her. But her words mirror Carl's sentiment from back at Cap's house. Her assertion that if I truly loved her I wouldn't have let her go for anything. Hell, it was my own words that put the idea in her head. And they're true.

Because I *haven't* let her go.

I've tried to, I really have, but despite how much she hurt me, I. Can't. Stop. Loving. Her.

That's what I came to tell her when I stomped into her room at Cap's. That she's fucking blind if she thinks I've let her go. That I may have broken up with her, but that I still belong to her in every way that counts.

"Yeah," Carl murmurs so softly it almost doesn't reach my clandestine spot outside the door. "I'm starting to realize that."

It's a knife to my heart. But it also sends my mind racing. She's starting to realize *what*, exactly? Is it the same bullshit she said back at Cap's about how I never loved her enough? Or is it something she's realizing about herself? About her own feelings?

Fuck.

"The more time passes, the more you'll realize how ridiculous it was for him to blame you for what Dad did," Nicole tells her.

"He didn't," Carl corrects her mother, and I thank God she at least knows that. But her voice sounds so small, so defeated, and it makes my chest ache. "I mean, maybe he would have, you know, resented me for it no matter what. Subconsciously, or whatever. But he broke up with me because I'm a liar." She lets out a self-deprecating laugh. "He used to tell me everything. Things he never tells anyone. And I sat there and never said a thing."

My arms tense at my sides and my hands clench into fists. I don't want to fucking hear this shit. I don't want to be reminded of how she hurt me. I need it to not be true. Because I'm already realizing I have no choice but to forgive her.

"What could you have said?" Nicole scoffs. "You didn't know there was any connection to the Greens."

Wait, *what*?

"I did know." I have to strain to hear Carl's response, but at least it makes sense, unlike Nicole's comment. "And even before that…He told me all kinds of things, and I *wanted* to tell him the truth, but you'd drilled it so deep that we couldn't. That everyone would judge us. The same things you've told Billy. And I'd been selling the lies for so long—about Dad being away on business, or traveling…By the time I realized I wanted to confide in Tuck…" Another scornful laugh. "I didn't want him to think I was a *liar*."

I dig my fingernails into my palms just to do something with my agitation. It's fucked having to just stand here, unable to correct either of them. Because, yeah, it stung to realize she'd spent years spinning lies right to my face, but it was hearing her admit she knew about her father's connection to mine, that while I'd spent the past year telling her about him—about his *suicide*—she knew the whole time her own father contributed to it, that I found unforgivable. Until recently, at least.

"So it's my fault, then?" Nicole says with a righteous indignation she never earned.

Carl's tone deflates again with her sigh. "No. It's nobody's fault but my own. I was scared that if I told Tuck the truth about Dad, and he knew I'd been lying to him since day one—that I wasn't the *Princess* he'd made me out to be all these years…I thought he'd just like, be over it."

"You can't blame yourself for that. Men haven't exactly been a stable force in your life," Nicole says matter-of-factly, but Carl continues like she didn't even hear her.

"It wasn't until spring break that he told me how he felt, and we were actually, you know, official. And I was thinking to myself that I was finally ready to tell him about, just, everything. But he told me before I had the chance. About his dad being Dad's client."

My heart stops beating in my chest. *I* told her? *No.* She knew the whole time. That's what she said. *She knew.* That was the whole fucking point.

"I mean, he didn't know he was talking about Dad. He just called him *Stanley*, and all this stuff about how he deserved worse than prison. And then that his family deserved to suffer like Tuck and his mom did." Carl chokes on a small sob, and I want so desperately to see her face and know for certain that what she's saying is real. But I can't. Because I can't be caught eavesdropping, and because my world is spinning so fast I'm not sure I could find my footing.

"And how is that your fault?"

Carl's deep breath is audible even in the hall. "I should have just told him," she says resolutely. "The second I realized what he was saying. The second he said *Stanley*. I should have told him. I should have told him a hundred times since. And I tried. I really did. But every time I opened my mouth, I just saw that hate in his eyes all over again, heard those angry words. I didn't think I could bear him looking at me like that."

Nicole mutters something I can't make out.

"Turns out I could bear it, though. Since he ended up hating me anyway."

"I thought you were friends now."

"I guess."

Carl huffs before dissolving into some rant about how Billy should be able to talk about his life and his family to whoever he wants, and how Nicole should be around more, but I stop listening.

Or I can't listen anymore. Because it's all muffled by the sound of my blood rushing through my ears as I try to make sense of what I just heard.

Carl didn't know until Miami?

No. That's impossible. I fucking asked her. I asked her and I will never forget hearing the sound of the two words that clawed my fucking heart out of my chest, leaving behind a worthless, gaping, bloody hole.

I knew.

But...*when* did she know? And does it matter? She said it herself—she should have told me that morning in Miami. She should have told me a thousand times since. I shouldn't have had to find out the way I did.

But as I recall our exchange that morning on spring break, the hateful words I hadn't known were about her own father—about *her*—I'm not sure I can even blame her. I'm not sure I would have done things any differently if it had been me in her position.

Fuck.

I need to move. I need to make sense of what I just heard. Because my entire life was destroyed on those two words—words that told me she'd known all along—and if they aren't true...then I might have ended us for *nothing*.

I make my way through the automatic double doors, desperate for the frigid late-November air to breathe some life back into me.

I think about the morning I learned the truth. When Cap came over that morning, it took all of two seconds of seeing his face for me to know my world was about to be catapulted off its axis.

He didn't want to tell me what his father had discovered. But more than that, he didn't want to witness what he knew it would do to me, and I had to practically bulldoze it out of him.

I lived less than ten minutes from Carl, but that drive took an eternity. The whole time I kept telling myself she didn't know. She *couldn't* know. Her parents must have woven an elaborate lie about why her father was in prison. Or at the very least she couldn't have known about his business alias. That when I'd told her what happened to my dad, said the name *Stanley*, she hadn't made the connection. I told myself she was innocent in all this. She *had* to be.

I knew it was crazy, but no crazier than her being the one weaving the lies. Or so I told myself.

But one look at my face told her why I was there, and one look at hers shattered my pathetic, delusional fantasy.

And in that instant, we were destroyed. I'd never had a whole lot of faith in relationships in general, but I had all the faith in the world in my girl, and she obliterated it with those two words.

I knew.

But she *didn't* fucking know. Not the whole time, at least. Not until I'd decided to unload my family's dirty laundry on her back in Miami, and inadvertently told her it was her own father who'd ruined mine, before I ever even knew it myself.

I lean back against the brick façade of the hospital, still trying to make sense of what I've done.

But my mind is still lost in that morning, battered by the memory of my own scathing rant, and the stunned look on Carl's face as I watched her cry freely, telltale tears of guilt just rolling down her beautiful face.

I was so sure she'd earned that guilt. That she'd known all along what her father did to mine. That she'd kept it a secret to manipulate me—to trick me into believing she was really the perfect princess I'd always seen her as—desperate to maintain the picture of wealth and success she and her mother had painstakingly painted all these years. The one where her father's only crime was neglecting his daughter in favor of creating *more* wealth and success.

I let myself believe she'd done it all on purpose. Taken advantage of my affection for her, skillfully played the role of the poor little rich girl to steal my sympathy. That she'd fucking conned me into loving her.

But even as I try to rationalize my thought process that day—and so many days since—I know I was disastrously wrong. What's worse is realizing I should have known it all along. Because everything I've ever known about the girl has been at odds with the narrative of manipulation and betrayal I've tried to piece together since that morning. The truth is it never fit Carl. And now I fucking know why.

Regret and frustration buzz through me, and I turn to face the wall, searching for the calm I need to go back upstairs. But it evades me, and instead of finding composure, I slam my palm into the unforgiving brick in front of me. Because how could Carl have just stood there and let me say that shit to her? Why didn't she fucking *defend* herself?

But I already know why.

Carl thought I was *right*. That she deserved my wrath and my contempt. So that morning, when I asked her if she knew, she had no idea I'd meant *all along*. She'd known since I told her in Miami and never spoke up, and in her mind that alone was an unforgivable betrayal.

And I didn't help things any when I called her a liar, and—*fuck*—accused her of spreading her legs to distract me like she was some kind of goddamn common whore. And yet she's spent months accepting my scorn as if she fucking deserved it.

I think of the horrible things I've said to her, the way I've treated her, and I can't fucking breathe. I told her she was a *stranger*. That we were fucking *nothing*—that we never were.

I don't know what the hell to do. Carl is up there thinking I never even really loved her; meanwhile it was just hours ago that I finally realized I never stopped—that I never could. And now—*now* I find out I never had a reason to *try* to stop? What the fuck do I do with that? Run up there and beg her forgiveness?

I know what I *should* do. What a better man would do. He would accept his failure, and let her go. But I already know I'm not capable of that. I'm far too selfish.

My phone buzzes with a text.

Are you still giving blood? 8:52 am

God, I suck. I'm supposed to be here for her, and I fled like a damned coward.

All done. Was a little lightheaded, went outside to get some air 8:53 am

Are you ok?? 8:53 am

And now I'm making her worry. Fuck me.

I'm good Princess. On my way up now. Billy ok? 8:54 am

Yeah, just waiting for him to wake up 8:55 am

When I walk through the door to Billy's hospital room, Carl is curled up in an armchair, texting. She startles when she notices me staring at her from the doorway. She's so beautiful, even in her uncertainty, and it takes me a moment to pull myself together. She stands up, smoothing my shirt, and I can't help my small smile. The sight of her affects me in the usual, physical way, and I hope it isn't noticeable. Her gaze darts between mine and the phone in my hand as it buzzes with a text.

You don't have to stay, if you don't want.

I frown. "Do you want me to go?"

She quickly shakes her head, uncharacteristic nerves etched in the creases around her eyes. She thinks I'm here out of pity, and why wouldn't she? I look at Billy, so small in the hospital bed. He's got tubes running every which way and he looks like he may never wake up. Before I can even process the horror of that thought, I hear someone say my name, and I get the feeling it's not for the first time.

"I said hello, Tucker."

My shoulders tense and I try to conceal my distaste. I offer a cordial nod. "Mrs. Stanger." *Stanley*.

Carl's anxiety is palpable, and I don't want to be the cause of it. I don't know what role her mother did or didn't play in her father's crimes, but I know the woman well enough to suspect that even if she didn't encourage him—which I find hard to believe—she more than likely knew what he was up to.

A smile as artificial as her lips themselves stretches wide, no other part of her face moving so much as a twitch. "You can still call me Nicole. No need to be formal just because you and Carleigh aren't dating."

No thanks.

Carl pulls nervously at a loose thread on the hem of her— *my*—shirt, glancing between her mother and me as if anticipating some sort of blowout. Her mother scarcely notices.

"Rory's coming in a bit," Carl murmurs, and I recognize she's offering me another out.

"Oh good," her mother replies without so much as peeking up from her phone. "Have her stop by the house and bring you something to wear. And perhaps some makeup and a hairbrush. Since you obviously rushed out of bed."

I have to hold in my snort. Nicole Stanger can't see that her daughter is a nervous fucking wreck, but *this* she notices.

Carl chews her bottom lip, a rare demure blush painting her cheeks, no doubt recalling just whose bed she rushed out of.

"Carl looks beautiful," I challenge, unable to stop myself, and they both stare at me.

Nicole turns back to her daughter and gives her an obvious once-over. "Surely you'd agree that she could make herself a bit more…" She gestures breezily. "*Presentable*," she finishes.

I can't help my eye roll. I sure as shit would *not* agree. Carl looks gorgeous as fuck in my shirt. But Nicole's attention is already back on her phone.

"Do you want to grab a cup of coffee?" I ask Carl, wanting to get both her and myself away from her obnoxious mother.

Carl nods. "You want some, Mom?"

"Hmm. I doubt they have anything remotely drinkable here."

Carl doesn't argue. She seems just as eager to escape that room. "Text me if Billy wakes up before I'm back." And she grabs my hand and pulls me away.

"You okay?" I ask her.

She breathes out a long-winded sigh. "Yeah. Just…You know how she is."

"Sure do," I agree. "Can't fucking stand how she criticizes you."

Carl shrugs. "Whatever, I'm used to her. Honestly, Tuck, I don't even care right now. I'm just glad Billy's going to be okay."

Yeah, me too. It would've absolutely killed me to watch Carl go through that—to see her suffer that kind of anguish, completely powerless to do a damn thing to fix it for her. But beyond that, I really do love that kid. And after last night, I realize I didn't just bail on Carl, but I abandoned Billy, too.

It's just more regrets to add to the pile—*the fucking landfill*—and more mistakes I vow to correct. That is, after I kick his ass for taking such a stupid fucking risk and scaring the living shit out of his Carl. And me.

Speaking of correcting mistakes…

I spot a small, empty waiting room and change direction without warning, pulling Carl inside. "I've been thinking about what you said back at Cap's—"

She shakes her head anxiously. "We don't have to do this, Tuck. I get it—"

"You get nothing."

She blinks at me.

"You're wrong." *Shit.* I'm in such a fucked-up position. I need to apologize—to tell her I was wrong for doubting her. For assuming the worst, and letting myself vilify her when I fucking *knew* better. But it's not the time for that. And until it is, I can't exactly tell her she was wrong back at Cap's, either. Instead, I need to work on rebuilding our friendship. I need Carl to start seeing me the way she used to. As someone who cares about her, someone she can lean on—someone she can trust, and talk to—instead of the guy who only ever spits spite at worst or ignores her at best.

In the back of my mind I realize I'm doing the same thing I crucified Carl for—waiting until I'm ready to confess something that might affect us both deeply. I only hope she can forgive me for it in turn.

I blow out a slow exhale and offer her an apology far less sufficient than the one she deserves. "But look, you're also right. I should be more sensitive. And I'm sorry, okay?"

"You're sorry…" Carl looks like she can't quite believe what she's hearing.

More fucking sorry than you know. I take a step forward, suddenly standing too close for the *friend* I insisted I could be.

I'm scared she'll retreat. But she doesn't. Her breathing picks up and she licks her lush, pink lips, making my blood rush south.

My hand cups her face all on its own volition, and between the blood donation and my hard-on I'm lucky if there's any blood left for my brain to function. But mercifully there appears to be just enough to stop myself from doing something dangerous like kiss her.

But my thumb strokes her cheek and I start to get lost in my favorite emerald color. Carl gasps at my touch, and my T-shirt slips off of her shoulder. *And there goes the rest of the blood.* Other than our mutual labored breathing, the room is blaringly silent, so the sound of Carl's phone buzzing in her hand is sudden and jarring.

My gaze automatically lands on the source of the interruption, and though I honestly don't mean to peek at the screen, some words—or names—just jump out at you.

Zayne.

I try to keep the snake of jealousy in its coiled slumber, but that fucker has the same reaction to Zayne's name as I do. To strike.

"You should take that," I murmur, fighting not to let my emotions show as I walk out the door.

I wait in the hall, because I told her I wouldn't leave until she told me to, and I won't abandon her ever again. But I'm not going to beg for her attention either. If she wants to talk to Zayne, then what the fuck does she need me for?

Chapter Twenty-six

Tucker

Present Day

We linger in the cafeteria after we finish our coffees, but I know Carl wants to be there when Billy wakes up, so we head back to his room before too long. It's still a few hours before he finally stirs, and I hang back in the corner while Carl and Nicole crowd his bed, softly calling his name and trying to get hold of his attention.

Rory, Cap, and Beth showed up sometime during the past couple of hours, and they decide to go down to the gift shop to "find something to brighten up Billy's hospital room." It's a thinly veiled excuse to give the Stangers some family time, and rationally I know I should go with them, but I need to make sure Carl is okay first.

A nurse comes in and checks Billy's vitals, which appear to be strong, and warns us to "keep the excitement down." It isn't until she's long gone that Billy starts with questions about his accident, and Carl bursts into tears.

She sobs through her account of Thanksgiving night and the following morning, but Billy remembers most of what led him to be in that car with Kyle. I was worried he might hold on to his resentment from his fight with Carl, but he doesn't. He apologizes and apologizes, still pretty dazed, and I take their emotional exchange as my cue to give them some privacy after all.

I take a walk around the hospital, unable to stop myself from wondering if Carl actually still wants me around. I head back to Billy's room for the third or fourth time—I've lost count—and find Nicole out in the hall talking to a doctor, and Carl still at his bedside, the two siblings laughing about God only knows what.

I hang back in the doorway, not wanting to interrupt them, especially now that they both seem to be in better moods. But Billy spots me, and I wait an interminable beat for his reaction to my presence. But he doesn't say anything, he just stares, gaze impassive, if a little unfocused from the drugs.

"Glad to see you giggling like a little girl again," I tease him. I can't help it. This is the ball-busting brotherly relationship we've always had. At least until the breakup.

To my great relief, Billy's mouth twists into an uneven smirk. "Whatever, Mother-Tucker. You're just jealous they gave me the *goooood* drugs."

I make my way to his bed, standing beside Carl, who looks up at me with a relieved smile. I crack a few more jokes through a strained smirk, and Billy and Carl laugh and laugh like last night—or this morning—never even happened. Nicole pops her head in to tell us she's going to Kitchen Cabaret to pick up some soup so Billy doesn't have to eat the "hospital garbage."

My phone buzzes with a text from Cap saying they're on their way back up. *Good.* They can keep Carl company while I talk to Billy.

I brush my palm over Carl's partially exposed shoulder, rubbing my thumb into the muscle at the base of her neck the way she likes. She automatically turns into my touch, and meets my gaze.

"Cap texted that they're on their way up. Do you think I could have a minute with Billy?"

Carl's brows pinch together in vague confusion, but she doesn't question me. "Yeah. Of course," she murmurs, and climbs from her armchair. She forces an unsure smile and tells Billy she'll be right outside.

I hate her uncertainty, especially when it's about me, and I grab her hand as she passes, squeezing once to reassure her. *Trust me.*

She squeezes back—blind faith I don't deserve. But I fucking will.

Billy watches me cautiously as I approach the chair Carl just vacated. If I wasn't sure whether or not he remembered what he said last night, his wary expression would easily give him away. I take the seat at his bedside, raising my eyebrows with mock melodrama—an attempt at easing the stress of these insane circumstances we've landed in—and Billy's lip twitches in an affirming half-smile. "How you feeling?" I ask.

He tries to shrug, but winces. "Sore," he admits. "But not too bad, thanks to modern medicine." He grins sloppily and gestures to the IV currently delivering the morphine that's making his injuries tolerable.

I scoot forward in my chair. "Modern medicine did a lot more today than make you high, you know."

Billy's grin fades instantly. "I know." His somber tone speaks volumes.

But I don't hold back. I tell him. I tell him how Carl reacted when she heard about his accident, how she broke down in the car ride over. I explain how she fought to keep it together while we waited in purgatory for news, and how she blamed herself for everything. I describe her face when his doctor walked into that waiting room to deliver the verdict of his surgery, and her palpable relief at the outcome. I tell him she took such a deep breath that I swore I felt her suck the air from the room.

And then I tell him how it feels to get the opposite news, and what it's like to know you'll never see someone you love again. I describe what it's like to wake up having forgotten for just a second they're gone forever, only to have reality come crashing back, again and again, every day for months…years.

I tell him all of it.

He cries. My eyes might water a bit. But he gets it. And I know there's more going on under the surface with him, and at some point I hope to talk about the underlying reasons for his acting out. But now is not the time for that. I'm just grateful that when Carl returns to Billy's room with our friends, her brother has a little more insight into how much she loves him, and how his actions affect her. And I can only hope that whatever he's dealing with, he'll think twice before he risks his life, or his sister's heart.

* * *

Now that Billy has been released from the hospital and Nicole Stanger has apparently decided to stick around and be a mother for a change, Carl is back at school and finally acting more like herself.

I cornered Ben in our garage our first day back on campus, and listened to him swear up and down that he had no ill intentions. That he knows giving Carl the meds and not explaining exactly what they were was stupid. I know that as an athlete he's taken them many times for injuries, and I also know plenty of people end up using them for reasons they weren't prescribed for. Others, still, take them recreationally. So it's possible he really didn't think it was a big deal. *Fucking idiot.*

He admitted he was wrong, and apologized profusely to both me and Carl. He understands how dangerous what he did was, or so he claims. I'm not so sure. I still want to kick his ass, but Carl asked me to back off. I begged her to report him, but she fucking believes him, and she doesn't want to ruin his entire future over one stupid mistake. She's way too compassionate. He didn't think twice before potentially risking her fucking life, and he deserves whatever punishment he'd get. But reluctantly, I have to let Carl make this call. And at least for now, she has. So I focus on other things.

We present our creative marketing project this week, and as we film our final scene at the lax house of a couple hooking up in the laundry room—or trying to—I can't stop staring at Carl. She caught me twice already, and the third time I don't bother looking away. I just blatantly eye-fuck her until she has to bite her bottom lip red to suppress her self-satisfied smile. It's her own fault. She knows what those flouncy little skirts do to me—the way the hem flirts with her supple thighs—and I doubt I'm imagining that extra sway in her hips as she walks to and from the kitchen to get a cold bottle of water. I can use a little cooling down myself, and I grab it from her and suck down half the thing in three big gulps.

"Hey." She swats me on the biceps and takes it back from me.

I'm so distracted by her that I barely notice Julia call cut, and thank our volunteer-actors. She has an evening class, so she says good-bye and walks them out. Manny checks today's file on his computer, making sure it automatically uploaded from his camera via the Cloud, as he's programmed it to do.

"Are these our releases?" Carl asks, staring wide-eyed at the organized mess of paperwork I have on the table. They are my responsibility, and though Carl has helped with a few of the guys who were reluctant to sign, we also needed signatures from the random girls who were in the background at our parties, and that is where I shined.

"Yup."

"Ugh, Tucker. You're so messy," she admonishes, and she starts alphabetizing them.

"Hey, my job was to get them signed, not make them pretty," I remind her, and she rolls her eyes. My chest swells. I've missed this. Having Carl not be afraid to talk back to me. To challenge me.

"While you two perfect the form of argument as foreplay, I'll be over at my dorm creating a masterpiece," Manny teases a little bitterly as he packs up his computer.

"What?" Carl gasps, but I just grin. She can deny it all she wants, but there's only one part of that Manny got wrong—we've had this shit perfected for years.

Manny rolls his eyes and salutes us before he leaves, but his calling us out has obviously unsettled Carl, and that bugs me.

"These are all crinkled," she complains as she tries to flatten a sheet of paper on the folding table we keep in the laundry room for—well—folding.

"At least they're all signed," I counter.

"Not *all*," she corrects me, but she's wrong.

I come up behind her and reach around her on both sides to find the release that had given us so much trouble. A particularly entertaining reaction by a girl who hadn't gotten the memo that the jokes were scripted. She heard half a line about spiking the punch with roofies and she lost her shit on Manny and me. It's gold for our video, but without her release, we couldn't use it. Neither Carl nor Manny could convince her to sign, but two days ago I discovered her weakness—a little begging and a big smile—and got the job done.

I find the paper in question and smooth it out in front of Carl.

She spins to face me. "You got it!"

I smile smugly down at her, so close my chest brushes hers with every inhale.

"How?"

"Employed my secret weapon." I shrug.

"And what's that?" I don't miss her breathy tone, and my jeans feel infinitely tighter as a result.

"What do you think?" I raise my eyebrows. I'm just fucking with her at this point, but what can I say? I can't resist. "Fair is fair, right? A release in exchange for…a *release*."

She eyes me dubiously, like she's actually considering whether or not I would do something like that, and admittedly, it stings a little, but I'm also massively amused.

Carl shoves at my chest, but I don't let her move me. "Ugh!

You're so disgusting," she hisses, and accepting she can't push me away, she turns away from me—never mind that she's trapped between me and the table as she pretends to busy herself with the paperwork again.

I lean down to her ear. "What's the matter, Princess? I thought you'd be pleased. I took one for the team."

"Don't fucking call me that."

I ignore her ire. *God* do I love riling her up. But if she's going to believe that I whored myself out for a goddamn school project, then she's going to fucking pay for it. "What's wrong, Carl? You jealous?" I taunt her with my breath on the back of her neck.

Her aggravation doesn't hide the goosebumps that rise—or the flush that sweeps over her skin. I grit my teeth to stop myself from tasting it.

"Why would I be jealous, Tucker? I've fucking had you, haven't I? Plenty of times," she sneers.

I love her wrath, but hate the whisper of vulnerability—the aggrieved undertone I know would kill her to know I've picked up on.

"I guess your secret weapon is losing its magic."

Oh, hell no. I keep my mouth close, letting my lips lightly graze her earlobe as I speak. "Is that why your breathing's gone shallow?" I lean farther down and brush them over her carotid artery. "Or why your pulse is racing?"

Both her breathing and pulse respond by accelerating even more, but her shoulders stiffen in an attempt to resist the effect I have on her. "No. *That's* because you're making me uncomfortable," she lies. Fortunately, I have mastered the art of reading Carl Stanger.

"The feeling is fucking mutual," I growl, and I close my hands around her sensuous hips, pulling them back the half inch that separates our lower bodies, and I lightly press the evidence of my raging *discomfort* into her enticing ass.

Carl gasps before she can stifle it, her head lolling against my shoulder in a fleeting surrender before she regains control and squares her stance. "Too bad I have standards."

"Have they gone up in the past week?" I scoff, gently scraping over the skin of her throat with my teeth, soothing it with my tongue, unable to resist a taste.

"Fuck you, Tucker."

I spin her to face me. Now I'm fucking pissed. She tries to look away so I grip her jaw and force eye contact. "How well do you know me?" I demand.

"Not as well as I thought!" she seethes.

My gaze narrows. "Clearly fucking not, if you actually think I would fuck some stranger to get her to sign a damn release form!"

Carl's eyes widen so slightly and briefly I know anyone but me would've missed her combined relief and remorse, but it's instantly crushed by a wall of defensiveness. "Well, how the hell am I supposed to know who you do or don't fuck." It isn't a question.

I know her attitude is out of self-preservation, born of insecurity, and I also know I'm to blame. I bend enough to level with her, softening my tone. "You're the *only* person who knows that, Carl." *You're the only person I'm fucking*. Even though we've only hooked up twice in the past few months, so we're not technically *fucking*. But as I try to get our friendship back on track, even if I know it's too soon to pursue something more, I see no reason for us to torture ourselves with abstinence. We've never been ones to do things in traditional order.

I can see the moment I win her over, but I've gotten her so worked up that her chest heaves with her aggravated breathing, and her gorgeous tits surge with every inhale.

"My eyes are up here, Tucker," she scolds, biting her bottom lip to conceal her mirth.

I continue to stare at her chest. "Yes, baby, but your perfect tits are right here." I step away to lock the door, then return to her, enjoying her wide-eyed stare. My hand slowly skates from her hip, up along her side until my fingers tease the outline of her breast. I meet her gaze, finding hers glazed with desire, letting her see how much I want her. My fingers follow the edge of her top, trailing along her neckline, my middle finger slipping just under the cotton fabric.

Both of us stare at my hand, and I take my time, but she does nothing to stop me. I let only the tip of that one finger explore the silky skin just under her neckline, watching with satisfaction as it leaves a trail of goosebumps in its wake. She has the most beautiful cleavage. Her breasts aren't the biggest, but they are perfectly round and full—an ample handful of pale, unmarred flesh, untouched by the sun or anything else. Except me.

I take the half step that brings me flush against her irresistible body, and my other hand reaches up to cup her jaw and angle her face upward. She seems so delicate—breakable.

"Tuck," she breathes. I love the sound of my name on her lips—always have.

"You make me crazy," I admit. I've said it before, many times, and it's no less true now than it ever was before. "I want you so much I can't even think straight when you're around." I drop my hand from her chest to her thigh, tracing the line where hem meets skin. "You knew exactly what this skirt would do to me."

She unconsciously licks her plump, pink lips, calling to me like a fucking siren, and my mouth crashes down on hers without another thought. Her arms fling around my neck as we consume each other, our breaths mixing and our tongues wrestling.

I pin her against the table, desperate to get closer, my tongue ravaging her mouth with impatience. Carl is practically gasping with need, and when her hips grind into my thigh, I lose all sense of control. I grab hold of both ass cheeks and lift her, lining our bodies up just right and guiding her long, gorgeous legs around my waist, and I place her on the table.

Better. But still far from good enough. The table is too low—or I'm too tall, so without disentangling from her hot mouth, I pick her back up and spin us around, setting her on the washing machine instead.

Perfect. Our hips are perfectly aligned, and I swell to the point of pain, my dick knowing how close it is to its target. Its *home.*

Her knees part and I charge between them, grabbing her hips and hauling her forward, but she pushes me back, startling me until I realize she means to rid us of the barriers separating our bodies.

Good fucking thinking.

Carl gets to work on obstacle number one—my jeans—unfastening my belt buckle. Her hands don't stop long enough for me to remove her shirt, so I just push her cardigan over her shoulders and shove her tank top up over her bra.

Fuck. Me.

She *knows* how much I love her in white lace. Most girls think a black or red bra is hotter, but Carl introduced me to the erotic appeal of white—a color I'd never considered sexy before I saw it on her when we first hooked up. And it's no less powerful right now, her pert, pink peaks peeking through the transparent fabric, and my mouth lowers to the swell of the bounty it holds, kissing and tasting.

Carl moans, and the sweet, sexy sound shatters the last of my patience. I shove my jeans and boxer briefs down my thighs, freeing my furious hard-on, and flip her skirt up around her waist.

I nearly come on the spot.

White. Fucking. Lace. Panties.

I have to close my eyes and suck in a gulp of air to regain control of myself. Carl makes matters worse, boldly wrapping her fingers around me, and I forcefully snatch her wrists before she can stroke me and end this before it begins.

She peeks up at me from beneath her long, lacquered lashes, mouth slightly parted and eyes hooded in lust. It strikes me that I am the only man who has ever seen her like this, and in this moment I know that I would do absolutely anything to keep it that way.

I run my hands up her thighs, spreading them further as I go, losing myself more and more to my lust with every inch they separate. My fingers grasp the thin, sheer material, and I yank them from her body in one swift tear. Carl gasps at my savagery, but with her most intimate of places bare and open for me, she can't hide how turned on she is.

I take her mouth in a fierce kiss, and she surrenders to me, her mouth as open as the rest of her, and I can take no more. "No man will ever make you feel like this, Princess. Only me." I need her to know this. To make sure that she knows there's no point in looking at other men while we're not technically together.

She winces, as if I said it as a punishment of some kind.

"I know." Her tone is resigned, almost sad, and it makes my chest ache. She still thinks I'd never be with her again, not for real, and I want so much to tell her she's wrong. That I would take her back today if she'd have me. But then I'd also have to tell her I treated her like garbage for months for no fucking reason. That I had the audacity to believe she knew about my father all along, and chose to keep quiet. And I know her well enough to foresee the indignation, the hurt that would cause, and I'm not ready for that. First I need to remind her how good we are together, make it up to her before she even realizes I've fucked up. And I know one way to start.

I stroke between her legs, marveling at how ready she already is for me. "I'm going to fuck this hard, Princess," I breathe gruffly into her ear. "I'm going to come so deep inside you I'll still be there next fucking week." I stare down at her, my eyes bright with my promise.

"You're always inside me, Tucker," she whispers, her words an arrow straight to my heart. Here I am making dirty little vows, and Carl says something so transcendently beautiful.

She leaves me fucking speechless. But I can express myself in other ways. I capture her mouth with mine, and kiss her with everything I feel—every desire, every regret. But right now it's the need to possess her that's strongest, and I pull her hips to the edge of the washing machine, and guide myself into her welcoming body.

I swallow her long, strangled moan, tasting its perfection as I hold myself still inside her. She grips me tight and hot, and I close my eyes and just feel. I've missed this. I miss this every single goddamned moment I'm not doing it.

"Tuck," she whimpers.

Carl wraps her legs around me in encouragement, like she wants to keep me a part of her, as if without me she's missing something vital. At least that's how it feels, and I love that, too. *God*, I love every fucking thing about her. I always have.

I gently fist her hair, pulling her head back so she's forced to lie down, and follow with my body covering hers. She grabs the hem of my T-shirt and tugs it up, and I reach back and yank it off in one quick motion, desperate to get back to where I belong.

I lean down over her, and then, finally, I move. I rear my hips back until I nearly withdraw, and then push slowly, deliberately in until I bottom out. Again, I pause. I'm struck with a wave of overwhelming humility. I don't deserve this, but fuck if I could ever bring myself to walk away. Not again. Not for real.

"Please, Tuck." Carl's voice is a breathy plea, and it obliterates my free will. There is nothing in this world like hearing her beg, and there's no other place she would ever do it. It's a heady thrill, and my body takes control, giving her what she's asked for.

My hips start pumping, gradually increasing in pace and force, and she meets me thrust for thrust. As always, my words pour out without a filter, and I tell her how good she feels, how tight and hot, how my favorite place in the world is inside her perfect body.

I feed on her moans of pleasure, letting them fuel me, until we are slamming our bodies together like animals, trying with everything we have to leave a piece of ourselves in each other.

She goes off first, exploding around me in pulses and ripples that do me in, and I burst inside her, marking her as deeply as I possibly can.

We both gasp for air, suspended in time. Right now, in this moment, she is still mine, and I don't want to return to a reality where we have come full circle. Where we are back to being fucking friends with benefits.

"Tuck…"

I lift my face from where it's hidden in her neck, and stare into a sated emerald sea. I want to get lost in it.

"We should go."

I sigh. I can't believe I'm back in a laundry room being rushed away from the girl who should be in my bed every night. Fuck my fucking life.

I reluctantly peel myself off of her and start getting dressed, pocketing her ruined panties. I know my silence is discomfiting to her, but I don't know what to say. I don't know how much longer I can do this. I need to tell her how I feel. I keep waiting for some way to prove to her that I deserve her—some way to guarantee that when I confess my fuck-up and profess my love, she will take me back. But maybe I'm just being a coward.

I look over at her, smoothing down her rumpled skirt, running her fingers through her tousled hair, and I wish I could wipe away her uncertainty. And I will.

Just not right now.

But when the moment is right, I'm going to tell her.

Soon.

Someone knocks on the door.

"Yo, Green! I know we said you could shoot in there, but some of us need clean clothes!" Sherman shouts from the other side of the closed door.

"Just a minute!" I call back. "Getting some B-Roll!"

Carl has herself back together in seconds, and then busies herself organizing the release forms while I fasten my fly.

"Dude, my girl's got class in an hour!"

Carl shoots me a puzzled look, and I roll my eyes. "She does his laundry," I explain with a smirk, knowing how she'll react to that.

Her scowl makes me grin.

I turn to go unlock the door.

"Tuck."

"Hmm?" I reach for the handle.

"Tuck!"

I turn back to Carl, at her panic-stricken, wide eyes, directed right at Manny's tripod, still in the corner of the room, camera still aimed at the washing machine, its recording light still blinking ominously.

Mother. Fucker.

"Tuck."

"Fuck."

"Tuck, *it's on*."

"*Fuck*."

I pounce on the thing like it's alive and hit the power button, and then rip out the memory card and glare at it. But I already know that the camera automatically uploads to the Cloud, and then to Manny's laptop.

"Tuck."

"I know!" I snap. "Shit, I'm sorry." I reach for her, but she dodges me. Great, now she's freaking out. Shit, *I'm* freaking out.

"What do we do?" she asks. She's looking to me like I have all the answers, and I don't know what the fuck to do.

"Maybe the footage didn't upload," I offer.

"You think?"

I don't think. I *think* Manny is walking around—albeit probably still unknowingly—with a video of me plowing into Carl like my life depended on it. But her anxiety stabs me in the gut, and I can't stop myself from reassuring her, even if it's a lie. "Yeah. He already down-loaded today's footage to the project file. So even if it did upload to the Cloud, there's no reason for him to find it." I hope.

"Yeah." Carl wants to believe me, but she's unsure. "Tuck…"

"It's going to be fine," I reassure her, but she shakes her head.

"Ben told me one of your teammates got benched last year because he got a bad peer review and Zayne docked his grade."

Huh? What does that have to do with anything? "Yeah. I know. Crauper. Screwed some girl on his team and it came back to bite him in the ass." I smirk at her. "Are you threatening to screw up my grade?"

But she's not amused. She shakes her head frantically like I'm miss-ing something. "No. Listen. I mentioned it to Zayne, and he said it didn't matter that the girl lied on her review because him sleeping with a teammate was unprofessional in its own right."

"Okay?"

She closes her eyes and takes a deep breath like she's growing im-patient with me. "Manny doesn't like me. Or you, for that matter. And if he sees this…"

I finally get there. "Then he has proof we fucked up."

Fuck. My heart races in my chest and I worry she can hear it. Be-cause if I blow the grade on this project, then it's half the grade in the class. It could be the difference between keeping my scholarship, or having to leave school. But I don't tell Carl that. I don't need her to worry any more than she obviously already is at the thought of a bad grade or losing that internship she wants so much.

I reach for her again and this time she lets me wrap my arms around her. We ignore the angry banging from the other side of the door. "It'll be okay," I promise her. "I'll make sure it's okay."

"How?"

"However the fuck I have to."

Chapter Twenty-seven

Tucker

Present Day

I walk into creative marketing with Carl a little over a week later. It's the second to last class of the semester and we're about to make our presentation for our group project. I've been keeping an eye on Manny, searching for signs he's seen footage of my naked ass, but he's given me no indication that he has, and it's a relief. I can't be sure, but I think he probably would have mentioned if he stumbled upon a video of Carl and me going at it, or I'd at least have picked up on some cryptic glances or something.

The rest of the class filters in and sits with their groups. I hand Carl our note cards and Manny boots up his laptop. Zayne calls up the first group, who picked the Quality of Life Foundation. Their video isn't bad, but it's amateur hour next to ours. It focuses on family milestones—birthday parties, holidays, etcetera—and sets them in hospitals using the kind of supplies the foundation's funding provides. It's obviously meant to pull at the heartstrings, but it feels more than a little unoriginal, and falls equally short. Zayne sits off to the side, taking notes, his expression inscrutable.

The next four groups are called and each presents. Two are actually pretty good—one sentimental and one pretty damn funny—but ours is the only one that's both serious and funny, and I still think it's the most creative. Manny's edit is brilliant, and I'm ninety percent sure we're winning that prize.

I peek over at Carl, who happens to glance at me at the same time, and her lips pull into a wry smile. She knows we've got this. I grip her shoulder and rub it firmly the way she likes, and I feel the small dose of tension dissolve. She's not lacking in self-assurance, but still, she is human. "You're gonna kick ass, Princess."

Carl winces so subtly I nearly miss it.

Shit, I keep forgetting not to call her that. But it only hurts because she still thinks I don't want to get back together. We've been getting along better than I could have hoped, and I think I'm finally ready to tell her the truth.

Soon.

The moment I'm confident it will go our way.

Fuck, I'm such a pussy.

The fifth group's video comes to an end, and the group claps perfunctorily. Zayne makes some notes as Manny clicks around on his keyboard to set us up. "Oh, I made a small edit last night, by the way," he murmurs nonchalantly.

Huh?

"Why?" Carl asks. "The cut you showed us yesterday was perfect."

"It's still perfect. I just made one small addition at the end. No worries, it's still under two minutes," he assures us as he clicks away.

He's such a perfectionist and he's done this so many times—made changes on details that to laymen like me felt so insignificant and immaterial to the actual content that it seemed like a total waste of time, but I guess that's why he's the expert.

Carl shrugs and Julia rolls her eyes, and Manny just keeps working. I give Carl's shoulder one last squeeze as she gets up to make our presentation, and move over into her empty seat as Manny brings the final file up on the screen and connects to the room's main screen.

"You better not have fucked it up," I tease Manny.

He laughs under his breath. "*I'm* not the one who fucked anything."

My heart freezes. "What did you say?"

But Carl's about to speak and Manny doesn't even meet my gaze,
he just looks casually at his laptop waiting to hit play.

Fuck! I'm not willfully delusional enough to convince myself his
comment was a coincidence, but I can only hope that his words
weren't related to his last-minute edit.

Because there is no reason on earth he'd show that video in class.

Would he?

"So who here has ever heard a friend or acquaintance make a joke
about rape?"

As predicted, no one raises their hand, and several mouths gape
open at Carl's brusque question.

"No one?"

Still nothing.

Carl nods. "Well, that's good. Because we'd all agree, it's nothing to
joke about, right?"

A murmur of affirmative answers.

"Except, I'd venture to guess that you've all heard these kinds of
jokes, or snide comments. You know, about getting a girl drunk so
she'll be more...*fun*. Or what about slipping something into someone's
drink?"

Slowly one guy raises his hand. Then a few more. Carl waits pa-
tiently until half the room raises their hands.

"I thought so," she says. "Well, the thing is, it seems there's this
weird phenomenon where some guys—and girls—think the idea of
incapacitating someone and taking advantage of them is cool...But we
think it's pretty lame for someone to have to resort to any type of force
just to get some. You know what's cool? Getting laid because someone
wants you when they're good and sober."

A few cheers and a whistle, and in the corner of my eye I see Zayne laughing, his eyes fixed on Carl like he could just fucking eat her, and it makes me want to pummel him.

"The thing is—and no offense, guys—we know you're not always the most original bunch."

There are a few guys pretending they're offended, including one who shouts "hey," but most of them are in complete agreement.

"So we realized that if we're going to change your humor, we'd have to write you the material."

Someone shouts "Thanks!" And several people laugh.

"On behalf of Sexual assault Awareness and Victim Empowerment, or SAVE, we present 'She Wants Me So Bad.'"

The lights go off, and Manny hits play.

The video begins with upbeat music and a fade-in to a party scene. Manny, me, and a couple of guys who volunteered are mixing the alcoholic punch and I repeat the same joke I heard Leo make before that first party at the house about lacing it. On the video the guys laugh and agree, but in the classroom, everyone boos. It's the most interaction a video has gotten and it bodes well.

Then Carl shows up on camera, and asks why I need to drug girls to get laid, whether it's a size issue, an endurance issue, or both. The room breaks out into laughter.

Then the scene starts over, with a joke about making the punch nonalcoholic so the girls don't go home with some loser by accident when they can have me. Sure I come off like a cocky asshole, but the guys who make these jokes in the first place are all cocky assholes.

The scenes continue like that, first with jokes we've heard, then with our suggested corrections, and it's effective both in message and entertainment value.

The text before the final scene is serious. It reads, *When you joke about sexual assault, you never know who's listening, and who might take you seriously*. But the scene itself is far from serious, as we have a gay couple, both of whom are in earshot of a roofie-joke, each separately spiking each other's drink without the other's knowledge. They go into the laundry room to "talk," each obviously planning to take advantage of the other, until they both go in for the kiss and promptly pass out on the floor.

The room bursts into a cacophony of howling laughter, and I smile proudly up at Carl, waiting for the final text and fade to black.

But it doesn't come. Instead, with fifteen seconds left of the video, a new scene comes into view.

I instantly recognize the lax house laundry room. Shots of the washing machine...and legs. Bare, feminine, familiar legs, wound around either side of a denim clad backside. My throat goes Sahara dry and my pulse rockets to the fucking moon. My hands curl into fists as I resist shooting Manny a death glare. I can't bring myself to look at Carl either.

The text on the screen reads, *But look what happens when we're sober...*

Splices of the camera zoomed in on smooth skin glistening with a thin sheen of sweat, in images reminiscent of one of those overtly sexy cologne commercials.

More text, *She wants me so bad...*

The scene cuts back to Carl's nails raking my naked back, my muscles rippling beneath them with exertion, her barefoot heels pushing against my ass that—*thank fucking God*—is still covered by the back of my jeans. The text of the final frames, *The only thing I slip her...*

I hold my breath, because if Manny added vulgar text to go along with his edit, then we're all fucked. Our video is risqué enough as it is.

Is mutual respect. Looks like it worked.

Now how cool is that?

Fade to black.

The video concludes to roaring laughter, a few catcalls and whistles, and a round of applause. No particularly intimate body part or discernible feature had been visible at any point, and, at realizing this, I release the breath that hasn't left my lungs since the scene began. *Thank the fucking Lord.* No one knows that was Carl and me except Carl and me. And fucking Manny.

I turn to him with a glare that foretells of his impending doom, but I have to hide it quickly, because the room's attention is on our group, and the last thing I want is to give away who that couple at the end was. Finally I peek over at Carl, whose mortified blush and stunned gaze makes me wonder how she's going to finish the presentation. I'm about to get up and do it for her when she clears her throat and slips on a mask of composure.

"Who still thinks it's cool to drug someone for sex?" she asks the room.

A chorus of chuckles.

"That last guy got it right!" one kid shouts, and I grit my teeth until the hinges of my jaw throb painfully.

"Hell yeah! Did you see those legs? I'll totally take that washing machine for a ride!"

Carleigh hides her embarrassment behind a smile that's only obviously fake to me, and for once I'm thankful for Zayne, who unknowingly comes to her rescue. He gets up and thanks our group, does the short question-and-answer session he did after each video, then starts going over what he liked and what he didn't about each one.

I lean subtly into Manny. "Do you have a death wish?" I whisper.

He tries to act unaffected, but his nervous swallow is audible. "Do you think it's *professional* to fuck someone you're working with?"

Now I'm the one with the anxious swallow. But he's overplaying his hand. Because as important as this grade is—as much as it could ruin my future—that's barely even on my radar right now. Because all I can think about is that he's just shown the whole fucking class splices of my girl getting fucked, and he should be more worried about his life than my grade.

"Do you think I give half a fuck about that shit when you just exploited my fucking girl?" I growl into his ear, and he finally has the brains to look scared.

Carl sits next to me like a statue, refusing to look anywhere but the front of the room.

"Manny, that was sick!" Julia gushes. "Where'd you get that footage? That was the laundry room from the lax house, right?"

I stiffen in anxiety.

"My friends from performing arts. They're both actors. They agreed to do it at the last minute," he says. "I thought it would be a funny ending. Sorry I didn't have time to show you guys."

I'm relieved he lied, but if he thinks he's sorry now, he should wait until after class, because I'm going to fucking slaughter him for putting Carl through that. Still, I take a deep breath and compose myself.

I lean over and whisper in Carl's ear. "No one knows, Princess."

She nods uncertainly.

"They couldn't see anything," I assure her.

Another shaky nod.

But Manny did see. He would have watched the entire thing in order to cut the edits, and knowing that he saw Carl like that—heard her like that—makes me want to tear his fucking head from his body.

"That was some serious acting." Julia giggles. "I wouldn't mind doing a scene like that, *Jeez*! He looked like he was trying to actually climb inside her! Carl, did you see those muscles in his back?" She dramatically fans herself and licks her lips, and I can't help but laugh.

"Yeah, Carl," I tease in my best impression of a girly voice. "He's *so hot*, isn't he?"

She cracks a small smile. "He was hot," she agrees. "But you know guys like that. I'm sure he's a total player."

Ouch. I lightly pinch her thigh in retaliation, but at least I've got her smiling again.

Zayne's been talking this whole time, and when he announces our group as the winner, there are cheers and applause.

Zayne says we'll be presenting our video to the ad execs next Wednesday, and he'll tell us then who gets to interview for the internship. I glance sideways at Manny, and realize this was his move to intimidate us so he can get it for himself. He's about to learn that's not how I work. But Carl is focused on our win, and her smile is genuine, and it's breathtaking.

Zayne dismisses us, and Manny is out the door in a flash.

I race after him, only vaguely aware of Carl calling my name from behind me.

I spot him halfway down the hall, and I burst into a sprint, catching up to him before he can turn the corner and try to lose me.

"Not so fucking fast, motherfucker," I growl, grabbing him by the collar. There's a janitorial closet a few feet away, so I push open the door and shove Manny inside.

He throws his hands up in surrender. "No one knows it was you, dude!" he defends.

"Until you threaten to fuck up Carl's and my grade by showing it to Zayne, is that right?" My tone tells him to tread carefully.

He shakes his head. "I wasn't really going to. I was just fucking with you, I swear!"

I don't believe him for a microsecond. I bet he wants that fucking internship badly enough that he'd have showed Zayne that video if it meant taking Carl out of the running. But I believe he won't now. Because he can see in my eyes that some things are more important than grades.

"You showed a video of my girl to fuck with me? Do you think that was fucking *smart*, Manny?"

His eyes go wide. "No one saw anything scandalous, and it was great material for the project!"

"*Fuck* the project!" I roar. "You think it was okay to put clips of me fucking in a school project and play it for the whole class? You think it was okay to do that to an innocent fucking girl? *My* innocent fucking girl!"

"No one can tell it was you—or her. No one saw anything!"

"Except you!"

"Dude—"

"You watched *my fucking girl?*" I'm utterly blinded with rage.

"I'm not the one who had sex in front of a camera!"

I swing.

Manny's head snaps sideways, and I throw him by his shirt into the wall, needing him away from me before I swing again and do real damage. He rubs his affronted jaw, holding his other hand up in an attempt to block my assault, but I just stand there glowering at him.

The door opens behind me.

"Tuck!" Carl steps into the room and her small hand closes around my tensed biceps.

I glance back at her horrified expression.

"Tuck, don't. Please," she pleads.

Manny rolls his injured jaw. "Too late," he murmurs.

I heave in angry breaths. "Apologize to her!" I demand.

Manny doesn't hesitate. "I *am* sorry. But you would've watched it too if you were me—you *know* you would. And it just worked so well for the project, and I wasn't going to use it against you, I swear to God. And no one will ever know who it was!"

"They better fucking not, Manny. Because if a single person on this campus makes even one sly remark about Carl—gives her so much as a questionable look—I will hold you responsible, and I will fucking *end* you. And if either of us gets so much of a fraction of a grade docked because of a fucking peer review, I'll know exactly who to come looking for. Do you understand me?"

He nods. His gaze lands behind me. "I really am sorry, Carl. My intention wasn't to hurt you."

"You should have just deleted it," she mutters. Her fingers tighten on my arm and I exhale a harsh breath, turning to face her. "Let's go," she says meaningfully.

I nod. Yeah, we should definitely go. Before I get myself fucking expelled.

"We'll see you at the presentation Wednesday," Carl says to Manny, far calmer than me, and infinitely more forgiving. "No more surprises, okay?"

"Yeah. I swear," he says.

"And you better delete that fucking footage," I add.

"Already done."

Chapter Twenty-eight

Tucker

Present Day

Finals pass uneventfully. Between cramming for tests and the tests themselves, I haven't seen much of Carl. But now that they're over I'm feeling impatient. Every moment she's not mine makes my chest ache, and at some point I realized I've just been stalling. That there will never be a way to ensure she'll forgive me with any certainty, no opportunity that will allow me to prove I'm worthy of her. If I want my girl back, I'm going to have to bite the bullet, and I've made a promise to myself that when we return to campus next month, we'll be doing it as a couple.

Overhearing Carl and Zayne chatting like old friends after our last creative marketing class served as its own motivation. Carl called me crazy when I suggested it, but I see the way Zayne looks at her, and it wouldn't surprise me if he was just waiting until he wasn't her professor anymore to try something with her.

Everyone had already gotten their grades and left, and with our group all receiving perfect peer reviews, we all ended up with A's on the project. Which means two things—that Manny was smart enough to take my threat seriously, and that all four of us will interview for the internship.

I couldn't bring myself to thank Zayne, so I just said "bye," and I was waiting outside the door for Carl, hoping to walk her to her next class. She obviously didn't know I was waiting, and she stopped to talk to Zayne, who'd been standing on the other end of the door, saying good-bye to each student as we exited.

"Hey, Carleigh. I'll see you tomorrow at the presentation," Zayne said, a little too warmly for my taste.

"Definitely," Carl replied. "Listen, in case we don't have a chance to talk then, I just wanted to thank you. For, you know, everything."

"Thank you for being a fantastic student."

"Yeah, well, I really enjoyed the class. I feel like I learned a lot, and...to tell you the truth, it's the first time I feel like I've actually learned something practical."

"Well, it is. Every business needs marketing, right? You can own the most phenomenal chain of salons in the country, but if no one hears about them, you won't be successful. Same goes for your makeup."

I was stunned, and honestly, a little hurt. She'd only confided in me about those dreams after we'd made our relationship official.

"And frankly, Carleigh, you have a knack for it. Some things can be learned, but others you just get or you don't. And you have an innate grasp of how to connect with an audience."

"I don't know about all that." Her voice was small—humble. But she's not the self-deprecating type, which meant she actually doubted herself. Zayne didn't pick up on it. He doesn't know her like I do. He never fucking could.

"Humility is a good thing, Carleigh, but it's okay to take credit when it's due, too. Important, even. I didn't get where I am by just accepting the hand I'd been dealt, or by letting others take advantage of me. We have to show others what we're made of, yeah? Take what we deserve." Zayne was emphatic and passionate, and as a teacher—I hate to admit—not *un*inspiring.

"Yeah," Carl agreed. "You're right."

"I'm glad you think so." Something in his tone rubbed me the wrong way, though I couldn't put my finger on what.

Zayne proceeded to ask after Billy, and the fact that they seem to have formed a sincere connection hit me hard. I suspected his interest in her from the minute I saw him lay eyes on her that first day of class. The way he looked at her, how he seemed to notice her presence just a little more than everyone else's—it unsettled me from the start, and I can only hope their relationship ends with the class.

Except, of course, we'll be seeing him today.

I drive Carl to the sleek, modern office building that houses Steepman and Boyle, the big-time advertising firm where we're going to present our campaign. Julia suggested we all ride together, but Carl thought it unwise for me to be in such a tightly enclosed space with Manny. Smart girl.

We head to the eighth-floor office suite and tell the receptionist our names. The rest of our team has yet to arrive, and Zayne is apparently already in with the ad execs, so we're told to have a seat.

Julia and Manny show up minutes later, and Zayne comes by with two men and a woman, introduces us all. They tell us they'll be with us shortly, and we all sit back down to continue our wait.

I excuse myself to use the restroom. After I do my business, I straighten my tie in the mirror. We were told to dress professionally, though I doubt anyone will be looking at me, not with Carl wearing that almost-sheer white blouse and sexy navy skirt. I can't help but wonder what's underneath, and as I picture pretty white lace, I have to force my focus onto lacrosse drills, lest I have to walk into our meeting plagued with a monstrous hard-on.

I exit the bathroom to head back to join the group, and as I'm about to turn the corner I hear Zayne in conversation and I pause.

"You sure we can't entice you to come back to work for us?" some vaguely familiar voice asks, and I think it's one of the men we were introduced to in the waiting room.

"Thanks, Todd, but my mind's made up," Zayne replies.

"You're positive? I thought the whole point of getting your master's was to be eligible for the next salary bracket? I'm pretty confident I could talk Marcy into implementing a raise early for you. You know she's a—uh—*fan* of yours. If you were willing to feed the cougar, I bet you might even get yourself a quarterly bonus—performance-based, of course." The Todd guy chuckles as if he's delivered some hilarious quip, and Zayne returns a forced parody of good-natured amusement.

"Appreciate it, but like I said, I'm coming into a substantial inheritance fairly soon. Nothing personal."

"But you're still teaching that class at the college, so it's a little personal," Todd jokes.

Zayne laughs. "What can I say? I enjoy shaping fresh young minds."

"You mean fresh young *meat*," Todd corrects, and to my very slight relief, Zayne doesn't laugh.

"You are something else," he admonishes instead.

"Hey—they're legal," Todd defends, and I feel bile rise in my throat. The only *fresh young meat* he's laid eyes on from Zayne's class are Carl and Julia, and no offense to Julia, but I have no doubt it's Carl who's caught his eye.

Zayne sighs. "You know that isn't why I'm there."

Todd exhales his concession. "Yes, yes, I know. I was just having some fun."

Zayne seems happy to change the subject. "Anyway, this was my last semester teaching. So I'm free. To relax, or travel on a whim—whatever I choose. I can't say I'm not looking forward to it. I've been working since I was thirteen."

"Right, right," Todd agrees. "Maybe it's a blessing that your father lost his company when you were a kid, yeah? You've had some adversity, learned some work ethic instead of becoming one of those spoiled, sniveling trust fund brats." Todd laughs, but Zayne doesn't.

"I'm going to have to disagree with you on that one."

"Fair enough. Well, you're getting that inheritance now, so all's well that ends well and all that."

"So they say."

Great. So Zayne is a good-looking guy, and now he's about to come into what sounds like a serious load of cash. And he clearly has a connection of some kind with Carl. I know Carl isn't remotely superficial, but I'm not naïve enough to think that an attractive, rich, ex-professor wouldn't hold a certain appeal to any girl. And just because Zayne doesn't appear to be the amoral dog this Todd character clearly is, now that he's no longer Carl's professor, if he wants to date her, there's no ethical reason for him not to. Hell, he doesn't even work for the school anymore. He literally has nothing to lose.

And me? I have everything to lose.

Fuck. I could lose her.

Yeah, that proverbial fire under one's ass? Consider mine lit. Consider it a blazing fucking inferno.

I pass the men still talking in the hall, and without another thought, march over to Carl and grab her arm.

She starts, her hand flying to her chest, and her eyes close briefly in relief when she realizes it's me.

"I want to have dinner tonight," I blurt. *Damn it, Tucker. A little more fucking finesse.*

Carl's brows pinch together and she blinks at me.

"What I mean is…will you let me take you out to dinner tonight?" I rephrase. Not an order, not a statement, but a request. "To celebrate our win. And…to talk."

It catches her off guard, and her pretty lips part and close twice before she speaks. "Sure, Tuck. I…" She exhales, and runs her bottom lip between her teeth—*nerves*. "I would really like that."

And suddenly I think we might just have a chance after all.

* * *

The presentation went better than I expected. I was surprised by how seriously we were taken. I won't pretend I didn't feel out of place in the massive conference room, all contemporary sleek lines and minimalist decor, but the meeting itself was decidedly less intimidating.

Carl talked about our concept and the inspiration behind it, I explained our strategy for writing the jokes, and Julia discussed the filming process while Manny got technical about his editing program and technique, and they seemed sincerely impressed. Carl, in particular, was in her element, and I think again about what I overheard Zayne say about her having a knack for marketing. He was right, but I should have been the one to notice it—to point it out to her, give her that confidence. But I'm grateful to have that opportunity now.

After our presentation they interview us one by one, and I spend mine talking up Carl.

I take her hand once we're back in the waiting room. She is positively beaming. She knows she owned that meeting, and probably her interview, too, and she's proud of herself. She's never sexier than when she radiates confidence and self-assurance like this, and I stare at her a moment, trying to find the words to tell her how magnificent she is, how impressed I am with her, how incredibly proud.

"Carleigh, you got a minute?" Zayne calls from behind me.

I reluctantly release her hand, trying not to let my resentment show.

Zayne pats me on the back and my muscles tense. "Good job in there, Tucker," he praises, but his eyes are on Carl. "Carleigh, do you have some time to stick around? Marcy wants to talk a little more to you about their internship program."

Carl's eyes go wide. "*Really?*"

Zayne chuckles. "Don't act so surprised, Carleigh." He winks.

I grit my teeth.

Carl's eyes slide to me, and I take care to hide my discomfort. This is an amazing opportunity for her and I can't begrudge it just because it's coming from Zayne. But Carl looks uncertain, and I realize she's worried about our dinner plans.

"Go, Princess. I'll meet you after, okay?" *Shit*. I just called her *Princess* in front of our fucking professor. Well, ex-professor.

Whatever, fuck him.

*   *   *

Two hours later I'm sitting at Kumo, the sushi restaurant I told Carl to meet me at before I left the office building. My mood is a strange combination of regret and hope.

I look around the red and black decor, accented with Japanese cherry blossoms. This place holds so many memories for Carl and me that it feels almost surreal to be sitting here.

The hostess knew right where to seat me, and I get settled in the corner table where Carl fed me sea urchin for the first time, and I joked that it looked like monkey brains. It's the same table where I got censuring looks from a middle-aged man for hauling her onto my lap and shoving my tongue down her throat. And an entirely different time when an elderly couple laughed and cheered me on for doing the very same thing.

This is where Carl told me about her salon dreams, where I promised her she'd make them come true. It's where I realized it had been exactly one year since we'd first hooked up, declared it our anniversary, and when she was skeptical that it qualified, ordered her cake and had the entire waitstaff sing *Happy Anniversary* to the tune of "Happy Birthday." Her mortified smile was fucking gorgeous.

I tap my chopsticks against the edge of the table, grinning to myself at the memory. Tonight, it will be where I tell her I never stopped loving her. That I never could. I will tell her I was wrong to assume she knew about my father's connection to her own, and apologize. And it's where I will fucking beg until she forgives me—until she agrees to give us another shot. Because I will never let her go.

By eight-thirty I start texting her. I assume she got caught up with those marketing executives, and I know it's probably a good thing, which is why I let half an hour pass before trying to get hold of her.

She doesn't text me back.

For a brief, disheartening moment, I wonder if she's blowing me off, and for an even briefer, even more disheartening one, I worry she's blowing me off for fucking Zayne. But I've already made the mistake of believing things about Carl that were entirely contradictory to her character, and I've paid for it dearly. She wouldn't blow me off. So where the fuck is she?

By nine, I start to get anxious. I've texted and texted, and called several times, each of which have gone straight to her voicemail. My messages have progressed from a casual request for a callback to desperate pleas for her to just let me know she's okay.

Could she have forgotten she was supposed to meet me? It's doubtful, but it's the only explanation that doesn't terrify me.

By nine-thirty, I give up and leave the restaurant. I consider calling Billy, but I don't want to worry him for nothing, especially with all the shit he's been dealing with lately. So I drive the twenty minutes to her dorm. Carl and I both had our last finals today, but there's another day of testing tomorrow and half the student body is still on campus. I text a girl I know from my economics class to get her to sign me into Stuyvesant, and then spend another ten minutes slamming my fists against Carl's door, shouting her name until I've pissed off half her floor, and gotten cursed out repeatedly by pissed-off people trying to study.

By the time I climb back into my car, my heart is pounding with fear. I don't even know where to go, so I sit in park.

With no options left, I dial Billy's number. I've seen him a couple of times since his accident, but it's still a little weird between us. He apologized for Thanksgiving, and on the outside our relationship has pretty much gone back to normal, but I still sense a hint of resentment. After all, it's well deserved.

"What's up, Tuck?" he answers.

"Is Carl home?" I ask abruptly.

"Uh…hello to you, too, asshole," he halfjokes.

I love the kid, but I don't have fucking time for this. "Listen, she was supposed to meet me at a restaurant almost two hours ago, but she didn't show."

"Maybe she decided to blow you off," Billy offers—again, only halfkidding.

"Yeah, I considered that. In fact, I'm fucking hoping for it. But she's not answering my texts and her phone's going straight to voice-mail. Tell me she's home," I practically fucking beg him.

There's a pause where I can feel Billy's mirth turn to anxiousness. "I don't think she is," he says quietly.

"Are you sure?" *Where the fuck is she?*

"Well, no. I'm not sure. I'm stuck in fucking bed, dude," he grumbles. He's still recovering from his surgery and he's supposed to take it easy. "But she would've come to see me. If she was home."

He's right. Billy's room would have been her first stop. "When was the last time you talked to her?"

"Uh…this afternoon. She said you were picking her up to go to some meeting."

Great. "What about your mom? Has she heard from her?"

"How the fuck should I know?"

"Is she home?"

"I think so."

"All right, I'm gonna call her." Fuck my life that I'm about to call Nicole Stanger.

"Mooommm!" Billy is already shouting for his mother, but that house is enormous and unless they're in the same wing, she won't hear him. "Damn, she must be downstairs. I'll call her, you keep trying Carl," he suggests. "Did you check her dorm?"

"Yeah, just left there. I'm gonna drive around to where she usually parks and see if her car is still here."

I find Carl's Audi in her usual spot, and my stomach rolls with dread. I should've asked her if she needed me to pick her up when she was done meeting with Zayne's old boss. I knew she didn't have her car, but she's always been so damn independent. I just figured she'd call an Uber or get a ride. The growing likelihood that she is still with Zayne unsettles me deeply, but at this point that conclusion is fast becoming a best-case scenario. I'm not ready to entertain other possible conclusions.

I drive to Carl's house, calling both Manny and Julia on the way to see if either of them have Zayne's number. They don't. Like me, they only have his e-mail, and I already e-mailed him before I left campus, giving him my number and asking him to call me. He hasn't yet.

I pull through the open gates and into Carl's circular drive, and jump out of my car. I ring the doorbell an obnoxious number of times, and Janet, their housekeeper, answers the door.

She used to greet me with a smile, but today I get thinly veiled animosity, and I'm reminded again how much I must've hurt Carl when I left her. Another time I would try to charm Janet, but right now I just rush upstairs to Billy's room.

I hear the raised voices from down the hall, and I enter to find him and Nicole scowling at each other.

"Just calm down, Billy," she says.

"What's going on?" I ask. "Have you heard from her?"

"No," Billy replies. "And our mother doesn't think there's a reason to be concerned."

My jaw clenches, but I try and tamp down my aggravation. "Mrs. Stanger, she was supposed to meet me at eight. It's now almost eleven."

"And she's not answering her phone," Billy adds.

I raise my eyebrows to emphasize Billy's point.

Nicole rolls her fucking eyes. "She's not *not answering*—her phone is obviously off. She probably forgot to charge it. You know she does that."

I do know that. But that doesn't explain why she seems to have fallen off the face of the fucking planet. "Something's not right. We need to call the police," I tell her.

"That's what I said!" Billy says, exasperated.

"You boys are overreacting."

I ignore her blasé attitude. "You're her mother. You need to call them and report her missing," I insist.

She glares at me. "And say what? My almost nineteen-year-old daughter was supposed to meet the ex-boyfriend who broke her heart, but decided against it at the last minute? Oh, and that she forgot to charge her phone for the billionth time this week?"

"Then where is she, Mom?" Billy more accuses than asks.

"Since when does she include me in her plans? Have you tried her friends?"

Well, *no*. But if she was with any of her friends, surely she would have borrowed their phone to let me know she's okay. Right?

Nicole sighs. "Why don't you try calling around some more, and if we don't hear from her in a few hours, we'll call the police, okay?"

"Fine," I all but growl.

I make myself comfortable in Billy's room and start texting everyone I fucking know. Many of our friends are home for break already, and I send feelers out to them all, asking if anyone has heard from Carl since six o'clock when I left her. Billy uses the time to call the local hospitals, to no avail.

Frustrating *no* after *no* trickles in over the next few hours, and I'm not even sure how much time has passed when some strange calling app appears on my phone out of nowhere, and a number I don't recognize starts flashing on my screen, indicating it has sent me a message with a photo.

Chapter Twenty-nine

Carleigh

Present Day

I groan as unnatural light slowly filters in through my fluttering eye-lids, my temples pounding in protest. Immediately I know something is very, very wrong. Each moment that passes provides another ter-rifying clue in time with the rhythmic heartbeats blaring behind my eyes—

Beat—the throbbing in my head.

Beat—the heaviness of my limbs.

Beat—the fact that two of those limbs, my arms, are restrained above my head.

Beat—I'm lying down.

Beat—on a fucking bed!

My pulse races in pure, unadulterated panic.

Where am I? What the hell happened?

But I can't concentrate enough to remember; all of my focus is drained on trying to calm the fuck down so I don't pass out.

"Relax," he orders, his tone unfittingly nonchalant.

Wait, *whose tone*?

My eyes, unable to latch on to anything more than a few feet away until now, finally take in the average-sized bedroom, unremarkable in every way except for the man standing against the far wall, leaning against the frame of the shuttered window.

"Zayne?" I gasp his name, as if I need a verbal confirmation of what my eyes can't possibly be getting right.

He smiles, like he's actually amused by my denial. And then the hazy, dreamlike memories come flooding back. Flashes of Zayne convincing me to have a drink with him to celebrate the internship I'd just landed blink in my mind like a strobe. I declined at first, but he insisted, and offered to drive me to meet Tuck afterward. I had almost an hour to kill before I was supposed to head to the restaurant, so I agreed. Zayne wanted to talk to Todd quickly, he said, and asked me to wait outside the garage, where he met me with his car not long after. At least I think it wasn't long after.

It gets fuzzy after we left the office building. Did we actually go somewhere and have that drink? But no matter how hard I try, I can't seem to recall. I suppose it doesn't much matter now. Here I am, either way.

But *why*?

Why would he do this? Why am I here?

Of course, the obvious answer assails my thoughts, but if he just wanted to rape me, then surely he could have done that while I was conveniently unconscious, couldn't he? And I'm quite certain that hasn't happened.

Somewhere in the back of my mind I register that he drugged me. My college professor fucking *drugged* me.

The oversized mirror that hangs over the dresser gives me a pretty good view of myself, and the sight of me, though utterly foreboding, supports my theory that whatever is going to happen hasn't happened just yet.

And then I realize that may not be a good thing.

I seem to have lost my blazer, but I'm still wearing my skirt and blouse from…whenever the presentation was. Today? Last night?

The window is tightly shuttered, allowing no outside light in, and the result is even more unsettling. To not know if it's day or night, or have any indication of the passage of time—it puts me at an even greater disadvantage. I keep my eyes trained on my own form reflected in the mirror. My clothing and hair look somewhat disheveled from lying in this bed, or from being unconsciously transported. Which makes me wonder—how *did* he get me here? How do you carry an unconscious girl to…wherever we are, without raising suspicion? God, where the hell are we?

I grit my teeth so hard my jaw aches, fighting to keep my mouth shut, sucking desperate breaths in through my nose instead. But I know he's waiting for me to ask him these questions, probably to beg for an explanation, and it's against everything in my nature to give him the satisfaction of my helplessness.

Instead, I glare at him with such fiery hostility I'm surprised he doesn't ignite on the spot.

But it only seems to amuse him, and finally, he sighs. He pulls a phone from his pocket—and I notice it isn't his usual phone— something I never would have known had he not helped me with Billy on Halloween.

Has he been planning this since then? Did I just walk right into some sinister plot to do God knows what to some naïve little college freshman?

He points the phone at me and snaps a photo.

What the fuck?

I turn my face away in defiance and shame. Suddenly my stomach lurches and I gag, my eyes wide and frantic.

I don't even realize I've made eye contact with Zayne until he's rolling his, and he brings me a small waste bin from under the writing desk.

"Relax, Carleigh. Nausea is a common side effect of rohypnol. You'll feel better in a couple hours. But if you're going to vomit, don't do it on the bed."

You'll feel better in a couple hours. I heard the same flippant words from Ben after he drugged me. And suddenly, all I know is wild fury. Who the fuck do these men think they are, drugging women at their damn leisure?

"What the hell is wrong with you?" I erupt in rage. "Let me fucking go, right fucking now!"

Zayne's mild amusement vanishes, replaced by a mask of irritation. He takes a step toward me, and it threatens the fight right out of me.

His gaze rakes me from head to toe with intent he's never shown before, and I hold my breath as his legs hit the edge of the bed. He makes no effort to hide his blatant arousal, and I'm terrified when it brushes my hip as he leans over me.

Oh, God. This can't be happening. "You don't want to do this," I hedge, but my voice is shaky, my fear undeniable.

"I do." He reaches for my bindings.

My pulse races frantically.

"But I'm not going to fuck you, Carleigh." He pulls on my restraints, tightening them further until I wince. He brushes the hair from my forehead in a parody of affection, and I turn away from him, revolted by his touch.

"Not unless I have to," he amends, and gets up from the bed. "Though it would *not* be a hardship, I assure you." He spares me one more lustful glance before looking unhurriedly through his phone, as if there isn't a kidnapped girl tied to his bed. Or *a* bed.

I swallow anxiously. "W-why would you have to?"

His patience expires without warning. "What is this—a fucking Q and A? Lie back and behave, and you may get out of this unscathed."

"You don't have to do this, Zayne. My family has money. They—"

"Oh, I know they do," he says cryptically.

I blink at him in confusion. But then, he saw my house, so he must assume it's built on wealth and means. I exhale my nerves. If all he's after is a ransom, then maybe he was telling the truth—maybe I can get out of this unharmed after all.

"My mom will pay anything, Zayne, just please don't hurt me. I'll get you however much you want. I swear." I hate how desperate I sound. But I *am* desperate.

He reaches down for the hem of my skirt, and I squirm helplessly, but all he does is push it up a couple of inches to reveal that much more thigh. He goes for my blouse next, undoing the two top buttons and untucking it from my waistband, and then proceeds to snap another photo.

"I thought you might say that. I only hope you're right, because I want the twenty million that's fucking owed to me." His voice is low and ominous.

Panic rises in my gut. *Twenty million?* That's all that was left after the feds seized everything they were able to find. Well, that and the house. But for the first time, I wonder what is worth more to my parents, the funds they refused to surrender in exchange for my father's freedom, or me.

They wouldn't intentionally risk my life of course, but kidnappings for ransom go wrong all the time, don't they? If it were a couple hundred thousand Zayne was demanding, or even a couple million, they'd hand it over in a heartbeat, I'm sure of it. But *all* of their money? Every last cent?

The unbidden thought that strikes me now is Tucker. That I may never see him again. And for the first time since I awoke to find myself in this precarious predicament, the well overflows and tears stream down my cheeks. Because I know if it were him and not my parents, he'd choose me every time. Even now.

I suck in deep breaths and try to stay rational. I'm going to have to keep my wits about me to get through this.

Twenty million.

Twenty fucking million. That he thinks is *owed* to him?

I stare at him, puzzle pieces clicking ominously into place, one by one, but too many are still missing. "Who are you?" I ask. "Were you one of my father's clients?" But he's too young for that, surely. "Or were your parents?"

Zayne laughs humorlessly. "Screw his clients. Oh, wait. He already did that, didn't he?"

"Who are you?" I ask again.

"Do you remember Art Stevens?"

Art Stevens? He was my father's business partner. They started Stanley Stevens Investments together, but fell out before I was even old enough to have remembered him, and though they remained business partners, they started working out of different offices, and rarely even saw each other.

"I know who he is," I answer hesitantly.

Zayne's eyes narrow subtly. "And who is he?"

I swallow nervously. "He was my dad's partner."

"You mean, the man your father ruined?"

I almost want to laugh. That could describe a lot of people. But I won't be put in a position to defend my father. I'm not him.

"My father was a respected businessman. The only wrong he ever did was trusting a fucking crook," Zayne spits.

Ah, so Art is Zayne's father? *Zayne Stevens.* I knew it was his last name, but it's such a common one that the thought never crossed my mind. Of course, I haven't heard the name *Art Stevens* in well over a decade, and even then I was just a little girl.

"When the business's assets were seized, it included any assets my father acquired from the firm. He started it when he was twenty years old. Everything he had was from Stanley Stevens, including my trust fund. And the irony is, that because my father is an honest man, he lost everything, while your criminal father did what criminals do and stashed enough away to ensure you're all still living the good life. Your father has his wife waiting for him, happily spending as much as she likes without a care in the world, while my father can only get out of bed in the morning by the grace of antidepressants."

"Your mom…" *God*. He told me his mother left when the money was gone. How horrible that must have been for him. I can't believe I feel pity for my kidnapper, but I do. How many lives has my father destroyed?

"Good memory, Carleigh. Indeed. Your family is also responsible for the destruction of mine, and while as an adult I've come to realize that losing a money-hungry whore of a mother wasn't a great loss, I'll admit I felt differently at thirteen, and my father does still. She was the love of his life, you know."

"I'm sorry." Vaguely I wonder if I will always be apologizing for my father's transgressions, and just how dearly I will be paying for them now.

Zayne sighs. "I'm afraid your remorse is neither here nor there, Carleigh. I'm a reasonable man, and I'm acutely aware that you are not to blame for what your father did when you were just a child. But I told you earlier that sometimes we have to take what we deserve, and I deserve retribution. I want what I'm owed, and I want your father punished."

"He's in prison," I remind him.

"As he should be. But he chose his sentence, so I wouldn't exactly consider it punishment. Punishment would be losing something dear to him, and clearly his own freedom took second place to money."

"Well, you said it yourself, Zayne. He cares about the money. If he gave a shit about me he would have chosen to be around for my fuck-ing childhood." My words bleed with the bitterness I feel.

"Well, for your sake, I hope you're wrong. Because it's his daughter or the money. He can't have both."

"So you mean to trade me for the value of your trust fund?"

"The company was valued at forty million. I simply want my half."

"You know they don't have that," I hedge. In truth, I have no idea what he knows.

"It's all very simple, sweetheart. I'm not here to hurt you. In fact, I've rather grown to like you. Trust me, if I didn't, there are plenty of ways I could make your stay here far more traumatizing. You're a means to an end, and I'll do what's necessary to achieve that end."

"Or what? You'll kill me?" Vaguely I know I probably shouldn't challenge him, but in my current terror I'm not exactly thinking strategically.

He reaches behind him and retrieves something from his waistband, and I realize belatedly that it's a handgun.

Holy shit.

He sets it on the table beside him, and I automatically start tugging at my bindings again, twisting in a desperate rally to get away.

"You'd be unwise to underestimate me, Carleigh."

He looks back to his phone and snaps another photo as I continue to squirm in a feeble attempt to get free. Idly I know it's futile, especially with him in the room—with a fucking gun—but my fear is finally catching up to my attitude, and my survival instincts are kicking in as Zayne snaps a fourth and fifth photo.

"You finally look appropriately scared. These photos will be far more motivating," he mutters to himself. "Well, time to get this show on the road!" He fiddles around on his phone. "Wouldn't want your mother to report you missing."

Like there's a chance of that. I swallow nervously, my heart pounding faster and faster with each passing moment. "You're going to call my mother?" *Will she even answer?*

He scoffs. "The woman who couldn't be bothered to answer her phone when her son was vomiting half the volume of the Long Island Sound? *That's* who you think my plan hinges upon? No, Carleigh, actually I have someone a little more reliable in mind."

"My father isn't exactly available," I remind him. *Nor is he exactly reliable...*

Zayne smirks as he sends off a text. He looks between me and his watch and then comes to sit beside me on the bed, and brings up an app I've never seen before. "Stealthcom. It's completely anonymous," he says proudly. "It auto-installs onto the other party's phone, and pings off of false towers so it isn't even traceable, at least not within a useful timeframe. I can use it for calls, texting, video, and it has features to disguise voices, among other things. An old classmate of mine developed it—it isn't even on the market."

"Impressive," I say dryly.

"Now, now, sweetheart. No need to be so cranky. As long as they cooperate you won't have anything to worry about," he assures me. I'm not reassured. "Now, I think the photo's had enough time to do its job. Time to follow up."

He uses the app to make a call. I recognize the number he dials immediately and my eyes widen in shock. But before he hits send, he glares at me in a way that makes my throat go dry. "Carleigh, I would think this goes without saying, but just in case...If you try to screw with my plans—try to tell them who I am, or attempt even a hint, for that matter—I will change my mind about not hurting you really fucking quick. Are we understood?"

I swallow thickly, and unable to form words, simply nod.

Zayne makes the call.

"Who the fuck is this?" Tucker growls.

"Someone who has something I'm betting you want to see again." Zayne's voice is unrecognizable through the disguise feature, and there's a pregnant pause where Tucker's heavy breathing is audible.

"Where the fuck is she? Is she okay?"

"I assume you received my photo?"

"Let me talk to her!" Tucker demands. His desperation is palpable and I can hardly stand to hear it.

"I'm fine, Tuck!" I lie. "I—"

Zayne cuts me off with a threatening glare, and it does its job, silencing me. He may not be planning to hurt me, but for the first time I wonder if a part of him might actually want to.

"Carl, where are you? I'm coming to get you—"

"No, you're not," Zayne corrects him. "Not quite yet. First you need to do something for me."

Tucker's voice lowers, deathly foreboding. "If you hurt her, I *will* kill you. Slowly."

Zayne laughs. "I'll make you a deal, Mr. Green. If I'm not given a reason to hurt her, then I won't hurt her, all right?"

Tucker doesn't respond. "Who are you?" he asks instead. "What the fuck do you want?"

"Who I am isn't relevant. What *the fuck* I want is twenty million dollars."

Silence.

"If you think I have twenty million dollars, then you definitely did not do your homework. I have a few grand saved up, max. Let Carl go and I will gladly hand over every damn cent."

Zayne grins widely, not that Tucker can see it. "I have no doubt that you would, Mr. Green. But it isn't your money I want. You see, Carleigh's parents have funds hidden in an offshore trust that they've managed to shelter from the federal government for years. If you want Carleigh back, then Nicole Stanger needs to wire twenty million of those funds within twenty-four hours to the account numbers I will provide. Your job is to make her understand that this is non-negotiable, and to keep her motivated. If the police are called—and I have failsafes in place to alert me if they are—Carleigh will disappear, and none of you will ever see her again. Do you understand?"

"Let me speak to her," Tucker demands.

"Do. You. *Fucking*. Understand?" Zayne roars so suddenly and viciously that I spring into a fetal position, my knees curled into my chest, my face shielded between my outstretched arms, still bound to the headboard.

"Yes!" Tucker hastily shouts. "Yes! *Fuck*. I understand."

"Good." Zayne recovers his composure just like that.

Tuck's labored breathing is audible through the phone, and it fills my chest with lead. "Please let me talk to her. I…I need to know she's okay," Tucker pleads.

Zayne mutes the microphone. "Remember what I said," he warns me, and then unmutes the phone and holds it near my face.

"T—Tuck…"

"Carl? *Baby*." His voice breaks, and he pauses a beat to collect himself. "Are you okay? Did he hurt you?" Tucker asks frantically.

"I'm fine, Tuck," I lie again. "He hasn't hurt me. But…you need to make sure my mom gets him the money, okay?"

I don't want him to hear how scared I am, but Tucker knows me better than anyone else in this world, and I'm afraid he can sense every ounce of my fear.

"I will. I promise I will." He chokes on an exhale. "I will figure this out, Carl. I will get you out of there." I don't know if his vows are to himself or to me, but I'll take them either way—they're all I have to hold on to.

"Well, it seems we're all on the same page," Zayne interrupts. "I'll be in touch." And he hangs up just like that.

Minutes pass and he doesn't look at me. I lie still on the bed, not moving a muscle, barely so much as breathing.

Eventually he turns to me, and just watches me, as if he's waiting for me to speak. I don't. I have boundless questions, and yet, I'm not sure their answers even matter.

"I suppose you're wondering why I called him," Zayne says eventually.

"Kind of, yeah," I admit. "I'm not sure he's the best choice to communicate with my mother. They're not exactly buddy-buddy."

He sighs. "Tucker Green wouldn't let anyone risk your life, including your mother."

If the situation wasn't so inherently sobering, I would laugh. "I think you may have misjudged my relationship with Tuck, Zayne. We barely even get along most of the time."

Zayne cocks his head at me. "Are you serious?"

I blink at him.

"You just heard him, did you not? Did he sound like someone who doesn't get along with you? *Baby?*"

Just hearing him mock the endearment makes my blood run cold. Hearing him mock Tucker at all. Tucker, who is superior to him in every possible way.

"He's a good person." *Something you know nothing about.* "But I told you he was my ex, remember? There's a reason for that."

Zayne chuckles. "Wow, Carleigh. I never realized how naïve you are."

I scowl at him.

"It took me fewer than five minutes to notice the way he looked at you the very first class of the semester. I told you this. Tucker Green loves you. In fact, sometimes, from his expression, it appears he loves you so much he hates you for it. But I doubt there's anything he wouldn't do to ensure your safe return. If anyone will get this done for me, Carleigh, it's Tucker. In fact, I'm counting on it."

My heart beats faster at his words. I want so much to believe they're true that I try to remember the way he looked at me that first class, but all I recall is pure, brutal contempt. But if Zayne is admitting he himself looked at me that first class, then that must mean he's been planning this at least since then, right?

"Tuck is just a victim in all this, too; you know that, right? Why would you put him through this?" I hate that Tuck is being used this way, against a family who has brought him nothing but devastation, and I don't understand why Zayne couldn't just leave him out of it.

"I do know that, as a matter of fact, and frankly, I'm rather puzzled by Tucker's feelings for you."

I flinch as if he's struck me, even though I know his point is a valid one.

"Oh, don't take such offense, sweetheart. It isn't personal. When I noticed his staring I did some research. It took some digging, but I was pretty surprised to realize the son of one of your father's own victims was in love with you. It's almost Shakespearean, no?" He laughs.

"I wish you'd stop calling me that," I murmur under my breath.

Another laugh from Zayne. I'm glad I can be of such amusement to him.

"I'm not saying I don't understand the attraction. Of course I do. It isn't surprising he fell for you. What surprises me is his ability to look past the history. Surely you both know that no amount of love will change what your father did to his, right? And even if you could get past that, his father certainly put the final nail in that coffin—pun and all—when he took his own life."

I close my eyes. I have no other choice. It's either close them or let Zayne watch them rain with the truth of his statement. But at least it works, and I don't cry just yet.

He gets up without another word, and heads inside what appears to be an en suite bathroom, closing the door behind him.

Eventually I hear his muffled voice, presumably on a phone call, but I don't even try to listen. I fear that, whatever he's up to, I'm better off not knowing.

Chapter Thirty

Carleigh

Present Day

I wake with relief, because I must have been dreaming the kidnapping. There's simply no other explanation. Things like that don't really happen. Friendly, helpful professors don't just turn psycho one day.

"Good, you're up," Zayne murmurs the moment my eyes blink away the intrusive light. "I brought you a sandwich, but I'll have to feed it to you."

"Not hungry," I croak, my voice hoarse from sleep. I expect Zayne to argue, but he simply shrugs, as if he couldn't care less whether or not I eat. And why would he? But I do need something from him, and it crushes my pride to ask. "I…need to use the bathroom."

Zayne rolls his eyes as if I've exasperated him with my basic human needs, and for a moment I think he means to deny me. Instead, he retrieves his gun from the table by the window, holding it balefully close as he undoes my restraints. He uses it to guide me to the bathroom, and to my complete and utter humiliation, keeps it trained on me even as I sit on the toilet with only my skirt helping me retain the slightest shred of dignity. He returns me to the bed the moment I finish washing my hands, redoing my bindings even tighter than before.

"Don't look so glum, Carleigh. Everything is going to work out. For both of us. In fact, now's as good a time as any to check in with loverboy, don't you think?"

I glare at him as he retrieves his phone.

"No talking for this one. Understood?" He doesn't wait for my agreement. He just makes the call, and like last time, puts it on speaker.

"Are we making progress?" Zayne asks, as if he and Tucker are some kind of team.

"I'm doing my best," Tucker replies. But I know him, and the uncertainty tainting his voice makes me anxious.

"I sure hope your best is good enough, Mr. Green. Is Mrs. Stanger being cooperative?"

"We'll get you the money," Tucker grits out. I can tell that what he really wants to say includes a barrage of expletives, but he keeps calm for my sake. "But, look, we might need a little more time. William Stanley is in federal prison—we can't exactly send him a text. Carl's mom e-mailed him and is waiting for his call. Once he tells her how to access the funds we can figure out how to wire it, but I don't know that that's all going to be accomplished in the next eighteen hours."

"I find that when people are properly motivated, they manage to accomplish things they never imagined possible."

"You think I'm not fucking *motivated*?"

"Then you better get it done. I have faith in you, Mr. Green. Carleigh has faith in you. She knows you won't let her down."

I scowl at Zayne, wanting to scratch that smirk right off his face.

"But what if it takes just a little—"

Zayne's switch flips, instantly menacing. "I see I wasn't clear earlier. If you want to see Carleigh again, it's twenty million within the twenty-four hours I gave you."

"If you fucking hurt her—"

"I don't plan on hurting her, Mr. Green. That would serve no purpose. Don't get me wrong, if you do something stupid like contact the authorities, I will have no choice but to dispose of the evidence, and that would include Carleigh."

He glances at me, but there isn't even a hint of shame at the fact that he's talking about ending my life so callously.

"I told you from the beginning—I'm in this for the money. And if you don't comply with my demands, then I will have to get it elsewhere."

"What do you mean?" Tucker carefully asks the question I'm too afraid to verbalize.

"I *mean*, I will make a profit off of Carleigh, one way or another. And I certainly prefer it's from the ransom, because twenty million is a hell of a lot more than I'd get from selling her. But a pretty, young, blond little thing like her? She could go for close to six figures at auction. Maybe more, to the right buyer."

"You motherfucker! I *will* find her! I will find *you*!" Tucker's threat crashes through the speaker, rocking the entire room.

But Zayne only laughs. "Honestly, friend, your energy would be much better spent elsewhere. If you call the police, she dies. If you fail to get me the ransom, she'll be on another continent before the next sunrise. Either way, you will never see her pretty green eyes again."

I can practically hear Tucker seething through the phone. "You'd sell her for a few thousand dollars rather than wait a few extra hours for twenty million?"

"Well, it'd definitely be more than a few thousand. It'd be enough money to hold me over for quite a while, and of course, the Stangers do have another child whose life they may take more seriously after losing the first."

My pulse races in panic. *Billy*. Vaguely I hear Tucker's rage echoing from the phone, but I register none of it.

I close my eyes to try and get hold of myself, and by the time I've mostly gotten my bearings, Zayne has already hung up.

He stares at me curiously, and I can't stand that I've given him the satisfaction of witnessing my panic. I rally all of my considerable fear, and mold it into fury. "So you're in the sex trade now?" I hiss with open disgust, and Zayne has the gall to laugh.

"No, Carleigh. I'm a college professor who's just finished his graduate degree in marketing. No one will ever suspect me in your disappearance. No one knows that I know someone who knows someone who knows people who know exactly what to do with a girl like you. But as long as your mother values her daughter over her lifestyle, you'll never have to meet them."

"You're delusional if you really think you'll get away with this," I spit.

"You mean, Tucker won't get away with this."

What?

Zayne shrugs. "Your group heard him ask you to meet him for dinner last night. The cameras in the office building will show I left alone, more than twenty minutes after you did. And I'm sure there are plenty of people to testify to your tumultuous relationship."

I gape at him. "You would really do that? Kill me, or...*sell* me. And let an innocent man go to jail for it?" I don't know why I ask. He's already proven the lengths he would go to.

"I doubt he'd go to jail. All the evidence would be circumstantial at best. But it would be enough to hold suspicion, which would, in turn, keep it from heading in other directions. Namely, toward me...I wouldn't worry about Tucker. He would be heartbroken to lose you, certainly, but he won't go to prison for it, and eventually, he'll move on. That's how grief works."

I don't respond. There's no point. Zayne is insane, and the more I try to find a rational person within him, the more I realize none exists.

*   *   *

I'm staring at the wall in some kind of timeless trance the next time Zayne determines it's time to "check in." The bed dips as he sits beside me, but I ignore him until I hear him making a call, and hear my mother's voice on the other end of the phone.

I'm vaguely aware of Tucker—and I think Billy—shouting in the background, and I stiffen.

"She's my daughter and I want to speak with him!" my mother shouts back before returning to the call.

This can't be good.

"Ah, Mrs. Stanger," Zayne greets.

"I'm afraid you have me at a disadvantage." My mother's voice is far too calm—her confidence filling me with unease.

Zayne chuckles. "I have you at several, in fact."

My mother expresses her displeasure with a stretch of silence. "Indeed," she concedes. "And what would you have me call you?"

"I don't suppose it matters much. Why don't you call me *Sir*." He shoots me a smirk.

"Hmmph." Unsurprisingly, my mother does not comply. "Well, it seems you are right. You do have me at several disadvantages. You see, I want my daughter back—unharmed—and you want an exorbitant amount of money."

"Well, we can't put a price on those we love, can we?" Zayne mocks her.

"Well, no," my mother agrees. "I cannot. But it seems *you* have. And while there's no amount of money I wouldn't give for my daughter's safety, unfortunately you've chosen a number we simply don't have."

I stop breathing. There's a violent commotion in the background that fades with the slam of a door. Vaguely we hear Billy and Tucker yelling frantically and banging their fists from the other side of what must be a locked door, but my mother seems to pay them no mind.

Zayne seems equally shocked by my mother's response, and with each passing moment his expression morphs that much more into anger.

"You seem to be familiar with my family's financial strain. It's all a matter of public record, after all. I assume you've done your homework…"

Zayne makes some affirmative grunting sound.

"You communicated to Tucker Green that you believe we have hidden assets in the way of twenty million dollars, and while I certainly wish that were true, unfortunately it couldn't be further from reality."

Zayne's eyes narrow, and I wish I could shout at my mother to shut up. But he has never looked more threatening, and I'm afraid if I so much as open my mouth, he might change his mind and kill me after all.

"I've just spoken to my husband, whom you are aware is in prison. As we speak, he is calling in favors from family and old associates, and will collect loans totaling five million dollars. I will wire that amount into the account of your choosing before your deadline."

"Five million," Zayne breathes incredulously.

"It is a great deal of money," my mother says proudly. "Once it's wired, I expect my daughter—"

"Give the phone to Tucker Green," Zayne says softly, employing a cryptic calm that unnerves me far more than his anger ever did.

My mother startles. "Excuse me? Did you hear what I said?"

"Indeed I did. Now hand the phone to Mr. Green. Immediately. Or you will hear your daughter scream."

My mother's gasp is audible, and my heart pounds in terror.

We know my mother has opened the door when Billy's and Tucker's voices grow in volume. They're shouting, and cursing, and threatening my mother, but I fear it's too late—the damage is done.

"Hello?" Tucker says frantically. "Don't listen to her. We'll—"

"You'll do *what*?" Zayne cuts him off. "It isn't your money. Nicole

Stanger must access and wire it. Your job was to make sure she understood her role and took it seriously. But apparently neither of you realizes quite how serious I am."

"I do!" Tucker says in desperation. "I fucking told her! I'll talk to Carl's dad myself. She wouldn't let me explain things to him. But I—"

"I was clear about my terms being non-negotiable, but it seems you need a lesson in what happens when I am not taken seriously."

"Don't hurt her," Tucker begs. "I swear to God—"

"God isn't interested and neither am I, Mr. Green. You knew the stakes, and if you ever want to see your precious *Princess* again, you won't make the same mistake twice."

My eyes blur in a well of tears that I refuse to let fall, but I start trembling uncontrollably. I can't know for sure what he means to do, but I suspect. He hinted at it earlier.

I'm not going to fuck you, Carleigh...Not unless I have to.

Zayne looks at me meaningfully, and I'm idly aware he hasn't ended the call. "I'm afraid you might have been right, Carleigh. I may have overestimated Tucker Green's feelings for you, after all."

"Please just let me go. Please," I plead with him.

"I can't do that, sweetheart. I've been consistently clear from the outset, have I not? The only way you walk out of here alive and free is if I get my money, on time. And not five fucking million. But this brazen attempt at negotiating the amount?" He shakes his head in disapproval. "It must hurt—his willingness to risk your life like that."

Tucker's angry voice thunders in the background, but I'm too distressed to make out his words. It doesn't matter, though. I know it was my mother who chose to risk my life, not Tucker.

"Clearly he did not effectively communicate my demands. But what it shows me is that Tucker and your mother, or whoever's asinine idea this negotiation was, doesn't quite understand the seriousness of your predicament."

"I know you're serious," I assure him. "Please. I *told* you—the money—"

"But I'm not a man who gives up easily. And there are ways to prove my commitment to this plan without killing you, and my money with you." His gaze rakes my body with carnal intent, and my eyes widen in horror.

I shake my head madly in denial.

But his eyes are grave and resigned, and without so much as a nod of confirmation I know what he's about to do, and I can do nothing to stop him.

I start begging anyway.

Zayne pushes the table from beside the window to the foot of the bed, enables the video feature on the app on his phone, and sets it on the table, facing the bed. The camera can clearly see me, tied to the bed, shaking and furiously trying to hold back tears. But Zayne makes sure only his back is visible, and though I silently will him to accidentally turn and show Tucker his face, I already know he will be too careful for that. Idly I consider shouting his identity, but he will kill me then; I know it.

I thrash and twist hysterically as he climbs over me, my wrists burning against their binds, my legs kicking wildly as my only defense.

"No, no, no!" I plead over and over, only vaguely aware of Tucker's continued furious bellowing through the phone—vicious threats and violent promises. But they're just that. Words. Because here, in this impersonal room, with just this heartless man, I am truly alone. No one will come to my rescue. The only hope I have at salvation is myself—a girl tied to a bed, kicking in vain at an enemy I never earned.

Zayne's large hands grip my hips in an effort to still me, and my pleading turns into rage as I begin to sling threats of my own. "Don't touch me! Don't you *fucking* touch me, you bastard!"

I'm grabbed and shoved so hard against the mattress that it knocks the air from my lungs, briefly shocking me still. But it only galvanizes me, and my knee makes contact with Zayne's rib.

He reacts with a wince and an *oomph*, but it's only a momentary reprieve, and it isn't like I can use it to get away, not with my arms restrained like they are.

I cry out as I take a backhand to the face, so hard my entire head jerks sideways, and stars dance behind my vision.

"Stop this, Carleigh! You're not going anywhere—you know that. Stop being stupid."

"Let her go, you motherfucker!" Tucker roars. "Leave her alone! Leave her *the fuck* alone!"

"I didn't want to have to do this," Zayne says to both me and the phone with a sincerity that nauseates me. "But at the same time, I think a part of me did hope I'd be given a reason to punish you," he admits. "You are exceptionally attractive. Like I said, I get the appeal."

He looks around the room with a strange nostalgia. "And how fitting that it should happen where it all began."

What does that even mean? He's crazier than I thought, and it's a frightening realization.

He reaches for the buttons of my top. I try kicking him again, but he pulls a knife from his pocket and switches it open in one quick motion, holding it to my throat. I gasp, freezing in place.

"Now that that's settled," he murmurs.

I want to growl more threats, sling more curses, but they lodge painfully in my throat. Instead I focus every effort on keeping the river trying to rush from my eyes securely dammed. My failure at this is my greatest shame. I hate crying, and Tucker is the only person I've ever given my tears to. He deserved them. He was worthy of them. Unlike this fucking monster.

I don't so much as breathe as Zayne uses the knife to fling the buttons from my shirt, drawing it open.

"If you kick me again, I will repay you in kind with this." He holds up the knife. "Do you understand?"

I don't nod. I don't give him the satisfaction. But he accepts my compliance anyway. He lifts my skirt, bunching it around my waist, leaving my white lace panties exposed.

I hear my mother weeping softly now behind the record of Tucker's fury, and even her reaction sounds contrived. I focus on Tucker's words, clinging to his promise that my kidnapper will pay for this with his life.

Zayne starts removing his own clothing, but he stops to retrieve the phone from the table. Careful not to show his identity, he aims it down at my distraught face as he climbs purposefully atop my body, straddling me. And then without warning, he ends both the call and the video.

But even as I lose the comfort of Tucker's rage, I also can't help but be thankful that he will be spared the visual of what is about to happen, even if I don't know why. I can only assume Zayne wants privacy for his own lustful pursuits, and I close my eyes for whatever he's about to do, my mind traveling far away from my present, chasing Tucker's voice and a memory of a better time, when there wasn't a monster using me as a means to a nefarious end, and when Tucker was still my future.

Chapter Thirty-one

Tucker

Present Day

My chest explodes in agony, and for the first time since my father died, tears leak from my eyes.

Some bastard is going to rape Carl, and there isn't shit I can do to stop him.

Billy stares at me with wide, horror-filled eyes, and I can't meet them. I can't offer him any comfort. Instead I turn to Carl's mother, whose tears may be real, but they are far too few, far too late, and all I want to do is shout at her again that this is all her goddamn fault.

But Carl's kidnapper was right. I am just as much to blame. I knew what kind of person Nicole was, and I still allowed her to talk to her husband and decide on a course of action without me. Yes, she was adamant that it wasn't my place to explain things to Carl's dad, but I could have insisted. I *should* have insisted. But I never guessed she planned to negotiate Carl's fucking price tag as if she was some prize racehorse.

I'm afraid you might have been right, I may have overestimated Tucker Green's feelings for you, after all.

It was like a blade to the chest, effectively slicing my heart right open. She doubted me. She doubted me because I gave her good reason to doubt me, and now she's suffering. Being touched by another man for the first time. Being *violated*.

Fuck! I can't just stand around waiting. I have to *do* something.

I decide to call Cap. I didn't call him earlier because I was afraid he'd insist on calling the police, but I can't handle this on my own anymore.

He answers on the second ring, and I start rambling like a madman. I tell him what happened from the moment I got the photo of Carl, tied to a bed, utterly terrified.

I tell him everything her kidnapper said to me, about selling her into the motherfucking sex trade if we don't meet his deadline, and killing her if we report it. I explain Nicole's disgusting attempt at a negotiation, and my voice cracks as I try to find words to describe his retaliation.

"He's *hurting* her, man. Right fucking *now*. And I can't do jack shit to stop it!" I choke on a sob.

I cry like a little bitch as Cap tries to help me think things through, but no matter what angle we approach it from, it just doesn't make any goddamn sense.

Cap has his car with him in the city, and making an excuse to Rory, he promises to meet me here as fast as possible. I know how much he hates lying to his girl, but Carl's one of her best friends, and she doesn't need to hear this shit. It's not like there's anything she can do to help right now.

I end the call, and try to think of what to do next. But there's nothing. Fucking *nothing* I can do to help my girl. My girl, who's currently under fucking *attack*—being tortured, violated and defiled. My legs give out, and I slide to the floor, dropping my head in my hands.

I think about what Cap said—about how I must know the guy. Enough that he knows what Carl means to me. It's a thought I've had before. Because he didn't just randomly decide to contact me over going directly to Carl's family—*no*, that was a calculated maneuver. But who the hell do I know who would do something like this?

My first thought was Ben, but he doesn't know anything about Carl's family. Still, I called him last night, and the background noise supported his claim that he was out in a crowded bar with four of our teammates. Two of those teammates also confirmed it when I called them to follow up.

No one has heard from Carl since we left her at that office building, including Zayne, who this morning responded to my second e-mail asking if he'd seen her, saying he hadn't—that he was busy grading final papers, and that he'd let me know if he hears from her.

I think again about calling the police. He could be lying about having mechanisms in place to alert him if we do. But I can't risk it—not with Carl's life at stake.

I grilled Nicole about potential suspects, but it's hard to narrow down a list of enemies for someone like William Stanley, a man who has more than he will probably ever know. She also pointed out that I am as good a suspect as any, and that if I wasn't standing right next to her, I would have been her best guess. We made no progress whatsoever, and no matter how I rack my brain even now, I can't think of anyone I might know who would do this.

Kidnap. Threaten murder.

Rape.

My heart clenches painfully in my chest. How will Carl ever get over this? My beautiful, strong girl, reduced to a helpless victim, at the mercy of some sick fuck. It will forever scar her, and that's if she survives.

A shrill ringing echoes from Carl's bedroom, and I jump up and rush inside to find Nicole answering her cell. She looks at me warily, and I know it's him. I know it's the motherfucking asshole who ruined my father, and who just risked his daughter's life to save some fucking money. I march over to her and snatch the phone from her hands. She doesn't even try to stop me. I think I'm starting to scare her a little. Well, *good*.

"…Nik? Is she okay? Did you speak to her?"

"You motherfucker," I growl.

"Tucker?"

Apparently his wife has ensured I need no introduction. "How could you?"

"Did you talk to Carleigh? Is she okay?" Will Stanley sounds nothing like I imagined—the pompous millionaire businessman who cares about nothing but his money. He sounds desperate, and small, and frightened, and it takes me aback.

"No," I grate, barely able to unclench my teeth enough to form words. "She's not fucking *okay*!"

"What—"

"How could you choose your money over your own fucking child?" I try to focus on my anger, but my voice cracks, and it's all I can do not to fucking cry like a damned child again.

"What? What are you talking about?"

"You had your wife offer five million dollars for her? Your daughter's life is something you *bargain* with?"

"*What*? No. That wasn't the plan. She was supposed to wire twenty million."

Huh?

I glare at Nicole, who is trembling with anxiety and shame, and I know. She risked Carl all on her own.

"Well, your wife went rogue, and told your daughter's kidnapper she would only pay five million."

"Shit."

"The bastard rejected the offer."

"Oh, God. *Carleigh*." His voice trembles with horror.

"He was concerned we weren't taking him seriously. He decided to force himself on Carl to make a point."

Silence. Not even a breath.

"Did you hear me?"

A broken sob echoes through the phone, echoing my own sentiment.

"You tell Nicole I'm going to kill her! That's it! I'm fucking *done*."

"Give her the wire instructions, and tell her to wire the full
amount," I demand.

"She already has access to everything! All of the accounts. She has
for years."

I turn to face Nicole. If a glare could be used as a weapon, she
would be riddled with wounds right now. "She's had access to the
money this whole time…" *Motherfucker*. She's had the power to end
this all along. Wire the ransom and be done with it. But she acted like
she couldn't do anything without her husband—that he was the only
one with full access.

"Damn it, Tucker, you have to get my little girl back!"

"That's what I'm trying to do!" I roar. But I'm confused. Because
the newspaper articles made it sound like he refused to return the
money against the will of everyone around him. That he opted to
do significantly more time in favor of holding on to as much money
as possible. But if Carl's dad cares so much about his *little girl*, why
wouldn't he have taken the plea deal with the shorter sentence so he
could be with her?

"Why didn't you just give it back? The money, I mean. Wouldn't
you already be out of there? Don't you want to be with your family?"

"Of course I do…more than anything." He sounds so sincere.

"She needed you," I tell him. "Carl. Billy, too. She *needs* you. Not
just now that there's some psycho threatening her life. She needed a
father.'"

"She had Nicole. She had means—"

"Nicole Stanger is no fucking parent."

A pause, then, "I know," he says defeatedly. "I hoped for more from her. She needs certain things to be happy. She wasn't always like that, or at least I didn't always know it. But when I told her I was giving it back to reduce my sentence, she couldn't handle it. She was going to take the kids and move across the country to be near her sister. I wouldn't have been allowed to leave New York State. She didn't give me a choice. She promised to bring them up to visit as often as I asked, but if I returned the funds…" He sighs. "I would have lost them anyway, but they would have lost everything else, too. Their home, everything."

"You were going to give back the money?"

"Initially, yes. But Nik, she was adamant that the right thing for my family was to provide for them by doing the extra time. She promised to do right by the kids—that she would be enough parent for both of us. And I wanted to believe her. You know, Tucker, you're young. When you're older you'll understand. When you love a woman, there's nothing you wouldn't do to make her happy. Even when that woman threatens to take your children and leave."

Fuck that. I couldn't love a woman like that. The woman I would love would be one who would choose her family over any amount of money.

And then I remember, I already love that woman. And her life is in danger.

"You shouldn't have trusted her. And I won't make that mistake again. E-mail me the instructions directly, and when he calls back I'll tell him we have the full amount."

"You love her, don't you?"

I swallow audibly.

"Nicole told me a little about your relationship, and that you ended it because of what I did to your family. I can't tell you—"

"I really don't want to fucking hear it, Mr. Stanley," I grit out.

"Still, you need to know that Carleigh—she was as much a victim in all this as anyone. She is everything that is good in this world, despite who her parents are."

"I know that," I say quietly.

"I know I have no right to say it, but I'm counting on you, Tucker. I can't do anything from in here. You have to help her."

"I will," I swear. Not for him, but for the girl I love. I tell him my e-mail address and hand the phone to Nicole.

His shouting echoes through the phone, and Nicole winces. I head into Carl's bathroom and splash some cool water on my face and look around for a towel. I find one in the top drawer. Under it is her hairbrush, and I stare at the fine, long golden strands stuck in its bristles. It smells like her shampoo, and the scent chokes me with regret.

A glimmer from the drawer catches my eye, and I reach down and slip my fingers under the chain that'd been hiding under Carl's brush. It dangles from my hand, taunting me with my own foolishness. The white gold crown charm I bought her for graduation, the one that should never be anywhere but around her delicate neck, shoved carelessly into a bathroom drawer.

I trace the shape of the crown with my forefinger. It caught my eye in the jeweler's window, and I dipped deeply into my savings to afford it, but I wanted her to have something special to remind her who she is to me. My Princess.

If you ever want to see your precious Princess again…

How did we get here?

Again, my eyes glaze over with tears.

And then my heart fucking stops.

If you ever want to see your precious Princess *again*?

He knew. He knew what I called her.

And like my brain has suddenly unlocked a memory it didn't think pertinent before, the truth hits me like an eighteen-wheeler.

I called her that yesterday. In front of Zayne. When he asked her to stay back to meet with the marketing execs, and she was concerned about our dinner.

Go, Princess, I'll meet you after.

I shove the necklace into my pocket and race out of the bathroom. Nicole is sitting in Carl's armchair, bawling dramatically, and I can't muster even the slightest ounce of pity for her. Billy sits in the corner, on the floor, refusing to so much as look at his mother. I can't really blame him.

"Nicole." I try to get her attention.

She doesn't even look up.

"Nicole!"

She peeks up at me, fearful of what I might do to her.

"Do you know someone named Zayne Stevens?"

Her brows attempt a thoughtful frown. "Stevens?"

My brows raise with impatience.

"Zayne Stevens. Yes. That's Art's son. Will's old business partner."

Bingo.

"He has Carl."

She blinks at me. "Art's son? Are you sure?"

"Tell me, does it make sense?" I ask.

She swallows anxiously. "Art didn't know what Will had been doing. He lost everything when Will went away. But they were already barely speaking long before then. Last I heard he suffered from pretty bad depression."

"And his son?"

Nicole shrugs. "He was ten or so the last time I saw him. But Art's wife left when he lost his money. I think Zayne stayed with Art."

Yeah, that's fucking motive if I ever heard it. "He was our professor for a marketing class."

Billy jumps up. "Zayne? As in the guy who drove her here on Halloween?"

I nod.

"He was here?" Nicole screeches.

"Yeah, Nicole. He was here. And if you were any kind of parent you would have been here, too. You would have recognized him, and he never would have had the opportunity to take Carl."

But as much as I want to continue to lay into her, I don't have time.

"Do you know where Art lives?"

"I have his old address, but I'm sure they would have had to sell that house."

Unlike you. You just had to send your husband to prison to keep it.

I call Manny, who is as talented with hacking as he is with digital editing, and remind him that he fucking owes me. He still grills me about why I'd want to find out Zayne's address, but the truth would take time I don't have, so I offer him money instead. One hundred buys his interest, but not without curiosity, but five hundred buys his services no questions asked. He agrees to help, and minutes later he e-mails me the information for Zayne's on-campus apartment. I doubt that's where he's keeping Carl, and I ask him to try and track down any other addresses he's had, including any under Arthur Stevens.

Then I grab my car keys and hurry down the stairs.

Billy stops me in the foyer. "I'm coming with you."

"No you're motherfucking *not*." I don't have time to argue with him.

He chases me into the driveway. "She's my fucking sister!"

"And she would kill me if I put you in danger, Billy."

"You can't go alone!"

"I'm not." I shove him out of my way, jump into the driver's seat, and dial Cap as I peel out of Carl's driveway.

"It's our professor, man," I tell him. "Zayne Stevens. His dad was Carl's dad's old business partner."

"Shit."

"Is that Glock still in your dad's old safe?" Cap and I guessed the combination when we were fifteen, and broke into the safe in Mitch Caplan's study, shocked to find the handgun.

"Yeah, I doubt he's moved it since he's been back around."

"Does Bits know the combo?"

"Do you think I'd give her access to a fucking *gun*?"

Yeah, fair enough. "Call her and give it to her. Tell her to grab the gun and the bullets, and to meet me out front in ten minutes."

"You sure about this, Tuck?"

"Do it. Now."

I get a call from Manny just as I hang up. He tells me Art Stevens is in an assisted living facility for the mentally ill, and their family home was sold almost nine years ago.

Fuck, where the fuck are they?

I doubt Zayne would use his own apartment, but I send Cap there anyway, since he's on his way from the city and he's closer to campus than I am. Bits is waiting for me when I pull into her driveway, hesitantly holding a bag like it might explode at any second, eyes darting around like she's worried she's being set up or something. I almost want to laugh, but there's nothing funny about any of this shit.

I fly out of the car and grab the bag from her, checking inside to make sure it contains both the gun and bullets.

"Tuck? What's going on? Sammy said you needed this, but...you guys are really scaring me."

"I don't have time to explain right now, Bits. But thank you." I race back to the car. "Stay in the house and don't tell anyone about this!" I call back to her.

And then I'm driving toward campus. Cap should be there by now, and just as I'm thinking it, he calls. "No one's here," he says. "The apartment is empty, and his neighbor says he hasn't been home in days."

Fuck.

"Okay. I'll call you back."

I try to stay calm, but I'm out of ideas. *Where the fuck are they?*

My phone buzzes. It's that fucking stealth app, and my pulse races in terror as I go to answer.

But it isn't a call.

It's a text. With a photo.

I click it open, and my stomach boils over with nausea and contempt at the sight of Carl's half-naked body, marked with the evidence of Zayne's possession, his release spattered over her bare stomach.

I have to pull over, and I open my car door just in time to vomit onto the pavement.

Zayne will fucking pay for this. He will *die* for this.

Nicole chooses that moment to call me.

"What?" I rage at her. She is the perfect place to direct my fury.

"Did you find her?" she asks shakily.

"No."

She sniffles.

"I need you to *think*, Nicole. Where else could he have taken her? Did they have a vacation home? A close relative who lived nearby?"

"I...No. I don't think so."

"Think harder!" I snarl at her, but she just cries harder instead.

Then I remember something he said. Right before he violated Carl, he said some weird, cryptic shit about how it was fitting that it would happen where it all began. I didn't think anything of it at the time.

Manny already said their family home sold years ago, but Art would have bought that house after they started making money. I read that Will and Art started the company the summer after their sophomore year at UPenn. So he could have still been living with his parents then.

"I gotta go." I hang up on Nicole and get Manny back on the phone. I ask him to find out Arthur's parents' address the year they incorporated Stanley Stevens, which takes him about five minutes since it's a matter of public record.

I'm about to make a very dangerous U-turn to head there, but then Manny tells me that house also sold. That a new family currently lives there.

Fuck!

Nicole beeps in and I answer with a short-tempered grunt.

"Maybe…maybe we should just call the police, Tucker."

"We're not risking her fucking life. Will e-mailed me the wiring instructions, and I'm going to wire the money."

"Yes, yes, you should," she says hastily. "But…what if he still doesn't let her go?" She voices my darkest fear.

"He has to." But he doesn't. And we both know it. "I have to find them." But I don't know how. "He said something about being back where it all started. But the house his parents owned back when they started the business—it sold years ago. I can't figure out where he'd take her."

"Art wasn't living with his parents that summer."

What?

"No, they'd gotten into some big fight about Art wanting to take a leave of absence from school to start the business with Will. They gave him an ultimatum, so he ended up staying with his grandparents. They actually started the business there—in the garage."

Where it all started.

That's it! It has to be.

It takes Manny minutes to find the address, which is on the company's original incorporation documents. The house is still in Morton and Edith Stevens's names.

I slam my foot on the gas pedal and race up Old Country Road, flying through the tail end of a yellow light and nearly getting T-boned by a driver too impatient to wait for his light to actually turn green. *Asshole.*

I call Cap, read him the address, and tell him to meet me there. He tries to make me promise to wait for him, but I can't. He doesn't want me going in alone, and while I know he's probably right, I can't let Carl suffer a moment longer.

The ten-minute drive is the longest of my life. Every other car on the road is my worst fucking enemy, and I swerve around them, changing lanes like a lunatic. I honk at the jerkoff who doesn't pound the gas the second a light changes, and cut off car after car without a second thought. All I can think about is getting to Carl, and I silently pray that she can forgive me for not getting there sooner.

Chapter Thirty-two

Tucker

Present Day

The sun is setting by the time I reach the address, and sure enough, his stupid fucking premature-midlife-crisis-mobile is sitting out front, parked right on the street. The house is nondescript in every way, a mid-century colonial just like every other one on the block. The once-yellow paint has faded to a urine-like hue that has peeled and chipped away in an obvious lack of care. The grass has been cut at some point, but other than that, the house doesn't appear to have seen any landscape work in years. And the windows are all shuttered up.

I park across the street, pull the gun from Bits's bag, and carefully load the magazine. I've never been more grateful for my visits to Pennsylvania to see my cousins, because without Uncle Jerry taking us shooting all those times, I would have no fucking idea what to do with this thing.

But as it is, I'm a pretty damn good shot.

With the windows covered tight as they are, it's impossible to tell if there's any light coming from the inside, so I decide to take a cautious walk around the perimeter. I keep my gun held out in front of me, silently praying I don't have to use the thing, but ready to do whatever the fuck it takes to get Carl out of there. I'm a long way from my comfort zone, and I try to tell myself I can do this. But in the back of my mind I know that firing a bullet at a bull's-eye is a far cry from shooting a living, breathing human being.

But then, Zayne is not human. The man who took my girl, hurt her, *violated* her...he's a motherfucking *monster*. And the thought makes my fingers tighten around the trigger.

There are only two entrances—one in the front and one in the back. But I can't exactly just bust one of them in and rush inside, gun blazing.

My phone buzzes with a text from Cap, announcing his arrival.

Thank fucking God.

I meet him at his car, parked two houses down, and we make a plan. It's a shit one, but it's our best shot, and we have the element of surprise, so we have no choice but to hope it's enough. Cap FaceTimes my phone, and I put mine on mute so nothing can be heard from his end. He'll have to hold it casually so Zayne won't guess it's on, but it will give me insight into where he is, and hopefully a view into the front of the house. I head around to the back and position myself beside the door, keeping my gun at the ready as I wait for Cap to ring the doorbell.

Ding dong.

It echoes through the house, and I wait. There's no guarantee Zayne will even answer it, and we don't have a Plan B if he doesn't.

I lower the volume on my phone and hold it up so I can see the close-up view of the front door.

"Who is it." The voice is muffled through the door, but it's definitely Zayne's.

"Mike, your neighbor," Cap calls back.

Then the door opens, and my screen displays Zayne's jeans, and behind them, the house's entryway.

"Yeah?" Zayne asks. He already sounds suspicious. Not good.

"Hey, man. Uh, sorry to bother you, but is that your car out front?"

A pause. "Yeah…"

"Oh. Yeah, I thought so. I just wanted to let you know—the front tires are slashed."

"What? What the fuck?"

"Yeah. Uh, there were a couple of kids walking around drinking a forty. They were being loud so I yelled at them—you see, my grand-mother's sick and she was trying to sleep. I think they thought it was my car. They whipped out a Swiss Army knife and went at two tires before I chased 'em off."

Cap sounds good. Convincing.

"Motherfucker!" Zayne shouts.

From my view on the phone, I watch him run down the walkway toward his car, where I know he will find the tires we sliced up before making our move.

Cap follows him slowly, directing the camera behind him so I can see into the house, and I instantly see the only door with light flowing under it.

Cap's phone moves again, showing me Zayne at his car, and I make my move.

I jam my foot just below the doorknob, leaning all of my weight into the kick. I feel the door give, but it isn't enough. Two more heavy kicks send the wood splintering and then the door flies from the frame, bouncing loudly off the opposite wall. I wince as the bang re-verberates through the house, but a glance down at my phone shows that Zayne is still at his car, ranting and cursing about the *little shits* who slashed his tires.

The house is small. One story, no more than two bedrooms. There is only one closed door I can see, the same one with the light on. I pray Carl is in there, and I rush down the hall, gun drawn.

The door is unlocked, and I go right in, and even with the pictures I saw earlier, the motherfucking video, nothing could have prepared me for the sight of the girl I love, eyes wide and terrified, gagged and tied helplessly to a bed. Her shirt has been draped over her breasts and her skirt pulled down over her thighs, at least offering her some semblance of modesty. But her day-old mascara paints shadowy watercolors under her eyes where her tears dried in abstract shapes of fear and hopelessness.

Her face registers shock that shifts to the most beautiful shade of relief when she realizes it's me. I hurry over to her, conscious that we don't have much time. She tries to talk through the gag, but all I make out are desperate whimpers. I shove the gun in the back of my waistband and retrieve the pocketknife I used to slash Zayne's tires, and proceed to carefully slice through the gag before hastily moving on to the cables binding her wrists to the headboard.

"Tuck," she breathes my name with such reverence you'd think I'm some kind of divine being, and her word, a prayer.

"I'm here, Princess," I assure her, and as soon as she's free, she flings her arms around my neck. I grab her waist and haul her into a crushing hug so fierce I fear I may do her harm. But she clings to me with equal ferocity.

Carl buries her face into my chest, my shirt growing damp with her tears. "You're really here," she mumbles into my shirt.

"I told you I was coming for you," I say meaningfully.

She sobs louder.

"Shh. We have to go. He's still out front. We need to sneak out the back. Can you walk?"

Carl nods. My strong, beautiful girl.

I draw the gun, and wrap an arm around her shoulder. "Cap's out front distracting him. We need to make our way around the side of the house, and then Cap will make an excuse to get out of there. Once the coast is clear, we haul ass to my car. Got it, Princess?"

She swallows anxiously. "O—okay."

She's obviously overwhelmed, but all she really needs to do is stay close, and I will get her home. "Come on."

I lead her out of the room and turn left toward the back hall. "Almost there."

But I speak too soon. Suddenly I hear Cap through my phone. "Are you sure you don't want me to help you find them, man?"

"No."

And then Cap's whispering urgently, directly into the phone. "Get the fuck out of there, Tuck, he's coming back."

But we can't move fast enough.

"Not another step!" Zayne shouts.

In one smooth motion I shove Carl behind me and aim the gun at Zayne, but his is already pointed right at my head.

"Get out of here," I order Carl. "Find Cap, and go!"

"I can't!" she wails.

"Go!"

"That's right, Carleigh. Run away, and leave loverboy here to fight your battle for you. I'll put a bullet right in his fucking head," Zayne sneers.

"This was her father's battle, asshole!" I spit. "Not hers." I'm tempted to turn to Carl, to convince her to get out of here, but I can't let Zayne out of my sight for even a second. "Baby, please. I love you. I've always loved you. If you care about me at all, then you need to listen to me for once in your goddamn life, and get. The fuck. Out of here."

"If she leaves, I fucking shoot you," Zayne threatens.

"Not if I shoot you first, motherfucker," I growl.

Carl lets out a whimper. *"Tuck."* My name is nothing but a broken whisper resembling an apology. And I know. She's not going anywhere. My heart sinks. "I can't, Tuck," she cries. "I love you, too. And I can't leave you."

Fuck. One of us is going to get shot. And I can't let it be her. "Let us go, Zayne. I have the wire instructions. Let us leave and I'll still get you your money."

He laughs. "Why would you wire the money once I've released

your entire incentive for doing so? Wire it now, here, in front of me, and I'll let you both walk out of here alive."

Yeah, not falling for that. "Not a chance, Zayne. I'm not putting the gun down until my girl's safe."

"I'll let Carleigh go, then. You stay, give me the gun, and wire the money. Once it hits my account, we go our separate ways."

"Deal," I readily agree. I'm aware the chances of him actually letting me go aren't great, but I'll worry about that once my girl is out of the line of fire. Nothing else matters until then.

"I'm not leaving you here, Tucker!" Carl shrieks hysterically.

My heart pounds like a snare drum at rapid-fire speed, my adrenaline spiking dangerously. In most fights, the side with greater numbers has the advantage. But in this situation more people just means more targets. I may have no choice but to shoot and hope Zayne doesn't notice my aim and pull his trigger first. But he's watching me so damn cautiously, just like I am him.

And then I see Cap in my peripheral, edging through the door, careful not to make a sound. He could have waited safely outside, or even left, but I never thought for a second he'd do either.

I keep my eyes trained painstakingly on Zayne so I don't give away Cap's position. But Cap is unarmed, and I need to keep Zayne distracted to give my boy a chance at helping us all walk out of here. So I continue trying to convince Carl to flee, inwardly praying that she either doesn't notice Cap, or has the presence of mind not to draw attention to him.

"Princess, I need you to listen to me, okay? Once I wire Zayne his money, he will let me go. He has nothing to gain by hurting me."

Cap charges. He pounces from behind and Zayne falls forward from the force and surprise. He manages to flip onto his back, and Cap delivers punch after punch to his face and gut, Zayne grunting with the impact. A resounding *crack* resonates through the hall as Cap's fist shatters Zayne's nose, blood spraying everywhere.

Zayne doesn't have a good grasp on his gun, but he gets a grip on the barrel, and slams the butt into Cap's jaw.

Shit.

Carl gasps behind me, and I wish I could reassure her, but I can't turn around. Every instinct I possess tries to thrust me forward to help my friend as I have so many times before, in fight after fight, first in schoolyards then in bars, but rationally I know my advantage lies vastly in the weapon in my hand.

But Cap knows how to fight, and he can take a couple of blows, and though it feels all fucking *wrong* to stand on the goddamned sidelines while my best friend fights my battle in my stead, I have no choice but to be patient—something that doesn't exactly come naturally for me. But my utmost priority is protecting Carl, and knowing I'm a wall between her and Zayne's gun makes it easier to just stand here and fucking aim, readily waiting for a clean shot as Cap and Zayne wrestle for it.

I try to keep my gun trained on Zayne, but the two of them are a single unit as they each struggle for the upper hand.

Zayne's elbow nails Cap in the stomach and he finally gets a firm grip on his gun, but instead of focusing on his assailant, he turns his back to him. A maniacal smirk stretches across his face, and he ignores Cap as he points the gun at me.

No. not me. *Carl.*

I hurl myself in front of Carl just as Zayne's gun goes off.

My arm explodes with searing, blinding pain as the bullet rips through muscle and tissue.

Motherfuck that hurts!

But it isn't enough to take me down, and just as Zayne shoves Cap off his shoulders and turns to aim another shot, he gives me a clear line to his fucking chest.

I don't hesitate. I pull the trigger.

My bullet hits about two inches south of my target, and for a moment Zayne just stands there in shock as wet crimson gushes from under his shirt, the spot growing and growing until, without warning, his gun falls from his hand and he collapses to the ground. Cap dives for the gun, but Zayne's fight is over.

I lower my weapon, and Carl is on me in seconds. "Tuck! You're shot! Oh, God."

Fucking fuck!

Agony shoots through my arm as she tries to touch it, and I shrug her off.

"It won't stop bleeding!" she cries.

It fucking hurts like death, too. But I can't think about that just yet.

"Don't move," I order her. Keeping my gun at the ready, I tentatively approach Zayne.

A river of red rushes to paint his formerly white shirt, its mirror image flowing in a puddle beneath him.

Not good for him.

But he is alive. His face contorts with a grimace of torment, his eyes blinking in shock at his turn of fortune. Randomly I recall overhearing him boast to his ex-boss yesterday about coming into a large inheritance. I realize now he'd meant Carl's ransom. Well, it didn't quite work out that way. But even in his failure, he stole something vital from my strong, innocent girl. Something she can never get back.

My hand tightens around the gun's grip, my trigger finger itching with intent.

"He's down, man," Cap points out the obvious. But I know what he's really saying. That it can be over. Carl is safe and Zayne isn't in any shape to threaten us anymore. But he's also saying that it's my choice. And I know the one he would make if it was Rory.

I raise the gun.

"Tuck!" Carl screeches.

"Get her out of here," I order Cap.

He hesitates, but moves toward Carl, ready to guide her outside. She's been through enough trauma; she doesn't need to see this shit.

But as Cap wraps a supportive arm around her shoulder, she wrenches defiantly from his hold. "No! I'm not going anywhere, Cap. Tuck, you're *bleeding*. We need to take you to a hospital. Like *now*. And we need to call the police."

But I don't respond. Because Zayne isn't going to jail, he's going to the fucking *morgue*.

Carl's fingers close around my uninjured biceps and I turn to face her. "Tuck, I know what you're thinking. But you can't. Okay?"

Fuck. I shouldn't have met her eyes. They affect me far too much—they always have. And as I gaze into my beautiful emerald sea, all I see is her concern for me. My caring, thoughtful, loyal, selfless girl. And I once thought her none of those things. I destroyed us because of it. And, I realize, as much as I despise Zayne for what he's done, it's me I hate most. But him—*him* I can punish.

I cup Carl's jaw, letting the pad of my thumb trace the angelic line of her cheek, grazing over the swell and blush from where he hit her. "He hurt you," I breathe, and I mean far more than just the blow to her face.

"You're better than this, Tucker," she says pleadingly.

I shake my head. It's so like her to think so, but she's so very wrong. "No, Princess. *You're* better than this. I'm actually *not*." I brush my lips tenderly over hers. Because I'm not. At least not when it comes to Carl. There's no line I wouldn't cross for her. "He violated you, Princess. And there's just no way I'm going to let a man take that from you and live to see another fucking day."

Her eyes go wide, and suddenly she shakes her head. "No. No, he didn't."

What? Is she seriously trying to lie to me to save the life of this piece of garbage?

"He fucking broadcasted it to my phone, remember?"

Another adamant head shake. "He wanted you to think he did. He wanted you to know he was serious. So you'd get him the money. But—"

I drop my hand, not wanting to have it on her as I succumb to my anger. "He sent me a fucking photo, Carl! Of *you*, with his…his…" My throat closes, refusing to finish the sentence.

Carl's eyes close, and her shame strikes me right in the chest. She swallows audibly and lifts her face, but she can't quite meet my eyes. "He climbed on top of me, and…he used his hand…on himself."

It's repugnant in its own right, but as soon as she says it, every cell in my body wants so desperately to believe it's true.

I grip her chin and demand her gaze. Strangely, the room spins. "You swear to me he didn't rape you?"

She nods.

I know better than to doubt her honesty. I've already learned that lesson. The fucking hard way.

A weight that would have burdened the remainder of my lifetime lifts from my shoulders. But what he did was still disgusting and most definitely assault. "He still hurt you, baby."

"Yeah, Tuck, he did," she admits. "But I'm really okay. He could have gone through with it, you know."

"You're defending him?" I growl.

"No. I'm not. I'm just saying that if he wanted to do it, he would have done it, instead of come up with a convoluted plan to convince you he did while sparing me the trauma."

I swing my gaze over to Zayne's still body, and the quick glance makes me stagger. I'm fucking dizzy.

"I don't know that it's going to matter in a few minutes," Cap murmurs. He's staring at what was once a puddle of blood beneath Zayne, but is quickly beginning to resemble a small pond.

But my vision dances uneasily, and, frankly, Carl's revelation that the worst didn't happen—it makes me feel almost elated. Or it would, if my arm wasn't throbbing with brutal pain.

I grit my teeth and use my good arm to reach for my girl. I pull her into my chest and roughly press my lips to her forehead. "You crazy, stubborn, beautiful fucking girl," I rasp.

She shakes her head, unapologetic. "I couldn't leave you."

I swallow down the emotion threatening to make me look like even more of a pussy. "I know."

Vaguely I'm aware of Cap in the background, on the phone with the police, and suddenly it feels really fucking cold. It's because my arm is soaking wet, I realize.

"Cap," Carl calls. "Cap! He's bleeding too much."

Finally I look down. My arm has been tattooed with a crimson tide. *Shit.*

I look ridiculous, and vaguely I know it isn't good, but it's Carl's distress that worries me most, and I'd do anything to fix it for her. "Looks like my arm is PMS-ing."

She shakes her head and rolls her eyes at me.

"Sit down, man," Cap says, guiding me to sit on the one step that leads to the small kitchen.

Carl stands beside me, her thighs at my eye level, and I stick my tongue out for a lick. She scolds me, but I just smirk and pull her down onto my lap. She shoves her hand in my pocket and pulls out my knife. She uses it to cut fabric from my shirt, and then ties it around my biceps, making a tourniquet.

"Look at you—my sexy little nurse, trying to rip my clothes off," I tease. She really is so fucking hot.

"My hero." She smiles, but it's forced, and I double down on my efforts to cheer her up.

"That's right, baby, I'm Prince fucking Charming," I grin down at her.

But instead of another smile, her brows pinch together, all dramatic. "Cap, help me get this tighter." She tugs desperately on the material around my wound, until Cap takes over, tying it so tight his grip turns white with the effort. "Why won't it stop bleeding?" Carl asks tremulously.

"It must have hit the brachial artery," Cap says.

"Really working that A you got in anatomy and physiology," I joke. But I took that class with him junior year, and I remember enough to know that isn't good, either. That it's a major fucking artery. But nothing feels real right now—nothing except my girl's ass perched on my lap, and I belt my good arm around her waist, binding her to me where she belongs.

"I hear the sirens!" Carl announces with palpable relief, and Cap gets up to go meet them.

When I look back at Carl, she's staring at me with unfathomable emotion, and it strikes me in the chest.

"You took a bullet for me," she says softly.

I'd take a hundred more.

I stare meaningfully down at her. "When you love a girl more than your own life, you don't let her go—not for anything, not even a motherfucking bullet."

She stops breathing, and I swipe at the tear that trickles down her cheek with my thumb.

"I thought you let me go a long time ago," she breathes.

"I tried, Princess. I really fucking did," I admit. "But it was never going to happen. I think a part of me always knew it."

"You hated me so much."

"I loved you. I hated what I thought you did. It broke my heart."

"What you thought I did?"

I swallow down my nerves. There's no time like the present, and in the back of my mind I know that the dizziness and the way my vision is starting to blur—it could mean there might not be a future. "I thought...you knew," I choke out.

"I did know." Her voice is so small. Or maybe it's the low thrum of white noise muffling the world around me.

"No. About my dad. Thought you knew everything."

Her eyes go wide, stunned. "You thought I knew your dad was my dad's client? And that it was why he—" She slams her mouth shut, staring at me with aggrieved indignation. And I've earned every bit of it. She deserved more from me, and I will always regret my lack of faith in her.

"I'm so sorry." Do I really sound that hoarse?

"How do you know I didn't?"

"Heard your mom. And you. In the hospital—after Billy's accident." I sound drunk. I *feel* drunk.

Carl suddenly shakes her head. "It's...it's okay, Tuck. Just take it easy. The EMTs are coming in."

"'S'not okay. I'm an asshole. Love you. So much, Princess. Always."

Her eyes water as she stares at me with the aftermath of the betrayal of my distrust, but also with forgiveness and boundless love. Because that is who she is. Like her father said—she is everything that is good in this world, despite who her parents are, despite who I am—the man who's supposed to love her. Despite all those who have tried to hurt her. And even as I feel myself about to slip from consciousness, I can do so without regret, knowing she knows the truth—that she was never to blame for leaving us in ruins. That it was all me. That I do love her more than my own life, and if that means losing mine for the sake of hers, then I am absolutely fine with that.

Epilogue

Carleigh

Six Months Later

"We're meeting them there," I murmur to Billy, who sits between Beth Caplan and me in the backseat.

Cap is driving, his arm stretched over the center console to hold Rory's shaky hand. She lost someone close to her once, and cemeteries make her anxious as a result.

The bright, sunny day seems strange considering where we're going. For some reason I always picture graveyards under shadowy, gray skies. But we're not headed to a funeral, and maybe the sun has decided to pay its respects by presiding over the unveiling of the new headstone—a memorial for someone who was very much loved.

We park behind Tucker's mom's car. I see her in the distance, standing with her sister's family—the only other people who were invited today. She runs her fingers over the large marble stone, tracing the top of its elegant shape.

Even from here, I can see the heartache staining her face. There are some losses you never get over.

We make our way over to them, but thirty yards to my right, I see the pond Tucker once told me about, and I tell Billy to go along with our friends, and make a detour. The water glitters in the glow of the afternoon light, and I can't help but think that Tucker was right—it is incredibly peaceful.

I spend too much time just staring at the ripples in the water made by the light breeze, and then suddenly that same breeze carries a familiar scent. I close my eyes and breathe it in.

I don't turn, though I know he's there, right behind me.

"It's nice, right?" his deep voice rumbles.

"You were right," I murmur. "He would be happy to know you made sure he got to be near the pond."

Tucker's arms come around my waist. "And now he finally gets the headstone he deserves, too."

I turn in his arms, and stare up into his beautiful army green eyes, wistful and adoring. "Hi," I breathe.

His leans down and skims his lips over mine. "Hi, Princess."

He takes my hand and wordlessly leads me over to where his family and friends stand around admiring his father's new headstone. It is a stunning pink marble, engraved with his name and his roles as a loving husband and father, the dates of his birth and death, and a beautiful etching of the symbol of his religion.

I can't help but think of how close Tuck came to be lying beside his father. My hand comes up to his biceps, my fingers absently tracing the spot on his suit jacket that lies above the scar the bullet left behind. You don't think of an arm wound as potentially fatal. But when it decimates a major artery, your body loses too much blood. Even the EMTs had a tough time staunching it, and by the time Tucker got to the hospital, he needed two transfusions before the doctors deemed him likely to survive. It reminded me so much of Billy's accident, and I doubted I had the luck to be granted a miracle again so soon. Still, I prayed and prayed, begging God not to punish the man I loved for saving my life.

He awoke a day later cracking jokes and flirting in true Tucker form. But just hours later he was begging my forgiveness for our breakup—for his assumptions about what I knew, and his rash reaction. But I never blamed him for it in the first place, and we were back together before he was even discharged.

The fallout from Zayne's actions and his subsequent death had far-reaching effects. I was still in the hospital, refusing to leave Tucker's side, when I got a call from my father's lawyer, asking me to go see him. By then, Tucker had told me everything. About how my mother was the one who forced my father to accept the plea deal, threatening to take us from him if he gave the money back. It was an explanation that made more sense than the last decade of my life.

It wasn't until Tucker was released that I finally made it upstate to visit my father, and by then he'd already made quite a few arrangements. The federal prosecutor, it turned out, was still immensely interested in recovering the rest of the funds, and agreed to negotiate a new plea deal in exchange. While he wasn't willing to offer the original six-year deal, he agreed to eight. My father had already served nine.

His release hearing was scheduled a couple of months later, and while he waited, he had divorce papers drawn and filed.

We were due for a lifestyle change, but it didn't exactly leave us destitute. The house was all we were left with, and after it was listed and sold we had its eight-million dollar value to hold us over.

The funds my father returned were divided between his victims, and about a month and a half later Tucker and his mom got the call alerting them that they were due restitution.

He'd been joking about how he would spend all of his newfound wealth when I suggested he start by replacing his father's headstone. He agreed that he couldn't think of a better idea, and when he brought it up to his mother, she agreed as well.

So here we are.

Tucker's mom shares the story of how she and his father first met, and it's decidedly sweet and swoon-worthy. I never knew that they were high school sweethearts, and I can't imagine her pain at losing him. I grip Tucker's hand a little more tightly.

* * *

Later that night I drop Billy off at the apartment my father has rented for us, and then go meet Tucker at his house. It's still uncomfortable for him to be around my dad, and I can't blame him for it. I've spent most nights over at Tucker's anyway.

It's late, and it's been a long day, and as I stare at my Kindle and read the same line from my romance novel for the third time over, I decide to call it a night, and hit the power button.

"How about this one, Princess? Two bedrooms and two full baths, so Billy has his own room when he stays over. It even has an eat-in kitchen."

I sigh noncommittally. Tucker has been trying to convince me that we should get an apartment together. He doesn't want to live in the lacrosse house next year, and with summer just beginning, he doesn't want to spend it like we did in high school. Sure, his mom is fine with me staying over, but he has no interest in spending time at my dad's place, and I'm not exactly speaking to my mom currently. The truth is I think Tucker still feels guilt over our breakup, and he's been working hard to make up for lost time.

But that doesn't mean we have to rush things by moving in together.

"We just got back together six months ago, Tuck." It's bullshit. We may as well be cohabitating for all the time we spend together. But even after these happy months, a part of me is still so terrified to trust it. What if things blow up again? What if signing our names on a lease puts too much pressure on our fledgling relationship?

Tucker takes the tablet from my hand and sets it on his night table, out of my reach. I roll onto my side to face him. "So fucking what,

Princess? You've been my girl for as long as I can remember, even if we took a while to get our shit together."

"Tuck, you know I love you…"

He scowls. He knows I'm going to say we shouldn't rush, and all the other practical, reasonable things I've been saying for weeks that my heart doesn't actually agree with.

Tuck's features soften as he leans over me, his mouth covering mine softly, sweetly. "You say six months, I say a lifetime. We've been through this. I'm not letting you go, not for anything. We both already know I couldn't if I tried. I've proven that." Army green eyes shine with sincerity and hope, and I just don't have it in me to deny him anymore.

And, of course, I don't actually want to. "Okay," I breathe.

Tuck's eyes widen in surprise. "Okay?"

I nod, and he smiles triumphantly before bringing his lips back down to mine.

Please see the next page for a preview of *In Pieces*, the next
book in the Something More series!

Chapter One

Beth

Present Day

I take my seat in the enormous lecture hall, settling in for an hour of tedium. If you thought Psych 101 would be interesting, you'd be wrong. Or, at least, the lectures aren't especially interesting, but I suppose that's more the fault of Professor Fawning than the actual subject matter.

The class itself is a mixed bag. Freshman and sophomore psych majors, like me, sit in the first few rows, intent on succeeding in a course that will be the foundation of our studies here at Rill Rock University. But there are also plenty of upperclassmen just looking to get an elective out of the way—something they'd hoped would offer easy credits. Which it probably will. It's only the third class of the semester, but so far it doesn't seem especially difficult, just, like I said, tedious.

My eyelids droop, threatening to lead me into an inconvenient nap, so I straighten my spine, abandoning the comfort of my seat-back.

I was up late. Not partying, like most of the other students half-asleep right now, but manically trying to finish the first assignment for my Shakespeare class in a manner that would earn me at least a B.

I'll need to get an espresso or something before Abnormal Psych this afternoon. That one actually requires brainpower. It's mostly for upperclassmen, and I was only able to take it as a freshman because of how many college credits I earned while still in high school. Well, *my* version of high school, which after ninth grade consisted of the best in-home private tutors money could buy, and when you don't have a social life, it isn't hard to overachieve academically.

I peek at my watch. Professor Fawning will cut off his droning any minute now, and it couldn't come soon enough. I need to get my legs moving to ward off this late-morning lethargy.

"There he is, like fucking clockwork," my roommate, Elana, murmurs from beside me, never one to miss an opportunity for a well-placed expletive. "Your sexy-as-fuck bodyguard."

But I already knew he was there. I've always had an inexplicable kind of sixth sense for his proximity, and I glance over to the doorway, where his six plus foot, looming form casts a towering shadow into the room.

I can't help but roll my eyes. Because David isn't here out of his own interest, or even concern. He cares about me, sure, in his own big-brotherly way, but that isn't the reason he's here. My brother's oldest friend is outside my psych class, waiting for me like he did on Tuesday and last Thursday before that, because he promised Sammy he'd look out for me, and it would appear he's taken that to mean babysitting. But I don't need a damned babysitter. Or *bodyguard*, as Lani put it.

Fawning dismisses us, and I dutifully march over to my de facto on-campus big brother, Lani keeping step beside me. I barely meet David's eyes as he hands me a coffee. They're too disarming, and they affect me ways no big-brother type should. They always have.

"You don't have to keep checking up on me," I grumble.

I don't know if Sammy actually asked him to look after me outright—though I suspect he did—or if David just took it upon himself as his implied duty. But I've survived freshman orientation and the first week of classes intact, so I'm hoping he'll back off soon.

There's nothing like having the guy you've crushed on since childhood seek you out out of obligation and not desire.

"You can check up on *me*, anytime," Lani suggests, her lashes batting dramatically.

That's her. No poise, no guile. She thinks David is hot, and she wants him to know it. Not that he could miss it.

"No sweat, kid," he replies, ignoring Lani's comment as he slings a friendly arm around my shoulders, and we fall into step toward the building's exit, sipping our coffees as we head in the direction of the student union.

"You know, *I* like coffee," Lani interjects, refusing to be ignored. "I like toned and inked-up arms around me, too."

I can't help my laugh. David does have fantastic arms. The tattoos are mostly new, having amassed over the past two or so years, an array of religious symbols, admired figures, and quotes.

"Don't you have your own friends, gnat?" David murmurs absently to Lani.

I wince inwardly. I don't like that he's given her a pet name. Even one that implies she's annoying and unwanted. Because she's not the kind of girl who goes unwanted. She's freaking beautiful. All deep red waves and chocolate eyes, curvy in all the right places. Yeah, she knows what guys see when they look at her, which is why she takes David's teasing in stride.

"*Friends*, yes. My own personal bodyguard? Not since I ditched my last mistake, but I'm in the market for my next one," she says cheekily.

I let out another laugh. She really is something else. Fortunately for me, David ignores her.

I probably should have said something to her about him earlier, when I first noticed her interest. Or maybe I should have anticipated it. David is the kind of guy who attracts crushes—he always was. But now he's something different. Something more.

Back when we were kids he seemed content to hang in the shadows of his friends, goofing around, playing girls, living like the future was a lifetime away. And I suppose it was. But it's closer now, and he exudes his awareness of the fact with a kind of maturity most people in his life had probably never expected of him.

I saw David less frequently over the two years since he finished high school, and while he did still come around on school breaks and summer vacations, between my brother's new apartment in Manhattan and his committed relationship, his friends didn't come around our house as much. Still, over that time, just as surely as I watched him fill out from a leanly built teen, gradually amassing muscle and ruggedness and artfully decorated skin, I noticed him slowly embrace his newfound maturity as he left the stage of *in-between*. He wears it all now in an impossible mixture of confidence and aloofness, and it is pure aphrodisia to the women around him, something I'm more aware of than I care to admit, even to myself.

I did not follow David to school here, and I'm glad no one has ever noticed my crush enough to presume otherwise. RRU is a state school here on Long Island, where we all grew up, and though it isn't big, it is renowned for its School of Arts and Sciences, which includes the psychology and social work program that brought me here. After everything I've endured in my short lifetime, I know what saved me, and I want to be that—to do that—for other kids someday.

David, on the other hand, is here for the creative writing program. Words have always been his thing, though he kept his passion mostly to himself up until it was time to disclose college plans. In fact, I doubt even his closest friends—my brother included—knew all that much about his interest or talent before he won that national short story competition their senior year.

But I knew. I knew a long time ago. Because he told me, and I can't help but wonder if he even remembers. I wouldn't blame him if he didn't. It feels like a lifetime ago. Back before the world got so complicated—when the worst kind of heartache was a schoolyard crush, the angsty sting of unrequited love. Turns out, love gets far more dangerous when it's actually returned. It doesn't sting—it cuts. It makes you feel unfathomably whole, before shredding you into pieces.

I'm not even looking to date. I got started in relationships way too young, in one far too serious, and all it did was slice me right open. I know all of the psych behind it now—my seeking out an older man, my extreme reaction when he left me...*Talk about fucking abandonment issues*. But it didn't just cut me, it gutted me and left me to bleed out on the floor, with no way to staunch the flood of life from my body. I survived by sheer luck, but only barely, and though I've come a long way in my recovery, the invisible scar is enough of a reminder to put me off dating indefinitely.

Not that David would ever want to date me.

But just because I can't date him, doesn't mean I want my friend to. I've grown tougher these past few years, but I'm still human, my heart still beats, and even after a lifetime of trying to train it away, it still echoes the first name that ever sent it racing. *Da-vid, Da-vid, Da-vid.*

I try not to be so affected by his arm around me, reminding myself of my place with him—which is his best friend's kid sister at least, and a friend at best—but when you've carried a torch as long as I have, it doesn't take much to spark its flame.

Random people greet him as we pass, guys lifting their chins in the way they do when a wave would take too much effort, and girls smiling or blushing—or both.

It took about an hour of being on campus with David to see that he has come into his own here. He stopped by my dorm on the first day of classes, offering to take me to the student union for coffee, and Lani tagged along. We couldn't walk ten feet without someone stopping to talk to him.

"So, kid, no morning classes tomorrow, right?" he asks.

I narrow my eyes, wondering where he's going with this. David always has some kind of rebellious plan or motive. "Not until noon," I confirm warily.

"Perfect. *B. E. G.*'s hosting its first party of the year, and you're my guest of honor."

"What in the actual fuck are you talking about, David?" *Looks like a week of living with Lani has started to rub off on me.*

The corrupter of my language herself doesn't tamper down her eagerness at the word *party*.

David startles vaguely at my colorful response, but recovers his breezy composure almost instantly, and I barely catch the amused smirk that tugs at his mouth. Before he can answer me, however, Lani's enthusiasm bubbles over.

"Uh, *yes*. Yes, yes, yes! We accept your generous invitation to be your *guests* of honor!" She emphasizes the plural, and again, I laugh. This time David also cracks a smile, and deep in my belly the vicious snake of jealousy lifts its ugly head.

I urge it back to sleep. "A frat party? Really, David?" I arch a skeptical brow. David's in Beta Epsilon Gamma, a fraternity notoriously filled with athletes—and decidedly different kinds of *players*. But he doesn't live in the house—*not his style*, he told me.

He hooks his arm further around me so he can turn me to face him, and we all stop walking. "Bea…Come." His eyes—a green-and-honey hazel that have fascinated me since I was a little girl—grab hold of me, disarming and imploring.

"Why?" I breathe.

David sighs. "You need a fun night out, where you don't have to worry about anything, or anyone."

"And you think a frat house is the place to do that?" My skepticism returns. I'm not naïve. I know what goes on in places like that. And David knows me well enough to know my social anxiety gives me more than the usual reasons to be leery of a frat party.

"*My* frat house, kid. With *my* brothers. And more importantly, *me*." He looks at me meaningfully.

I look away, my eyes inadvertently landing on his defined biceps, and I notice ink I haven't seen before peeking out from beneath the hem of his short sleeve. My fingers reach out to stroke it before I can help myself. A quote in beautiful black script, matching the others.

There are more things in heaven and earth than are dreamt of in your philosophy.

"Hamlet." It's one of my favorite quotes from one of my favorite plays—more words from the master to add to David's collection

"Shakespeare, really?" Lani says.

He cocks an eyebrow. "You got a problem with the Bard?" he retorts, but he's looking at me. They're the exact same words he said to me when he got his first tattoo—another quote from *the Bard*, back in high school.

My eyes automatically shoot to his T-shirt, envisioning the ink right over his left pectoral muscle, engraved into his skin back when he was legally too young to even get one. It made him seem like a real badass, even though it was a quote from Shakespeare.

But it's this new one that's got me thinking. Because there *is* more to life than I can learn in a classroom, I know that.

"Beth's taking a Shakespeare elective this semester—maybe she can study off of your body," Lani smirks. We both ignore her.

"Look, Bea, college isn't only about academics, okay?"

Bea. Not *kid*.

"And I'm not saying you need to make up for lost time all in one night. Just to try and keep an open mind and try to have some fun. You trust me, don't you?"

"Of course I do." My answer is honest and immediate. And the thing is, part of me knows he's right. I missed out on a normal high school experience because I never knew how to find any balance.

When I wasn't surrendering to social anxiety, or the debilitating emptiness that flared more and more, I was diving into a relationship I was ill-prepared for, experiencing too much too early on. I can't pretend I haven't wondered what it would have been like to feel young and carefree like everyone else my age. To drink a little too much, smoke an occasional joint, or engage in a hookup that had no greater meaning. I've still only ever slept with one guy, and that was over three years ago.

"Great. Show up at nine."

And I will. Because David called me *Bea*, and even if it was just a slip of the tongue to him, it is a magic word to me, and I wonder if he even remembers when he first called me that.

* * *

Abnormal Psych is in a smaller lecture hall. Professor Bowman is a practicing social worker, and she also runs the student help-line in the mental health offices of the on-campus health center, where I stopped by during orientation to look into volunteering.

I don't want to wait until I have a degree and a license to help people. I know better than most how empty life can feel at times—how despairingly hopeless—and the difference one can make by simply providing someone to talk to in those moments.

When I was first diagnosed with depression barely months before my sixteenth birthday, I wouldn't have counted myself lucky. But I was. Infinitely. I had access to the best professionals money could buy, and an endlessly patient family to support me through the taxing and terrifying process of whittling down the right combination of medication and therapy.

It was a steep uphill battle, one not without its trips and tumbles, and while I stumbled through the inevitable process of elimination, there were still times when it was myself I wanted to eliminate.

I was already familiar with the vicious world of neuroses, thanks to the social anxiety that's plagued me since childhood. But if there's anything I've learned over the years, it's that there's no getting used to having your thoughts and emotions hijacked by the chemicals inside your own brain—having your life sabotaged by a invisible rogue force inside your own body.

It was thanks to my mother and Sammy, and not least of all to Dr. Schall, that I found a treatment that works for me. And it's still a struggle some days, but while I've accepted that it will always be a part of me, I've also learned how to embrace it—how to channel it into something positive. In fact, David actually helped with that, even if he doesn't know it.

But I'm fully aware that many others aren't so lucky, and I don't underestimate the power of simply having someone to talk to when the hopelessness starts to take over. Which is why I respect Professor Bowman so much for donating such a great deal of her time to the student help-line. With her credentials, and—according to Google—her five-hundred-dollar-per-hour session fee, surely it would be more lucrative to focus on her private practice. But the amount of time she spends on campus tells me she really cares about her work, which makes me admire her even more.

It's only the third class, but it's already obvious that she also happens to be a great teacher, and I don't have to feign my interest in her lecture, or fight to stay awake. Bowman is knowledgeable and engaging, and the class flies by.

But despite my interest and her competence, I find myself distracted by an inexplicable sense of unease.

I feel strangely unsettled. Like someone is watching me.

A vague shiver creeps down my spine and I'm struck with the urge to turn around.

So I do. I peek over my shoulder from my seat in the first row, and my gaze automatically lands on the culprit.

My stomach flips as I try to place the stranger. He isn't even watching me—he's *glaring* at me.

Aren't you supposed to look away when someone catches you staring?

Glaring.

A beat passes. Two. A third, and then he looks away with irritation, as if he doesn't feel particularly compelled to submit to this social demand, and only does so reluctantly. I return my eyes to the front of the room.

What the fuck was that?

Who *the fuck was that?*

If I've ever seen him before, I have no memory of it.

I decide to sneak another peek.

This time he has the grace to look away faster, but his eyes were most definitely on me a split second ago. And what eyes they are. Completely foreign, and yet somehow unfathomably familiar. Deep blue, similar to mine in shade, but different in every other way. His are like the ocean. Not the translucent aquamarine of the Caribbean, but a dark ocean. A stormy, turbulent one. An ocean hiding secrets below its depths, its murky waters concealing the dangers within.

The kind of ocean that will drown you if you're not careful.

But I have no intention of getting caught in a riptide, by him or any other man. I've been there, done that, been drowned and reborn, and I'll stick to the safety of swimming pools, thank you very much.

But then, this guy didn't seem to be staring at me in the usual way a boy stares at a girl, which is all the more off-putting. He wants something from me, I've no doubt, but I don't think it's what most guys want, and that frightens me.

I take advantage of his attention being elsewhere, even if he's faking it, and take a moment to check him out.

I hadn't noticed him before today. Which is strange. Not because I've taken note of each of the fifty or so students in the room—I haven't—but because he's the kind of guy a girl notices.

Even seated, his stature is unmistakable. He's got to be at least six feet, probably a few inches over. He's bulky in a way that makes it obvious he's committed to his fitness, but I doubt it's out of vanity. He seems intense—the kind of guy who works out to release hostile energy, and his sculpted muscles are simply a happy byproduct. His face is all sharp lines and hard planes, his dark, prominent, masculine brow furrowed in what seems to be perpetual agitation. He positively radiates disquiet.

It raises my hackles even more.

I'm about to look away when he resettles his glare right on me, this time brazenly meeting my eyes. It's shameless, but instead of averting my gaze, I find myself returning his glare.

And why should *I* back down? *He's* the one challenging me with his inappropriate fucking staring.

A lightning bolt of familiarity strikes in my gut like a wave of déjà vu, and it makes no sense. He must remind me of someone. David, maybe. Or my brother, who definitely has his intense moments.

And then, so subtly I almost miss it, the corner of the stranger's mouth twitches, as if it wants to smile, but barely knows how.

Big surprise that the glarey asshole doesn't know how to fucking smile.

I narrow my eyes, refusing to surrender, because regardless of what he thinks I look like, I am not some weak little girl.

I am a *survivor*. And he will not intimidate me with a fucking glare.

"Okay, guys. See you Tuesday." Professor Bowman dismisses us, and glarey asshole looks away first—*victory!*—grabs his notebook, and pushes his way down the aisle, students scampering out of his path as he moves. Yeah, he has that kind of presence. I'm done wasting my time on him, so I approach Bowman to ask her about volunteer hours. She offers to meet me tomorrow morning, which is perfect since I don't have a class until noon. Sure, I agreed to that party, but it isn't like I'm planning to nurse a hangover or anything, and I'm used to getting up early.

Glarey stranger is gone when I leave the room, much to my relief, and I head to my last class of the day wondering if there's any way of getting out of the party altogether. Of course, David would probably show up at my dorm and drag me by my hair. I blush at the prospect. It doesn't sound all that terrible.

Acknowledgments

Firstly I have to thank all of the readers who fell for the Something More series with Normal, and who continue to show these characters nothing but love. Your support is everything.

Infinite thanks to my editor at Forever, Amy Pierpont, for her endless patience, and for still being kind when that patience starts to run out. Thank you for loving Carl and Tuck as much as I do. And to Madeleine Colavita for the gentle nudges when deadlines came and went.

A million thank you's to Erica Silverman at Trident Media Group for believing in this series, and for always being in my corner.

Thank you to my betas, Becky, Gabi, Drew, Morgan, JC, Margo, Paula, and Christie for your time and honest feedback.

To the bloggers and their blogs, big and small, who got the series out there in the first place, and who continue to devote so much time and effort for the simple love of literature; I am in awe of you. Bianca at *Biblio Belles*, Celeste at *The Book Hookup*, Jordan at *Young Adult Book Madness*, Michele at *Devilishly Delicious Book Reviews*, Trish at *Bedroom Bookworms*, Kristin and Amber at *A Beautiful Book Blog*, Stacy at *Books Unhinged*, *Lost to Books*, *Prone to Crushes*, *Crystal's Many Reviews*, and so, so many more I couldn't possibly name them all.

To the entire indie community, for all of the book-love and support for authors—whether indie, "hybrid," or traditional—and for providing authors with a platform to get our books out there. To everyone who takes time out of their busy day to post reviews, share book news, engage on social media, attend signings, etc. Your passion for our characters and their stories gives authors the fuel to keep going during the inevitable times of self-doubt.

Above all, I have to give a special thank-you to my family. To my mom, Margo, who has encouraged me to write—quite literally—since I could hold a pencil, and who is quick to jump on Grandma-duty when deadlines strike. To my Aba, Jay, who is always my biggest and most vocal fan. To Lana and Mike, my second pair of parents, who take on so much for the love of their children and grandchildren, and who are always ready to play babysitter, chef, driver, and whatever other roles they can take on to help, always. None of us would accomplish half of what we do without you there to help us keep it together.

To my two incredible, gorgeous future-book-boyfriends; you both inspire me so very much. To little miss good-luck-charm, whose birth not only landed on the one-year publishing anniversary of my first book, but also brought with it my first book deal. I'm not usually one to believe in signs, but some things can't be ignored. I guess I'll have to keep her around.

The one person this book simply would not exist without, however, is my handsome, loving husband of ten years, Roman. Thank you for picking up my long and winding slack, and for playing *Mommy* when Mommy disappears into the writing cave. For being the father every girl dreams of having for her kids, and for being the husband I don't always deserve. But most of all, thank you for our first decade of true, perfectly imperfect love and marriage. You have been the center of my world since I was nineteen years old, and writing love stories is easy when I have my own, real-life version as inspiration. You do put the "*Roman*" in "*romantic*."

And the "antics".

About the Author

Danielle Pearl is the bestselling author of the Something More series. She lives in New Jersey with her three delicious children and ever-supportive husband, who—luckily—doesn't mind sharing her with an array of fictional men.

She did a brief stint at Boston University and worked in marketing before publishing her debut novel, Normal. She writes mature Young Adult and New Adult Contemporary Romance..

You can learn more at:

DaniellePearl.com

Instagram @daniellepearlauthor

Twitter @danipearlauthor

Facebook.com/daniellepearlauthor